Sarah's Story

ALSO BY LYNNE FRANCIS
FROM CLIPPER LARGE PRINT

Ella's Journey
Alice's Secret

Sarah's Story

Lynne Francis

W F HOWES LTD

This large print edition published in 2019 by
W F Howes Ltd
Unit 5, St George's House, Rearsby Business Park,
Gaddesby Lane, Rearsby, Leicester LE7 4YH

1 3 5 7 9 10 8 6 4 2

First published in the United Kingdom in 2018
by AVON

ISBN 978 1 52886 902 7

Typeset by Palimpsest Book Production Limited,
Falkirk, Stirlingshire

Printed and bound by
T J International in the UK

To the Writing Matters group for all their encouragement and support.

PART I

MAY – SEPTEMBER 1874

CHAPTER 1

Sarah had watched the bird of prey awhile, shading her eyes against the midday sun. It was hunting from the edge of Tinker's Wood, scattering small birds from the hedgerows where they had taken refuge from the heat. The hedge-hawk had had no success so far, and she wondered at the energy it was expending, but it was patient. It returned to the shelter of the woodland canopy each time, waiting for the scattered birds to settle, then launched another attack. She didn't want it to succeed, but she couldn't tear her eyes away, either.

Just when she thought it must have given up and flown away without her noticing, it startled her by skimming up over the hedge, so close to where she was sitting that she could have sworn she saw the intent in its yellow eye as it swept past. There was a muffled squawk, a flurry of fine feathers and calls of alarm – and it was all over. The hawk sped off, taking its prey to a plucking post deep in the woods.

With a sigh and a shudder, Sarah jumped down from the wall where she had perched herself and

3

shook out her skirts, craning her head back over her shoulder to check for any mossy stains. She tied her bonnet back in place over her curly brown hair which, in honour of the unusual warmth of the weather so early in May, was loosely caught up on top of her head rather than hanging halfway down her back, then she turned back to the track. She'd wasted enough time and the plants in her basket were beginning to wilt. Her grandmother would not be pleased. With the sun in her eyes, Sarah didn't notice the man until she was almost upon him. She cried out in shock and almost stumbled as she tried to avoid him.

His arm shot out and he held her in a firm grip. 'Watch out for yoursen here, miss. 'Tis a rough track you tread and your ankles look a sight too dainty for it.'

Sarah, her heart beating fast at the close and unexpected encounter, felt her colour rise. It was wrong of the man to make a remark about her ankles, which in any case he couldn't have seen, encased as they were in sturdy, though patched, boots.

She made to shake him off but he'd already let go of her arm and stepped back to a respectful distance. He held both hands up, placatingly.

'I only thought to save you from a fall, miss. No offence.'

Now that she was no longer blinded by the sun she could see what manner of man he was. And she rather liked what she saw. He was barely taller than she was – unusual in itself as she was petite – wiry with dark curly hair and a deeply tanned face. His eyes shone bright blue and they seemed filled with an amused expression, while a smile played around his lips. She had no idea how she could read so much into a countenance, but she had the distinct impression that he was laughing at her.

'I'll thank you to stand aside and let me on my way,' she said, with as much dignity as she could muster.

He regarded her gravely, then bowed. 'The track is yours.' He stood back to let her pass and she had gone but ten paces before he called after her, 'But I'd be honoured if you'd let me keep you company along the way. I fear 'tis not safe for a young girl like you to be abroad along this path. 'Tis used by all manner of ruffians and vagabonds, heading to and from the water.'

His words echoed those of her grandmother, who had warned her never to use this route, tempting though it was as a short cut, for the very same reason. She faltered in her stride. How could she know whether or not he was the very same vagabond whom he was proposing to guard her against? She turned and regarded him.

'And where are you from, if I might make so bold as to ask? Are you from these parts, or a stranger here?'

The man chuckled. 'My name is Joe Bancroft. Today I am just passing through but I've spent enough time here in Nortonstall to know that the canal dwellers do have a fondness for this track here, using it to get them most directly into town, and they be, for the most part, company 'twould be the wisest for you not to keep.'

By this time, he had fallen into step beside her and, reassured by his manner, she had allowed him to keep pace with her until the track widened out. Here, a path struck out over the fields, climbing up towards Nortonstall, and she felt quite safe to take it alone. It was an open track and her progress along it would be visible for miles, not hidden as they were right now between two high hedges laden with May blossom.

He'd talked about all manner of things as they'd walked, about the hedges and the birds and the creatures hiding within, and she'd reached the end of their journey together knowing no more about him than she had at the start, nor he of her.

'I thank you for your company but I must leave you now and make haste. My grandmother will be vexed.'

'We must hope not,' Joe said. 'I, too, thank you for your company. I daresay I'll not be able to pass this way again without remembering you.' He smiled, a rich and joyous smile.

Sarah, rather taken with the thought, smiled back.

'Might I know your name?' Joe asked.

'Sarah,' she replied, all at once reluctant to part but turning to climb the stile nonetheless. 'Sarah Gibson.'

'Well, Sarah Gibson, I hope our paths may cross again, if not here then in t'near neighbourhood.' And with that Joe tipped his hat to her and strode off.

Sarah, almost cross that he hadn't offered to hand her up, mounted the stile, jumped down on the other side and retrieved the basket that she had pushed beneath, before striking out up the hill. She looked back once and could just make out the top of his hat as it passed between the hedgerows. A melodious yet jaunty whistling drifted up to her, causing her to smile again. Joe Bancroft appeared to be a man of the greatest good humour, something that his very presence seemed to spread and share. She rather hoped that she would see him again, and soon.

After that first encounter, Sarah had arrived home to Hill Farm Cottage breathless and flushed, easily accounted for to her grandmother, Ada, by her fear that she was very late and might have caused her to worry. She described at great length how she had wandered further afield than usual and discovered lungwort and comfrey, waxing lyrical about the great quantities there and promising to return for more at the first opportunity.

She made no mention of her route home by Tinker's Way, nor of her encounter with Joe Bancroft. That was something to be kept to herself, a memory to savour in private moments when no one else was around. Having examined the chance meeting from every angle, Sarah concluded that it was something she must repeat, despite having no way of knowing how this could be achieved. As it was on Tinker's Way that she had first seen Joe, she decided that it was to Tinker's Way she must return, risking the wrath of her grandmother if her disobedience were to be discovered.

CHAPTER 2

Sarah had lived in Hill Farm Cottage, along with her grandmother Ada, for as long as she could remember. Sarah's mother, Mary, had lived there too for a while. Mary had married a weaver from Northwaite, William Gibson, who – having made himself unpopular for one reason and another at the local mill – had been forced to look further afield for work, in Manchester. He left behind his wife Mary, along with Sarah and her two younger sisters Jane and Ellen. He sent home what he said he could spare from his wages each week but, even so, without additional financial help from Ada the family wouldn't have survived.

Ada's role as a herbalist gave her some status in the village, and a little wealth; enough to afford the rent on the cottage. It was a little way out of Northwaite but was big enough to house them all and to provide a garden for Ada to grow the herbs she needed. The distance from the village meant that Ada paid a lower rent, but it was a disadvantage for the less able of her patients, who struggled to make the journey. So, from an early age, Sarah had been employed to deliver remedies to them as necessary.

Ada cut a stern figure despite her diminutive size, dressing all in black in honour of her long-dead husband, Harry Randall. When Sarah was small, the approaching rustle of Ada's bombazine dress had filled her with dread for she always feared that she was about to be caught out in some behaviour considered worthy of punishment. In later years, Sarah got to wondering whether Ada's joy had died along with Harry, for she smiled little and scolded a good deal.

It was partly this that made her eager to offer to run errands for her grandmother, so that she could leave the cottage and its frequently strained atmosphere. She learnt very quickly that if she was swift in the execution of the errand she could dawdle her way home, stopping on the bridge over the brook to look for minnows or sticklebacks darting about in the shallows or, in spring, to watch fluffy young ducklings quack anxiously after their mother as she shepherded them on an outing. And if she loitered in the doorway of Patchett's, the baker's, she would often be rewarded with a treat.

'Been out delivering for your gran again? You're a good girl. You must be hungry – here's a morsel for you.' Mrs Patchett, the baker's wife, would wipe her floury arms on her apron and beam, handing over a roll that she said was misshapen, or a sweet tart where the pastry had caught and burnt a little round the edges. The one thing the treats had in common was that they were all somewhat larger than a morsel and Sarah would eat them quickly on the last stretch of her journey home, taking care to wipe her mouth on her sleeve and to lick her fingers to remove the evidence.

As Sarah grew a little older, Ada sent her on errands beyond the immediate village and she quickly came to know her way around the countryside and to delight in exploring it. By this time Mary had left her mother's house, taking the two little girls with her to join her husband in Manchester. Sarah, aged ten, was left behind to act as her grandmother's companion.

Sarah wasn't entirely sorry at this turn of events. Her grandmother and mother clashed constantly and Sarah's loyalties were torn. Although she found her grandmother formidable, she was at least consistent. You knew where you stood, and you knew to expect punishment if you did wrong. Sarah's mother was harder to fathom. At times she was emotional, gathering her three children to her and telling them how much she loved them all. At other times she was cold and cruel, denying them food for childish misdemeanours. Or worse: Sarah had found her sister Ellen shut in the cellar one day when she chanced to go down there to find jars for the ointments her grandmother was making. Ellen, her eyes saucer-like with terror, could barely explain what she had done to deserve this and Sarah was unable to discover how long she had been down there. Ellen spent the rest of the day clinging to Sarah's skirt while she worked.

Mary returned quite late that day, unusually flushed and looking happier than Sarah had seen her in a while. That evening, harsh words passed between Ada and her daughter and within the week Mary was gone, taking Jane and Ellen with her. Sarah discovered that the household was a calmer place without her mother, although she missed Jane and Ellen terribly. Now she had no companions to spend her days with, and her distance from the village meant that she made no close friends there. She thought she ought to miss her mother, too, but since her grandmother had been such a strong presence throughout her formative years all went on much as before, although perhaps a little more quietly. If Sarah was missing affection in her life she didn't notice, it having been in short supply before.

Ada wrote to her daughter in Manchester once a month and received news in return. She shared this with Sarah, who, noticing her grandmother's pauses as she read aloud, suspected that much was being kept from her. Jane and Ellen were now lodged by day with a neighbour as Mary had gone to work in the mill alongside her husband. A frown creased Ada's brow as she read this out to Sarah, who was old enough herself to worry that her younger sisters wouldn't be properly cared for.

'What need do they have of yet more money?' Ada muttered. Sarah kept quiet, aware that she was speaking more to herself than to her granddaughter. 'Is what I send not enough? It must be the drink. The devil's work.'

With the rest of the family gone, and without her mother's presence to create and inflame tensions, Sarah and her grandmother quickly settled into a mutual understanding. Ada grumbled and complained but Sarah came to see that it meant little.

Sarah dutifully accompanied her grandmother, staunch in her Methodism, to the chapel in Northwaite every Sunday but, if truth be told, she was barely a believer herself. She learnt the art of appearing to worship, whilst all the time she was far away in daydreams in which she wandered the surrounding countryside, spending time with the sisters she missed so much. She feared they would be so well grown as to be unrecognisable the next time they met.

Her grandmother would try to draw her into conversation about the sermon on the way home, but Sarah was always ready to distract her or to divert her thoughts. Usually she would ask a question about some remedy that they were making but once she had thought to enquire more about Ada's, and the family's, faith.

'Did my mother go to chapel with you when she was young?' she asked. She was well aware of Ada's high standing in the chapel community yet Mary had attended chapel rarely, simply refusing to be ready on time, and she had prevented Jane and Ellen from attending too. Sarah, as the eldest daughter, had accepted her own role as her grandmother's companion and gone along without questioning it. Now she wondered whether the strained atmosphere in the house had been caused by arguments about religion, or whether it was something else entirely.

'Your mother came to chapel until she was about sixteen, when she met your father,' Ada said. 'William Gibson didn't hold with the Methodist beliefs, in particular where drink was concerned, and within three months he had your mother rejecting them as well.'

Ada's dislike of Sarah's father was clear, Sarah thought. Could this explain why he was such a shadowy presence in her own life? He had been working in Manchester as long as Sarah could remember; certainly since Jane was born and probably before that. They had been a household of women for what seemed like the whole of Sarah's life.

Something else that her grandmother had said had lodged in her mind, too: her mother and father had met when Mary was sixteen. That was younger than Sarah was now. The thought had worried away at her – living in an out-of-the-way cottage with just her grandmother for company, how was she ever going to meet a young man, let alone marry and have a family of her own?

CHAPTER 3

The day after her encounter with Joe, Sarah suggested to her grandmother that it would be wise to go back and gather as much of the remaining lungwort as possible before someone else discovered its whereabouts. Ada was suspicious of Sarah's eagerness to go herb gathering, when before she had considered it an unwelcome imposition, but she was always grateful for supplies of the plants that she didn't grow herself. So it was that within the week, Sarah set off again for Tinker's Wood. She'd dressed carefully, choosing her second-best blouse and skirt in the knowledge that wearing her best clothes for such an errand would have alerted her grandmother to the fact that something was afoot. Even so, she'd been careful to slip out of the house before Ada had the chance to scrutinise her too closely.

As she made her way down the garden she paused at the rose bed to sniff deeply. She thought about taking a rosebud or two to tuck in her hair, then rejected the idea, instead scooping up a handful of newly fallen petals, keeping them in her pocket until she was out of view of the house.

Then she scrunched up the petals and scrubbed them against her cheeks, hoping that their deep crimson colour would bring out the roses there. At the very least, she felt, her skin would take on some of the glorious scent.

Sarah tried hard to pretend that she was undertaking a normal outing but she was nervous and giddy, shrinking back into the hedge at the sound of horses' hooves on the lane and appearing so flustered that the carter was moved to observe to his mate, 'Isn't that young Sarah Gibson? She's a bold lass, always ready with a greeting. Whatever can have afflicted her today?'

Sarah simply wanted the first part of her errand to be over, and to remain unobserved throughout, convinced that her guilty longing for a meeting with Joe Bancroft must be written all over her face. She couldn't have explained why it was that she wished to see him so much, nor what instinct made her wish to keep it a secret. All she knew was that she had thought of little else but Joe's smile since she had seen him last, and the way that it lit up his eyes. And, without fail, the memory of the way those eyes lingered on her brought a blush to her cheeks.

Now, in a hurry to complete the legitimate part of her errand, Sarah gathered the lungwort along the edge of Tinker's Wood with great haste, barely noticing as her hand plunged in amongst the nettles to grasp the flowering stems of the herb. It was here that Joe Bancroft came upon her unexpectedly, seated at the edge of the wood, ruefully sucking fingers made swollen and itchy by the surfeit of stings.

'Oh, it's you!' Sarah, caught unawares, blurted it out. She had hoped and expected to see him a little later in her outing, along Tinker's Way, where she would have been more composed and in control of herself.

Joe – who had been poaching in the woods – had taken care to tuck the rabbit that was destined for the pot into one of the capacious pockets of his jacket, and it was hidden from Sarah's sight. He gestured to the ground beside her.

'May I?' he asked.

'Why yes,' said Sarah, arranging herself as prettily as she could and hoping that the dappled shade under the trees was showing her to her best advantage.

Joe loosened the red neckerchief from around his neck and used it mop his forehead.

''Twill be a right hot 'un today, I reckon,' he said. 'Yon herbs will be after wilting.' He nodded in the direction of Sarah's basket.

She hastily pushed the basket further into the shade with her foot and just managed to stop herself from saying, 'Yes, I must get them home to my grandmother,' which was the first thing that had sprung to mind. For she had rehearsed a second meeting with Joe over and over in her head, and in her imagination the conversation flowed freely. She now found herself tongue-tied, with not a single sensible thing to say to this man.

Joe leant towards her and she shrank back a little. 'What hast thou done to thy hand?' he asked and, reaching out, he took Sarah's small hand in his. She was aware of the calloused roughness of his skin as he gently opened out her fingers, turning her hand back and forth as he examined the raised and reddened areas. Then he lifted the sore fingers to his lips and blew on them with extreme gentleness. Sarah, who had been half expecting him to kiss them, was startled. The sensation was both soothing and cooling, and something else entirely. Joe kept his eyes fixed on hers as he repeated the action. This time he finished by kissing the tips of her fingers.

Later, Sarah could barely imagine what had come over her. Her lips had parted involuntarily but she did not speak. She felt as though her insides had turned to liquid – a liquid that was charged with fire.

'Well, Sarah Gibson,' Joe said, 'what are you doing out here, a young girl like you, roaming alone again? Anything could happen to you.' He said it teasingly, but as he spoke he let go of her hand, setting his free hand on her neck and gently drawing her face towards his. Her eyes were locked with his as he kissed her, at first gently and then deeply. She did not know what to make of the feelings that this created within her; the fire had turned to ice, then fire again. When he let her go she wanted both to have him kiss her all over again, and to run away.

Joe sat back and studied her. 'Well, well, Sarah Gibson. You're a one and no mistake.' He took her hand again and sucked her fingers almost absent-mindedly, looking perturbed all the while.

Sarah, who was now feeling that their encounter had not gone at all as she had intended, snatched her hand away and scrambled to her feet, uttering the words she had repressed earlier.

'I must get back to my grandmother.' She indicated the basket of lungwort. 'She'll be needing this.'

Joe got to his feet too. 'Let me walk along of you.'

'No, no,' Sarah said. 'I must hurry.' She picked up her basket and ran down the hill, feeling unaccountably close to tears. As she turned to mount the stile from the field to the footpath she saw Joe standing just where she had left him. His bright waistcoat made a vivid splash of colour in the shade of the trees and he raised his hand in farewell. He called out and Sarah wasn't sure whether she had heard it correctly, but she thought he'd said, 'Goodbye, Sarah Gibson. Until tomorrow.'

The meeting had not played out according to plan at all, Sarah thought as she made her way home. In her often-imagined version, he had begged to accompany her on her walk and been solicitous and reverential towards her. Her cheeks burnt with indignation. How dare Joe Bancroft act in such a forward manner towards her? And what did he mean by 'Until tomorrow'? She had no intention of seeing him ever again.

An hour later, with the lungwort delivered to Ada – who had given her granddaughter a sharp look on registering both the clothes she was wearing and her flushed demeanour – Sarah was consumed with longing to see Joe again. The memory of his kiss had returned to her and she shifted restlessly as she tried to settle to the sewing tasks that had piled up in the workbasket. She longed to head out into the sunshine again and roam across the fields where she could explore her thoughts. Inside the house she felt stifled, but she knew she must stay there and act as normally as possible. Her grandmother must not suspect that anything out of the ordinary had happened.

CHAPTER 4

'There's a man at the gate, Sarah. We're not expecting visitors, are we?'

Ada's tone was querulous. She'd had a bad night, in pain from the rheumatism that plagued her hands and feet at different times of the year, and she wasn't in the mood for the niceties that a social visit would demand. Sarah peered out of the window over her grandmother's shoulder and had to suppress a gasp.

Standing at the gate, cap set at a jaunty angle, a bright-red neckerchief tucked in the neck of his canvas shirt and wearing a different waistcoat, but no jacket in recognition of the warmth of the day, was Joe Bancroft.

'I'll go and ask him what he wants,' Sarah said. 'Don't worry. I'll send him on his way.'

Without waiting for her grandmother's response, she opened the door and marched down the path. Joe swept his cap from his head with a flourish and bowed at her approach.

'Good day, Sarah Gibson. I was just passing by and thought to ask whether you or your grand-mother had need of help? Aught to be fixed around the house or garden?' The expression on Joe's face was one of guileless friendliness.

'How did you find me here, Joseph Bancroft?' Sarah was quite fired up. 'It's most forward of you to call on me at home in this way.' She was almost spluttering with indignation at his behaviour.

Sarah had quite forgotten how she had sought out Joe the previous day, as well as how she had been longing to see him again ever since. Now, concerned that he had tracked her down in her own home, she felt quite wrong-footed. Joe, who seemed mildly amused rather than put out by her greeting, was looking over her shoulder.

'Those roses there –' he pointed at Sarah's favourite crimson blooms '– would they be the ones scenting your cheeks yesterday?'

Sarah's blush was as crimson as the rose petals. She was caught out in her vanity and embarrassed by it. But Joe's face had changed in an instant. He spoke low and urgently.

'Sarah Gibson, I must see you again. I've not been able to get thee from my mind the whole night through. Meet me tomorrow at the edge of Tinker's Wood.'

Sarah shook her head, half turning as she heard her grandmother open the door.

Joe spoke again. 'I must go away awhile tomorrow night. But first I must see you.'

'Sarah, come away back inside.' Ada's tone was sharp and Sarah turned at once to go in.

'Tomorrow. At midday. I will wait,' Joe said.

Sarah turned back in time to catch Joe doffing his cap to both her and Ada, before he assumed his air of jaunty insouciance once more and went on his way, whistling.

'What did he want?' Ada demanded as soon as Sarah stepped over the threshold. 'He looked nothing better than a tinker. I hope we'll not be robbed in our beds tonight.'

Sarah's mood switched quickly once more and she felt rage welling up inside her at her grandmother's words. How could she refer to Joe in this way, as a tinker and a potential thief? She did her best to remain calm, however, determined not to reveal that she had any prior acquaintance with Joe.

'Oh, he just wondered whether we had any jobs around the house or garden that required a man's hand. He was most polite in his manner. I don't think we have anything to fear from him.'

Sarah busied herself with folding laundry, hoping that she had allayed her grandmother's worries, all the while prey to violently mixed emotions. Despite her cross words to Joe, she knew without a doubt that she would try to meet him at Tinker's Wood the next day. When he had said that he'd been unable to get her from his mind the whole night through, a thrill had run through her. No one had ever said such a thing to her before. It was a secret, and she must keep it to herself, yet it gave her a delicious feeling of power.

She wished her sisters still lived there with her

– she would have shared Joe's words with them and asked them for their help. The laughing and giggling this would have provoked would no doubt have irritated Ada but, as it was, she had no one to turn to – and no one to help her effect her plans. At midday the next day her grandmother would expect Sarah to be at home, preparing their meal, not heading off over the fields to a secret assignation.

Although Sarah tried very hard to apply herself to the tasks set by her grandmother for the remainder of that day, her concentration was woefully lacking. While transferring the herbal distillations to smaller containers she overfilled the bottles, allowing the liquid to pour over the sides unchecked and so earning a scolding from Ada. She let the potatoes boil dry while preparing the midday meal, being too busy staring unseeing out of the window to notice anything amiss until a smell of burning snapped her out of her reverie. Sent out to gather may blossom from the hawthorn hedge bordering the garden she wandered off and came back empty-handed after an hour, having been distracted by watching a weasel hunting baby rabbits in the field beyond.

Ada was quite exasperated by the time bedtime arrived. 'Well, child, I don't know where your head has been today. I hope tomorrow brings a better state of affairs. After you have helped me to Nancy's house in the morning, I suggest you use your free time usefully to consider your behaviour today. When you fetch me back later you can tell me what you have learnt.'

Sarah stared in astonishment at her grand-mother, then collected herself. Having spent most of the day trying to work out how she could find an excuse for yet another herb-gathering trip to Tinker's Wood, she was both amazed and alarmed at being given the solution to her problem by the very person she had expected to be an obstacle to her plan.

Sarah always found it difficult to sleep on summer evenings, when it was still light outside while the household was abed. That night was no exception and she tossed and turned, hot with anxiety and anticipation, until she could have sworn that she'd slept not a wink and here it was, already light again but this time with the freshness of dawn.

In the morning she helped her grandmother into her visiting clothes, doing up the tiny and fiddly buttons without complaint, and took extra care over breakfast. She even brought in a rose from the garden to set on the breakfast table. Sarah had washed up the breakfast dishes and finished her chores long before her grandmother consid-ered herself ready to leave, but she did her best not to show any signs of impatience.

The sun was high in the sky before they set off to walk to Nancy's cottage in Northwaite and Sarah calculated she would need to hurry if she was to reach Tinker's Wood within a half-hour of

Joe's appointed meeting time. Despite feeling faint with apprehension, she did her best to be attentive to her grandmother as they made their way to Nancy's house.

'Now, child, I will be expecting you not a moment past four in the afternoon,' Ada said. 'You know that I can't abide the way Nancy goes on, but with the sorrow she's had, well . . .' Ada sighed. Her bag held a variety of remedies requested by Nancy, whose husband's death had been followed not long after by the deaths of her daughter Jean's youngest children. Jean's subsequent nervous collapse had left Nancy to care for the family until her daughter regained enough strength to return to the farmwork that had supported them, albeit in the most meagre of ways, since her husband had walked out on them.

Ada had expressed a belief that the loss of the two youngest had been a blessing in disguise. 'Two less mouths to feed,' she'd said, and looked surprised when Sarah had shushed her with an expression of horror.

Now Sarah kissed her grandmother on the cheek and wished her a pleasant afternoon, waving a greeting to Nancy as she stood at the door, before she took herself off at what she hoped was a seemly pace. Once out of view of Nancy's house she broke into a run, stopping only once to retrieve her bonnet, which she'd failed to fasten well enough, so it had shaken itself free of her curls.

She slowed her pace when she reached the field that led up to Tinker's Wood, the trees on its northern edge perched on the crest of the hill. If Joe should be watching, she didn't want to appear over-eager, nor did she want to arrive too promptly, which would also have suggested too obvious a desire to please him.

As she reached the brow of the hill, she scanned the edge of the wood for a flash of colour, a sign that Joe was waiting there. But no one was to be seen. Sarah slowed her pace yet more. Was she early? A glance at the sun showed her timing to be correct, so it had to be that he was late.

She sought out the spot where they had sat before and settled down, plucking disconsolately at the grass around her. She felt half-inclined to go home, since he couldn't be bothered to keep an arrangement he'd made, but all the nervous anticipation that she had endured over the last day kept her there. Scanning the field and the path that skirted it, she looked for signs of move-ment, but there were none. The countryside drowsed in the heat and she began to feel sleepy herself after her restless night. She wondered whether it would spoil her clothes if she lay back in the grass for a nap.

The hands placed over her eyes took her totally by surprise but the sensation of the rough skin on the fingers told her who it was, even as she gasped out loud. Joe had crept up behind her with the practised silence of a poacher.

'And what might you be doing here on such a fine day, Sarah Gibson?' Joe asked.

'You know well enough, Joseph Bancroft,' Sarah retorted. 'And where, may I ask, have you been?'

Joe held up his hands in supplication. 'Ah, I had things to attend to that took longer than I thought. But here I am now.'

Sarah noticed his failure to offer an apology but, aware of the time already lost from the little they had available to spend in each other's company, she refrained from remarking on it.

'Look,' Joe said, 'I brought us summat to share.' He pulled some bread, cheese and a couple of bottles of ale from the pockets of his jacket. Sarah regarded the ale doubtfully but was glad of his forethought in bringing food; the sight of it made her realise how hungry she was, having been too nervous to breakfast well.

'And,' Joe said, holding out his hand to pull her to her feet, 'I know a place in t'woods where we can eat, away from the heat and prying eyes.'

Sarah was glad of this too; she had been fearful that one of the villagers might have cause to pass along the track below and spy her there. She shook out her skirt and followed Joe into the wood, wondering at his surefootedness when there seemed to be barely a path.

CHAPTER 5

Joe led them deep into the wood, to a small clearing hidden a little way from the nearest path. Sarah marvelled that he could find it. The narrowest of tracks suggested that animals were the only ones to pass this way and, when the path opened into a clearing with a wall of rock behind it, Sarah saw there was a small pool at the foot of it. ''Tis used by the deer,' Joe answered when she questioned him, and he busied himself spreading out his jacket for them to sit on, and laying out the food.

The first time he offered her the bottle of ale, Sarah demurred. Her grandmother never touched a drop and expected her to follow suit; she'd tried it once at a village celebration and had not been at all taken by it. After Joe had taken several large swigs, he offered her the bottle again and she felt it might seem churlish to refuse. So she took it from him, wiped the neck and took a couple of sips before offering it back.

Joe laughed at her. 'Why, tha's barely let a drop past thy lips. Here –' and he handed it straight back to her '– tha' needs more'n that when it be so hot.'

Sarah took a bolder swig and tried not to splutter. It did, it is true, have a pleasing effect. It seemed to help ease the anxiety that still knotted her stomach, so she drank deeply once more. Joe laughed again and reached over to take the bottle from her, his fingers brushing hers as he did so.

'Now you have a taste for it,' he teased. 'And I must fight for my share.' He pulled her towards him playfully and cupped her chin, gazing into her eyes. 'Will tha' miss me when I'm gone, Sarah Gibson?' He used his hand to make her nod her head and they both burst out laughing. In the next instant, his lips were on hers and her hands were in his hair.

'Ah, Sarah, Sarah,' he murmured into her neck. He ran his hands up and down her back and she shivered at his touch, lost in the sensation. His hands found their way beneath her skirt to caress her legs, her thighs. She stiffened and tried to pull away from him but he kissed her again and undid the buttons on her blouse one by one, running his fingers over the curve of her breasts and whispering 'Sarah, oh Sarah,' over and over until she found she had allowed herself to be laid gently on the grass whilst his hands explored every inch of her beneath her clothes. She took delight in his touch and in the secrecy of the situation. She had never been the focus of anyone's attention before – certainly not in such a way – and she didn't want it to stop.

Afterwards, it was as if she had emerged from

some kind of enchantment. Joe had his back to her, tucking in his shirt, and she lay and gazed up at the trees overhead, watching the patterns that their leaves made against the sky. There was something about the quality of the light that made her sit up suddenly, fearful of what time it was.

Joe was silent on their way back to the edge of the wood, but when they reached it he turned her to face him. 'I was your first.' It was a statement rather than a question but Sarah nodded, at a loss for words. He pulled her to him, in a rough hug that all but knocked the air out of her, then held her away from him at arm's length.

'Look after yourself, Sarah Gibson. And look out for me when I get back.'

Then he set off at a great pace down the hill and did not turn round once, leaving Sarah to watch him go, fearful of how late she might be to meet her grandmother. With Joe no longer at her side, she wasn't sure that what had just happened was such a good idea, after all. She felt in desperate need of some time to herself to think it all over but, once Joe had reached the bottom of the hill, Sarah set off in the same direction. When she arrived back at Nancy's house, her grandmother and Nancy were in the front garden, talking, and Sarah was suddenly hopeful that she wasn't too tardy.

'There you are, girl! I was beginning to wonder what had become of you.' Ada didn't sound particularly annoyed, so perhaps it had been a good visit.

'I'm sorry, Gran.' Sarah hesitated. 'I fell asleep at home. I hope I'm not late.'

'You'd have done better to make time to tidy yourself up before you left,' Ada said, giving Sarah a critical look.

She blushed, hoping that what had just occurred by the deer pool wasn't as obvious to others as it felt to her, but her grandmother had turned back to Nancy to discuss some aspect of the garden, leaving Sarah free to indulge in her thoughts until it was time to go home to Hill Farm Cottage.

CHAPTER 6

The weather turned while Joe was away. The early promise of summer was washed away in week after week of rain. The farmers were in despair as their crops failed to prosper and began to rot in the fields. Cows and sheep huddled together, taking whatever shelter they could. As time passed with no sign of the rain abating, their owners were forced to drive them back to their winter quarters, worrying all the while about whether they could afford to feed them for the rest of the year.

Sarah, although not oblivious to the weather, was unaffected by the misery around her. She was too wrapped up in her own private longing, which created a purgatory all of its own. She had no knowledge of when Joe might return, but also no knowledge of how and when to find him if and when he did. She trudged through the mud on errands for Ada, returning each time with skirts soaked and muddied and boots that had barely dried out before her feet must go into them again for another journey.

After the first week of rain, people ceased to

notice it, enduring it instead with a kind of stoical despair. The weather gave Sarah an excuse to be abroad – head down, shawl drawn over her hair and face – without it being remarked upon. She was sustained in her forays outside by vivid memories of her own glimpse of summer, coloured by her two encounters with Joe. She revisited the meetings time and again, until every word and every nuance were etched on her memory. The one thing she couldn't bring to mind was what he had said about his return. Was it a week? A month? Had he even given any indication? She simply couldn't remember.

So Sarah made a point of making detours on her journeys to come back via Tinker's Way, this being the only fixed location in her encounters with Joe. It felt as though it was the one place where she might happen on him again. Yet after only a week she was forced to abandon this. Two fields ran along the edge of Tinker's Way, both set on hillsides, and the run-off turned the track into an increasingly muddy morass. At first Sarah had stuck to the grassy edges of the track, persevering in her quest, until these, too, became consumed by mud, at which point she had to admit defeat. Tinker's Way was impassable and she was going to have to settle with the knowledge that, although she didn't know where to find Joe, he knew where to find her.

In the end, Joe *did* find Sarah, just when she was least expecting it. She'd taken advantage of a break in the weather to hang out some washing in the garden, keeping her fingers crossed that the wind, which had accompanied the sunshine, wouldn't simply push in yet more black clouds. She was busy calculating whether it was worth washing more of the pile of dirty linen, which had grown considerably during the rainy spell, when she was seized around the waist from behind and a hand was clamped over her mouth.

'Sssh!' a male voice whispered in her ear and Sarah, heart beating fit to burst, found herself spun around and face to face with Joe.

'Joe! When did you get back?' Sarah immediately glanced behind her, back towards the house, fearful that her grandmother would spot her. As she had hoped, the billowing sheets hid them both from view.

'Just last night,' he said. 'And Sarah Gibson was the first person I wanted to see.'

Sarah blushed and bit her lip. 'How did you get into the garden?'

'Over t'wall.' Joe indicated the sizeable dry-stone wall that ran along one edge of the garden. 'I've been waiting out here a while for thee.'

His smile lit up his eyes, just as Sarah remembered, and she felt a huge wave of relief and happiness wash over her. He was back, and he'd come straight around to find her.

'You mustn't stay here,' she said, common sense taking over. 'If my grandmother sees you, there'll be trouble.' She glanced anxiously once more over her shoulder.

'Later then,' Joe said. 'This a'ternoon. I'll wait by Two-Ways Cross.' He named a crossroads familiar to Sarah, one that she passed regularly on her way into Northwaite. Then he was gone, vaulting over the wall with ease, before she could gather her wits and reply. She could hear him whistling as he headed away back towards Northwaite.

Sarah struggled to fulfil her household duties that morning. She was glad of the washing, which gave her an excuse to be in and out of the house, for her hands were shaking with nervous excitement and Ada would surely have remarked upon it otherwise. As she had half-expected, the clouds blew in again by late morning and Sarah hastily gathered the washing back in. As she shook it out in the kitchen and found a place for it to dry near the range, the rain came down heavily once more.

'I do hope this doesn't last,' Ada said. 'I've promised Mrs Shepherd that she will have her remedy this afternoon and it looks as though you will get drenched yet again.' She looked out at the rain and let out a long sigh.

'No matter,' Sarah said. 'I've become used to it.' She made an effort not to appear too cheerful or eager at the prospect of venturing out, whilst silently thanking Mrs Shepherd for giving her the excuse she needed to see Joe.

By the time dinner was eaten and the plates cleared away, the rain had eased a little but threatening clouds promised yet more to come.

'I'll take shelter if it comes on too hard,' Sarah

said, preparing her grandmother for a possible delayed return. She departed swiftly, heart beating fast at the prospect of seeing Joe. But he was nowhere to be seen at Two-Ways Cross, and although she waited a while, walking up and down to see whether she could observe his approach, she didn't like to loiter too long. Wondering what might have kept him, and feeling very disconsolate, she made her way to Mrs Shepherd's house, declining her offers of refreshment with the excuse that she'd like to get back home before the rain came on.

Sarah hurried back through the streets of Northwaite, slowing her steps as she passed The Old Bell. Was it possible that Joe was in there, oblivious to the passage of time? She had no way of finding out; entering would be inconceivable, and loitering with the intention of asking a departing customer whether Joe was there would likely cause a scandal. The door swung open and she peered in, but could make out little of the interior other than figures huddled at the bar, so she put her head down against the rain, which had resumed, borne on a driving wind, and headed back towards home.

At Two-Ways Cross she paused again. After a few moments she could hear whistling, faint at first but drawing ever closer along the road she had just traversed. Her heart leapt. 'Joe,' she thought, and sure enough he strode into view shortly after.

'Well, lass, a' thought it were you in Northwaite just now.'

She could smell the ale on his breath, but told herself that since he'd been forced to bide his time before meeting her, then of course it was likely he would be in the tavern. She was expecting a kiss but instead he seized her hand and pulled her through a gate leading into the field beside them.

'We'll be drownded like rats if we don't take shelter,' he said, taking her hand to guide her through the sticky, slippery mud – made even worse by the passage of hooves of cattle – towards the barn, which provided a trysting place less attractive than the deer pool, but no less welcome.

Joe stamped his feet and waved his arms to drive the cattle out into the field to allow them access. The cows had sheltered glumly under a tree at first but then edged back, gathering around the door and bumping into each other as they jostled for space, the breath from their nostrils hanging in the damp air.

As soon as Joe had Sarah safe within the barn, laid on the straw, he fell on her like a man ravenous. She felt a sense of disappointment that he hadn't wooed her and coaxed her, followed by a feeling of detachment from the situation. Afterwards, he was silent, head turned away from her, and she thought he had fallen asleep. Just when she was beginning to feel that she couldn't bear the weight of him a moment longer he turned towards her.

'So, hast thou missed me?' he said, stroking the

side of her face and allowing his fingers to linger as he moved to caress her body. Finally, she felt the stirrings of the feelings that had both sustained her and tormented her over the last few weeks. He trailed his fingers across her belly, then laid his hand flat on it. He looked at her questioningly.

'With child?'

She shook her head, willing him to go on with his exploration of her.

He bit the flesh on the back of her hand lightly, gazing at her all the while, then grazed her shoulder with his teeth. She shivered and he stopped.

'Ist thou cold?'

Sarah shook her head again. The weather was chilly for a July day, sodden and damp with rain as it was, but her skin burned. She reached her hands up around his neck and pulled her down to him.

'If it's a baby you're wanting, then you must do something about it,' she whispered.

He was kissing her more gently now and Sarah was barely aware of the scratch of damp straw against her skin, but a thought she wanted to express kept rising to the surface even though her whole being wished to be simply swept along on a tide of pleasure.

'You must marry me,' she murmured.

Joe paused and pulled away to look at her. Had she been too bold? Sarah wondered. Had she made a mistake in voicing this thought out loud, a thought that had taken root and nagged away at her all the time he had been gone?

'Aye, well, happen I must,' he said, and fell to kissing her again so that Sarah barely knew whether she had heard him aright.

CHAPTER 7

Within a week of Joe's return, summer was back. He'd joked that the skies had been crying over his departure but now all was well, and it was certainly true that each day brought increased sunshine, a rise in the temperatures and a rapid drying up of the mud.

Sarah used the excuse of needing to see how the herbs that she collected from the wild had fared during the rain as a reason to absent herself from the house. This, along with the delivery of remedies around the area, found her able to arrange meetings with Joe nearly every other day. Ada, absorbed in the nurturing of the herb beds at home, and in the creation of the ointments and remedies, didn't seem to notice the length of Sarah's absences. But Sarah found herself made greedy. She had so longed for Joe's return that now she had him back, an hour or so of his company two or three times a week wasn't enough for her. She wanted to spend more time with him, to do ordinary things with him. Although she didn't regret one minute of their fevered assignations, she did find herself wondering what it might be like to sit across the table from him at breakfast, or to prepare a meal for him at the end of the day.

As July and then August passed, and the weather held out, she waited for Joe to speak again of their marriage. Come September, as the month wore on and the leaves started to fall, colder, wetter weather swept in. Outdoor meetings would soon be impossible, Sarah reasoned, and she resolved to raise the subject of marriage with Joe once more. Two events forced her hand. As she straightened her skirt and buttoned her blouse one autumnal afternoon, sheltered this time from the blustery winds by the enclosed nature of the deer pool, which had become their regular trysting place, Joe spoke. He had his back to her as he pulled on his jacket and his voice was casual.

'I'll be away from next week. There's work to be had for a while.'

Sarah stilled her fingers. 'Will we be married before you go?' she asked.

Joe still had his back to her when he spoke again. 'Nay, why the hurry? We can talk on it when I'm back.'

Sarah felt her colour rise along with a rush of anger. 'And when will that be?' she demanded.

Joe swung round to face her. 'Why, tha' knows I canna say for sure.'

By now, Sarah knew that Joe worked on the canal, taking boats with their loads of cotton, wool and coal up to Manchester. She'd been shocked at first; her grandmother always spoke badly of the canal dwellers, deeming them uneducated, low and thieving folk. Sarah would have liked to be able to refute this but Joe had described his life on the canal to her in the time that they were able to spare for talking when they met. He'd joked about the vegetables that they took from the gardens alongside the canal, and of his prowess as a poacher. He'd offered her pheasants and rabbits but Sarah had laughingly refused, asking him just how did he think she could explain them away to her grandmother?

He'd told her how jobs on the canal could run on for weeks and months, when the arrival of a delivery at its destination could be met with a demand for the boat to transport a new cargo back to the other end of the canal. He'd declined work over the summer in order to be free to spend time with Sarah, he'd said, but could no longer afford to miss the wages.

This time, Sarah had a pressing need to be sure of his return date.

'I've a baby on the way,' she said.

Joe looked at her with an expression she couldn't fathom. She would have hazarded a guess at a mixture of pleased, alarmed and wary.

When he didn't speak, she pressed on.

'I don't think I can wait five or six weeks for your return, Joe. I will be showing by then.'

He nodded slowly. 'Afore I go, then. Afore I go, we will marry.'

He stood up and pulled her to her feet and

43

hugged her close to him. They both stood without speaking for some time, wrapped in their own thoughts.

'Must I tell my grandmother?' Sarah spoke hesitantly. She could see no way round it, but couldn't bear to guess at Ada's reaction.

'Nay, lass. Not yet. Let me think on it.'

In fact, it was Sarah who went home that day to think about it. And her thoughts persuaded her that it might be foolish to wait for Joe to organise their wedding, with so little time remaining before he was to go away again. With no idea herself, though, of how to go about organising such a thing, she could see no alternative to telling her grandmother of what had befallen her. This was not an easy conclusion to reach and she passed a restless night, with a good deal of it spent watching the shadows change on the wall as the darkness of the night lifted to reveal a grey dawn.

Even with breakfast on the table, Sarah was no clearer in her mind as to how to approach the topic. She only knew that Ada was likely to be angry; indeed, very angry. Would she forbid the wedding? Sarah wasn't sure, but she would have to endure much scolding before it could be agreed upon. She could see little point in waiting any longer though. So, as soon as Ada had taken her seat and Sarah had poured tea into her cup, she spoke.

'I'm to be wed.'

Ada laid down her knife and the piece of bread she was about to butter.

44

'I don't believe I can have heard you correctly. I thought you said you were about to be wed.'

'Indeed I did,' said Sarah.

'And am I to know the name of the bridegroom?' Ada's calm reaction was not what Sarah had been expecting.

'Joe Bancroft. From . . .' Sarah hesitated, reluctant to mention Joe's abode, which would reveal his line of work. 'From Nortonstall.'

'And where did you meet this Joe Bancroft?'

'While I was out gathering lungwort and comfrey.'

Ada picked up her bread and buttered it carefully before speaking. 'You're too young, Sarah. You may ask this Joe Bancroft to come to the house to meet me, to see whether he might be a suitable match. With your father and mother away it falls to me to decide such things.'

Sarah looked down at her plate, concentrating hard on the faded painted twists of flowers around the edge while she fought back tears. 'I must be wed. And within the week.'

Ada's knife slipped from her fingers and clattered down, striking her plate and falling to the floor.

'Am I to understand . . .' She couldn't bring herself to finish the sentence.

'There's to be a baby, yes.' Sarah tried hard to stay in control but her voice shook and tears spilled down her cheeks.

'Have you no sense? No shame? Like your mother before you. As if I hadn't already been shamed once in my own community.' Ada shook her head.

'You're throwing your life away. Like as not he's a ne'er-do-well, or you wouldn't find yourself in this situation.' Her voice rose along with her anger. 'And why married within the week, might I ask?'

'He's to go away for work,' Sarah said, her voice dwindling almost to a whisper. 'By the time he gets back, the baby will be well on the way.'

'Aye, and how well that will look before the altar. So, do you think he's going to stand by you? Or has he made off already?'

'No!' Sarah protested. 'He said he would arrange things. But I thought . . .'

'It's as well you did, my girl.' Ada's tone was grim. 'I think we had better find this Joe Bancroft and make sure he does right by you.' She pushed her chair back from the table, tea now cold and her breakfast untouched. 'Where does he live?'

'I don't rightly know.' Sarah faltered. 'By the canal, I think.'

Ada's mouth tightened into a thin line. '*By* the canal? Or do you mean *on* the canal? Is he one of those narrow-boat folk?' She almost spat out the words.

Sarah could only nod. 'But he's a good man,' she countered. 'Thoughtful, kind and gentle.'

'Aye, no doubt,' Ada said. 'And how will he provide for you and a baby? Where will you live? Are you to join the boating folk?'

Sarah was startled. She hadn't considered this. It had never occurred to her that she might live on the canal. She'd spent her whole life in this hilltop village, surrounded by fields and wide-open skies. Narrow-boat life, down in the damp, dank valley, suddenly seemed restrictive and, if truth be told, frightening.

'I thought I'd live here,' she said in a small voice.

'It seems to me that thought has had very little to do with any of this,' Ada said, tying on her bonnet and shrugging off Sarah's attempts to help her fasten her shawl in place.

'I'll thank you for staying here for the day and keeping house,' she said. 'If you'd done more of that and less gallivanting off over hill and dale you might not be in the position you find yourself in.' And Ada left the house, shutting the door with some force behind her.

Sarah cleared up the breakfast things, glancing constantly out of the window as if she expected her grandmother to reappear at any moment with a shamefaced Joe in tow. What had seemed such a delightful secret over the last two months felt shabby and demeaning now that it was revealed to public scrutiny. And could her grandmother be right? Was it possible that Joe had already left?

CHAPTER 8

By the time Ada reappeared it was late afternoon and Sarah was in a fever of worry, trying to imagine what might have happened. Three times she herself had put on her bonnet and got as far as the garden gate before retreating inside. She was mindful of Ada's words and fearful of angering her even more, should she return to find the house unattended.

How would her grandmother locate Joe? she wondered. And when she did, what would she say to him? Her thoughts flitted from one possible scenario to another and, when Ada finally appeared at the gate, Sarah could have sunk to the floor in a mixture of fear, apprehension and relief. Instead, she hurried to set the kettle on the hob. When Ada opened the door and was blown in on a flurry of leaves, whipped up by the stormy weather brewing outside, Sarah was ready, solicitous. She helped Ada remove her bonnet and shawl, meeting no resistance this time, and pulled up a chair close to the warmth of the range.

Her grandmother looked grey-faced with exhaustion and Sarah noticed how her fingers trembled slightly as she raised her teacup to her lips. Sarah busied herself with the tea and setting out slices of her grandmother's fruitcake, feeling sure that she would be in need of sustenance.

Then she asked her, 'Did you . . . did you . . . find Joe?'

Ada gazed unseeing through the window, where the wind was lifting the autumn leaves from the trees so that they rained down in fluttering flashes of orange, red and yellow.

'Yes, I did,' she said, after a lengthy pause. 'It seems that there are folk around here who know more than I do about what my own granddaughter has been up to.'

Sarah winced at the barbed comment, feeling a flush rise to her cheeks even as her heart sank. She had hoped that she and Joe had been discreet in their meetings, conducting them as far as possible from any prying eyes in the neighbourhood.

'Your precious Joe, it seems, likes a drink just like your father did.' Ada had colour back in her cheeks now, but her expression was stern. 'And, just as in the past with your father, I had to go into The Old Bell to fetch him out to make an account of himself.'

Sarah's hand flew to her mouth as she stifled a gasp. Had Ada really gone into The Old Bell? Had she faced down the stares and the remarks of the men who drank there in order to find Joe? Sarah was filled with a mixture of admiration for her grandmother's fearlessness and spirit, and

49

embarrassment for Joe. Surely he would have been humiliated in the eyes of the other men? How would this make him react at the mention of marriage?

Ada registered Sarah's reaction. 'Oh, as I said, it's not the first time I've ventured through those doors, you can be sure. Your father's fondness for drink meant that I've fetched him from there more than once to stop him spending the last farthings that your mother needed to feed you all. And I've spread the word of the Methodist faith both inside and outside those doors. There's men in there who'd do better to spend their time by their own firesides, rather than The Old Bell's.'

Sarah wished for a moment that she could have witnessed Ada, the indomitable widow, as she berated the men in the safe haven that they had created for themselves away from their wives and families. But her feelings were short-lived.

'A pretty piece of work the pair of you have made,' Ada said. 'And what a time it has taken me to set it half to rights.'

She was looking angry now and Sarah, barely understanding what she meant, quietly poured her more tea. The windows rattled as the rain gusted harder and the rain came on, splattering against the panes with such force it was as though hand-fuls of gravel were being thrown against them. Sarah shivered, despite the warmth of the room.

'So, I've spoken with the minister and it is agreed. As a favour to me there will be a quiet ceremony in the chapel on Wednesday afternoon. I'll write to your mother to let her know, but you're not to expect her or your father to give up a day or more's wages to make the journey here. Nor will you have your sisters as bridesmaids.'

Sarah, who hadn't even considered the latter as a possibility, was suddenly tormented by the thought. How Jane and Ellen would have loved it: bridesmaids, in their Sunday-best frocks with flowers in their hair.

Ada went on, 'Joe tells me that he can furnish a best man and we'll find someone from the chapel to give you away. There'll be no wedding breakfast though: your new husband has to be away to work that very afternoon.'

Sarah was struggling to comprehend the extent of the planning and arrangements that had taken place in Ada's few hours of absence.

'So Joe . . .' she faltered, struggling to express herself without revealing the fears that she was starting to feel.

'Joe will be there,' Ada said firmly. 'He has met with the minister and provided an account of himself.' She paused and frowned. 'He's a sight older than I expected. He must have ten years on you. I left him in no doubt as to how I feel about the situation, and about how he has exploited you.'

Sarah was moved to protest, 'It wasn't like that . . .' but Ada cut her off.

'I don't wish to know how it was. I thought your

upbringing had prepared you for better than this. But what's done is done and we must make the best of it. I suggest that you see that your best dress is in a fit state to be worn. And take a look at the fit of it.' She cast a critical eye over Sarah's figure. 'It won't do to make it too obvious why there is a necessity for such a haste to be wed.' She stood up. 'Now, I'm going to take a rest and I'll thank you for not disturbing me until suppertime.'

She climbed the stairs slowly and Sarah heard her close the bedroom door, then the creak of the floorboards as she moved about overhead before settling on the bed. For the next hour, both women were fully occupied with their own fears, hopes and imaginings for the future, thoughts that took them down very different paths.

CHAPTER 9

Sarah felt that time was dragging its heels on its way to Wednesday. Joe had shared the news of his departure with her on the Thursday, her grandmother had spoken to him and all the plans were in place by Friday, but there were still four whole days to be got through before her wedding day. Four days in which she had no chance to see Joe, for Ada as good as kept her under lock and key.

'You've brought quite enough disgrace on our good name,' she said. 'I'll not have you flaunting yourself again around the countryside.'

Sarah cast her eyes down, unable to meet Ada's gaze. In the words that came out of Ada's mouth the meetings between her and Joe, which had felt so happy, joyous and full of love, had become sordid and shameful. But she ached to see Joe and to be able to discuss plans beyond the wedding day with him. She comforted herself with the thought that they would get themselves a cottage somewhere, either in Nortonstall or Northwaite, and she could keep house for him without having to endure her grandmother's bad humour.

Sarah got through the days by trying her best to stay on the right side of Ada, to avoid causing further upset, and daydreaming about her future at every possible moment. She accompanied Ada to the chapel on the Sunday, stealing covert glances at the congregation to see whether anyone was paying them undue attention. If they were, surely one glance at Ada, sitting bolt upright in her pew and wearing a forbidding expression, would have discouraged any further observation.

As they departed, the minister shook Sarah's hand in his usual cordial fashion and made no reference to her forthcoming wedding, presumably to spare her blushes in the face of the congregation. It took every ounce of her will not to look back as they walked down the path away from the chapel but she told herself that the gossipmongers were welcome to have their say; soon she would be Mrs Joe Bancroft and they could still their tongues then.

On Tuesday letters arrived to break the monotony of Sarah's enforced imprisonment. Ada opened the first one, which had come from Sarah's mother in Manchester. She skimmed the contents, frowning, then read it out to Sarah.

'My dearest Sarah,
I do so wish that I could be with you on your wedding day. A day that should be a joyous occasion but that, if I understand your grandmother correctly, has had to be arranged in

haste. Sarah, I am sorry that you have followed in my footsteps and I wish I could have been there these last years to offer you guidance –'

Here Ada made a contemptuous snort. *'I hope you have made a better choice than I did –'* here Ada was moved to snort again *'– and wish that I could be there to meet your new husband. The fact is that neither the girls nor I are well, barely well enough to make it to the mill each day, so afflicted are we with coughing. So we must postpone our visit until the spring or summer, when we can come and see the baby as well.*

All my love, and from your loving sisters Jane and Ellen too.'

Sarah listened intently. Just as her grandmother had predicted, there would be no other family at her wedding. More worrying was to hear that they were ill. But where was her father in all of this?

'My father?' she asked tentatively. 'Will he come to give me away?'

Ada shook her head. 'There's no mention of him here. I don't know why. It will take another letter to ask her, with no time for a reply, so you must resign yourself to the fact that I will be your only family tomorrow.'

Sarah, seeing how tired her grandmother looked, and made anxious after hearing the news of her mother's and sisters' illness, was moved to get up and go over to her, to stroke her shoulder.

'Never mind; they have said they will come in summer to see the baby and meanwhile we will be quite content, just the three of us, tomorrow.'

Ada only absent-mindedly acknowledged Sarah's attempt at a conciliatory gesture. She had picked up the second letter and was frowning at it.

'I don't recognise the writing on this,' she said, turning it this way and that between her fingers as though hoping for clues.

Sarah, although wishing to suggest she could discover the author by opening it, held her tongue.

'It's addressed to you, Sarah. Do you wish me to read it to you?'

Sarah flushed. She had never paid any attention to schooling and found her letters baffling. She'd long ago declared that she didn't need to know how to read and write, a decision she had come to regret, never more so than now. She nodded slowly. 'Yes, please.'

Ada spread the letter flat on the table, skimming over it as before, then read:

'My darling Sarah,
It seems odd to address you this way, by means of a piece of paper rather than face to face, but your dragon of a grandmother has forbidden it.' Sarah bit her lip, but Ada read on. *'I wish we could have met in the last few days but I look forward to seeing you tomorrow. There will be so little time to spend together before I must leave, but I know you will be safe with the*

dragon until my return. Be patient, until tomorrow,

Your loving Joe.'

Sarah was very embarrassed by the flippant references to her grandmother, but also confused by the tone of the letter. It simply didn't sound like Joe's voice. Her grandmother was clearly also suspicious. She turned the letter back and forth in her hands, delivering her verdict.

'I suspect your husband-to-be has employed someone to write this for him.' She paused. 'It's a shame that whoever he chose didn't persuade him to mind his manners.'

Sarah, once over her initial embarrassment, felt cheered that at least Joe had made the effort to make contact with her. It dispelled her tiny nagging doubt that he wouldn't show up the following day. What was less pleasing, however, was that he seemed content for her to remain as she was, living with her grandmother. She resolved to try to find a moment to raise this with him tomorrow, after they were wed.

CHAPTER 10

The day of the wedding dawned full of promise. Sarah was awake early, having passed a fretful night full of nervous anxiety. She thought that she had heard Ada moving about in the night, but decided not to venture from her room herself until dawn had broken. She didn't want to have to hear anything further on her wedding day itself about how she was a disappointment to Ada, and to the family.

When Sarah went downstairs, rejoicing at the sight of the first blue sky to be seen in several days, she found Ada already seated at the table.

'Are you all right?' Sarah was concerned, hurrying to stoke up the range to ease the chill in the kitchen. She feared she hadn't escaped a lecture, after all, but Ada didn't seem to be disposed to be critical. She sat quietly and accepted a cup of tea with thanks, after Sarah had hurried upstairs to fetch a bed quilt to wrap around her. It looked as though Ada had been sitting there for some time; her hands and face were thoroughly chilled.

Ada accepted the breakfast that was put in front of her without question and Sarah, feeling if anything more unnerved by her grandmother's strangely quiet behaviour than by her anger or contempt, noted that she didn't eat a great deal of it.

'I had a troubled night,' Ada said, once breakfast was over. 'I'm going to try to rest a little before we must go. Be sure to wake me in plenty of time to dress.' And with that she left the table, trailing the quilt behind her as she slowly mounted the stairs. Sarah was struck by how her grandmother seemed to have suddenly aged: it was as though ten years had been added to her overnight.

She busied herself tidying the kitchen, glad of something to keep her occupied until it was time to leave the house. Her dress for the day was hanging in her room and so, once she was satisfied that there was no more housework to be done, she took off her apron and went upstairs.

She felt that she should be making a special effort with her appearance, something that there had been little call for in the past, so she unpinned her hair, letting it fall halfway down her back. She brushed it well before pinning it back in place. If it had been summertime she would have left it long and dressed it with flowers, but there was nothing much to be had from the garden at this time of year, other than a few berries. So she settled on a tortoiseshell comb, decorated with artificial flowers, as an adornment.

Sarah took her dress off its hanger, spread it out on the bed and scrutinised it. It was plain in style, the fabric lightly sprigged with cream flowers on a brown background. She wished that it could have been a little more elegant for such a special day but, once she had pulled it on and done up the buttons, pinning a brooch at the throat of the high neck, she felt it would do. Appraising herself critically in the freckled glass of the mirror, Sarah wondered whether her appearance was a little sombre for the occasion. She supposed that she would, at least, have colour in her cheeks after their walk to the chapel, for the blue skies and sunshine had brought with them a chilly wind.

Mindful of the time, Sarah went to wake Ada. Her grandmother, who was lying on the bed, already awake, nodded approvingly when she saw how Sarah was dressed.

'How well you look! No one can criticise your appearance on your wedding day, Sarah. Joe is a lucky man to have you.' Ada sighed and shook her head but said no more, simply holding out her hand for Sarah to assist her from the high iron bedstead. 'Help me with my dress then we must be on our way,' she said.

Within the half-hour Sarah and her grandmother were making their way down the garden path. Sarah had wondered whether, once they reached Northwaite, her grandmother would choose quiet alleyways rather than their usual Sunday route to reach the chapel. But no, she marched along the road through the village, greeting everyone whom they met. The conversation never strayed beyond commenting on the weather, but Sarah could see the villagers' curiosity as to why she should be abroad on a weekday with her grandmother, both of them dressed in their best clothes. She felt relieved when they had turned off to take the quieter path down to the chapel, then became filled with anxiety as to whether Joe would be there.

She needn't have worried. As they entered by the main door, the small group waiting at the altar turned around to look. Sarah felt Ada stiffen slightly, then she withdrew her arm from Sarah's.

'You should go forward. I will take a seat. Now, don't rush.' The last words were uttered as an admonishment to Sarah who, legs made shaky suddenly from the overwhelming nature of what was about to happen, had started forward down the centre aisle, almost at a trot.

'Oh, Sarah, I almost forgot.'

Sarah turned back towards her grandmother, who had opened her reticule and, to Sarah's surprise, taken out a tiny posy. There were no flowers, just plants and herbs of different hues of blue and green, some with spiky leaves, some with soft, silver-furred leaves, all tied with a cream satin ribbon. Sarah recognised rosemary, sage, bay and ivy. She buried her nose in the posy, then smiled her thanks at her grandmother. The aromatic scent seemed to steady her sudden agitation and the posy gave her something to do with her nervous hands.

Sarah turned back towards the altar and walked

at a more measured pace down the aisle. As she did so, she took in the appearance of her groom-to-be and his best man and realised why her grandmother had reacted as she had when they had entered the chapel. Joe and his best man made a poor show against the smart, restrained appearance of the minister and his chaplain. The latter looked at ease in their Sunday suits; Joe and his friend looked as though their attire had been borrowed from a number of different acquaintances. It was all mismatched, the jackets being of a different tone to the trousers, and Sarah couldn't help but notice that the sleeves of Joe's jacket were a good few inches too short for him and that the fabric strained slightly across the back.

He'd made an effort to slick down the wave of his hair, she observed, finding it comical and trying not to laugh. She caught a glimpse of one of his bright waistcoats, partly hidden by his tightly buttoned jacket, and he'd given his love of bright colours full rein in the red neckerchief that he wore at his throat.

Sarah gave Joe her biggest smile, feeling a little lurch of her heart as he reached out his hand to grasp her fingers and pull her towards him. His hands were warm and dry; hers felt clammy and sweaty by comparison. She stole a glance past him at his companion and her smile faltered. No amount of slicking down his hair with water or trying to adopt a smarter dress could disguise the fact that he looked, as her grandmother would have described it, 'rough'. His nose had the appearance of having borne many a punch in a fight and, when he smiled at Sarah, the gaps in his teeth only backed up that impression.

Sarah raised her posy to her nose, breathed deeply and turned to glance back at Ada, the only guest, who had seated herself halfway down the hall, before letting her gaze roam around the octagonal chapel. Light was streaming in through the windows on each wall, and splashes of colour fell to the floor in front of her from the single stained-glass window behind the altar. Someone had recently polished the pews and the wooden panelling: Sarah could smell the rich scent of beeswax on the air.

Joe squeezed her arm to draw her attention to the minister. Her senses seemed heightened as she waited respectfully for the minister to begin, and so the sudden crash of the main door being flung open, and just as quickly closed again, made her start violently.

CHAPTER 11

All heads swung round to see who had entered the chapel and for the second time that day Sarah was aware of the reaction of the person beside her. Joe had stiffened and shaded his eyes against the bright sunlight flooding the room in order to take a better look at whoever had entered. She felt him relax as it became apparent that the visitor was a young man who looked flustered and was making apologetic motions with his hands as he slid quickly into a pew near the back of the chapel.

The minister cleared his throat and Sarah, Joe and his best man turned around to face him. Sarah found herself distracted; who was this young man who had just arrived and why was he here, an uninvited guest at her wedding?

Joe had to nudge her to make her responses and so it was in a kind of daze that Sarah found herself married and on the receiving end of congratulations from the best man, whose name she still didn't know, then ushered out into the sunshine by the minister who clearly had other things he wished to attend to on a Wednesday in the working week.

Sarah was aware of the young man hovering in the background as Joe introduced his best man as Alfred, then took both her hands in his, looked her deep in the eyes and told her that he must leave, that he was already running late with the cargo that he must deliver. Alfred nodded his head in vigorous confirmation of his words.

Sarah had known that this was going to happen but she still couldn't help feeling a stab of bitter disappointment. The lack of a wedding celebration after the build-up of tension over the last few days felt like a major let-down.

Joe took her head between his hands and kissed her hard on the lips. 'I'll be back with you as soon as I return,' he said. 'And my thoughts will be with you every moment I am away. Sarah Bancroft – my own wife!' and he laughed as if he found it hard to believe. Then he kissed her again, nodded in acknowledgement to Ada and strode away, Alfred scurrying to catch up.

Sarah stood and watched him leave, feeling hot tears well up. She willed him to look back but her concentration on his departing back view was broken by an exclamation from Ada.

'You don't say! Sarah, did you hear that?'

Reluctantly, Sarah tore her eyes away from Joe and turned towards her grandmother.

'This young man has come all the way from Manchester at your mother's behest. She couldn't be here today, as you know, but she has asked Daniel to return with news of the day.'

Sarah took in the young man's appearance: he was as smartly dressed as she suspected his pocket would allow and his freckled countenance was friendly and open. His dark brown eyes seemed to view her with some sympathy and on impulse she said, 'Why, then you must come and celebrate with us and share whatever news you have. As you can see I have been abandoned already on my wedding day and so we must make our own entertainment.'

Daniel began to protest. 'I came but to witness the event and I must apologise for the lateness of my arrival and the manner of my entry. I'm unfamiliar with the area and found myself by mistake at the church in the village rather than the chapel. Now, I'm afraid, I must set out again on my return journey.'

'Nonsense!' Sarah, thwarted in her wish to celebrate her marriage with her new husband, had now seized upon a different plan. 'You must at least take tea with us before your return. Let it not be said that the Randalls –' she paused '– and the Bancrofts lacked manners and sent a traveller back on his homeward journey without sustenance of any kind.'

Ada looked a little bemused by the turn of events but lent weight to Sarah's invitation and promised that means would be found to help convey him to Nortonstall later that afternoon so that he might journey onwards by train to Manchester. So Daniel found himself borne along on a wave of Sarah's

66

nervous excitement, back through Northwaite, where she was this time oblivious to the outright curiosity of any villagers whom they passed. Ada called in on Mrs Sykes to see whether her husband, the carter, would come by and collect Daniel in good time for his journey and then they made their way back to the cottage.

Ada and Sarah made tea and buttered slices of fruit bread, plying Daniel with questions all the while. How was Mary? And Jane? And Ellen? Was there any improvement in their health? How did Daniel know the family? Where did he work? Where was Sarah's father, William?

Daniel appeared embarrassed and clearly reluctant to impart too much in answer to the queries. Sarah had a suspicion that he was focusing on describing his own work to prevent further probing. He explained that he lived in the same lodgings as Mary and her daughters and worked at the same mill, but his skill with machinery had kept him away from the mill floor and in the office, where he was engaged in working with the owner on some new designs to improve the efficiency of the waterwheel. It was on the pretext of visiting a mill in the area, which was known to have recently made major improvements in its output, that he had managed to make his visit that day.

'But surely you will be in trouble on your return if you do not have the expected information?' Sarah said, not a little troubled on Daniel's behalf.

She wondered also why he was so willing to undertake this journey on her mother's behalf.

'I was able to make the visit this morning,' Daniel said. 'I had fully expected to be turned away but, in fact, they were keen to show me around. It was this, and my mistake in going to the church, that caused me to be later in finding the chapel than I had intended.'

'And the affliction affecting Mary and the children?' Ada asked. 'Is she receiving treatment?'

Daniel looked uncomfortable.

'It is something that has swept through the mill and troubled the women most particularly. I think their lungs are weakened by constant exposure to the cotton dust. Mrs Gibson was perhaps not in the best of health when she fell ill and she has taken it hard.'

'And my father?' Sarah demanded. 'Where is he? Can he not help?'

Daniel looked even more uncomfortable.

'Ah, Mr Gibson no longer lives at the lodgings. I think perhaps he has gone to work at a mill on the other side of town and taken lodgings there for convenience.' Despite his best attempts to dress up the truth, it soon became apparent that Mary had revealed less than she might have done in her most recent letter.

There was a silence while Sarah and Ada digested this news then Ada said crisply, 'Do you mean he has left the family, Daniel? Is that what has happened?'

Daniel blushed scarlet. 'I really couldn't say for certain, Mrs Randall.'

'Humph!' Ada looked down at her plate, chasing a few crumbs around with her fingertips, then reached a decision. 'I must go to Manchester. Sarah, you will be all right here on your own for a few days, won't you? I think that I must see with my own eyes what is happening.'

The half-hour before the carter was due to arrive passed in a flurry of activity. Sarah tried hard to maintain polite conversation with Daniel whilst running up and down the stairs, helping Ada to pack a few things together and searching in the larder for provisions to send to her mother and sisters.

'Why was she not more honest in her letter?' Ada was hunting through her cupboard of remedies. 'I could have prepared something for her if I'd had a better idea of the situation, and of their struggles. As it is, I will just have to take whatever I think may come in useful.'

Sarah barely had time to tie the remedies securely into a cloth bundle before the carter was at the door.

'Sarah, take care.' Ada, distracted, was tying on her bonnet as Sarah handed her another shawl for the journey. 'I'm sorry to leave you like this but hope to be back before the week is out.'

Sarah, overwhelmed by all that had happened that afternoon, tried very hard to remember her manners. 'Daniel, it was very nice to meet you and so good of you to have come all this way.'

'I can assure you, the pleasure was all mine. I wish you every happiness in your marriage, Mrs Bancroft, and hope that I may be lucky enough to be in a position to visit again.'

'Do come. Perhaps you may have cause for another visit to the mill here.' Sarah was preoccupied, speaking half over her shoulder as she handed her grandmother's belongings up to her while she settled herself behind the carter.

Daniel sprang up into the front seat and doffed his cap. 'Goodbye. Goodbye,' he called. She sensed that he wished to say more but the carter shook the reins and they were off. Sarah watched the lamp on the cart as it dwindled away into the gathering dusk and was visible no more, then she went into the kitchen and began clearing up through force of habit.

She looked out into the darkness, aware that she needed to light the lamps inside, and thought of both her husband and her grandmother somewhere out there, wending their separate ways to great cities. Now she was left totally alone on her wedding day and it seemed like a cruel blow. She sat down suddenly at the table, rested her head on her arms and burst into tears.

PART II

SEPTEMBER 1874 – FEBRUARY 1875

CHAPTER 12

While Ada was away a spell of damp, cold weather swept in. It brought with it a morning fog that frequently lingered until midday unless there was any autumn sunshine to burn it away. Darkness seemed to arrive each day by five o'clock, and on some days it felt as though it barely got light at all.

The change in the weather also brought a steady stream of visitors, all looking for Ada. Mostly elderly, they were out of breath by the time they had climbed the hill out of the village to reach Hill Farm Cottage. At first, Sarah wondered whether their appearance was due to curiosity at the state of affairs surrounding her marriage, but she quickly realised that in all cases the visit was prompted by a need for a consultation with her grandmother, caused by a flare-up of rheumatism or the onset of a troubling cough.

Sarah invited in each arrival and, when they had regained their breath and offered their congratulations on her newly married state, they had (without exception) turned querulous over Ada's unexpected absence. Sarah could only reassure them that she was expected back any day now and offer to pass on a message about the nature of their illness to her grandmother as soon as she returned.

It wasn't long before Sarah was regretting, yet again, her lack of literacy. If she had only paid attention to her letters she could have written down the name of everyone who called, as well as the nature of their business. As it was, she was reduced to memorising the details and forcing herself to recite them out loud each morning on waking.

The arrival of the week's end found Sarah in a state of anxiety. She had expected her grandmother's return by now, but there was no sign of her and no word from her. Once again, Sarah had cause to regret her inability to read and write. Otherwise Ada might, perhaps, have sent her a note of explanation. But she knew only too well that her granddaughter would be unable to read it.

Sarah took to imagining what might be happening in Manchester. She convinced herself that Ada must have felt the need to stay on to nurse her daughter and granddaughters back to health. Surely there could be no other explanation? But as a new week began, her conviction was sorely tested. She found it hard to put on a brave face for the trickle of visitors who continued to arrive and her assertion that she expected her grandmother's return any day now sounded, even to her, as though it had a hollow ring to it.

She tried not to dwell too much on the fact

that, although she was married now, it had made no difference at all to the way she lived her life. She was lonely by day, with Ada away, and lonely at night, when her thoughts turned to Joe. How cruel it was that her new husband was forced to be away from her at this time, when she had need of him! Her vision of how contented they would be in their domestic routine remained untested; indeed, her own routine fell to pieces with no structure to her days and too much time to spend in wild imaginings.

By the time Ada did come home, one week and a day after her departure, Sarah was frantic with worry over what might have happened to her family. She had also become consumed with anxiety as to how she would be able to pay the rent or afford food and household necessities should her grandmother fail to reappear.

One look at Ada's face, however, was enough to make the angry words that had rushed to Sarah's lips die there. Her grandmother was in no fit state to be on the receiving end of Sarah's distress at being left without news for so long. Ada's face was grey with fatigue and her eyes were sunken hollows, suggesting that she had struggled to get enough sleep while she had been away. She had lost weight; as Sarah helped remove her travelling shawl she could feel the sharpness of her grandmother's collarbones beneath her hands and, on giving her a wordless hug of welcome, she was startled by how frail Ada felt.

'Come and sit by the range. You look worn out by your journey. The kettle has not long boiled. I'll make some fresh tea.'

Sarah bustled about, filling her grandmother's silence with a pointless running commentary on mundane domestic things. She was desperate to ask about her sisters and her mother but Ada's continued silence didn't encourage questions. Finally, with tea set down in front of her grandmother, along with a slice of bread and butter on her favourite plate, Sarah felt she could wait no longer.

'How are they?' she asked tentatively. 'You were gone so long I became worried. Were they very sick?'

Ada sighed deeply. Sarah was sure that she must be thirsty after her journey but she hadn't even reached for her cup.

'Yes, they were,' she said.

Sarah waited expectantly.

'Yes, very sick,' Ada repeated. 'Daniel was quite right to come and fetch me, although he was clever enough to make it appear that Mary had asked him to come. In fact, from what I could gather, she had done no such thing.'

Ada paused and finally reached for her cup. Sarah noticed that her hands were trembling so that the cup rattled against its saucer before she raised it to her lips. Her wedding ring, still worn in memory of her husband Harry, was too big now, slipping along her finger and barely kept in place by her knuckle.

Ada rested the cup on her lap, gazing at the range before speaking again.

'I do not know how they came to be in such a sorry state. Although it's easy to guess.' There was a sudden flash of anger. 'William Gibson had cleared off and left them, sharing one small room, nay, even reduced to sharing one bed in their lodging house. It's not surprising that they fell ill one after the other. Too sick to work, they had run out of food by the time I arrived and what little bit of coal they had to heat the room must have come from Daniel. If it wasn't for the kindness of the neighbours, sharing a bit of soup with them of an evening, I don't know what they would have done.'

Ada sat on, staring at the range as if she saw something there other than an austere black-leaded stove, its fire safely housed within. Sarah shifted in her seat, waiting for her grandmother to speak again. She was conscious of the wind gusting outside and she shivered involuntarily. She hoped no one was struggling up the hill in expectation of finding Ada at home. Her grandmother did not look well enough to be listening to someone else describe their ailments; in fact, she looked as though she might be sickening for something herself.

'Would you like to go up to bed?' Sarah asked gently. 'I can light the fire in your room. You look worn out. Perhaps a rest would see you right.'

'It will take more than a rest.' The edge in her

grandmother's voice made Sarah start back in her chair. Ada noticed her reaction.

'I'm sorry, Sarah,' she said. 'I didn't intend that to sound as it did.' She shook her head slowly from side to side.

'So how are they now?' Sarah asked. 'Were they well when you left? Were you able to heal their sickness?'

Ada turned an uncomprehending look on Sarah before she shook her head again.

'I'm so sorry. It feels as though I have been away a lifetime. Of course, why would you know what has been going on?'

She stopped and Sarah waited, frowning. Her grandmother was talking in riddles.

'Sarah, they've gone.' Ada's voice caught on a sob.

It was Sarah's turn to look baffled. Gone where? What did she mean? Had they moved somewhere else to find work?

'Sarah, they're dead. They lasted barely two days after I arrived. First Mary, for she must have fallen sick first, then Jane, then Ellen. Daniel and I took it in turns to sit up with them through the night but there was nothing to be done. They were too weak when I got there. If that useless wastrel of a father of yours had only thought to get in touch, perhaps I would have got there earlier and things might have been different. But he was too concerned with protecting himself. He scarpered at the first sign of illness. Went off to his fancy woman on the other side of town, by all accounts.'

Ada's voice was scornful, then her tone softened. 'I thought Daniel's heart would break when Ellen left us. Turned out he was sweet on her even though she's –' Ada paused and corrected herself '– she was but fifteen years old.'

Sarah had sat in numbed silence throughout. Was she hearing aright? Had she really lost her mother and sisters for ever? She swallowed hard and tried to find her voice, but it came out as a croak.

'Where . . . How . . . Are they . . .?' She couldn't put into words what she wanted to ask.

'They're buried,' Ada said. 'I was able to save them from a pauper's grave, at least. They're in the churchyard at St Faith's. It turns out that Mary had been known to go there on occasion. It seems she felt more of a welcome there than at the Methodist chapel, on account of her drinking.' Ada's mouth had twisted into a grimace.

'All buried?' Sarah's voice was little more than a whisper. She couldn't believe that she would never see Ellen or Jane again. She could see her sisters as clear as day, just as they were the last time she had seen them as she was waving them off to start their new lives in Manchester. They were surrounded by sunlight and waving and blowing kisses from the back of the cart, promising to come and visit soon, telling her to come and see them as soon as they were settled.

'Yesterday,' Ada said. 'I'm sorry that there was no time to send word.' She spoke flatly; the last few days had drained her of all emotion.

Sarah got up slowly, went over to her grandmother and wrapped her arms around her.

'Was it terrible?' she asked.

'Yes. Indeed it was.'

Ada clung to her granddaughter, who stayed there, awkwardly bent over her. Neither of them shed a tear but both of them were staring into their own personal abyss of horror, Ada's consisting of what she had witnessed, Sarah's of what she imagined.

CHAPTER 13

That night Ada, exhausted by her journey and the emotion of the last few days, slept well. Sarah, in the bedroom next door, paced the floor and wept. The fire in the bedroom grate cast a welcome glow around the room, which only served to remind Sarah of how her siblings had ended their days. Starved of food and heat, and so stricken by poverty they were huddled together in the same bed in the one room they had to call their own. How had they arrived at such a state?

She felt a surge of hatred towards her father, whose callous behaviour had surely made a bad situation much, much worse. Other than him, Sarah wasn't sure where next to direct her anger. Towards the mill-owners? She felt sure they had overworked her sisters and her mother until they were exhausted, their health damaged to such an extent that they were unable to fight off the sickness that afflicted them. Towards her mother? Why had she failed to protect her family? Towards her grandmother? Why had she not thought to visit and to check on her daughter and granddaughters?

Finally, Sarah chastised herself. Why had *she* not gone to see the family in all the time that they had been in Manchester? She'd sent messages in the letters that her grandmother wrote and she'd often thought about Jane and Ellen as she'd gone about her daily business. A walk over the fields on a hot day had reminded her of the time when she and her sisters had set about picking every flower in that particular field that they could find. When they'd arrived home with armfuls of blooms, most of them wilted beyond help, they'd been roundly scolded by Ada. She had explained to them that their actions might prevent the same flowers growing in the field in future years because they'd robbed them of the chance to set seed.

Whenever Sarah passed that way in the summer now she would automatically check, with a sense of anxiety, how many flowers she could see. She would mentally tick them off: yellow rattle, field scabious, hedge parsley, creeping buttercup, ox-eye daisy, meadow saxifrage, tufted vetch.

She could visualise the scene on that day now, as if she was watching it from above with herself within it. Three young girls, dressed in faded pinafores and summer blouses, their hair different shades of brown and pulled back into pigtails and a little unruly, with curls escaping and sticking damply to their foreheads and necks under the heat of the sun. She could hear their squeals and giggles as they darted here and there, in search of new varieties to add to their flower bunches, batting away the bees that followed them, puzzled by the constantly moving sources of pollen.

Ellen, who had something of the artist in her, had contrived a bunch in which the different shapes and colours of the flowers somehow seemed to complement each other, and she'd surrounded the bunch with feathery grasses picked from the edge of the field. Jane and Sarah had simply greedily grabbed everything they could find and the result was a mishmash of colour, quickly spoilt by the tightness of the grip of their small hands.

It was Sarah, as the eldest, who had got into the most trouble for their actions that day. Now, nearly ten years on, she was pierced by a terrible sense of failure. As the eldest, why hadn't she made it her business to know what was going on in her sisters' lives? If she'd imagined their life in the city at all she'd thought it must be better than her own, had assumed that they were earning enough money to live reasonably well.

Now she wondered why some sixth sense hadn't told her what was happening. She'd been disappointed that they had been unable to come to her wedding and now . . . now, she was faced with the knowledge of what they had been going through in their own lives while she'd been oblivious to it, selfishly focused on herself. When she finally climbed into bed she tossed and turned, racked with guilt. Why was she still alive while they were dead?

Dead – she found it hard to even contemplate

the idea, the fact that she would never see them again. She was alone in the world now, or so it felt. Her father was still alive, but what part had he played in her upbringing? None that she could recall. He was as good as a stranger to her. So now she just had her grandmother.

With a sense of shock, Sarah recalled that she was a married woman now. She had a husband, and soon she would have a child. The memory surfaced of how she had felt over the past few days, while her grandmother was away. She remembered the sense of desperation she had experienced, of not knowing how to provide for herself. Drifting into a fitful sleep as the grey fingers of dawn edged around the curtains, she resolved that she could not be reliant on her grandmother or on Joe. She needed to be sure that she could take care of herself.

It seemed that Ada had been prey to much the same thoughts. When Sarah came down to a late breakfast, her eyes gritty from lack of sleep, she found Ada already at the table with a sheet of paper set before her, a list written on it in her neat copperplate hand.

'How did you sleep?' Ada gave her a concerned look.

'Not well.' Sarah rubbed her eyes hard with the heel of her palm. 'There was a lot to think about. And many questions I want to ask. But first, you ought to know that we had a lot of visitors while you were away, all in need of your help.'

She cast a glance out of the window, where a clear, cold blue sky promised a much brighter day than of late. 'I'm sure that some of them will be back now that the weather has improved. But these are the ones who came,' and she reeled off the list that she had memorised.

'Goodness!' Ada seemed quite taken aback. 'Let me have the names again, but more slowly this time so that I can write them down.'

Once she had finished she looked over the list, and shook her head. 'It will be a lot of work,' she said, clearly thinking of all the remedies that would be required. Then she looked at Sarah. 'This brings me to something that I have been wanting to say to you.'

Sarah had cut herself a slice of bread and was about to butter it but laid down her knife at the seriousness of Ada's tone.

'Don't look so worried. There's nothing to fear.' Ada paused. 'Now, I know you have just got married and so you can expect your husband to provide.' She hesitated. 'I don't wish to speak out of turn but, since your husband's work will take him away a great deal your income may, perhaps, be . . . unreliable.'

It was clear to Sarah that her grandmother was picking her words with unusual care.

'And if, God forbid, an accident should befall him, well . . . in a few months' time you will have an extra mouth to feed. And I won't be here for ever.'

Ada held up her hand as Sarah started to protest. 'No, I'm not as spry as I used to be and, after what has befallen the family in the last week, well, it has made me think how important it is for you to learn some skills, so that you are able to earn money and look after yourself in the future, should the need arise.'

Sarah interrupted her. 'I had been thinking much the same thing. While you were away I was so worried. What if you never came back? And it made me cross with myself that I had never learned to read and write. I had no way of making contact with you. I could have made that list for you –' she gestured at the piece of paper '– if only I had learnt my letters. But, apart from learning how to read and write now, what else can I do?'

'Well, I have a plan.' Ada drew towards her the piece of paper that had been on the table when Sarah came down for breakfast and outlined the idea that she had formulated during her long hours of vigil over her daughter and granddaughters.

'I will teach you how to read and write. And I will instruct you in the art of herbalism. I won't be able to do what I do for ever and someone must take over from me when I am gone. There is much to learn but I am sure that you will be up to the task.'

Ada made the last declaration in the manner of someone who was trying to convince herself.

'But do you really think I can?' Sarah was doubtful. She knew that her grandmother was disappointed in the lack of interest that she had shown in her profession; collecting herbs as instructed and decanting remedies into bottles made up the extent of her knowledge to date.

'I don't think there's an alternative, do you?' Ada said, after a short pause. 'Not with a baby on the way.'

They were both silent, considering her words. Then Sarah spoke.

'We must make a start today. Letters each morning, herbal instruction in the afternoon. Does this sound possible?'

'Indeed it does.' Ada managed a small smile, the first one since her return from Manchester. 'Now, let's eat something. You'll need a good breakfast inside you before we make a start.'

CHAPTER 14

So it was that Sarah, for the first time in her life, applied herself to work in a way that she never had before. Each morning, once the basic chores were out of the way, she and Ada sat down at the table and Sarah, with a grim determination, focused on learning how to read and write. She was encouraged and delighted to find that learning her letters proved relatively easy, and that she could write and recite the alphabet with ease by the end of the first week. But when it came to putting letters together into words, and words into sentences, Sarah's delight turned to despair.

'I don't think I will ever be the master of this,' she said, flinging her slate and chalk down on the table. 'It makes no sense to me. I can neither see nor hear how the letters are strung together into words.' Tears of frustration sprang to her eyes. 'And if I can't do it that means I will never learn to be a herbalist, either. If I can't write a label for a remedy, or note down how to make it, or record what has been prescribed for a patient . . .' Sarah broke down in sobs of frustration, her head in her hands, overcome by the enormity of what lay ahead.

'Ssh. Ssh,' Ada soothed. 'Don't let difficulties over one kind of learning be a bar to another. You can learn the ways of herbalism without needing to write down a word. So much of it has been passed on over the years by word of mouth. How do you think I learnt my skills? Although it is the way today to expect that everything must be written down, why, women have known these things for generations and passed them on, mother to daughter.'

Sarah stopped crying and considered. She'd never thought about how Ada might have come by her knowledge.

'Take your great-grandmother, Catherine Abbot, my mother. She was famous for miles around. Not just for her remedies, mind, but she was the one all the mothers turned to when their time had come. She must have delivered every baby in the area for nigh on twenty years. And she did all of this without knowing how to read or write.'

Ada must have noticed the frown that was furrowing Sarah's brow. 'But it's still a skill you should have,' she added hastily. 'Times have changed and folk around here respect the written word even if they don't understand it. I'm just trying to show you that you needn't think you can't learn one without the other. Reading and writing will come with time. You don't need to try to hurry things.'

Sarah didn't fully believe her. She was struggling to see how anyone could make sense of the strange combinations of letters; they clearly meant something to some people and this just confirmed her lack of self-belief. She must be stupid and incapable of learning. This was the reason, no doubt, why she had failed to learn her letters before. Sarah was forced to acknowledge to herself that her problem with reading and writing was due to her dislike of getting something wrong. Instead of resolving to learn how to get it right she became stubborn and turned away from it. If she was going to succeed, this was something she would have to learn to overcome.

Herbalism, though, proved to be another matter entirely. Sarah found herself looking forward to the afternoons; partly because it meant that the torture of the morning, the effort of forcing her unwilling brain to comprehend, was at an end. But also because she had discovered a genuine interest in what her grandmother did.

During the first week, the afternoons were spent in creating remedies for all the visitors who had called by while her grandmother was away. Ada seemed to know without needing to enquire further what they would need and, for the first time, Sarah concentrated hard on what her grandmother was doing. She asked questions about why Ada was using a particular herb, why it had to be prepared in such a way – pounded, steeped or used in combination with other herbs.

Ada had learnt her own skills over a very long period of time but Sarah's thirst for knowledge, combined with the feeling on both their parts that this knowledge needed to be acquired quickly, required a new approach. After a period of trial and error, during which Ada based her teaching around a specific herb, then around an ailment, she settled on working with Sarah's practical skills. They studied ointments and lotions, infusions and decoctions, powders and poultices, tinctures and tisanes. Sarah discovered that in many cases she somehow knew which parts of the plant would be efficacious, whether it was the flower, the root, the bark, the leaves or the seeds. She could only assume that it was knowledge that she had absorbed over the years spent living with her grandmother.

And, perhaps because the preparation of the herbs was a practical skill, not dissimilar to the domestic chores or food preparation that she was accustomed to doing, Sarah felt quite at ease in her work. She found herself enjoying the concentration required, the measuring and weighing of ingredients, the calm preparation and the scents that the herbs released. Absorbed, she would carry on working late into the afternoon, with lamps lit, and it would be Ada who generally called a halt to the proceedings by suggesting that it might be time for tea, or to make a start on the preparation of food for the evening meal.

As November progressed, so did Sarah's knowledge. She was eager to absorb whatever she could about the practice of herbalism and found herself irritated that in this winter month she could only work with the herbs her grandmother had dried and prepared during the summer. She longed for the chance to learn how to work with fresh herbs but, in the meantime, there was still much to take in.

Her deftness earned her grandmother's admiration and, to Sarah's astonishment, she discovered Ada's advice to allow her reading and writing to develop in their own good time to be sound. She started to recognise the words written on the labels of the jars that she was using on a daily basis, and to see the virtue of such labels. Even though she was learning to distinguish herbs by their scent, and discovering the importance of putting the bottles and jars back in their rightful place on the shelves as soon as she had used them, the possibility of making an error if she couldn't read what was written there was only too apparent to her.

Soon, the morning lessons ceased in favour of devoting the whole day to Ada's teachings on the nature and implementation of her remedies. Within the month, Ada trusted her to prepare the simpler remedies alone, with only basic supervision.

Each evening Sarah would retire to bed, head buzzing with what she had learnt. It would come to her then that Joe had barely entered her thoughts during the day. Indeed, her thoughts turned more often to the loss of her sisters and, if it hadn't been for the baby growing and making its presence felt inside her, she might have started to wonder whether Joe was a figment of her imagination.

CHAPTER 15

One late November afternoon, Sarah and Ada were working in companionable silence side by side in the kitchen. They had been making tonics suitable for nervous complaints and Sarah was packing away the unused herbs while Ada wrote up what had been prepared in her ledger. A knocking at the door was so unexpected that Sarah jumped and dropped the herbs, which scattered on the floor.

Ada laid down her pen. 'Whoever can that be at this hour, in the dark? Go and see, Sarah.'

Sarah's thoughts immediately flew to Joe and it was with a sense of trepidation that she went to the door. She hadn't considered his return and how he would fit into their household, an unfamiliar male presence in their little house. She wasn't sure how she felt about the routine that she and her grandmother had established being disturbed by another. And yet, now she thought of him, she felt a sudden longing for him.

She slid back the bolts and opened the door then stood for a moment, uncomprehending. The muffled figure at the door was too tall and too slight to be Joe, and not someone that she recognised as one of the villagers.

'Who is it, Sarah? You're letting in all the cold air.'

The visitor loosened his muffler, revealing his face, and at that moment Sarah recognised him.

'Daniel!' she exclaimed. 'Come in at once. You must be freezing!'

There was a sharpness in the air that heralded snow and, as Sarah seized Daniel's arm to pull him into the warmth of the kitchen, she was aware that he was shivering in his thin jacket. 'Here,' she commanded, drawing up a chair for him, 'sit by the range and warm yourself.'

'I must apologise for disturbing you without warning,' Daniel said. 'I was called upon to make a visit to the mill in Northwaite again and intended to return straight home by train from Nortonstall. But when I enquired at the station as to the next train, they told me that snow had blocked the track through to Manchester. It was clear that I must stay the night in town and try again in the morning. I thought to pay you a visit in the meantime.'

'And we are very pleased that you did!' Ada exclaimed. She had set the ledger aside and risen from the table to clasp Daniel's hand in hers. 'Sit yourself down, as Sarah bids you. The walk up from Nortonstall on such a cold afternoon is not one to be undertaken lightly.'

'I confess I almost lost heart and turned away when I reached here,' Daniel said. 'I saw through the window how calm and content you both looked within, so that I hesitated to disturb you.'

'I'm glad that you did.' Ada was firm. 'I would never have forgiven myself if you had turned away, after all the kindness that you have shown to my family.'

Sarah had busied herself sweeping up the spilled herbs and she cleared a space on the table to set out tea things. They passed an agreeable hour, talking of Daniel's work in Manchester and of Sarah's efforts to learn her grandmother's trade. After a while Sarah slipped away to light the fire in the parlour, feeling that they shouldn't entertain their guest in the kitchen all evening. She was well aware that if the snow came on it would be necessary to accommodate him for the night, and bedding down on the sofa in the parlour would be the only option for him. As she returned to the kitchen, Daniel leapt to his feet as she entered and she reflected with some surprise on his natural good manners.

It was clear that he and Ada had struck up a strong rapport during the time she had spent in Manchester. Sarah, observing them as they chatted, became pensive. Daniel knew so much more of Ellen and Jane's life during the last few years than she did herself. If things had turned out differently, perhaps he would have been sitting here as her brother-in-law. On cue, as if he had read her thoughts, Daniel reached into his pocket and pulled out a crumpled envelope.

He hesitated. 'I carried this with me when I knew I was coming to Northwaite, on the off-chance that I might see one of you, to pass it on.'

'What is it?' Ada asked, regarding the proffered envelope with some suspicion.

Daniel coloured up. 'It's something that's not rightfully mine to keep,' he said, looking embarrassed. 'I should have given it to you when you came to nurse your family but I didn't want to part with it after what came to pass. Now I feel that was wrong.' He paused. 'I have been given a better position at work, with an increase in salary, and so have been able to move out of those lodgings into more suitable accommodation. I came across the envelope when I was moving my possessions and was reminded of what I had done.'

Ada now held the corner of the envelope between her thumb and forefinger. 'But what is inside it?' She seemed reluctant to discover this for herself.

'It holds the few mementoes that I had of Ellen,' Daniel said. His cheeks were now quite scarlet, standing out in contrast to his sandy hair. 'There's a lock of her hair, a ribbon and . . . a photograph.'

'A photograph?' Ada and Sarah, both startled, spoke together.

'Yes. We visited a bazaar in Manchester on Ellen's birthday. I bought her a ticket for a chance to sit for a studio portrait and she won.' Daniel smiled sadly. 'I think the photographer had an eye for a pretty girl and he liked the look of Ellen. We had quite an argument about it. But she let

96

me go with her when she sat for her portrait. Here it is.'

Daniel took the envelope back from Ada, opened the flap and shook the contents into his hand. It gave Sarah an unpleasant shock to see a curl of Ellen's hair, much duller in colour than she remembered, but even more surprising was the photograph. It was a small head-and-shoulders portrait in sepia tones of a serious young woman who was staring straight at the camera. She was wearing a light-coloured blouse, neatly buttoned up to the neck, and her hair was piled loosely on top of her head, one long curl escaping to hang at her collar.

Sarah took the photograph and studied it. She found it hard to make the association with the Ellen she remembered. She supposed she had changed a good deal in the years she had spent in Manchester, and the formal pose had robbed her face of its lively character, of the characteristics that went to make up her much-loved sister.

She handed the portrait to Ada without comment. Ada moved closer to the lamp and spent a good minute or two in close contemplation of the image. When she looked up, Sarah could see the sparkle of tears in her grandmother's eyes.

'She was much reduced from this when I nursed her,' Ada said to Daniel. 'I wish I could have seen her in such good health. But I fear I am cursed to carry the image of when I last saw her with me for the rest of my life. I think you should keep these things, Daniel, unless Sarah has a use for them?' Ada turned enquiringly to her granddaughter.

Sarah shook her head. 'I have an image of Ellen, too. It dates from much further back than this and I can scarcely believe how much she has changed. This is the Ellen that you knew, Daniel. I think you should keep it.'

Sarah picked up the photograph from the table where Ada had laid it and tucked it back into the envelope. Then she handed it back to Daniel, who still held the lock of hair, tied with a narrow satin ribbon.

'They're yours,' Sarah said firmly. 'We all have our own memories and our own pictures of Ellen, even if they are in our minds. These belong to you.'

'But it was very thoughtful of you to wish to give them to us,' Ada said. 'We are agreed though: you must keep these things and remember Ellen in your own way.'

Daniel didn't try to argue with them but quietly stowed the envelope back in the inside pocket of his jacket. Then the three of them sat in silent contemplation for a good few minutes before Daniel got to his feet and said, 'Well, I really have disturbed you for long enough. I must make my way back to Nortonstall and take a room for the night.'

'Nonsense,' Ada said, at the same time as Sarah protested, 'No, no.'

'I won't hear of it,' Ada said. 'There's snow on

the way if it isn't here already.' All three of them glanced at the dark window and Sarah stood up, pressed her face close to the glass to peer out then started back as fat white flakes spattered against the pane.

'Yes, indeed it is snowing. There's no need for you to consider travelling further tonight, Daniel. I've made up the fire in the parlour; why don't you go through and I will prepare some supper for us.'

'We have been too much in our own company and it will do us good,' Ada added, forestalling further protests by rising to her feet and ushering Daniel through to sit by the fire.

Sarah attended to the cooking, thinking as she did so of her own situation. Her husband was gone from her and what did she have to remember him by while he was away? Nothing: not a lock of his hair or one of his neckerchiefs. Nothing except the baby in her belly and the memory of his laughing eyes. It worried her to think that even that memory was beginning to fade.

The contentment she had felt over the last few days was replaced by a sudden sharp longing. Did Joe ever think of her? she wondered as she chopped the vegetables ready to throw into the pot. Did he remember the curl of her hair, the colour of her eyes, the dimple on one side of her lips when she smiled? Did he long for her as she longed for him sometimes at dead of night when some noise outside the house awoke her? Or was she forgotten, the heady days of their summer love frozen into winter?

Her gloomy train of thought was broken by Daniel's appearance in the kitchen and his polite enquiry as to whether there was anything he could do to help. Sarah, used to taking charge of every-thing herself, was quite taken aback but assured him that all was in hand. He looked downcast so she hesitated before saying that he might take through another scuttle of coal for the fire, as it would no doubt be needed to guard against the chill of the night.

'Would you mind if I took a look outside first?' Daniel asked. 'I promise not to leave the door open too long. But the snow we have in Manchester is a grimy affair, marred with soot and smuts, and I feel sure it will be different here.'

He pulled the door open and exclaimed. 'Oh my goodness, look at this!'

Sarah, bemused by his enthusiasm, peered out too. The moon had risen and the path and garden sparkled and shone under a thick white carpet. Snow had been falling heavily throughout the time that Daniel had been there but it had ceased now and a hard frost was adding its own patina to the surface.

'It does look lovely,' Sarah agreed. 'But you will be hard-pressed to get back to Manchester tomorrow if it carries on overnight.' Sarah's years of living in the countryside had led her to view the snow from a practical angle, as a hardship to be endured, rather than a thing of beauty in itself.

Daniel looked momentarily worried, then brightened. 'No matter. I can return to the mill at Northwaite tomorrow and send word back to Manchester from there. And it will not hurt to spend more time with their engineer. We always have more things to discuss than we ever have the time for.'

Sarah chivvied him away from the door so that she could close it against the cold, then she joined Daniel and Ada by the fireside while the supper bubbled on the range.

CHAPTER 16

They dined at the kitchen table, Sarah laughing off Daniel's compliments on the quality of the stew, then they quickly returned to the warmth of the parlour fire. Sarah found herself marvelling at the way the evening passed in conversation and much good humour. Visitors to Hill Farm Cottage of an evening were non-existent in the winter and she couldn't remember family evenings in the past with her mother and sisters as being so enjoyable. Someone would have been angry or in trouble and an atmosphere would have been brewing. The contrast here was remarkable – was this how normal family life was conducted? Sarah wondered. Even though, of course, this evening's gathering wasn't strictly a family.

'Penny for them?'

Sarah realised that Daniel had spoken and both Ada and Daniel were looking at her enquiringly. She blushed and made a point of fussing over the fire to cover her confusion, then said on impulse, 'No, I will say it. I was just thinking how nice an evening we are having and how rare that is for us, usually so quiet and abed by nine o'clock.'

'You have been most hospitable to your unexpected guest,' Daniel said. 'And I have enjoyed myself too, far more than I have the right to expect. A plate of cold mutton stew and a draughty room at one of the inns in Nortonstall would have awaited me otherwise.'

'At least you would have had a bed.' Sarah smiled at him. 'I'm afraid that we can only offer you the couch. The room will at least be warm.'

Daniel sprang to his feet as he could see that Ada was making a move to rise. He extended a hand to help her then he turned to Sarah.

'I fear my staying here will be an inconvenience to you. And I would not like to be the cause of any unseemly gossip in the village.' He looked troubled.

Sarah laughed. 'I hardly think that staying the night as the guest of a respectable widow and her newly married granddaughter will give rise to much scandal. In any case, we are so far out of the village that your presence here is unlikely to have been noted.'

'You mustn't give it a second thought.' Ada was resolute. 'Now, Sarah will help me up the stairs. My old bones find the winter's cold hard to take these days.' She turned to Daniel. 'Sarah will bring a coverlet down for you and, now that the fire is stoked up, you should stay warm enough until the morning.'

After Sarah had provided Daniel with a quilt and a pillow she bade him goodnight, checked the bolts were secure on the kitchen door and turned off the lamps before making her way back upstairs. She smiled to herself as she thought back over the evening and then, as she drew her bedroom curtains, she paused to gaze out over the snowy expanse of garden. Where was Joe on such a cold night? she wondered. She shivered involuntarily as she thought of him on his narrow-boat some-where along the canal. She hoped that he had a warm fire to sit by and, as she climbed into bed, she longed briefly for the warmth of his arms around her, before falling into a deep, untroubled sleep.

When Sarah awoke in the morning, the chill of the room struck her at once. The low fire that she had left to burn in the bedroom grate overnight had long since gone out and she could see her breath in the air. She took a moment or two to gather her resolve, then she swung her legs out from beneath the covers, pulled on her boots and wrapped a thick shawl around her shoulders before heading downstairs to the kitchen.

Focused as she was on raking out the coals in the range and restoring the fire to bring some heat into the room, she didn't hear Daniel enter the kitchen. She almost dropped the ash bucket in shock when he spoke. She spun round, hand clamped over her mouth to stifle a gasp.

'Forgive me. I have startled you!' Daniel said.

'I had forgotten that you were here.' Sarah was mortified, aware of how she must look in her nightgown and boots, a shawl around her shoulders and her hair in disarray. She thought that Daniel looked hurt and she hastened to add, 'We are so unaccustomed to visitors and you are so unassuming. I do hope you slept well?'

'Indeed.' Daniel smiled. 'I feel thoroughly refreshed. I don't believe that any more snow has fallen overnight so perhaps I should try my luck at the station.'

They both looked out of the window. While it was true that no more snow had fallen, the previous day's fall still lay deep across the garden, so that it was hard to make out its features. The path and the gate were half-buried in a crisp white drift, now sparkling under winter sun.

'It's possible that the train may be running down in the valley,' Sarah conceded, 'but your difficulty will be in making your way there. Perhaps you should wait a little to see whether the sun will bring with it any chance of a thaw?'

She excused herself and hurried upstairs to dress. She remembered too late the water that she had set to boil on the range as she dipped her hand into the iciness of her bedroom water jug. She hesitated, then poured a little into the bowl and splashed her face, gasping as she did so. Having hastily dressed, she brushed her hair and then twisted it into a semblance of a top-knot. Back downstairs she made tea, moving around Daniel, who clearly didn't know what to do with himself in this small domestic space.

'Sit,' she commanded eventually, as he paced between the range and the window. 'There's nothing that you can do for the moment so you may as well have tea and some bread and butter.'

Daniel sighed and did as he was bid. Sarah poured tea from the big brown pot and laid out a cup and plate in readiness for Ada. As she poured milk into a jug a sudden wave of nausea overtook her and she had to stop, bent forward, the back of one hand pressed to her mouth as she supported herself on the table with the other.

'Are you all right?' Daniel half-rose to his feet in concern.

Sarah nodded her head and grimaced, hoping that the feeling would pass as quickly as it had come. It had started to afflict her in the mornings and Ada had promised that they would make a herbal tea that would, she felt, ease the symptoms.

'I'm all right, thank you. Just a little . . . sickness.' She hesitated, wondering how much to reveal, then added in a rush, 'I'm expecting a baby.' She caught Daniel's quick glance at her belly and lowered her hand there in a protective reflex.

Daniel looked puzzled. 'Did your husband not leave for work before your wedding night?'

There was a silence, during which Sarah felt a hot flush rise to her cheeks, mirrored on Daniel's countenance.

'I am so sorry,' he said, looking aghast. 'That was most rude and thoughtless of me. Please forgive me.'

When Ada came down to breakfast a few minutes later she found them sitting in an awkward silence, both their faces still bearing traces of their mutual embarrassment. She looked from one to the other but didn't comment, and the moment quickly passed as Sarah poured tea for her and they discussed what Daniel should do for the best. Ada was in favour of him waiting to see whether the sunshine would bring a thaw but Daniel was impatient to be doing something and, when he announced his intention of attempting to reach the mill, Sarah was secretly thankful.

'It's more than likely that the workforce have already made their way there this morning,' Daniel reasoned. 'They won't want to lose a day's wages. So there'll be some sort of passable route from the village. And once I am there I'll wager I can discover whether or not the trains are running from Nortonstall.'

He pushed his chair back from the table. 'I've imposed on your hospitality long enough. My boots are stout – I'm sure they will see me through a bit of snow.'

Ada tried to demur but Sarah quietly gathered together some bread and cheese and parcelled them up for him.

'Here, take this with you,' she said. 'If you reach the mill you'll be needing something to get you through the day.'

Daniel was already at the door, winding a muffler around his neck and preparing to slide back the bolts. He took the package gratefully with a nod of thanks then, promising Ada that he would return if the snow should prevent him making his way home to Manchester, he opened the door and stepped outside. The air was icy and, despite the sunshine, a hard frost still crisped the surface of the snow.

Daniel's progress was comical; his first steps were on top of the snow before suddenly his foot plunged through the layers, pitching him forward. He flung his arms wide to keep his balance, just managing to hold on to his lunch, before he took a few more steps on the surface only for the same thing to happen again. He turned at the gate, lifted his cap and gave them a cheery wave. His cheeks were glowing from the cold, Sarah noticed, but he was smiling broadly and clearly enjoying himself. She felt a pang of envy. He was heading off on an adventure while she could only wave back and close the door, in accordance with Ada's wishes that she should stop letting out all the warmth.

Whilst the novelty of a visitor had been very welcome, Daniel's visit had raised a sense of dissatisfaction in Sarah that hadn't been there before. She hoped it was something that would quickly pass. If the snow remained, she could see that she would be in her grandmother's company for the foreseeable future, following the same daily routine. Something that had once seemed so pleasurable now felt confining.

CHAPTER 17

That same evening, once her day of practical study was over and it was time to start preparing something for their supper, Sarah thought back to the previous evening and was reminded once more of the pleasure created by the change to their routine. A thunderous knocking at the door caused her to start so violently that she almost dropped the cooking pot that she was about to set on the range.

Her thoughts flew to Daniel as she wiped her hands on her apron. He must have found himself unable to return to Manchester after all and had returned to spend another night with them. Despite their earlier embarrassment, she found herself glad at the thought and opened the door with his name already on her lips, only to find a stranger standing there. Snow was falling again and a wind had got up, so that the figure was temporarily hidden from her in a blizzard of flakes and she could not make him out.

'Well,' the figure demanded. 'Will ye let me in or am I to freeze to death here on t'doorstep?'

'Joe!' His name came out as a gasp.

'Aye. Your loving husband. And who else might it be at this hour?'

Joe was through the door now, and shaking the snow off himself so that it settled on the flagstones and quickly turned into a puddle.

'It really is you!' All thoughts of Daniel were now banished by Sarah's sudden joy at seeing her husband after all this time. His hair was longer, his skin paler and his beard bushier than when she had last seen him but his eyes were the same vivid blue and they crinkled with pleasure at the sight of her.

'Well now, what a journey I've had for the pleasure of seeing you,' he said, sitting heavily in a chair that he had pulled out to face the range. 'My fingers are fair frozen. You'll have to get these off me,' and he indicated his boots.

Sarah knelt down and unlaced his boots then pulled them off, feeing the chill of his feet through his socks as she did so. 'Here,' she said, raising his feet to set them on the hearth of the range, 'sit closer. Your feet are like blocks of ice. Have you walked far?'

'Aye, all the way up from canal near Rawton's Wood, just to have sight of you,' Joe said. He laughed. 'And a right trip it proved to be. Why, I sat down on my arse more times than I care to count. The ice that has canal in its grip is a sight worse up here.'

'The canal has iced over?' Sarah was glad that her grandmother wasn't in the room to hear Joe's profanity. She wondered momentarily whether Daniel had been able to leave Nortonstall at all. It would be awkward if he should suddenly turn up on the doorstep, too.

'Is that Daniel back again?' It was her grand-mother, calling down the stairs from her bedroom, where she had been resting.

'Daniel?' Joe said, looking at Sarah with raised brows. 'And who might he be?'

Sarah was tempted to say that it was someone from the village in need of a remedy, then wondered why she had thought to lie. She supposed it would be easier if she didn't have to explain about Daniel right now, for it would only lead to her having to tell Joe about her sisters and her mother. She wanted to be able to focus on him, and his life over the last few weeks. She decided on a half-truth, giving him his full name, Daniel Whittaker, and describing him as an unexpected visitor from Manchester and a friend of her grandmother.

Hearing Ada coming down the stairs, Sarah went through to stand at the bottom. 'It's Joe, Gran. And a terrible journey he's had of it, it seems. The snow is coming down heavily now.'

'Do you have a glass of ale?' Joe called after her. He greeted Ada's entrance into the kitchen by rising to his feet and making a mock serious bow. 'A pleasure to see you again, Mrs Randall.'

He caught Sarah around the waist as she passed by and pulled her onto his lap. 'Now, I passed up on chance of a drink in Northwaite, to be sure of seeing you all the sooner. So can you find a thirsty man some refreshment now?'

'Not in this house, I'm afraid, Mr Bancroft,' Ada said crisply, moving past him to set the kettle on the hob. 'I hope some hot tea will be welcome on such a cold night?'

Sarah felt Joe's grip on her tighten momentarily and she saw that he was glowering at Ada's back. Then she felt him relax.

'Joe, ma'am, since we're to be under same roof.'

'How long is your visit to be?' Ada's tone was polite, but the implication was that the shorter the visit, the better. Joe was unmoved.

'Happen that's down to t'weather. Boat's stuck in canal and there it stays until t'ice be gone.'

'So you're not moored in Nortonstall?'

Sarah felt uncomfortable sitting on Joe's lap in her grandmother's kitchen; it seemed impolite and she wriggled free to busy herself with the supper.

'Nay. We left there on Wednesday on way back to Leeds but afore too long we found ourselves iced in.'

'Wednesday?' Sarah swung round to look at him. 'So you've already been back to Nortonstall but didn't think to come to visit?' She was puzzled and hurt.

'Nay.' Joe shifted uncomfortably in his chair. ''Twas a lack of time. We were straight on way back with t'next load.'

Sarah wondered whether he'd found the time to

visit the Packhorse Inn in Nortonstall but made no comment. He was here now and she must make the most of it before the thaw set in and sent him on his way.

'I wish I'd known you were coming,' she said. 'I could have made a special supper: the wedding celebration that we never had. Instead, soup is all we have to offer.' She looked despondent.

'No matter.' Joe was cheerful. ''Twill be enough of a treat to have food cooked by someone else. 'Tis a trial to have the boat out on t'water for a full day, then to have to scrat around for supper come evening.'

He sat there, facing the range, his legs stretched full-length, while the two women worked around him, Ada taking over the cooking while Sarah went to set a fire in the parlour. It was an extravagance to have a fire in there two nights running, but it seemed churlish to light one for Daniel and not one for her own husband, whom she hadn't seen in many a long week.

CHAPTER 18

With Christmas finally upon them, her first one as a married woman, Sarah felt a sense of nervous anticipation about Joe's second visit. He'd been able to spend so little time with her when she'd last seen him, just less than a month ago. She'd found it strange to have him there, and she had been uneasy about having him in her bed the whole night through, with her grandmother sleeping so close by. But Joe had fallen asleep before she had even joined him there, then snored the whole night, so what with the disturbance and the novelty of it all, she hadn't slept a wink.

Dawn had brought with it a steady 'drip, drip, drip' from outside and she had peeped out to discover that a thaw had set in overnight. The temperature had risen as quickly as it had fallen and Joe, on waking, had announced that he'd need to return to the canal, and his narrow-boat, right away.

He'd pulled her back down beside him on the bed and nuzzled her neck, then drawn his finger along the length of her nose, kissed her full on the lips and pushed her away again.

'I can't tarry. But I'll be back to spend Christmas so make sure you have a nice dish of beef for me, an' a slice or two of plum pudding.'

She trailed a length of ivy across the parlour mantel and tucked the last sprig of holly behind the one picture on the wall, a painting of the river below Nortonstall where it was crossed by the packhorse bridge. It had been painted by her great-grandmother, signed Catherine Abbot and dated 1805. Sarah examined it closely for the first time: it was an accomplished piece. She wondered whether other works by her great-grandmother existed and resolved to ask Ada about it, but first she stood back and looked critically around.

The scent of the foliage brought a sense of the crisp outdoors into the room. The dark-green glossy leaves and the red berries added a festive air, but it wasn't quite enough, she decided. A few more sprigs of holly to go in a jug, perhaps, then with the fire lit it would truly feel like Christmas Eve.

She took the scissors from the table as she passed through the kitchen, threw a shawl around her shoulders and slipped her feet into her boots before stepping outside. The chill of the air struck her. Surely it hadn't been this cold when she had been outside earlier that afternoon?

She glanced up at the sky; the clouds of earlier in the day had vanished and now the sky was shaded from palest blue over in the west to inky blue above her head, where a couple of stars were just peeping out. She knew her way well enough around the garden to have no need of extra light to locate the holly bush, and she swiftly cut a few more stems, sucking her finger where the spines on the leaves pierced her skin and drew blood. She was just trying to remember whether, in legend, the berries were meant to represent drops of blood when, deep in thought, she was startled by something hard hitting her full in the face.

She stepped back, dropping the holly as she did so, heart thumping. Then she started to laugh. Her assailant was a towel, hung out on the line earlier. Forgotten about, it had frozen and now hung there, stiff as a board. Sarah unpegged it and frowned at the rigid cloth, then she laid it on the ground and used it as a tray to carry the holly inside.

'What on earth have you got there?' Ada asked. She'd been resting upstairs, something that she had got into the habit of doing regularly of late.

'It's the kitchen towel, frozen solid,' Sarah said, standing the rigid piece of cloth on the draining board. 'We're going to have a hard frost tonight. I hope Joe gets here before the hill out of the village becomes too icy.'

'Well, I daresay he'll be none too steady on his feet, in any case,' Ada observed drily. 'No doubt he's made it as far as The Old Bell but stopped to wish a merry Christmas to one and all.'

Sarah ignored the comment and went through to the parlour to finish her holly decorations. Then it would be time to prepare the evening meal, which they would normally have had after midnight service in the chapel, but this year, for the first time, Ada had decided not to go.

'It's a way to walk there and back in the cold and dark. I'll content myself with the Christmas Day service this year,' she'd said.

Sarah had been puzzled. Ada had always enjoyed attending the evening service; the streets on the way there and back were busy with people all muffled against the cold and offering the season's greetings to each other. The abundance of lanterns, set on walls and in windows and carried by the churchgoers, added a magical feel and Sarah would be sorry not to see it. But Joe would be coming and she had a feeling that, once indoors, he would have little enthusiasm for heading out again to go to the chapel.

They were to have Ada's special beef broth for Christmas Eve night, along with a slice or two of ham and some pickles to add to the bread, freshly baked that afternoon. A few apples from their store in the outhouse and a bit of cheese would complete the meal.

'Not too much cheese,' Ada would always counsel. 'Otherwise you'll be complaining of the wildness of your dreams in the morning.'

Sarah began to lay the table, bringing out the best china and cutlery from the parlour cupboard. These things saw the light of day at Christmas, Easter and on birthdays, and the rarity of the exposure always made the event seem extra special. She took a linen cloth and polished the cutlery and glasses until they shone. Joe had only dined with them once before but tonight's table, which she'd also decorated with ivy, would impress him, she thought.

'We need another place set,' Ada remarked as she passed through the room.

'Another place?' Sarah was puzzled. She'd already laid out three place settings.

'Yes, for Daniel.' Ada looked equally puzzled. 'I enquired as to his Christmas plans when I wrote to him and, when I heard that he would be spending the day alone in Manchester, I insisted he should come to us. I'm sure I told you.'

Sarah experienced a momentary flash of worry at her grandmother's absent-mindedness. Ada had always been so sharp and never missed a trick; it was most unlike her to forget to tell Sarah about Daniel's visit. This thought was quickly replaced by another: what would Joe make of Daniel's presence? They'd never met, or had they? Daniel had been present at the wedding but now she couldn't remember whether he and Joe had been introduced. And Joe's previous visit had been so hasty that she had never found the right moment to tell him of her sorrow at the loss of her sisters and mother, nor to explain the important role that Daniel had played in their last days.

Would Daniel and Joe get along? They were very different characters. Sarah felt a wave of misgiving.

Suddenly she wasn't quite as excited about the prospect of Christmas as she had been just a few minutes earlier.

'Is that all right? Do we have enough food?' Ada was looking at her with concern. Sarah became aware that her own feelings were probably written too clearly on her face.

'Yes, of course. It will be lovely to have Daniel here. I was just surprised, that's all. And we have plenty of food. But I don't have a gift for him.' This new thought dismayed Sarah all over again.

'It's quite all right. I'm sure he won't expect anything. But I have knitted him a muffler, so all is not lost.'

Ada looked rather pleased with herself and it occurred to Sarah that Daniel had become the son or, more properly, grandson that she'd never had.

CHAPTER 19

When the knock on the door came, Sarah was apprehensive. Would it be Joe? Or Daniel? She hoped it would be Joe, so that she could prepare him for Daniel's arrival. When she unbolted the door, at first she couldn't make out who stood there, well wrapped against the cold. But when the person stepped forward into the light of the lamp that she held up she saw the frank, open features of Daniel, his nose pink with cold and his freckles standing out against his pale skin.

Her misgivings were forgotten in the change in the atmosphere that Daniel brought with him. All at once, there was excitement in the air. Daniel was clearly in the mood for celebrating. He'd barely shrugged off his overcoat before he was producing items from a cloth bag and laying them out on the table: a large pork pie, a pot of mustard, a box of dates, a bag of nuts and a couple of bottles of ale. He apologised to Ada for the latter and said that he would gladly drink them out in the garden if it offended her to have them in the house, but he was so happy to be free of work for a day or two, and to be spending time with them again, that he felt he couldn't let the day pass without a small celebration.

'I would have brought something to drink for you both, of course,' he added hastily, 'but I wasn't sure it would be welcome. I just wanted to make a small contribution to the dinner-table.' He gestured at the things he had laid out. 'The shops in Manchester were so full of good things for Christmas that I couldn't resist.'

Sarah paused as she was hanging up his overcoat. 'I've never been there. Never even been beyond Nortonstall. You must tell me more about it.'

So while the soup heated gently on the range, Daniel described the shops in Deansgate and Market Street to Sarah and Ada. When he told them about the Barton Arcade, Sarah was uncomprehending at first.

'Shops on two levels, under a glass roof, you say? How can that be?'

Daniel, who had lived in Manchester all his life, was used to the developments that prosperity had brought to the town and struggled to convey all the riches on offer. He described small shops designed for the purpose of solely selling furs or dresses, perfume or flowers.

'But how can folk afford such things?' A frown furrowed Sarah's brow. 'On mill-work wages?'

Daniel patiently explained that, while the mills and other industry had brought thousands of workers to the town, they had also brought riches and there were many wealthy people who could well afford to shop in the streets of central Manchester. He liked to wander the shopping streets and observe them, and it was something that Ellen had enjoyed too. This time he had determined to buy a few things as gifts for Sarah and her grandmother.

His expression grew sad when he mentioned Ellen and the mention of her sister's name struck Sarah to her heart. Although they hadn't spent Christmas as a family since before her mother and sisters moved to Manchester, this was her first Christmas without them being in the world at all. It felt wrong to be celebrating, somehow, no matter how quietly.

'You know,' Daniel said, 'Ellen spoke about you so often, and of her happy memories of living here. Even though I only knew her in Manchester, I feel her presence very strongly here because she described it to me so vividly. She would have loved to be here with us this Christmas. Perhaps she is, in a way.'

Sarah, caught up with the idea, looked around the room as if she expected her mother, Jane and Ellen to suddenly materialise. Ada broke the spell by moving over to the range to stir the soup.

'We should eat,' she said. 'Daniel must be famished after his journey and I confess to feeling almost faint myself.'

It was only as Sarah was setting out the ham and preparing to serve the soup that she started to feel the first twinges of anxiety again. This time she was worried as to where Joe could be. The evening was already well advanced. Could it be that her grandmother was right and he was to be found in The Old Bell? Resolutely she pushed the thought from her mind and concentrated on enjoying the evening ahead. Joe had always been a law unto himself. He would show up when he was good and ready.

'Are we waiting for someone?' Daniel asked once they were seated, the soup bowls steaming before them. He indicated the unused place setting.

'Joe, my husband,' Sarah said. 'We won't wait. His supper will keep.' And she picked up her spoon. 'Eat, before it cools.'

'Grace first,' Ada admonished, and they bowed their heads while she offered a few words of thanks, then they fell to. Daniel ate slice after slice of the crusty bread with his ham and cheese, exclaiming in delight over its freshness, until Sarah, fearful that there would be none left for Joe, wished that she had set some aside.

Once the table was cleared they moved into the parlour and Daniel produced a pack of cards and suggested a game of Whist. Ada would not hear of any form of gambling, even with matchsticks, so they contented themselves with playing purely for the pleasure of it. Sarah found she had done rather well when they tallied up the score at the end of the evening and she accused Daniel of letting her win. He was vehement in his denials and so, still disbelieving, she went upstairs to fetch bedding for him while Ada made her way up to her room.

'There is no word from Joe?' Daniel asked on her return.

Sarah paused, her hand on the door handle as she prepared to leave the room. 'No. But I would expect none. Who could be found to carry a message on Christmas Eve night? I am sure he has his reasons and we will no doubt see him in the morning.'

She made herself sound more cheerful than she felt, wished Daniel a good night and took herself up to bed. There she shed more than a few silent tears of disappointment into her pillow before she slept. Where was Joe? And why hadn't he thought to send word? The baby kicked in her belly and she laid her hands over it to soothe it, forcing herself to stop crying. Tomorrow would bring him, she was sure.

When Sarah awoke the next morning, she was struck by the cold quality of the light in the room. She was puzzled for a few seconds, until it dawned on her that it must surely have snowed in the night. As she summoned up the will to leave her warm bed and look out of the window, her thoughts strayed to the day ahead. It was Christmas Day and there was much to be done before dinner could be set on the table.

She counted to three, took a deep breath and flung back the bedcovers. Sure enough, as she pulled the curtains aside, she saw that a blanket of snow carpeted the garden. It was as deep as last time, just less than a month ago, but today it wasn't sparkling under a bright winter sun but lay instead under leaden skies. The curious yellowish tinge of the clouds promised more snow to come and indeed, as Sarah watched, a few flakes started to drift lazily from the sky.

Shivering, she turned away to take a shawl from the bedroom chair and to straighten the bedding. Remembering that Daniel was downstairs, and that last time she had appeared before him totally unprepared, she splashed her face with icy water and hastily brushed her hair, before loosely twisting it up and securing it with pins. When she turned back to look out of the window, the air was filled with falling snow, whipped into flurries by gusts of wind. As Sarah placed her hand on the bedroom door latch, Joe again came to her mind. She wondered what chance there was that he would be with them that day.

CHAPTER 20

With dinner over and Christmas Day rapidly drawing to a close, although the darkness of the snowy skies meant that it had never seemed to truly begin, Sarah had ventured out into the garden to scatter some crumbs for the birds before bedtime.

'Poor things,' she thought. 'Wherever do they hide from the bitter cold overnight?'

She kept the ivy untrimmed on the outhouse wall on purpose, in hope that the sparrows would make their roost there on winter nights, cosied up together without squabbling. She knew that the wrens were happy to band together to provide each other with winter warmth, for she'd found at least ten of them tucked in amongst old sacks stored in the outhouse. They, at least, were tiny enough to squeeze in below the eaves to find shelter on such harsh winter nights.

She was on the lookout, though, for her favourite garden visitor. The splash of red on the robin's breast would surely make him stand out against all this snow but, to her concern, there was no sign of him. He'd followed her around the garden towards the end of the summer, once his brood was raised, singing a subdued but no less sweet song and always but a few feet from her, whatever she was doing. He had a confiding air about him, his head cocked to one side as he watched her, and she was in the habit of chatting to him whether she was working in the garden or hanging out the washing. At morning and evening he sang his heart out from the topmost branches of the tree in the garden; it was the first thing she listened for on waking.

She shook out the crumbs from the tablecloth and broke up some extra pieces of bread for good measure, then waited anxiously. Had she left it too late in the day? Had he already found a roost for the night, feathers fluffed up to protect him from the bitter cold? She admonished herself for not thinking of him earlier in the day. 'And on Christmas Day, too,' she thought to herself as she turned to go back to the house.

Then a movement in the ivy caught her eye and there he was, muttering rather than singing his song. 'He means to scold me,' she thought, and called out to him.

'Hello, Mr Robin. Happy Christmas. I've brought you some crumbs and a special treat, just for you.' She reached into the pocket of her apron for the morsel of plum pudding hidden there, then crumbled the rich mixture between her fingers and scattered it onto the snowy surface. She caught a flash of the robin's rich red breast as he flew down and alighted on the snow, dipping down to eat then righting himself swiftly as if to guard against attack or possible intruders.

'It's going to be another cold night,' she told him. 'I hope you have somewhere warm to sleep. You are all alone, just like me. No one to keep you warm at night.'

Joe had not appeared that day. She hadn't really been surprised. The snow had fallen steadily all morning and she suspected they were as good as cut off. It hadn't stopped her looking up ten times an hour as she prepared dinner, or indeed while they were eating it, to see whether his face was pressed to the window, to check up on what they were doing inside, before he banged on the door demanding entry.

That morning, as soon as she had risen and seen how the snow was coming down, Ada had declared her intention of foregoing attendance at Christmas service.

'There's not a chance I could make it there and back,' she had said. 'If I need to speak to God I can just as well do it here on a day like today.'

Sarah had been relieved; she and Daniel had discussed it before Ada got up and he had stoutly declared himself more than happy to escort her if needed, while Sarah got on with the dinner. Privately, Sarah believed that they would be lucky to get beyond the garden gate, but she'd set about laying fires and had asked Daniel to make sure that all the coal scuttles were well stocked so that they wouldn't need to venture out later.

She had reason to be thankful again for Daniel's presence at dinner; it would have been a sorry affair with just Sarah and her grandmother, and no doubt swiftly over. Daniel was not only very good company but, since he was their guest, they were obliged to make sure that he was entertained. Otherwise, Ada would have withdrawn into her own world, which was something she did a great deal of late, and Sarah would have been brooding over where Joe might be.

As it was, they had dined well on beef with roast potatoes, carrots and greens and rich onion gravy, a speciality of Ada's. The plum pudding steamed gently on the range and, whilst it took longer to cook than Sarah had expected, this was no bad thing. Daniel had declared he would need to take several turns around the room if he was to find any room in his belly for more food, then decided that a vigorous bout of washing-up, despite Sarah's protests, would serve just as well.

She had sat back in contentment, happy to take a rest for twenty minutes, and caught Ada's quizzical gaze as she did so. Ada hadn't commented on Joe's absence and, although Sarah was upset that he hadn't joined them as promised, she also had to acknowledge that their day would have passed very differently if he had been there. Would Daniel have been so relaxed if Joe had been present? Would Joe have been difficult around

Daniel? She had no way of knowing, nor how she herself might have reacted.

Now Sarah, deep in thought in the snowy garden, was startled to hear, 'Whatever are you doing?'

The voice, just behind her, made her jump. She hadn't heard Daniel's approach. As she spun around he came towards her, holding out his overcoat to her.

'Here, put this around your shoulders. You must be frozen.'

Sarah realised that she was, indeed, thoroughly chilled and, as soon as she acknowledged it, her teeth started to chatter.

Daniel shook his head as he draped the coat around her shoulders and ushered her back to the house.

'You know, you mustn't worry,' he said suddenly. 'I am sure your husband would have been here if he could. But with this weather –' he gestured at the garden, carpeted by its thick blanket of snow '– why, it would be folly to try to get through. Indeed, I fear you may have to put up with my company for longer than I had intended.'

Sarah was thankful to be back in the warmth of the house but turned on the threshold to take one last look over the garden as dusk began to creep across the sky.

'Who were you talking to out there?' Daniel followed her gaze.

'Oh dear. You heard me! You will think me very

strange.' Sarah laughed. 'It was the robin. He's such a special creature. Listen.'

She held her finger up to her lips for silence. The robin had taken up his perch at the top of the tree and was singing; not his full-throated song, but loud enough to spread beyond the confines of the garden.

Daniel listened for a moment or two. 'It's beautiful. He's letting the others know who's in charge around here, I'll be bound. Now, come away inside. Ada would have us play some games and it can't be done with just the two of us.'

Sarah bolted the door and turned down the lamps then went through to the parlour where the evening passed in rounds of Happy Families, Snap and Snakes-and-Ladders, Ada having resolutely refused to play Whist again as she felt it was wrong to play a gambling game on Christmas Day, despite having very much enjoyed it the previous evening.

CHAPTER 21

It wasn't until a couple of days after Christmas that the cold released its grip on the land and the snow started to thaw. Sarah had mixed feelings as she waved Daniel off early one morning. She had enjoyed his company over Christmas, particularly in Joe's absence, but he had clearly started to suffer from cabin fever and an eagerness to return to work as his enforced imprisonment went on.

'I do hope my presence hasn't been a burden to you,' Daniel said as he left. 'Spending four nights instead of the two I had planned must have stretched my welcome to the limits.' As Sarah started to protest he held up his hand. 'I confess to being eager to return to work but I hope you will keep an eye on Ada. She seems much changed, even since my last visit just a few weeks ago.'

His words checked Sarah's protestations. Although she'd noticed that Ada seemed unlike her usual self the change had, she supposed, been a gradual one. It was clearly much more obvious to Daniel.

'The loss of my mother and my sisters has hit

her very hard, particularly since she was with them in Manchester at the end. But I will keep a close eye on her and try to make sure that she recovers her strength.'

Daniel made a mock bow of farewell then strode away along the path, leaving Sarah smiling as she watched him go. He was like a young colt released out into the field, eager to scent the air, kick his heels and make a bid for freedom. His enthusiasm for his work was a novelty to her, although she had little on which to base her judgement. Apart from Joe, she had no experience of working men other than those in the village, who were, in the main, shopkeepers, publicans, blacksmiths or farmers, with a few mill-workers among the younger men of her distant acquaintance.

Joe said very little about his work and seemed to undertake it with a kind of grim endurance. He had scarcely mentioned it when he was with her, other than to give her an indication of when he must depart again. Daniel, though, seemed fired up by his job; she'd found him only yesterday drawing diagrams in a book that he carried in his overcoat pocket. When she'd asked him about it, he'd replied that he was trying to help solve a problem with the waterwheel at the mill, to make it run more smoothly and efficiently when powering the machines, despite the fluctuating water levels in the river. He'd seemed surprised when she'd teased him about working during his holiday.

'Why, I'm always thinking about ways to solve problems,' he said. 'No matter whether it's a Monday or a Sunday.'

Now he was gone without a backward glance and Sarah knew that the house would feel quiet without him. She also knew that there was a danger she would start to brood about Joe. There had still been no word from him, although surely a message would come through now that the thaw had set in?

Three more days passed before Joe put in an appearance, on New Year's Eve. Sarah had reluctantly taken down the holly and ivy decorations, which were starting to dry out and curl up, feeling that the house looked bare without them. She'd wanted Joe to see the place at its best so she was disposed to feeling aggrieved when he made his appearance on New Year's Eve afternoon.

The smell of ale and smoke on his clothing when she had opened the door to his insistent knocking was in sharp contrast to the fresh chill of the air outside, and brought an unwelcome suggestion as to where he had been spending his time. But Joe swept her into his arms, then picked her up and carried her back into the kitchen while she shrieked and protested, half scared that he might drop her.

'Why, tha' barely weighs more than a feather, and wi' a bairn inside too. Is tha' sure, lass?' he asked, patting her belly then bending low to plant a kiss on the bump.

His presence, as usual, seemed to fill the room. Sarah was glad that her grandmother was taking her afternoon rest. She would have Joe to herself for a little while and hopefully in that time he would calm down from his present excitable state. His good humour was infectious, though, and Sarah found herself laughing and smiling despite herself, although she had to persuade Joe that it wasn't a good idea to take to her bedroom for a rest, as he put it. His hands on her body made it quite clear that a rest couldn't have been further from his mind but Sarah, only too aware of her grandmother resting upstairs in her own room, didn't feel enough at ease to take up his suggestion. Instead, she busied herself making a fire in the parlour and setting the kettle to boil so that Joe might have tea and some fruitcake, the only festive food that was left in the house.

Comfortably settled in a chair by the fire, Joe drew her onto his lap and began to cover her neck with kisses while his fingers sought to undo the buttons of her bodice. Sarah returned his kisses but, finding herself growing hot from the fire and by the feelings awakened within her by his caresses, she broke free and, with the excuse that the kettle was surely boiling, she escaped to the kitchen, hastily adjusting her clothing in case her grandmother should walk in.

Joe was dozing when Sarah returned to the parlour and, as she was closely followed by Ada, there was no opportunity to renew their intimacy.

'A merry Christmas to you,' Ada said by way of greeting to Joe. Sarah felt it was a rather pointed remark but Joe, leaning forward to select a piece of cake, didn't appear to be put out.

''Tis more like a Happy New Year,' he observed. He was clearly not disposed to pick a fight, nor to enlighten them about his whereabouts over the festive period, other than to say that he had thought that the snow would never cease and that he would be trapped on his boat in the perishing cold until the spring came.

'Do you not have a fire aboard?' Sarah asked. Then she wondered whether this was a stupid question. It was surely necessary, but dangerous?

'Aye, we have a fire right enough, for heat and cooking. But when the water is chilled to freezin' and the boat's arse – begging your pardon –' this with a nod to Ada '– is set in it all day and night, why, 'tis hard to stay warm. This is more like it.'

Joe stretched luxuriously, basking in the glow of the fire, and Sarah, feeling sorry for what he must have endured, hurried to fill his cup and cut him another slice of cake. Her heart, which had been in danger of becoming frozen against him, began to thaw. They sat in silence for a while, content to enjoy the present moment.

Then Ada finished her tea, stood up and said, 'Well, you two will no doubt be glad of some time together,' and withdrew to the kitchen, rejecting Sarah's offer of help with the evening meal. Sarah moved her chair to be closer to Joe and the pair of them gazed into the fire, Joe stroking the swelling of her belly until he fell into a deep sleep, only waking when summoned to eat.

He had little to offer in response to questions about his work during the meal, other than to say that it went on much as usual, with a load being put on in one place and then taken off further down the canal, only to be replaced by another. Sarah described the Christmas celebrations that he had missed, going into detail about the decorations and the dinner, and the games played in the evening. She wanted him to imagine what it would have been like to be there. She observed Ada watching Joe closely but he offered little reaction other than to grunt and concentrate on cracking the leftover nuts that she had put out at the end of the meal.

The mention of Daniel's name elicited the reaction, 'So he's become a regular around here, has he?' but he just shrugged when Sarah hastened to say that his work quite regularly brought him to the mill in Northwaite and that he, too, had been caught out by the snow.

With the plates cleared from the table Joe fetched bottles of ale, which he had stashed in his jacket pockets. Registering Ada's frown he said, 'You wouldn't deny a man a celebration to see out t'old year, now, would you?' He poured a little of the ale into a glass and pushed it towards Sarah. 'And it's rude to let a man drink alone.'

Sarah sipped at it, feeling torn: Joe was being

provocative but they were under Ada's roof. She found herself in a difficult position: wanting to relax and enjoy her husband's company after his long absence, but mindful of the respect due to her grandmother. It seemed that Ada was not unaware of her dilemma, however, and not disposed to sit late into the evening with them.

'She'd have stayed if Daniel was here,' Sarah thought ruefully as Ada made her excuses after less than an hour had passed, and took herself off to bed. Somehow, Joe's presence filled the room much more than Daniel's had, and it was something to which she and her grandmother were going to need to adjust.

PART III

FEBRUARY – APRIL 1875

CHAPTER 22

It was one of those rare February days that offered the alluring promise of spring, following on from nearly a fortnight of heavy cloud that had sapped Sarah's spirits, and her grandmother's, too. Ada had taken to her bed over the last day or so and Sarah, now big with child, had volunteered to deliver a remedy to the village.

She was glad that the pregnancy was slowing her pace; she was enjoying the feel of the sun on her skin and the birdsong all around her. The hedgerows were alive with activity; it was as if the birds had been holding their breath, waiting, but now they were firmly convinced that it must be time to nest. Even the air held a certain sweetness and it brought a smile to Sarah's face. She knew that the weather might change in an instant, that the clouds could roll back in and the gloom could return, but she was happy to enjoy it while it lasted, and to see it as a foretaste of things to come.

She was surprised at how tiring she was finding the walk, but she paused every now and then to draw breath and to take note of the plants starting to peep through in the hedge-bottoms. It was too early for much beyond the first leaves to be visible, but it was nice to be reminded of where the comfrey had been and where clumps of foxgloves had grown tall. The landscape was so changed by winter that it was hard to picture it as it had been through the summer – and yet Sarah knew that it would only take a few more days of weather like this and all the barrenness would be left behind.

She was grateful of the offer of a seat and a glass of water when she arrived at Martha Mitchell's house in Northwaite. Martha seemed concerned and told her to take as long as she needed to rest before heading home.

'When do you think you are due?' Martha asked Sarah, eyeing her bump.

'Oh, it will be a little while yet,' Sarah said. 'Around mid-March.'

'Hmm. It's nearly the end of February now. I know first babies are often late but you're a mere slip of a thing. I wouldn't be surprised if this baby shows itself sooner than expected. It's a long walk back up that hill to your grandmother's,' Martha continued. 'I can ask Wilfred Sykes, the carter, whether he has business that way, to save you the journey.'

Sarah smiled politely but disregarded Martha's concern. 'No, I'll be heading home as soon as I've drunk this. Gran hasn't been feeling too well and I'm keen to persuade her out into the garden when I get home. I'm sure the fresh air will do her good.' Sarah drained the glass and stood up, wiping sweat from her brow. It really was very warm for February.

She was aware of Martha's eyes on her as she walked down the path, and she made a conscious effort to walk slowly but surely. While she would have liked to stop at the gate and stretch a little to ease her back, instead she used the gatepost to bear her weight as she turned to wave farewell to Martha. Then, with grim determination, she set out again.

Now she was less keen to linger; her mind had locked on to Hill Farm Cottage and she wanted to get back there so that she could lie in the cool of her bedroom. Her body, though, seemed to have other ideas. Her wish to get home simply wouldn't overcome its apparent determination to prevent her, and she was less than halfway up the hill when she was forced to stop, at the gated entrance to a field. She held on to the top bar of the gate and leant towards it, allowing the weight of her belly to drop forwards.

'Please, not yet,' she whispered. Surely it was too soon for the baby to be coming? She looked longingly at the field; the lush grass might make a comfortable bed if she couldn't make it any further, but could she even summon the strength to push the gate open? Was she to have the baby here, by the side of the road, with no one to help her?

She let out a low moan of panic and pain as a contraction seized her. Feeling hot and nauseous, she tried to pull herself upright and think clearly. Could she make it back down the hill to Martha's house and ask for help there? Her feet were as good as rooted to the spot, though; no matter how hard she tried to force herself into action, her body had other ideas.

Sarah clung tightly to the gate as another contraction tore through her. She let out a low wail of fright then, as she became aware of the sound of horse's hooves, rumbling wheels and voices, she felt a sense of shame. No one must see her like this.

'Sarah!' It was Martha's voice, and no sound had ever been so welcome. 'I knew I shouldn't have let you leave. Here now, hold still, we'll work out a way to get you home.'

Martha's hands were stroking Sarah's back and she offered soothing words as the carter helped her to climb into the wagon.

'As quick as you can to Hill Farm Cottage,' Martha said, then turned to Sarah who was leaning against her. 'As soon as you left I ran in search of Wilfred here. I thought to follow you home, not liking the idea of you alone there if Ada wasn't well. I didn't think I would find you here like this. Heaven knows what might have happened.'

Sarah listened to her through a haze of pain and confusion. She wanted above all else to be at home in her bed and the motion of the swaying cart was agony; she felt every stone beneath the wheels and every footfall of the horse, but she told herself it must be endured. By the time they reached the gate of Hill Farm Cottage she was almost fainting. Martha and Wilfred helped Sarah into the parlour, abandoning any idea of getting her up the stairs to bed, then the older woman despatched the carter straight back to Northwaite.

'Fetch the midwife at once,' she said. 'And if she can't be found at home, then seek her out, but don't delay.'

Mrs Atkinson, the midwife, who had been assisting at another birth, arrived nearly two hours later to find that she had missed the main event. Sarah, with her hair plastered to her brow with sweat and wearing an expression of bewilderment, was already cradling a tiny infant. Martha, looking flushed, was bundling up the sheets she had seized in great haste from Sarah's bed.

'Well, it looks as though there's little for me to do here,' the midwife declared.

'There's the cord to be cut,' Martha said, and her voice started to wobble.

'Now then, you have a sit-down,' the midwife commanded. 'It's lucky that you've had three of your own and have some experience of babies. But the pair of you have suffered a shock, just the same.'

She bustled around making Sarah comfortable and checking the baby over before using some of the water that Martha had set to boil to make tea.

'You'll be needing it sweet,' she said, spooning

in the sugar despite Martha's protests. 'It's good for shock. I'd suggest a nip of brandy but, knowing Ada, there'll be none to be found in this house. Now then,' she said, addressing Sarah, 'you've a fine, bonny lass there, none the worse for making her entry into the world so suddenly. Have you a name for her yet?'

'I thought I would call her Alice,' Sarah said.

'Is she named for someone special?' the midwife asked, propping Sarah upright with cushions so that she might drink her tea.

'Yes, for my grandmother.' Sarah's smile was a little tremulous. 'She told me she'd always wished that she'd been called Alice instead of Ada.' She gazed down at Alice as if unable to believe her eyes, then looked up suddenly. 'Oh, heavens. I forgot about Gran. Wherever is she?'

Martha sprang to her feet. 'Don't move. I'll go up and see.'

A few minutes later Martha reappeared, with a slightly dishevelled Ada in tow.

'What's this I hear?' Ada exclaimed. 'Did no one think to wake me?'

The three other women in the room looked at each other and shook their heads. Ada must have been in a very deep sleep.

Sarah smiled at her grandmother. 'Meet your great-granddaughter Alice,' she said.

CHAPTER 23

Sarah lay awake the whole of the first night, euphoric and stealing glances at her daughter tucked in beside her. She missed Joe keenly, longing to introduce their daughter to him, wanting him there to kiss her and tell her how clever she was. She hoped that he wouldn't be disappointed that he didn't have a son; she wanted him to be proud of Alice. Perhaps he would suggest that the time was right for them to look for a house of their own, now that they were a proper family?

But Sarah was unprepared for the way in which the presence of a small baby could have such an effect on a household. After the first night Alice, having arrived a little early in the world, seemed intent on making up for lost time and began to demand feeds constantly. Her cries, though mewling, were insistent, and it felt to Sarah that no sooner was one feed done than another was required. Attending to Alice seemed to take up all of her time and, if it hadn't been for her grandmother, Sarah would not have known how to manage the cooking or housework. Alice's arrival, however, seemed to draw Ada out of the gloom into which she had sunk, and to give her a new lease of life. Sarah went from worrying about her grandmother's health to marvelling at her energy.

Sarah was apt to nod off if she sat down for too long by the warmth of the range whilst Alice was napping. Ada, by contrast, gave up her afternoon rests. She was always ready to take Alice off Sarah's hands, to walk with her and soothe her cries when she was fretful, and to undertake the domestic chores and cooking that had fallen increasingly to Sarah over the last few years.

She showed Sarah how to swaddle Alice so that she would sleep more soundly, made a remedy to give Alice when she was colicky, and generally seemed like a woman twenty years younger than her sixty-five years. It brought home to Sarah very forcefully how much Ada had been suffering over the last few months after seeing Mary, Jane and Ellen – her own daughter and granddaughters – into their graves.

The weather took a turn for the worse after the unusual spring-like conditions that had heralded Alice's birth. March came in, with icy rain brought on strong winds, frustrating Ada in her plans to take her great-granddaughter into Northwaite to show her off around the village.

One day, when Alice was a month old, the minister came calling. Sarah's heart sank when she saw him approach along the path, his coat flapping and his hat clutched tightly to his head whilst he attempted to stop the wind snatching it and hurling it away.

'Come in, come in, Minister,' she said, opening the door before he could knock. 'It's not a good day to be out visiting.'

'Well, with Easter upon us, I thought it was high time that I visited the newest member of our congregation,' the minister replied. Sarah took his coat and set it to dry over a chair close to the range. She ushered him to the parlour and knelt to light the fire even though he protested that there was no need.

'It will warm the room up in no time,' she said. 'And meanwhile I can get you a cup of tea. You'll be needing one after your walk up here in the wind and the rain.'

She hurried back to the kitchen, fearful that she was about to start babbling nonsense in an attempt to keep him away from the subject that was no doubt uppermost in his mind: Alice's baptism. So she fussed about, bringing in the tea things and begging him to set his chair a little closer to the fire, which was indeed drawing nicely with the strength of the wind now blowing outside.

Ada's appearance in the room with Alice was greeted by the minister leaping to his feet, almost spilling his tea in the process, and a relieved smile from Sarah, which she hoped had escaped the minister's notice.

'Mrs Randall, your presence has been much

missed at the chapel. Why, I believe we've barely seen you these last six months.'

'Well, Minister, I've been unwell of late. As you know, I lost my daughter and two of my grand-daughters just last October.' Here Ada paused as her voice threatened to crack. 'I think you will find I was a faithful worshipper even after that until the weather turned against me. I'm not as young as I was and the journey has proved taxing in the winter months. Then, of course, our darling Alice was born and I have been kept much at home, helping Sarah.'

Sarah was surprised by the note of reproof in her grandmother's voice. As Ada held Alice out for the minister's inspection, it dawned on Sarah that Ada had, indeed, been remiss in her attendance at chapel. Her welcome of the minister, while polite, was less than fulsome. Sarah found herself observing her grandmother covertly, struck by this revelation.

The minister, clearly a little uneasy around babies, made the appropriate complimentary comments before returning to his cup of tea and his slice of malt loaf, which he declared to be 'exceptional'. After some polite discussion of village events, the minister said, 'Well, I must confess that one of my primary reasons for visiting you was to discover what plans you have for Alice's baptism.'

'None,' said Ada, pleasantly. 'I think that will be a matter for Sarah and her husband Joe to decide. As you know, Joe is away a great deal and is as yet unaware that he has a daughter.'

'I understand,' said the minister, although his expression suggested otherwise. 'But perhaps we can agree on a date in the not too distant future when we might perform the ceremony? It would, of course, be delightful to see you all at Sunday chapel, once the weather improves.'

Ada rose to her feet, meaning that the minister had to hastily finish his tea and set down his cup in order to do the same. 'I'm not anticipating that that will be any time soon, given the weather just now. It would be quite impossible to risk taking a small baby so far in the chill and the wet. Sarah will consult with Joe on his return and you can be sure that you will be the first to know when a decision is reached.'

Sarah felt her cheeks burning with embarrassment. It seemed to her that Ada was managing to be rude in a very polite way to the minister and she hurried him into the kitchen, helped him on with his now dry coat and exclaimed about the downpour outside to distract him from taking offence.

When the minister had gone, refusing their half-hearted attempts to persuade him to stay awhile to see whether the rain might ease a little, Sarah turned to Ada with a look of enquiry.

'Is there something wrong? You never used to miss Sunday chapel. It hadn't occurred to me until just now how rarely you have been of late.'

Her grandmother remained silent, collecting up plates and teacups while indicating to Sarah that she should sit with Alice by the fire. After a while she sighed and spoke.

'I prayed to God every night, and every waking hour of every day, to spare your mother and sisters. He didn't see fit to hear me and I've found that my faith has been tested to its limit. I couldn't understand why they had to be taken from me and on my return I found no solace in the words of the minister or in the sympathy of the congregation. I can't say that I won't be drawn back to worship again in the future, but for now I find more to engage with in the new life that we have here.'

Ada's sombre expression was transformed as she reached out and hooked one of Alice's tiny fingers in hers. Sarah, who had been dreading a battle over Alice's baptism, convinced as she was that it was not something Joe would countenance, could hardly believe what she had just heard.

'So, you don't mind if I don't baptise her? For now?' she added hastily, mindful that Ada's lapse of faith might well be only temporary.

'She's perfect as she is. What will it add? How could I mind?' Ada said, taking the tea tray into the kitchen and leaving Sarah to sit by the fire, shaking her head in wonder.

CHAPTER 24

As it turned out, only a few hours separated the departure of the minister and the arrival of Joe. The minister's visit had set Sarah thinking about her husband's absence; he had known well enough that she was due to give birth in mid-March and now it was nigh on Easter. It seemed as though her thoughts must have somehow conjured him up because, glancing out of the window to check on the weather later that afternoon, she spied Joe walking up the path.

She met him at the door, Alice clutched to her shoulder.

'Well now, that's some expression to welcome a husband with, isn't it?' He was teasing, and Sarah tried hard to adjust her scowl but her frustration couldn't be contained.

'Joe, where have you been? I've been a mother for a month now and you've not even clapped eyes on your baby.'

'Well, I'm here now, aren't I? And how was I to know? 'Tis said that first-time mothers are more often late than early, so I was thinking myself right on time.'

Joe gave her his best smile, the one always guaranteed to win her round, as he shrugged off his coat and reached out his arms for the baby.

'So what have we got here? Am I to know if I have a son or a daughter?'

'This is Alice.' Sarah's pride in her newborn couldn't be held back.

'Alice, hmm. And am I to have no say in the matter?'

'Well, if you'd got yourself here a sight earlier you could have had first pick,' Ada said crisply as she came into the kitchen. 'But seeing as you're a month late, why, Alice has got used to her name by now.'

'The minister was here today, looking to set a date to baptise her,' Sarah said, in an effort to divert the conversation.

'We'll be having none o' that,' Joe said. He held Alice away from him. 'Let's be having a good look at ye.'

Sarah was about to warn him to be sure to support Alice's head when she realised he was handling her with every appearance of being an expert. Alice seemed to appreciate the new voice and presence in the room: she was staring at him intently.

'Well now, aren't you the serious little thing?' Joe said. 'I don't see much of me about her, do you?' he asked, turning to Sarah.

'She looks exactly like you,' Sarah protested. 'I can't see an ounce of me.'

Joe chuckled and settled himself by the range, Alice cradled along the length of his thighs. 'So, what does a man, and a new father at that, have to do to get fed around here? I'm fair starved,' he said.

'Since we weren't expecting you, there's nothing special to be had other than what we were planning for our own supper.'

Sarah sensed in Ada's words her irritation at Joe's presence and his instant usurping of her role as chief babyminder. 'Perhaps I can persuade Gran to make a rhubarb pie,' she said, looking pleadingly at Ada. Making the pie would keep Ada occupied and allow Sarah to devote a little time to Joe, and the baby.

In fact, Joe had limited patience with Alice. Once she started to grizzle for food he was more than happy to hand her back, taking himself off upstairs for a sleep before supper. Ada had to remind him to remove his boots before he climbed the stairs, which he did without a murmur, apologising and saying that stairs, and indeed dry land, were a novelty after so much time spent on the boat. Sarah noticed that his socks were out at the heel and resolved to take them from him for washing and darning before he had to leave again.

Alice slept through their suppertime, by the end of which Joe and Ada had overcome their initial prickliness and found a way to settle into a polite tolerance of each other.

At breakfast the next morning Joe announced

that he would be staying for a week. Sarah, frying an egg for him on the range, was delighted. It would be the longest time they had spent together, either before or after they were wed. After breakfast she set him to work on some of the tasks that she and Ada had struggled with. The outhouse door was half off its hinges, meaning it had to be lifted in and out of position, which Sarah had found increasingly difficult through pregnancy. The dry-stone wall at the end of the garden was in urgent need of repair in more than one place and there was wood to chop, too.

Despite the cold, Joe was cheerful in his work and Sarah enjoyed watching him from the kitchen. Ada was happy to have Alice to herself for a bit and so Sarah undertook pie-making and baking in honour of Joe's visit. After their lunchtime meal, which Joe declared to be the best meat pie he had ever eaten – even though Sarah knew that potatoes and carrots made up the bulk of its contents – he announced that he would take a walk into the village.

'Is there aught you require there?' he asked.

Sarah had to bite back a question as to what business he might have in Northwaite. She feared it was most likely to involve a visit to The Old Bell, but he had worked hard around the garden that morning and she wasn't sure that she had the right to deny him.

No sooner was he out of the door than Ada, who had been glowering since he made his announcement, turned to her. 'Has he given you any money yet?' she asked.

Sarah flushed. 'I never thought to ask him,' she replied.

Ada shook her head. 'It's the first thing you should have done. He's been working on the boats; he'll have had his wages. If you don't take them from him he'll feel all the better off and he'll be spending it. You should have taken it from him and given him back an allowance.'

Sarah was angry with herself for not thinking of this and now that it had been pointed out to her she was worried. She had a vivid picture in her mind of Joe standing rounds in the inn while his much-needed wages turned into a pile of rapidly diminishing coins on the bar. So it came as a welcome surprise when Joe returned within a couple of hours, seemingly none the worse for wear if a little inclined to be over-amorous. Embarrassed in front of her grandmother, she fended off his kisses, holding Alice out for his attention instead.

Ada donned her bonnet and shawl and announced her intention of delivering a remedy in the village and, as soon as she had gone, Sarah decided she must be bold and resolve the issue of Joe's wages.

'Joe, you haven't mentioned money since you arrived. I need money to keep house, to look after Alice and myself . . . and you, while you are here,' she added hastily, unnerved by the rapid change she observed in his demeanour.

'You went on well enough before, you and the old lady together. What's changed now?'

Sarah ignored the less than complimentary reference to Ada. 'We're married now,' she said, trying to sound firmer than she felt. 'You have a responsibility to me. And to Alice. I can't expect Gran to house us and take care of us for ever.'

With a grim expression, Joe dug around in his pockets, pulled out a small handful of coins and flung them on the table. ''Twill have to do until I collect my pay.'

With a sinking heart Sarah ventured, 'But were you not paid on delivery of your loads?'

'Aye,' Joe said. 'But the money isn't mine. It goes to my master and he pays me when he sees fit.' With that he went outside, slamming the kitchen door behind him, and Sarah saw him pick up the axe and start chopping wood with more vigour than finesse. She shuddered and drew Alice to her, hoping her warm presence would help calm the fast beating of her heart.

After ten minutes Joe threw down the axe and came back into the kitchen. Sarah shrank back against the range, fearful of his anger, but he strode over to her and gave her a rough hug.

'I had no call to take it out on you. Truth be told, my master ain't paid me yet and my ire should be saved for him, not you or the firewood.' Joe gave her a rueful smile. 'Am I forgiven? Come, let me make it up to you.' He took Sarah by the hand and led her into the parlour.

'It's too cold to be in here,' she protested.

'Then light the fire.'

Sarah hesitated. A parlour was for visitors and special occasions rather than family and Joe's proposal was at odds with this.

'I've just chopped firewood. I think we can afford the fire,' Joe said, not unreasonably. 'Sarah, we've hardly spent any time together since we were wed and I don't think your grandmother will be against us having a bit of privacy.'

Sarah still hesitated, less convinced of this than Joe.

'Well, would you rather we went upstairs?' Joe said, rising to his feet.

'No, no.' Sarah was shocked; this proposal seemed even stranger than their use of the parlour. 'Here, take Alice and I'll lay the fire.' She quickly deposited the sleeping baby into her husband's arms and went to collect the makings of the fire, passing her grandmother in the kitchen as she did so. Ada had returned from her errand and seated herself by the range, a pile of mending and her work-basket beside her. She raised her eyebrows as Sarah passed, but said nothing.

The sight had jogged Sarah's memory, however, and as she knelt down to lay the parlour fire she said to Joe, 'I noticed the heels were out in your socks yesterday. Do you have more socks, or any linen, in need of repair?'

'Nay, don't bother yourself,' Joe replied.

'It's no bother,' Sarah said, surprised. 'I'd like to

do it for you. Consider it a wifely duty.' The last was said in a light-hearted way; Sarah was only too conscious that she didn't feel like a wife, even though she was a mother already.

'Aye, well, it's a job I can do well enough mysen,' Joe said.

The fire lit, Sarah rocked back on her heels and swivelled to face him, pushing a strand of hair back from her face and leaving a trail of ash on her skin as she did so. 'Well, that's as may be but you don't seem to have done a good job of it up until now,' and she laughed, looking pointedly at his shirt-front, where one button was missing and another two were hanging by a thread.

'Aye, well . . .' Joe muttered. He seemed reluctant and embarrassed to give up his mending so Sarah didn't push the matter further, thinking that she would simply go through his things over the next day or two to discover the garments in need of repair.

'I can get us meat,' Joe said suddenly. 'A rabbit for the pot, mebbe, or a pheasant.'

'Where from?' Sarah asked, although she knew well enough.

'Tha' knows,' Joe said, in a tone of reproof. 'But thy grandmother need not.'

Sarah thought for a moment or two. There was no denying that some meat would make a welcome addition to their diet. She and Ada had become used to having meat just once or twice a week but she had a feeling that Joe would require

160

heartier fare. For herself, she didn't mind the idea of poaching. Why should it matter whether a rabbit or a fowl that was running free was caught on one side of a fence or another? She wasn't sure that her grandmother would feel the same, however. She made a sudden decision.

'We'll have to say it's a gift, or in exchange for monies owed to you,' she said. 'It can't be denied that it will help with the housekeeping.'

The following day Joe took himself off late in the afternoon, as it began to grow dark. Sarah steeled herself again to say nothing whilst fearing he was heading to the inn. He returned a couple of hours later, less flushed than the previous day and, as he entered the kitchen, he pulled a rabbit from his pockets and laid it on the table in front of Ada.

Sarah started and glared at him but he ignored her.

'Here you go, Mrs Randall,' he said. 'I met up with a friend in the village and he repaid a debt.' There was a touch of defiance in his voice; like Sarah, he was expecting Ada to give him a sound telling-off.

Instead, she gazed at the body before her then reached out to stroke its fur. 'A fine specimen,' she said. 'I haven't seen one as large as this, Sarah, since your grandfather used to bring them back. Hunter's Wood?' she asked, turning to Joe.

'Aye,' he said, with a broad grin.

Sarah was aware that her mouth had fallen open. At times like these, she wondered whether she knew her grandmother at all.

161

CHAPTER 25

'I told you not to do it.' Joe, who was staring down at a pair of his socks in his hand, frowning at the darning, had raised his voice.

Sarah had been concerned that her handiwork was poor quality but his reaction seemed a little extreme, even so. 'What's wrong?' she asked, shushing Alice, who, seemingly sensitive to the charged atmosphere, had started to grizzle.

Joe's week at Hill Farm Cottage, during which Sarah had at last begun to appreciate what it felt like to have a husband and to live together as a family, had come to an end. He had arisen early and was collecting a few things together while she nursed Alice. Sarah had laundered his clothes, fixed the loose buttons and repaired the rips in his shirts and darned the threadbare socks. Because he had been affronted by her original suggestion she had done this secretly, while he had been at work in the garden, away in the village or poaching in the woods. She hadn't given it a further thought, assuming he would be back on the canal before he even noticed.

Now he was glaring at her and she couldn't

understand his reaction. They'd had a good week, she thought. He and Ada had resolved a way to be around each other without too much unpleasantness. Ada had been mollified by how good he was with Alice, and the fact that he wouldn't be around for long had allowed her to be magnanimous towards him and resist her jealousy over his usurping her role in relation to her great-grandchild. That he failed to provide much of a contribution to the family purse other than by poaching had, however, counted against him.

For his part, Joe had been respectful around Ada and conscious of the fact that he was a guest in her household. He had clearly found this irksome at times, showing a disinclination to keep company in the kitchen with Ada and preferring to have a fire lit in the parlour. Sarah's unease at using the best room in this way had continued, but Joe had pressed her, citing long hours cooped up in the confines of a narrow-boat and a wish to be able to enjoy the company of his family when he could.

The previous evening, as they lay in bed talking in whispers to avoid disturbing Alice, sound asleep in her crib, Sarah voiced her wish that they might find a house to call their own. Even as they talked about it, cocooned in drowsy warmth, she felt a sense of disloyalty to her grandmother. After meeting Joe, and before she was married, she had longed for the day that she and Joe would live together as a family in their own place, away from Ada. Now she had become only too well aware of what Ada had done for her, over the years as well as recently.

Common sense told her that they had managed to make things work in the past and could undoubtedly continue to do so, at least until Joe had work that took him away less than at present. A wish to change the nature of Joe's work was something that Sarah hadn't dared raise with him as yet, but it had become a goal more real to her than taking on their own family home. Perhaps, she thought, if he could become a respected farm-worker on one of the local farms they might have a chance to rent one of the farm labourer's cottages? At the very least, he would be around much more and his income would be secure. But Sarah kept this to herself. She had decided to bide her time – and meanwhile it wouldn't hurt to indulge the fantasy of a home of their own, no matter how unlikely that might be.

Now, as Joe stood before her with the offending socks in his hand, she was puzzled by his petulance and had to ask herself yet again whether she really knew him.

'I'm sorry. I didn't intend to annoy you,' she said, even though her instinct was to pick a fight with him. She would have thought that thanks were in order, rather than anger, but for whatever reason Joe wasn't happy and he threw the offending garments into his bag. She laid her hand on his arm.

'Let's not part with a quarrel,' she said. 'Do

164

you know when we might expect you again? For Alice's sake, at least,' she added hastily, fearing that her attempt to pin him down in this way would further irritate him. 'She will grow so fast and you will miss so many important moments. And she will miss you.'

Joe sighed, and it was as if he let out all his anger with his exhalation. 'I hope to be back ere long. May or June, when we can hope for some better weather.' He cast a glance outside, where dark clouds chased across the sky and gusty winds were hurling rain against the windowpanes.

'It looks as though I'll be half-drowned afore I reach t'canal-side.' He shouldered his bag and bent to kiss his wife and daughter. 'Take care of this precious little 'un. And of yourself. I'll be back as soon as I can.' He turned at the bedroom door. 'And this time I promise to bring my wages with me.'

Then he was gone, away down the stairs and out of the bedroom door, leaving Sarah feeling the pressure of his lingering kiss on her lips. 'It's a long time until May. Or June,' she whispered to Alice, sleepy and contented after her feed. 'What will we do without him?' She gazed at the bedroom door as a sudden sense of bleakness swept over her.

CHAPTER 26

There was little chance for Sarah to mope about Joe's departure. The very next morning a note was delivered, addressed to Ada. As Sarah read the front of it before handing it over, she was uncomfortably reminded that her lessons in herbalism and writing had come to an end with the birth of Alice. She was about to suggest to Ada that they should be reinstated when her grandmother, who was reading the note, sat down suddenly, her hand clutched to her heart.

'Why, whatever is the matter?' Sarah asked, hurrying to her side. Wordlessly, Ada handed her granddaughter the note. She frowned as she concentrated on deciphering the writing then turned to her grandmother.

'Have I understood correctly? We're to be turned out of this house?'

'Well,' Ada demurred, 'I don't know that turned out is quite right. But yes, the farmer wants this cottage for his son, who is coming back to the area with his family. He wants us out by May.' Ada clutched her head. 'Why didn't I see this coming?'

Sarah sat down suddenly too. 'Can he do this?'

'Yes, he can,' Ada said. 'The terms of the lease are one month's notice.' She looked around in despair. 'I've been here for so long. It's full of so many things, so many memories. However will we find a new place in time? And somewhere nearby, at that.'

Sarah had rarely seen her grandmother other than totally in control of herself. Now tears were seeping from her eyes and coursing down her cheeks. She looked old and careworn and Sarah's heart went out to her despite her own anxiety.

'Don't you worry. We'll find something. I'll make a start on looking today. And we should start to pack a few things away. Maybe we can ask the farmer if he will give us a little extra time here, too. You've been a good tenant.' Sarah's thoughts were flying in several directions at once. She would go down into the village and ask around in case anyone knew of a cottage coming up for rent. And maybe she could take Alice with her on a visit to Hill Farm to ask the farmer whether they might stay a little longer. If only Joe was still here: he would have told them both not to worry, she was sure. Then Sarah realised that it was more than likely that they wouldn't be here for Joe's next visit. However would she get word to him to tell him that they had moved?

Sarah bit her lip. She could only do one thing at a time. First of all, she would go into Northwaite and make some enquiries there.

'The weather is good again today,' she said. 'I'll

take Alice and go to the village. If I spread the word that we are on the lookout for a new home it might lead to something.'

Sarah hoped that she sounded more convinced than she felt. The proximity of the mill meant that cottages, or even rooms, were hard to come by. As soon as anything became vacant it would be taken up by a mill-worker, eager to save time on the journey to work from one of the far-flung villages.

'I'll come with you,' Ada said. Sarah, noticing that her grandmother was trembling as she rose to her feet, thought about trying to dissuade her until she said, 'I don't want to stay here on my own. I'll just be fretting until you return.'

Progress around the village was slow. Sarah thought the shops would be a good place to enquire, as the shopkeepers generally heard all the news from their customers who passed the time of day in idle chat while they queued. But the appearance of Sarah with her new baby meant that everyone in the shop wanted to have a peep and to exclaim over Alice's bonniness, then to exclaim all over again and commiserate when Ada and Sarah shared the news of their imminent and enforced departure from Hill Farm Cottage.

'If good wishes were enough to find us a home we'd have a hundred by now,' Ada sighed, after they had visited the last shop and Alice's grizzling indicated that she was expecting a feed in the near future. They turned their steps homewards, Sarah thinking with some sadness that very soon their home would be in some entirely different place. It wasn't something she welcomed. A home was so much more than just the fabric of a house; it was everything within it, and even though these things could be moved elsewhere it was harder to take the feelings it evoked. Even though Sarah had been keen to move to a place of her own with Joe, she'd always thought that she'd still be able to visit Hill Farm Cottage, home to all her childhood memories.

Deep in thought, she didn't notice Martha step from her gate as they passed her house and she started at being addressed.

'Sarah! Did you think to head home without letting me have a glimpse of this little one?'

Sarah felt instantly guilty. She had been so taken up with Alice's early days that she had neglected to visit Martha and thank her properly for her kindness and all her help when Alice was born.

'Oh, Martha, I'm so sorry. I've been meaning to visit.'

'But someone has been keeping you busy, I'll be bound.' Martha peered at the bundle that was Alice and laughed at the screwed-up face she presented. 'She looks cross.'

'Hungry, I think,' Sarah said.

'Then you must come in and have a cup of tea. You can feed her so you don't have to suffer her wails as you walk home. And –' Martha turned to Ada '– you look quite done in. Come away inside and have a rest.'

Sarah made a token protest but Martha was

having none of it. She bustled them inside and Sarah, relieved to be able to attend to Alice's needs, discovered that she herself was also tired. 'It's my first proper day out since she was born,' she told Martha.

'So what brings you to the village?' Martha asked. Their lack of packages must have been sign enough that shopping wasn't their purpose, so Sarah enlightened her while Ada sat mute, sipping her tea.

'Why, that's shocking!' Martha exclaimed. 'After all those years, to be asked to leave at such short notice.'

'And there's nothing to be had nearby,' Sarah said. 'Or at least, no one has been able to tell us of anything.'

Martha was pouring more tea and didn't say anything for a few moments, before sitting back and saying, 'Well, there is one place.'

'Really – where?' Sarah asked eagerly as Ada lifted her head from gazing into her cup, sudden hope in her eyes.

'Why, next door,' Martha said. 'But it's been empty for years. I don't rightly know whether it's fit to be lived in any more, or whether the owner would prefer that it fell down.' She brightened. 'But I, for one, would be thankful to have it lived in and cared for, and I can't think of anyone that I'd rather have living next door.'

Sarah tried to suppress the rush of excitement that she felt. She had passed Lane End Cottage on every journey in and out of the village and she knew that Martha spoke the truth. It was very run-down. But if it should be available for rent then she felt sure that she and Ada could make something of it.

'Do you know who owns it?' she asked.

'It's a Mr Timothy Smallwood,' Martha said. 'He doesn't live in the area any more and I'm not rightly sure how you would get hold of him.'

Sarah's heart sank but Martha was frowning, deep in thought. 'I think Sutcliffe's, the solicitors in Nortonstall, might still have some dealings with him. It was a long time back but the solicitor's clerk came out here to get some papers signed, when old Mr Smallwood still lived here. I had to help him bang on the door and shout through the letterbox to get entry; the old man was deaf as a post. It's his son who owns it now but he's not lived here nor visited in all that time as far as I know.'

'Shall we take a look at the place?' Ada asked. She'd brightened up at the prospect.

'We won't be able to go inside,' Martha said. 'But there's no harm in taking a look around the outside.'

Alice was still sleeping soundly so Sarah left her behind, tucked into the wooden crib that Martha still kept, left over from her own children. They were now all grown but Martha lived in the hope of grandchildren before too long. Once outside, they paused at the gate of Lane End Cottage, taking it all in. Sarah had passed it many a time without paying it too much attention. If asked to describe it she would have said, 'dark and overgrown', without being able to provide much beyond that by way of description.

Now that they were standing before it, that description still stood. Ivy had smothered the front of the cottage and was starting to encroach on the roof, where it looked as though some of the slates might be in danger of being dislodged by the creeping, grasping stems. The front garden was a dispiriting mess, waist-high with skeletons of whatever plants had grown there last summer, still festooned with seed heads and dead leaves. They pressed on cautiously up the overgrown path. Sarah, leading the way, was aware of rustling as creatures that had been used to having possession of this wasteland slipped away at their approach.

A solid wooden door marked the entrance to the cottage, with a window set at its side. Ada peered in but announced that she couldn't see a thing, so Sarah tried, with the same result. Layers of grime on the outside of the glass and darkness from within effectively shuttered the room. They made their way around to the back, Sarah giving the round metal door handle a cursory twist as they passed, but to no avail. At the side of the house there was another door, unusual and only possible because it was the end of the terrace.

'I suppose this must lead into the kitchen,' Ada commented. 'Is there another door at the back?'

Sarah, still ahead, took a look. 'No, just a big window.'

'It works rather well to have the kitchen door here,' Ada said, reflectively, but Sarah was already stepping out into the back garden. This was a tangled mess of shrubs and plants, with ivy having taken over a good deal of it. Ada and Sarah looked back at the house from the garden, both feeling disheartened, but Martha would have none of it.

'Imagine how nice it will be all tidied up, with the ivy stripped away and the garden properly planted.'

Sarah tried her best, but in her mind's eye she could only see Hill Farm Cottage, with its neat borders within the grey stone walls and the wildness of the countryside beyond. Their home was pretty and inviting, with roses climbing around the door in summer and inside all polished wood, flagstone floors, limewashed walls and dark beams, brightened by the curtains and cushions that Ada had made, along with the rag rugs and bed quilts handed down through the family.

Sarah didn't like to think how Lane End Cottage must look within and she guessed from Ada's expression that she didn't either. Sarah's initial enthusiasm for the idea was draining away with every step that she took around the property but she knew that she couldn't let her grandmother see this. They didn't have any other options at this point and, appearances aside, it did have some things to recommend it. It was in Northwaite, their preferred location, and next door to Martha who had delivered Alice into the world. The cottage was a good size, as was the garden, and Sarah could see how it had potential for herb-growing. Her heart failed her again, though, as she thought of the well-established herb beds at Hill Farm Cottage, and how her grandmother had nurtured them over the years.

'What do you think?' Martha asked, once they were back inside her cottage where Alice was still sound asleep.

'It looks awful,' Ada said flatly, having only managed to raise enthusiasm for the side entrance, at the same time as Sarah said, 'I'll see if I can get in touch with the owner.'

'Oh, it will be lovely to have you living here,' Martha said, as they prepared to set off back to Hill Farm Cottage. 'No more hills for you!' she called after Ada, as they paused to wave at the gate and then turned their faces towards home.

Home, Sarah thought bitterly. It was going to be very hard to imagine replacing Hill Farm Cottage but replace it they must, and soon. She would have to try to make contact with Mr Timothy Smallwood the very next day.

CHAPTER 27

Awintry chill still cut the air, despite all the
evidence of spring, as Sarah made her way
home from Nortonstall the following afternoon. Worrying that Alice would be fractious and
undoubtedly in need of a feed, she hastened her
steps as she took the woodland shortcut back to
Northwaite. It saved struggling up the long hill
out of the town as the path threaded its way
alongside the stream in the valley but, once the
mill had been passed, it meant a steep, sharp
climb up to the edge of Northwaite and then on
to Hill Farm Cottage.

As she walked, Sarah turned over in her mind
the results of her endeavour to discover whether
they might rent Lane End Cottage. She'd left Alice
in Ada's charge that morning when she set off to
visit Sutcliffe's the solicitors, without much thought
of how to manage her errand when she arrived in
Nortonstall. She'd never had cause to visit a solicitor before, but remembered Sutcliffe's offices
well enough. They took up a prominent position
in the marketplace, housed in a stucco building
with steps leading up to a pillared frontage that

seemed at odds with the traditional grey stone facades surrounding it.

Her nerve had almost failed her as she mounted the stone steps and rang the bell beside the glossy, black-painted door. She observed the high polish on the brass knocker, letterbox and bell surround, so shiny that you could see your face in it, and at once regretted not having worn her Sunday best. The door swung silently open and Sarah made to step inside, but a gentleman in a frock coat held up his hand to bar her entry, enquiring what her business might be.

'I'm here to ask about Lane End Cottage in Northwaite,' Sarah said, feeling a little unprepared. 'To ask about renting it, that is. I gather that you have some dealings with the owner, a Mr Timothy Smallwood.'

'I believe we do handle Mr Smallwood's affairs,' the man replied coldly. 'Wait here and I will enquire as to whether anyone is available to see you,' and he shut the door in her face.

Sarah turned back to face the street, much discomfited at being denied entry and feeling as though all eyes must be upon her. She was thankful when the door opened again shortly after and she turned towards it, hopeful of entry, only to be denied once more.

'I'm afraid no one can see you today without an appointment,' the man said, and made to shut the door once more.

Sarah felt her colour rise. 'I've travelled from beyond Northwaite today to make this visit, leaving a baby barely a month old behind, and now must make the same journey back again on foot. Can a moment not be spared to see me?'

'I'm afraid not.' The man was determined to close the door but Sarah was equally determined to gain entry.

'I think Mr Smallwood would not be happy to hear that this interest in his property had been ignored.'

She wasn't sure what made her say it, but it had the effect of making the man hesitate.

'Wait here a moment,' he said, looking pointedly at the doorstep. Sarah saw him take a few steps across the hallway and consult, from the doorway, someone within one of the rooms.

He returned to his post as gatekeeper. 'You're to come back in an hour,' he said, looking less than pleased as he shut the door on her once more.

Sarah was unhappy with the delay; it would mean that Alice was more likely to be awake and needing to be fed by the time she returned, but there was nothing she could do. She spent a disconsolate hour trailing around the market stalls and looking in shop windows at things she couldn't risk buying, with little money to spare and the prospect of having to move hanging over them.

A cold shower of rain dampened her spirits even further and she was desperate to find somewhere to take refuge. She entered the draper's shop and spent a little while browsing the rolls of fabric, assessing the quality of the cloth between her thumb and forefinger until the shopkeeper asked her pointedly whether he could help her with anything.

Blushing, she refused and left the shop just as the church clock chimed the hour. She was still a little early, but surely the solicitors wouldn't still deny her entry? Feeling less brave than she had felt earlier she returned to the great door and rang the bell once more. This time a different face greeted her, a younger one, and the owner of it seemed less inclined to be dismissive of her.

'I've come about renting . . . I mean . . .' She paused, trying to remember how the unpleasant gentleman had phrased it earlier. 'I've come with regard to Mr Smallwood's affairs.'

'Ah, you must be the young lady enquiring about the cottage rental? Come in and take a seat.' The young man beckoned her in, indicating a row of hard-backed chairs against the wall. 'Mr Sutcliffe Junior will see you shortly.'

Sarah took a seat and looked around the room, rather overawed by its high ceiling and the grand doors, each set deep within a substantial and solid wooden surround. A series of portraits of well-to-do men, captured on canvas within heavy gilt frames, lined three of the walls, while on the fourth there was a sign, with 'Sutcliffe & Sons' picked out in fine italic script. She was expecting a man of a similar age to the one who had let her into the building but in the event, when she was shown into one of the offices a good twenty minutes later, Mr Sutcliffe Junior appeared to be in excess of forty, if not fifty, years.

His grey hair was quite bushy, as were his eyebrows, and he wore a high collar and a silk cravat, secured with a jewelled pin. His pinstriped suit was immaculate and Sarah was instantly conscious of how shabby she must look, her boots scuffed and too worn to hold their polish any more, her skirt and blouse faded from their numerous washes over the years, her shawl a homespun affair and her hair undoubtedly frizzy from the effects of the rain, despite her bonnet.

Mr Sutcliffe Junior put on a pair of gold-rimmed spectacles and peered over the top of them. 'I understand that you have business relating to Mr Smallwood.'

'Yes, sir,' Sarah said. 'Mr Timothy Smallwood. I believe that he is the owner of Lane End Cottage and I would like to enquire whether it is available to rent.'

'Lane End Cottage? And where might that be?'

'In Northwaite, sir.' Sarah was puzzled. Did this gentleman own more than one property? Or was Mr Sutcliffe Junior not very well acquainted with his affairs?

'I see.'

There was a pause, so Sarah ploughed on. 'It's very run-down, sir. It will need a lot of work to make it fit to live in. But I'd be willing to set it to rights.'

'I see,' the solicitor said, again. He leant back in his chair, hands on the table, fingers interlocked. 'And why would you be prepared to do that?'

'There's nothing else available, sir,' Sarah said. 'And my grandmother and I require a home within the month.' She wondered at the smile playing around the solicitor's lips as she spoke.

'Hmm,' he said. He looked at her and Sarah feared that he was about to dismiss her request out of hand.

'If we don't take it on, sir, why I fear it will have fallen to the ground within the year.'

Mr Sutcliffe Junior raised his eyebrows. Sarah judged it best to keep quiet. He stood up and Sarah reluctantly rose to her feet too.

'Well, Miss . . .' He paused.

'Mrs Bancroft,' Sarah said, feeling her colour rise once more.

'Well, Mrs Bancroft. Come back to the office this time next week and we'll see.' The solicitor had moved to the door, ready to show her out.

'Next week?' Sarah asked. She didn't think they could afford to wait a whole week for a decision.

'Mr Smallwood is on his estate in Ireland. It will require a little time to get his answer. Good day.'

And with that Sarah found herself back in the hallway, where the young man was waiting to usher her out into the marketplace once more.

180

Now, as she hurried home, she wondered at the wisdom of having made the lack of property available in the area apparent to the solicitor. He would surely tell Mr Smallwood, who would raise the rent accordingly regardless of the state of the cottage.

By the time she arrived at Hill Farm Cottage, out of breath after the steep climb from the valley and with a headache from turning what had just occurred over and over in her mind, she found her daughter in full voice and quite red in the face.

'Thank heavens,' Ada said, handing the cross infant to Sarah the moment she walked through the door. 'She's been crying for what feels like hours.' She noticed how cold Sarah's hands felt after the walk. 'Sit by the range. I hope you haven't caught a chill. Today's sunshine was deceiving; we're not quite done with winter yet.'

With Alice settled and suckling, Ada quizzed Sarah as to the outcome of her interview. When she heard that it would be a week before they even had an answer from Mr Smallwood, she fell silent. Both women contemplated the future with a certain amount of grimness.

'Perhaps it won't matter,' Sarah said with a determined effort to be cheerful. 'It may be that something else will come up in the meantime.'

'Perhaps,' Ada said, and they both sank back into silence.

CHAPTER 28

The little family awoke the next morning to discover that Ada's words about the weather had been prophetic and indeed winter hadn't done with them. Snow had covered the ground during the night – just a light covering but enough to make Sarah feel anxious about the birds in the garden, newly nested, and the tender first flowers adorning the borders and the hedge-bottoms.

'It will be gone by midday,' Ada said, as Sarah collected up the breakfast crumbs in readiness to scatter them for the birds. 'Provided we get a bit of sunshine.'

The grey skies outside promised little but by mid-morning a rising wind had blown the dark clouds away and sunshine was indeed melting the snow. Sarah had suggested to Ada that, since the weather looked likely to keep them indoors, they should make a start on sorting through all the items collected over the years, with a view to preparing to pack up. They'd made slow progress over the morning, Ada constantly stopping to reminisce as she pulled items from the back of cupboards.

Her exclamations of 'I'd forgotten that I had that!' didn't make her any more inclined to be rid of it; in fact it made her more inclined to keep it so that she could enjoy it once more. Sarah looked in despair as the pile of things to keep grew steadily, whilst the throwing-away pile consisted of a few items rusted and broken beyond repair.

Sheets pulled from the bottom of the linen closet, with brown marks all along the creases where they had been folded in storage for many years, were seized upon by Ada and declared perfect for use as backing for quilts.

'But we have no need of more quilts, Gran,' Sarah said.

'Alice will need one for her bed as she grows,' Ada said. 'And should you have more children, they will be in need of them too.'

Sarah was silenced; the likelihood of having more children hadn't occurred to her as yet, wrapped up as she was in caring for Alice. She wasn't sure whether it was an idea that appealed or not.

Ada was spurred on by the idea of quilt-making and was turning out drawers in search of fabric. 'Look for garments that are part worn-out,' she said. 'We can cut out the best pieces and throw away the rest.'

Sarah was about to demur and say that they had more important things to do, when she thought better of it. Her grandmother was looking better than she had since they'd had the notice to leave, so why deny her this small pleasure? She sighed and fetched the scissors; any further clearing out would have to be saved for another day.

Her grandmother's enthusiasm for the project proved to be infectious. She gathered fabric together until they had quite a pile of suitable pieces and, Sarah was pleased to note, a good amount of fabric scraps that could be thrown away once stripped of anything useful such as buttons.

The sunshine had served its purpose and melted the snow, but the winds brought another band of cloud and the afternoon looked set to be one of persistent rain.

'Why don't we make a start on the quilt now?' Ada suggested. With Alice content to lie on the rug and watch them at work, seemingly entertained by the flash of the scissors and the colour of the fabrics, Ada showed Sarah how to cut hexagonal templates from scraps of paper. She then placed these on the fabric and cut around them, leaving a margin of fabric all around the shape.

Then she showed her how to tack the fabric to the paper backing, folding in the extra around all the edges to keep the template in place. After a few false starts, in which Sarah used the fabric with the wrong side outwards or stretched it so that the shape was distorted, she began to amass quite a collection of patchwork pieces. The work had an addictive quality and she was almost resentful when she had to break off to feed Alice.

As the afternoon drew to a close, Ada called a halt. 'My poor eyes won't take much more today, I fear.'

Sarah was disappointed and all for continuing, but Ada said that in any case it was time to plan the next stage. She showed her how to form the patchwork pieces into a flower shape around a central hexagon.

'Once you have stitched these pieces together, more neatly this time but with the papers still in place, then you make up all the other pieces into flowers. After that, you can start to join all the flowers around the first one.' Her grandmother demonstrated, moving the fabric pieces around on the table top like counters on a game board. Sarah was fascinated and so was Alice, whom she held on her lap.

'How clever!' Sarah exclaimed. She became absorbed in trying out different combinations of patterns, using plain centres for some flowers with a mix of patterns around the edge, or using a different pattern for each piece. 'Look, that's my old pinafore, from when I was about five. Ellen and Jane wore it after me, I remember.' She paused, the sudden remembrance of her sisters conjuring up a wave of sadness. 'How well it looks set against this fabric. What's this from again?'

'It's left over from the old kitchen curtains,' Ada said. 'I used to look at that fabric every time I passed the draper's shop. He left it in the window for so long that it faded and I got it for half price.' She smiled and shook her head at the memory.

Sarah was still keen to get on. 'Can we sew some together now?' she asked.

'Tomorrow.' Ada was firm. 'If we don't think about supper now it will be midnight before we eat it.'

As Sarah began to prepare vegetables while Ada took care of Alice, she reflected on what a good distraction the afternoon's work had been. Neither of them had mentioned their predicament during the afternoon and, for herself, she hadn't thought about it even once. Now there was one less day to get through until she had to go back to Nortonstall to hear the result of her plea to the solicitor. She pushed the unwelcome prospect of the move to the back of her mind and resolutely concentrated on the task in hand. Fretting would achieve nothing.

CHAPTER 29

The quilt top was well advanced by the time the day dawned for Sarah's return to Sutcliffe & Sons. She knew she should have spent the time more wisely, in asking around the neighbourhood for any news of cottages to rent, or in clearing out and packing, but the weather had been dismal for much of the time. Every day brought rain, with barely a half-hour's respite morning or afternoon. As she listened to it lashing against the windowpanes, Sarah wondered how the folk down in the valley were getting on. Had the stream swollen and burst its banks? It seemed likely, with the amount of water that must be coming down off the moors, but she didn't think too much about it until her grandmother pointed out that no one had visited them in search of remedies.

Ada was looking worried. 'It's unusual. And it means we have no income.'

'It's the rain,' Sarah said. 'It's keeping everyone at home. They'll be back, once it clears up. And we've been living like church mice ourselves. We haven't bought a thing all week.'

The weather had made her disinclined to venture into Northwaite to shop so they had dined off whatever was stored away in the pantry or outhouse. Sarah hadn't noticed the lack of anything other than fresh milk, which she'd be glad to be able to get when she went out that day.

The sky, washed by days of rain, was a clear pale blue by the time Sarah set out for Nortonstall. She took the road through Northwaite rather than the path beside the stream down in the valley, feeling sure that it would be waterlogged and filthy underfoot. She had no wish to arrive in Nortonstall looking like a ragamuffin.

Northwaite was busy as she passed through it; it looked as though the inhabitants were taking advantage of a break in the weather to stock up on food and household necessities. Sarah exchanged greetings with all those she passed but didn't pause. She felt a sense of urgency in her quest; more so since she had passed Lane End Cottage on her way into Northwaite and it had occurred to her that the dreadful weather of the last few days could have wrought havoc inside a neglected house. Inscrutable as ever, the cottage had revealed nothing of what lay within as she went by.

Sarah was struck by the height of the muddy swirling water within the ditches as she headed down the hill towards Nortonstall. Once again, she wondered how the town would have fared with the volume of water flowing into it off the neighbouring hillsides. As she reached the edge of town she could hear the sound of rushing water. The stream that flowed through the valley below Northwaite broadened into something more properly considered a river as it reached Nortonstall, and from the noise it was clear that it was in spate.

She came around the corner towards the Packhorse Bridge and stopped, astonished at the sight of so many people gathered in the roadway. She joined the back of the crowd but found it impossible to get closer to the bridge due to the press of people. Unable to see over their heads she enquired of her neighbour in the crowd, a tall, burly man who would undoubtedly have a better view of the situation, 'What's happening?'

'The water's so high there's a fear that the bridge might give way.'

'Surely it's not safe to stand here if that's the case?' Sarah's alarm was compounded by the fact that, unable to see anything, she found it impossible to judge for herself.

'Aye, you could be right.' The man chuckled. 'But the town's never seen owt like it and after all t'rain we've had, well, it's a chance to get out and having something to neb at.'

Sarah left him to his 'nebbing' and pushed her way around the back of the throng to head towards the centre of town, fearful of time wasted. Yet her efforts to reach the marketplace were thwarted. The river had breached its banks already here, spreading across the square; she could see it lapping at the steps leading up to the grand entrance of Sutcliffe & Sons.

'But how am I to see Mr Sutcliffe?' In her distress, Sarah spoke out loud and a woman standing next to her, observing the flood, turned to her thinking she was being addressed.

'It's a right carry-on, to be sure. And on market day, too.'

'But how can I get over there?' Sarah pointed to the solicitors' offices.

'Well, unless you've brought a boat, 'tain't likely you'll be doing business there today.' The woman laughed then, seeing tears start to Sarah's eyes, added hastily, 'I heard tell that they've set up office temporarily in the backroom of The King's Arms. It's up Hill Street, away from all this mess. You might find what you're looking for there.'

Sarah thanked her before hurrying away up the street that had been pointed out to her. After a short, steep climb away from the town centre she came upon The King's Arms, set in a grey stone building up a flight of steps. Thinking to herself that many a head must have suffered a crack on these steps after a night's drinking in the establishment, she took a deep breath on reaching the top, squared her shoulders and pushed open the door. As she expected, her entrance attracted a good deal of attention and the customers, all male, stopped whatever they were doing, whether it was supping from tankards, playing cards or dozing by the fire, to turn and stare at her.

Feeling her cheeks start to redden from a combination of the heat of the room and the intensity of the stares, Sarah marched up to the bar. 'I'm looking for the solicitors, Sutcliffe & Sons. I'm told they've taken up residence here, away from the flood.'

The bartender put down the cloth that he had been using to wipe the glasses, Sarah observing as he did so that it was far from clean, and peered at her.

'Sutcliffe's, you say. Aye, well, you'll not find them in t'public bar. Go back out into t'passage and follow yer nose along to t'back and there they be, all set up nice in t'snug.'

Sarah, fighting down the feeling that she had made an error in coming here, stepped back into the passageway and followed his directions. They led her to a quieter area at the back of the inn where a fire was burning in a considerable hearth and several besuited men were seated at the few tables in the room, writing industriously in ledgers. Sarah recognised the young man who had let her into the marketplace offices, but of Mr Sutcliffe Junior there was no sign.

CHAPTER 30

'He's not here, miss.'

Sarah had approached the young man whom she recognised to enquire about the solicitor's whereabouts. The other clerks were still writing, but less assiduously she felt, clearly listening to what might be about to unfold.

'Do you know where I might find him?'

'Well, with the flood he might be back at the office checking that all is safe there. Or he might be out on business. I couldn't rightly say.'

'He asked me a week ago to return today.' Sarah felt a rising sense of desperation. Was there never to be a way of discovering whether Lane End Cottage could be rented? The clerk was looking blankly at her, clearly disinclined to continue the conversation but she stood her ground.

'It's about Lane End Cottage. Mr Smallwood's property.'

He smiled politely and shook his head. 'I'm sorry. I'm afraid I can't help you.'

Unsure of what to do next she was about to turn away when one of the other clerks spoke up. 'Wait, Mr Smallwood, you say?'

'Yes,' Sarah said, turning eagerly towards him.

'I believe we have had some correspondence from the gentleman in question.' The clerk was thinking, tapping his pen on the desk. 'I'm not sure, though, whether it has been brought over here or left in the office.'

Sarah felt her hopes, briefly raised, about to be dashed again. 'Do you know what it might have said?'

'I'm not at liberty to divulge that,' the clerk said, sternly.

It looked as though she would have to give up on Lane End Cottage. They must look further afield, away from the area altogether. It was all too much: Sarah burst into tears, turning her face away in shame at behaving this way in front of a roomful of strangers. Her vision blurred, she stumbled back towards the door and held one hand over her face to disguise her anguish while she felt along the wall with her other hand to guide her exit.

'Now then, what have we here?'

The voice was cultured, a little gruff but not unfriendly. Through her tears Sarah could just make out that she had all but collided with a gentleman who was entering the room as she was trying to leave.

'Excuse me, sir,' she muttered, trying to brush past him.

'Ah, but I must detain you a little longer.' The gentleman was taking up the doorway and she would have to push him out of the way to make her exit, which was unthinkable. Sarah cast her eyes to the floor and waited.

'What have my clerks been doing to upset you so? Hmmm?'

Despite her distress, Sarah could see that this wasn't the solicitor she had seen previously. This was a much older man, of average height and portly build with white hair and whiskers to match. What she could see with downcast eyes of his suit and the gold chain of his pocket watch spoke of prosperity; he was also in possession of a gold-topped walking-stick on which he appeared to be resting his weight.

'Come now, we require a chair for the lady. And a reviving glass of something. A little light ale, perhaps? No, I think brandy-and-water should do the trick. What point is there in being housed in an inn if we do not make use of it, hmmm?'

The last remark seemed to be addressed very much to himself, since the clerk he had button-holed had sped off to do his bidding and the others were bent to their work, pens busily scratching.

With a chair procured for her and a glass of brandy-and-water, which she sipped out of polite-ness, Sarah was persuaded to tell the gentleman, who had introduced himself as Mr Sutcliffe Senior, of her plight.

'Well, it is most fortunate that I decided to call in here today,' the solicitor said. 'My son is caught up at the office, with some of the other clerks, trying to make sure that all the files are stored well away from possible water ingress while we remain under threat from the flood waters. Meanwhile, as you can see, business must go on. The courts can't wait and so here we are.'

Mr Sutcliffe Senior gazed around the room. 'It reminds me of the early days of the business, when I first started out, all of us in just one room. Although not in an inn, of course.' He chuckled and Sarah tried hard to raise a smile. She wished he would get on and attend to the matter in hand, but she must indulge his reminiscences out of politeness.

'Well, but my ramblings don't answer your purpose in coming here today, do they now?'

Sarah feared that her feelings must have been apparent on her face, despite her efforts to disguise them.

'Since Mr Sutcliffe Junior isn't here for my appointment I really must return home.' Sarah's words came out in a rush. She just wanted to get away from the room and her pointless quest now and return home to where Alice was no doubt in need of her.

'Ah, but I do have some news for you,' Mr Sutcliffe Senior said. Sarah gazed at him, eyes wide. 'Partly good news, partly bad.'

Once more, Sarah's heart sank. Was there to be no end to the disappointment?

Mr Sutcliffe Senior continued. 'Mr Smallwood has let it be known that he would be prepared to consider a lease on Lane End Cottage.' Sarah's heart was beating so hard that she felt sure that all the occupants of the room must hear it. 'However, he needs to be sure of the tenants' abilities to meet their commitments. We thought it prudent to undertake enquiries on his behalf and have discovered that the leaseholder of your current residence, Mrs Ada Randall, is, ah . . .' the solicitor paused and coughed '. . . a little advanced in years. This would not suit our client. He requires a gentleman with an assured income as tenant, as is usual.'

Mr Sutcliffe Senior's gaze, while still benevolent, was tinged with a hint of sternness.

Sarah was astonished that enquiries had been made based on the very limited information she had supplied on her last visit. It came to her that this was likely to be her last chance to obtain the cottage, and so she steeled herself to speak up.

'I would propose, sir, that as a married woman and not being advanced in years I might take on the property. If this should not be to Mr Smallwood's satisfaction then my husband, Mr Bancroft, will of course be happy to have his name on the lease. He is away on business at present, though, and it may be in excess of a month before he would be able to sign anything.'

Sarah kept her gaze level; if her hands hadn't been so visible her fingers would have been crossed. She was hoping against hope that their

196

investigations hadn't stretched to Joe; if they had they would have discovered, as she now had, the precarious nature of his income. As the solicitor's expression remained unchanged by her representations, she pressed on.

'My grandmother and I would be happy to take on the cottage in its current condition and restore it to a habitable home. The garden would also benefit; my grandmother is a herbalist and our current garden bears testament to the work she has put into it. You would be most welcome to visit it, and inspect the cottage, to see what nature of tenants you could expect us to be. And, of course, my grandmother's practice has maintained us since her husband died.'

She added the last, knowing that in recent weeks the income from the practice would not bear examination but feeling that she had little to lose. If they were to get the cottage they would have to make it work.

Mr Sutcliffe Senior appeared to be considering her words. Finally he spoke, 'In my view, the best course would be to inspect Lane End Cottage and then make our decision based on this.'

It was Sarah's turn to consider. If the cottage turned out to be in a worse state than she hoped, would he refuse to lease it? And if not, would she and her grandmother be in a position to cope with putting it to rights? Her course established, however, there was nothing to do but continue.

'I am sorry for pressing you on this, sir, but when

might we expect a decision to be made? We have but three weeks until we must leave our home.'

Mr Sutcliffe senior smiled. 'I would that the young men that we employ had half your determination and tenacity. Not to mention such a forthright manner of speech.' He held up a hand as Sarah began to stammer out an apology. 'I find myself without an office to call my own at present, so I will visit the property in question tomorrow and after that I will ride on to visit you, if I may, with my decision.'

'Thank you sir,' Sarah said, faintly. 'Hill Farm Cottage. You will be expected, and most welcome.'

Leaving her brandy-and-water on the table, virtually untouched, she backed out of the room, then left the inn as quickly as possible, nearly knocking down a weary-looking Mr Sutcliffe Junior, who was mounting the steps. She hurried away, hopeful that she had not been recognised. Now that Mr Sutcliffe Senior had taken on their case she judged it better that it remained so. And she must hasten home, to tend to Alice and to warn Ada of the forthcoming visit, which would require a deal of cleaning, tidying and baking, she felt sure.

CHAPTER 31

Sarah and her grandmother passed the following morning in a fever of preparation. Having quite forgotten about their need for milk on the journey home the previous day, Sarah found herself despatched to the farm with a jug the minute that breakfast was over. Stung by the farmer giving them notice, she had managed to avoid Hill Farm until now, but there was no time for the walk into Northwaite; Ada was making scones which she felt would be most suited to serve to Mr Sutcliffe Senior, whatever time of day he arrived, and for scones she needed milk.

'I'll make half the batch savoury, then if it's a morning visit he can have them with a piece of cheese,' she said, half to herself. 'And if it's the afternoon we have a jar or two of preserves unopened – gooseberry perhaps. It has a tarter flavour that appeals to men; it's a recipe I'm particularly proud of.'

Sarah made haste, as she was bid, with the largest jug they had and a request for butter and cheese shouted after her. The farmer's wife greeted her cheerily, with a comment on the weather, a hope that her grandmother was well and an enquiry after Alice, then sent her off with the dairy maid in search of what she required. Neither of them mentioned the fact that Sarah's custom would soon cease; Sarah wasn't sure whether the farmer had discussed the matter of the cottage with his wife. She was a jolly lady; Sarah had no bone to pick with her.

It was perhaps as well that there was no sign of the farmer before Sarah made her way back home, for if she had seen him she would have found it hard to restrain herself from offering her opinion on his treatment of her grandmother. Although the errand had taken barely three-quarters of an hour, Ada was in a flap on her return, worried that the scones would still be in the oven and the kitchen not tidied before the solicitor made his appearance.

'I think he's likely to be a while yet, Gran,' Sarah said soothingly. 'He didn't look like the sort of man who would be up and out at first light. I'm sure he will have breakfasted well, read the news-papers and his post, before he even thinks about calling for his horse. We are more than likely to see him this afternoon.'

Although she gave every appearance of being calm, underneath Sarah was as anxious as Ada. Alice was sensitive to their moods, and became as fretful as they had ever seen her. She wailed and refused to be put down for her nap and Sarah and Ada had to take it in turns to walk around the garden in an effort to soothe her. Quite worn out,

Alice eventually fell asleep at midday, leaving her mother and great-grandmother to fly into a frenzy of last-minute preparations, dusting and polishing until the place sparkled. Sarah picked whatever flowers she could find in the garden – violets, primroses and a few stems of heartsease – and put them in small jugs on the windowsills.

After a lunchtime repast of bread and cheese, eaten in a rush in case their visitor arrived meanwhile, Sarah decided to light the fire in the parlour. Ada was unconvinced, fearing it might give the wrong impression and show they were profligate when they needed to convince of their economy and thrift, but Sarah overruled her.

'We wouldn't entertain the doctor, the minister or any such guests in the kitchen, so why should a solicitor be any different?'

As Sarah went to fetch the kindling she heard faint murmurings and cries from upstairs as Alice began to stir. Barely five minutes later, with the fire not yet lit and Alice's complaints beginning to grow in volume, she heard a horse's hooves on the road outside. She rose from her position in front of the hearth and went towards the window, feeling sure they must pass, but there was Mr Sutcliffe Senior, already down from his mount and tying the reins loosely to the gate so that his horse could crop the grass on the verge.

'Gran, he's here.' Sarah flew through to the kitchen, wondering whether to leave Alice to cry but finding Ada already halfway up the stairs.

'You let him in,' Ada said. 'I'll see to Alice.' She looked panic-stricken, so Sarah did as she was told, remembering to remove her apron and smooth back her hair just in time as she opened the door to the solicitor.

'I thought to come to the back door,' he said. 'No need to stand on ceremony.' He paused on the step and turned to look back at the garden. 'You spoke the truth yesterday,' he said. 'I've rarely seen a garden better cared for, and with so much in leaf and flower already. I think I must send my own gardener round to learn from you.'

Sarah hurried to relieve him of his hat and coat as he entered, whereupon he took a good look around the kitchen. 'Quite charming,' he said. 'Again, I cannot fault yesterday's boast. You clearly have more than a touch of the homemaker about you. Or should the credit go to your grandmother?'

He looked around the room, as if expecting Ada to pop out from behind a door or from within the pantry.

'Is she here today?' he asked, taking a seat at the table and indicating to Sarah that she should sit.

'Yes indeed, she's upstairs with my daughter.' Sarah was suddenly unsure whether the addition of an infant would further their cause or not but, as Ada arrived bearing Alice at that very moment, she didn't have to wait long to find out.

Luckily, Mr Sutcliffe Senior clearly had a great fondness for infants and, even more fortunately, they for him. He took possession of Alice on his

202

knee while Ada and Sarah laid out scones, jam and cheese, having failed to decide whether two o'clock in the afternoon was a savoury or sweet time of the day. Alice seemed mesmerised by the solicitor's white whiskers and gazed wide-eyed at him while he despatched a savoury scone with quite a hearty slice of cheese and a heavily buttered sweet scone piled with gooseberry jam, declaring that Ada's baking far surpassed that of his cook.

To Sarah's bemusement, the solicitor and Ada appeared to have a good deal in common, even to the extent of some mutual acquaintances, so she took herself off with Alice and attended to her feed before her daughter could become fractious. She returned to the kitchen to find the teapot exhausted, with no sign that Mr Sutcliffe Senior was ready to come to the point. However, with Sarah settled back at the table, he began.

'It pains me to have to report that Lane End Cottage is a deal less suitable than your current home. I confess that my spirits quite sank on entry, the place filled with gloom and dust and a chill that strikes right through to the bones. But, from what I could tell, the roof at least is sound, and although only spiders and mice have made the place their home over the last few years, I daresay it could be made habitable again.'

He paused, put his fingertips together and took a good look around the room. 'Whether it can ever be made as homely as here, I simply don't know. There's a darkness in there that oppresses the soul, although I have no doubt that while a gentleman can't see how to overcome it, a lady might. And it is true that in its latter years of occupation it was lived in by a reclusive widower, so it must be a good ten years or more since it has seen any proper attention inside.'

He paused again and sighed. 'The garden is much overgrown and the challenge of turning it into as pretty a patch as you have here is one that I think you will find requires help beyond the labour of your own hands.'

Sarah's hopes were rising, as the solicitor seemed to be talking very much as though they might be future tenants but, aware that his expression was grave, she still feared that some cruel blow was about to be delivered.

'All in all, I'm prepared to recommend your tenancy to Mr Smallwood. I would like him, though, to arrange to put the place into proper order before you take it on and for that reason I would suggest the lease commences six weeks from now.'

Sarah had to think quickly. While it was very good news that they were approved as tenants, they couldn't afford to wait for the proposed length of time.

'We must leave here at the end of the month,' she said. 'I do not think our landlord will be prepared to extend this lease as he wants the place for his family. Would you consider letting us take on the tenancy any earlier?'

Mr Sutcliffe Senior considered the matter. 'I must say I half-expected your response.' Sarah noticed the glimmer of a smile. 'In that case, my recommendation to Mr Smallwood will be that you take the cottage rent-free for the first month, at half-rent for the second month, then at the normal monthly rent thereafter. The lease will not reflect this. It will be an informal arrangement for those first two months. And, of course, we will need your husband to sign as a joint tenant with you.'

The last remark, addressed to Sarah, dashed her hopes once more.

'As you know he is away on business, sir, and I don't rightly know when to expect him back. But within a couple of months, I'm sure,' she added hastily.

The solicitor frowned, then brightened. 'In that case, you will sign the lease now, he will sign it on his return and we will date the commencement of the lease from then. I feel quite sure that I can trust you to honour the terms of the lease until then. As, to the best of my knowledge, Mr Smallwood hasn't left his estate in Ireland for nigh on five years, he need know nothing about it.'

Mr Sutcliffe Senior took his leave, with Sarah promising to come to the office the moment the floods had abated in order to sign the lease. They both thanked him fulsomely, aware that he had for some reason bent over backwards to help them.

As soon as he had ridden away, Sarah seized Ada and whirled her around the room, laughing and crying in excitement and relief while Alice looked on at them, wide-eyed.

PART IV

APRIL – SEPTEMBER 1875

CHAPTER 32

It was with some trepidation that, for the very first time, Sarah used the front-door key that Mr Sutcliffe Senior had given her. She had called in on Martha as she'd made her way back from Nortonstall on the afternoon that she had signed the lease. As she walked, she'd turned the great iron key over and over in her pocket, feeling nervous about what lay in store. By the time she arrived she had worked herself up into quite a state, imagining all manner of things that might be lying in wait within the neglected building.

Martha was delighted when Sarah begged her to spare a few moments to accompany her inside; she had been bursting with delight and curiosity ever since she had heard that Sarah and her grandmother were to be her new neighbours.

'Mr Sutcliffe said that the side-door key must be within the house as he doesn't have it,' Sarah said as she inserted the key into the lock of the front door. She had expected to have a struggle, but it turned without too much difficulty, perhaps because the solicitor had so recently visited.

As the door swung open, a cold, damp smell

greeted Martha and Sarah. Telling herself to expect the worst, Sarah led the way inside, taking note of a decent-sized if drab parlour and a large kitchen overlooking the tangled and overgrown garden. Everything was dusty and all the windows were festooned with cobwebs, but Sarah already felt a little surge of hope. It would require a lot of cleaning but she noted that the kitchen was home to a big dresser to house all their crockery, and the pantry was a good size.

Martha was beaming. 'I can see it already. All neat and clean. It will be a lot of work, mind, but I'll lend a hand and I'm sure there's others in the village who'll be glad to help out when they can. With a bit of luck the weather will stay fine – being able to open up the windows to air the place will make all the difference.'

Sarah stood at the bottom of the staircase and looked upwards. 'Shall we?' she said to Martha. Martha nodded, so Sarah mounted the wooden steps, taking care in case of worm damage. Luckily all seemed sound and soon they were viewing the three bedrooms that led off the landing. These were stripped bare but with decent wooden floorboards and views out over the fields at front and back.

Sarah turned around slowly in the biggest of the bedrooms, taking it all in. 'It has a nice feeling, I think,' she said. 'Although it is dusty and dirty it isn't as bad as I feared it would be. Of course, Mr Sutcliffe is used to much grander residences. He must have thought it a very poor affair. But I think Gran, Alice and I could be happy here. And Joe, of course,' she added hastily. 'At times I forget about him; he's here so little,' she apologised. 'Is that very wrong of me?'

Martha smiled. 'Not at all. Men are best forgotten about, on the whole.'

They both laughed, Sarah feeling some sympathy for Martha, whose husband was an irregular visitor too, working away in Leeds and, if village gossip held a grain of truth, preferring to stay there and sample the delights of the racecourse and inns rather than come home, even when a holiday presented itself.

Sarah didn't feel that she could keep her grandmother away from Lane End Cottage, even though she would rather have found a way to put it to rights by herself to spare Ada the exhaustion of it all. Her grandmother was waiting anxiously in the garden when she arrived back at Hill Farm Cottage, impatient to know whether she had the keys. A mop, scrubbing brushes and brooms and pails waited just inside the kitchen door.

'It's too late to make a start today,' Sarah protested. 'But I have visited and it's not quite as bad as I feared. Although that doesn't mean that it won't take a lot of work to get it to be anything like this place.'

'No matter,' Ada said. 'I've been well accustomed to hard work over the years.'

'Indeed,' Sarah said, scooping up Alice and

211

giving her a squeeze. 'Let's just hope that this little one behaves herself so we can get on with it.'

'We will at least have a bit of extra help.' Ada flourished a letter that lay on the kitchen table. 'Daniel writes to say that he is going to come and lend a hand. He will be at the local mill at the end of the week, and if we can give him a bed on the floor he can help on Saturday afternoon and Sunday.'

'A bed at Lane End Cottage?' Sarah was dubious. 'It's not really in a fit state and there's not a stick of furniture there.'

'We can sort that out,' Ada said briskly. 'It's but Wednesday today; I'm sure we can achieve something before he's due.'

And they did. By the time Daniel opened the gate to Lane End Cottage on a Saturday afternoon that was unusually warm for late April, the floor had been swept in one of the bedrooms, every nook and cranny dusted and the windows washed. The walls were still drab and there was just a straw pallet and a blanket for a bed but the room smelt fresh and sweet, the windows flung open to allow the breeze to blow in from over the fields.

Ada and Sarah had at first given in to the temptation of trying to do a little bit here and there, overwhelmed by just how much *did* need to be done once they looked closely, but before too long they had settled into working together on one room at a time. With a bedroom prepared for Daniel's use, they had turned their attention to the kitchen, which is where he found them, Sarah with her hair wrapped in a scarf to protect against the dust and up to her elbows in soapy water as she washed down the walls. Ada was concentrating on the windows, scrubbing away at layers of grime to reveal a vision of tangled ivy, brambles and weeds that made up the garden. Both turned flushed, hot faces to the door as Daniel entered and both were happy to drop what they were doing to greet him.

'Right, now that I'm here, how can I help?' He'd been welcomed and shown around the place; if he had any doubts about what they'd taken on, he was keeping them to himself.

'We must eat something first,' Sarah declared, 'then we'll make a plan.'

With the furniture still in Hill Farm Cottage, there was nowhere to sit. The garden was too overgrown to accommodate them, so they stood by the kitchen window and looked out as they chatted and ate the bread and cheese that Ada had packed, along with a pork pie that Martha had kindly provided. She had volunteered to care for Alice that day while they worked, and she popped round now to bring her for a feed, and to be introduced to Daniel for the first time.

Introductions over, Daniel announced that he would make a start on the garden as he had a wish to be outside after a week spent working indoors. Ada looked stricken.

'I didn't think to bring any tools for the garden with me,' she said.

Daniel declared himself happy to go up to Hill Farm Cottage and fetch them but Martha stepped in to offer the loan of anything that she had. Daniel worked in the garden until the light was all but lost, while Sarah and Ada scrubbed and swept, polished and mopped. Sarah would have carried on longer if she could have, but she was exhausted and there was still the road home to be climbed and dinner to be prepared. Once again Martha came to the rescue, summoning them all to her house for supper. They fell upon the food she had made, none of them able to speak until at least half of their plates were cleared and their energy partially restored.

Daniel having declared himself content to bed down for the night at Lane End Cottage, Ada, Sarah and Alice headed home. When they arrived the next morning he was already hard at work. With weeds, brambles and scrub already removed from a good third of the back garden he'd turned his attention to the front, saying that if they would be moving in soon they'd not want to be looking out on a forest of weeds, so they left him to it.

Sarah and Ada climbed the stairs to tackle the other bedrooms. They'd brought bread and cheese to see them through lunch and they were determined to go home that evening and make a proper dinner for Daniel to thank him for all his help. But whenever they thought to pack up for the day, another job presented itself. In the end, Martha came in to them.

'For heaven's sake, Ada, you'll not have the chance to live in this house, for it's an early grave for you unless you stop right now.'

Sarah looked guiltily at her grandmother, who did, indeed, look wan with exhaustion. She should have called a halt much earlier. Daniel was burnt by the sun, his forearms scratched and freckled with blood and his shirt torn in places where further battles with brambles had taken place.

'Now get your hands and faces washed and come away next door, all of you. I've been baking, so we have fresh bread and a ham pie, along with new potatoes and lettuce from the garden and I've stewed some rhubarb.'

Martha waved away their protests that they couldn't impose on her again.

'Am I to eat it all myself?' she asked. 'It'll only be a feast for the rabbits if I don't make use of it. I know you'd do the same for me.' She paused to take a good look around. 'My word, though, look at how much you've achieved.' She went over to the kitchen window and looked out. 'You can actually see the size of the garden now. It's much bigger than I'd remembered.'

Daniel had returned to the back garden after working on the front and it was now three-quarters cleared. He'd created a huge pile of brambles, ivy and weeds, all drying out under the sun and waiting to be burnt.

Lane End Cottage now looked and smelt clean, but the drabness of the decoration meant that the gloom hadn't lifted and so the full extent of Sarah and Ada's work wasn't revealed. Despite the endless buckets of dirty water that they had sluiced away they felt a sense of despondency, only increased by their weariness.

'I'm not sure it will ever be put to rights,' Ada sighed.

'Now, now,' Martha scolded. 'I won't hear a word of it. The place is sparkling clean and just needs a coat of limewash to make it fit for you. Come and eat, do. You'll all feel much better about it with something in your bellies. And Alice has been missing her mother.'

Sarah felt a second pang of guilt. She'd barely given Alice a thought throughout the weekend. If it hadn't been for Martha's kindness in caring for her, and for all of them, they would never have achieved half of what they had done.

CHAPTER 33

Sarah woke with a feeling of unsettling panic on the Monday morning. Daniel had said goodbye to them on the Sunday, standing in his shirtsleeves at the gate and waving until they were out of view as they walked homewards up the lane. He'd promised to leave the key with Martha when he left for work the next morning. Sarah and Ada had fallen into bed barely ten minutes after reaching Hill Farm Cottage and Sarah woke with a start at dawn, when Alice's grumbling cries turned into full-blown wails. She had fed her, then settled her back into her crib, where Alice had gazed a while at the patterns that the sunlight was making on the ceiling, before the pair of them had drifted off to sleep again.

An hour later, there was no ignoring the fact that Alice was well and truly awake again so Sarah rose once more, aware that every muscle in her body ached from the weekend's exertions. Her arms and shoulders were particularly sore, and her contemplation of the amount of work still required to make Lane End Cottage fit to move into had occasioned the sense of panic.

They had so few days left in which to prepare the new cottage and pack up Hill Farm Cottage as well, which wouldn't be a simple task. Sarah made her way downstairs to get the day underway, Alice clutched to her shoulder. She winced as each step pulled on her overworked calf muscles. Unusually, her grandmother was already seated at the table. Wordlessly, she poured a cup of tea for Sarah.

'How are you feeling this morning?' Sarah was concerned. Ada was a good forty-five years older than her and she had worked every bit as hard as Sarah the day before.

'My bones are creaking with every move I make and I could swear that my back is broken,' Ada complained. 'We can't go on in this fashion. We must simply do what we can over the next few days and then move in. Whatever work there is left to do we can complete once we are there.'

'You're right,' Sarah said, secretly relieved. 'I don't think I can face lifting a mop nor bucket, let alone a paintbrush, for a day or two.'

'There are remedies waiting to be made, too,' Ada said. 'The weather has been good so I must harvest whatever herbs have come into season and make use of them. If our income is lost, we'll not be long for Lane End Cottage in any case.'

Sarah and Ada crept around for most of that day, in such pain from their frenzy of work that Sarah was hard pressed to believe they would ever be well enough to undertake more.

'I'd best go and fetch the key from Martha,' Sarah said, as the afternoon drew to a close. 'She'll be wondering what's become of us.' But that day and the next slipped by in helping Ada and attending to neglected household chores and it was Wednesday before Sarah felt sufficiently recovered to head down the road into Northwaite.

'I'll deliver these remedies,' she said, tying on her bonnet. 'And then I'll pick up the key from Martha.'

Ada was going to keep an eye on Alice and Sarah felt quite sure that she would be taking advantage of Alice's nap-time to have a sleep herself. She hadn't regained her energy as Sarah had; she would have to insist that the working party was reduced to two for the coming weekend. She and Daniel could carry on, while Ada could stay with Martha and help her mind Alice.

Her mind busy with such thoughts, it took her a moment or two to recognise that there was no one home at Martha's house. She knocked at the back and front doors but the house had a silent, unoccupied feel about it. Thinking that Martha must have gone to Wednesday market in Nortonstall, Sarah was turning for home when a movement in the window of Lane End Cottage caught her eye. Puzzled she peered in at the front window, shielding her eyes against the reflections cast by the bright sunlight. There was definitely movement in the dim interior but it was hard to make out what was happening until her eyes adjusted to the gloom within. Martha, her hair bound up in a scarf, was in the front parlour with another couple of women from the village, industriously applying limewash to the walls.

Sarah rapped on the window to gain their attention and Martha jumped, then laid down her brush and came to the door.

'You weren't meant to find us here,' she said. She was flushed; whether from the hard work or embarrassment, Sarah couldn't be sure. 'We wanted it to be a surprise. You worked so hard over the weekend – I knew you must both be exhausted. Fanny and Agnes here –' she indicated the two women, whom Sarah now recognised as having children recently helped by Ada's remedies '– wanted to help you out after all that Ada has done for the village over the years. And you've done such a good job of cleaning that the limewash is going on a treat.'

It didn't take Sarah long to discover that they were now working on the final room, having worked in teams since Monday. She was overcome and could barely thank them, choked as she was by tears.

'You're to think nothing of it,' Martha said firmly. 'Nor must you think of coming to help. You have enough to do with the packing up and care of Alice. I didn't tell you because I thought you might just forbid it. The men are coming in over the weekend to finish off the garden and you'll be able to settle yourselves in after that.'

CHAPTER 34

After several days' hard labour packing up their home, Sarah had cause to be grateful all over again to Martha for her kindness in preparing Lane End Cottage. They arrived in their new home on the Wednesday, a week on from Sarah's last visit, the carter having set aside the morning in order to make several trips. Ada's boxes of bottles, jars, herbs and books made up one complete load and Sarah had given up the task of trying to persuade her grandmother to throw things away, reasoning that this might be best achieved once they were unpacking in the new place.

They'd arrived to find that Martha had been true to her word and the work that Daniel had begun on the garden had been finished, front and back. An area of rather scrubby lawn, complete with apple tree, had been revealed at the bottom of the back garden, but otherwise all was pristine earth, ready for planting.

The limewash had transformed the cottage interior, so that all was now bright instead of dingy, and Martha had thoughtfully placed flowers picked from her garden in the parlour and kitchen. Their moving-in day brought with it the blessing of further good weather, so not only were their household effects kept dry throughout their transportation, but the new cottage seemed filled with light as soon as they stepped through the door.

Ada had been particularly morose as she said goodbye to Hill Farm Cottage, her home for so many years. She had walked from room to room as their possessions were emptied out, then taken refuge in the garden, leaving Sarah to direct the operations. Sarah herself had expected to feel sadness, but the trials of organising the loads meant that, by the time she came to take one last look around the place, it felt as though it had been robbed of its memories. They had vanished along with the furniture and ornaments that had turned the place into a home.

She had, though, made a point of going out into the garden to say goodbye to the robin, keeping crumbs aside from breakfast for the purpose. Although she feared her friend might be busy with a nest and youngsters, the crumbs brought it down from the ivy.

'Goodbye,' she said, watching its quick, wary movements as it caught up the crumbs. 'We have to leave and are sorry to do so. We hope the new residents will watch over you.'

Ada had been very quiet as they walked down to Lane End Cottage, following the carter with his last load. When she saw the garden all cleared and ready for planting she brightened, however. And she was speechless when she walked into the cottage. Sarah hadn't elaborated on how much had been achieved by Martha and the other villagers, simply saying that a few of them were lending a hand and preferring to leave the extent of the transformations as a surprise.

'It's hard to believe that this is the same place that we left only ten days ago,' Ada exclaimed. 'How well everything looks here!'

Martha had been busy directing helpers where to put the furniture as it arrived on the cart so that the cottage was already beginning to look much more like home. Ada explored it from top to bottom and came downstairs smiling. She took Alice out into the garden and Sarah heard her grandmother describing to her great-granddaughter where the herb beds would be planted and how the fruit-tree would give them shade and how perfect the grass would be for her to run about.

Sarah oversaw the placing of the last few items and boxes, then tried to decide which room to begin unpacking first. The kitchen seemed like the obvious choice and so she set to, filling the dresser with the china so recently packed away and hanging the pans on the hooks to the side of the range. Ada came back into the kitchen, fired up with enthusiasm and ready to get to work on planting her herb beds at once. She'd brought as much as she could in the way of cuttings and seedlings with her.

'If I don't get them into the ground they'll wilt. Do we have the garden tools packed away somewhere?'

Sarah, standing in the middle of the kitchen surrounded by bags and boxes, opened her mouth to speak and burst into tears instead.

Ada looked at her in consternation. 'Why, whatever is the matter?'

Sarah wasn't sure that she could rightly say. Her head ached, as did her shoulders, and it felt as though everything she had bottled up over the last few weeks was now rising to the surface and must burst forth. There had been the shock of being given notice on Hill Farm Cottage, the uncertainty of whether they could take a lease on Lane End Cottage, the necessity of putting a brave face on things to convince her grandmother that they could turn it into a home despite its condition, the achieving of this goal and the effort involved in packing up their lives.

Now that all was successfully concluded and they were here, she should have felt happy – but Sarah had been fretting all the while she was unpacking. Her thoughts had turned to Joe and whether he would be able to find them now that they had moved, then to Alice. Her baby was barely two months old and Sarah felt as though she had neglected her badly over the last month. She had been so distracted by everything that needed organising that she'd handed Alice over to her grandmother or Martha with barely a moment's hesitation. Had it been a relief to do so? Had she been irritated when she had to devote time to giving her a feed? Was she, in fact, much like her own mother, unsuited to motherhood? She'd entered into the state with barely a thought as to what it entailed and now she didn't know how to go on with it.

Sarah became aware that Ada, watching her with concern as she sobbed, was waiting for an answer. She couldn't tell her the truth. It had dawned on her today that their roles had been reversed, apparently without either of them noticing. Her grandmother had become reliant on her for organising their lives. Was this the way it was to be from now on? It would only upset Ada to point it out to her, she felt sure. She sniffed and struggled hard to get her feelings under control.

'I can't believe we're finally here, that's all.' She wiped her eyes on the corner of her apron. 'I wondered whether it would ever happen but it has and we've been so lucky with all the help we've had.' The thought of this, and how on earth they could have managed without, threatened to make Sarah's tears well up all over again.

'Is that all?' Ada looked relieved. 'I thought something bad had happened. And now I see that you've been busy unpacking while I've been indulging myself with dreaming. Have we the makings of a cup of tea, I wonder? Let's take it into the garden and then I can help you set the kitchen to rights. My foolish nonsense about planting can wait until the weekend. Daniel says he will be with us on Saturday afternoon and he'll be glad to be outside after a working week in the mill, I'll be bound.'

Ada bustled around making tea while Sarah sank into a chair, taking Alice onto her lap and feeling as though her life was back on its rightful track once more. She was eighteen years old and a married woman with a baby, but for once it felt good to be just a granddaughter once more. The tea revived her and with two cupfuls poured and drunk she was ready to return to the unpacking once more.

'I'll finish up in the kitchen,' Ada said firmly. 'You go and set your room to rights. Alice will be unsettled enough tonight, what with her crib in a strange place and her no doubt picking up on your mood. You'll not want to make that any worse by trying to unpack around her as she sleeps.'

Her grandmother clearly knew what she was talking about, Sarah thought ruefully that night as she paced the floor with a cross and wailing baby. Alice hadn't taken her last feed well, seeming distracted, and Sarah, who was impatient to be off to do some more unpacking, had tried hard to appear calm and serene so that Alice wouldn't sense this. Later, she'd barely been in bed beyond an hour before Alice's wails roused her. Her daughter was not going to be pacified by another feed; she seemed alert to the difference in the room, refusing to feed for more than a minute before her eyes were drawn to the moonlight coming through the curtainless window, then craning her neck towards the shadows it cast on the floorboards.

'Well, little one,' Sarah whispered, 'there's no sleep to be had while you're in this mood.'

Pausing only to throw a shawl over her nightgown, she went quietly downstairs and let herself out into the garden. 'Look how bright the moon is,' she said, holding Alice in front of her so that she could see it. Alice waved her arms and kicked her legs with some force, making Sarah laugh in surprise.

'You're a strong one. You'll be walking before you think of crawling, I'll be bound.' She walked slowly around the garden, holding Alice so that she could see everything around her. 'Your father will see a difference in you when he's home,' she whispered into Alice's ear, drinking in her baby scent and loving the sensation of her little warm and wriggling body. Sarah felt Joe's absence keenly now. It wasn't just that there were jobs to be done around the place that were better suited to a man's strength. She didn't like to count how many days they'd spent together as man and wife in nine months of marriage but she feared it couldn't even amount to a month. It wasn't how she had imagined it would be and she missed him.

Sarah had returned Alice to her shoulder and was circling the garden, rhythmically patting her on the back. It was only when weariness caused her to stumble that Sarah realised her daughter was sleeping peacefully now and so she crept back up the stairs, fearful that a change in her rhythm of movement would wake her. She slipped Alice back into the crib and fell thankfully into bed.

Cooing cries that threatened to turn into a grumble and then a full-blown wail woke her to soft sunshine the next morning. Six hours had passed and although Sarah would have relished more, she was thankful for the rest she'd had.

CHAPTER 35

Despite the best season for planting having passed, Ada had such experience with herbs that her confidence in the cuttings and seedlings she had brought with her from Hill Farm Cottage had been rewarded. She'd worked with Daniel over the first weekend of their residence to mark out the beds, of which there were four in all, consisting of two rectangular ones on each side of the central path leading down the garden. She'd earmarked the borders along the hedges at the sides for fruit and vegetables and to grow herbs that required shade.

'There's no substitute for woodland, though,' Ada had declared, a month after planting. Assiduous watering had seen all but five or six of the seedlings take to their new home and the herb beds were beginning to prosper, although they were a long way off what she had enjoyed at Hill Farm Cottage. The plants that required moist shade had no place in the garden, and so Sarah still found herself despatched to search these out.

She had also managed, before they had moved, to find the time to broker a deal with Farmer Platt, the owner of Hill Farm Cottage. Swallowing her anger over what she viewed as their summary dismissal after having been good tenants for such a long time, Sarah had approached Farmer Platt to see whether they might be permitted to continue to harvest some of the herbs from the garden they were leaving behind.

Farmer Platt, a large, ruddy-faced man who looked at home in his working gear, but always appeared to be in danger of bursting out of his Sunday best when he was in chapel, was even redder in the face than usual when Sarah was shown into the farmhouse parlour. He wouldn't meet her eyes at first, but ran his hands through his thinning grey hair and confessed to being mortified at what had come to pass.

'I hope I can rely on you to assure your grand-mother, Mrs Randall, that if I had my way you'd be tenants still down the hill,' he said, having sat silently through Mrs Platt's cooing over Alice. Dressed in her prettiest sun-bonnet, Alice was on her best behaviour and quite entranced by Farmer Platt's number one sheepdog, Bonnie, who was the farmer's constant companion.

'Aye, if it were up to me you should have been tenants until she had no more need of the place,' he went on. ''Tis my son who is the cause of all this bother. He's after coming back to take up farming, having decided that life in yon city –' Farmer Platt jerked his head in the general direc-tion of Leeds '– don't have half the charm of country life. He's only gone and got himself a wife and four mouths to feed, the littlest 'un not a day older than your little lass, I'll wager. Mrs Platt was all for finding place for them here, but if truth be told it's his wife Eliza who'll have nowt to do with that. She's had her heart set on Hill Farm Cottage since Sam tell't her about it and as soon as she clapped eyes on it, why, she never let up. If I'm to keep peace in Sam's house then I must go agen my own wishes and give in to t'lady and forget being a master in me own home.'

Mrs Platt, quite taken aback by her husband's most unusual eloquence, and concerned by the fiery colour of his face, attempted to create a distraction by pouring tea and offering slices of seed-cake.

'Aye, but I want thy grandmother to know,' the farmer burst out again, as soon as every last crumb of cake was cleared from his plate, 'that I've not forgot her great kindness to my mother throughout all her years of pain, plagued with rheumatics as she was. She'll be turning in her grave at the way things are.'

The farmer subsided with a sigh and looked so miserable that Sarah seized her chance.

'It would be a great kindness if you would consider a request from my grandmother,' she said, swiftly fashioning a plea where none had existed. 'She'd be in your debt if you would consider allowing her to harvest from the herb beds when they fall ready. Provided Mrs Sam has no need of them, of course,' she added hastily.

'It would be a comfort to me,' the farmer said, the deep furrow in his brow easing a little. 'Mrs Sam will be told that any ideas she has for planting must be set aside until you have tek whatever you need. And she must grant you access with good grace, too,' he added grimly, no doubt thinking ahead to the prospect of a battle with his daughter-in-law.

So it was that Ada experienced little interruption to the supply of the essential ingredients to her trade. And her new home brought her additional business, from those who had previously used market days in Nortonstall as an excuse to visit the herbalist, but now found it more convenient to visit Ada in Northwaite.

Sarah had followed Ada around the garden on Daniel's third visit to Lane End Cottage, at the end of May, while Ada listed the plants she wanted to add to those already beginning to take root in the soil, which was proving pleasingly fertile.

'I thought blackcurrants here, at the back of the vegetable patch, so we can have leaves for a diuretic and berries to ease the throat. We already have blackthorn here.' Ada pointed to the hedge dividing the garden from the field, which swept down towards the valley and the mill hidden from view below. 'I can use the flowers, the berries and the bark.'

Ada turned to the new beds, nearer the house. 'I thought comfrey or knitbone here, along with feverfew for headaches and fever, coltsfoot to ease coughs, foxglove to help heal the heart, ground-ivy for nervous complaints, and St John's wort, of course. Then we'll have sorrel, lovage, sage, rosemary and thyme here . . .'

Sarah lost track of her grandmother's plans as she wandered over to the fence and looked out across the fields. Was Joe out there somewhere, down on the canal in the valley, making his way back to find her? It had been eight long weeks now – she hoped he would be home soon.

CHAPTER 36

'Well, she's a skinny, mealy-mouthed piece of work!' Sarah came into the kitchen to find Joe seated at the table, looking somewhat ruffled and in the throes of regaling her grandmother with a tale that Ada thankfully seemed to be finding amusing.

'Why could you not have tell't me that tha'd moved?' Joe demanded on seeing Sarah.

'And how was I to do that,' she fired back, 'when I never know where to find you from one day to the next? Where would I have sent word?'

Joe subsided into indecipherable muttering, which Sarah took to be recognition that his wife was right but he had no intention of acknowledging it.

'Let's not start with a quarrel,' Sarah said, swallowing down the feelings that his words had raised and focusing instead on her gladness at having her husband home.

'Joe was just telling me how he discovered our whereabouts,' Ada said, trying to suppress a smile. 'He's just had an encounter with Mrs Sam.'

'Ah, that explains your ill humour!' Sarah

exclaimed. 'Farmer Platt has had a lucky escape. If he'd had to put up with that woman sharing his farmhouse, as Mrs Platt wished, he'd have taken to sleeping in the cowshed, I'll be bound.'

Sarah and her grandmother had developed such a fondness for Lane End Cottage that they could talk of their previous home now without any sense of loss. The trips to harvest herbs had become less and less frequent as neither Sarah nor Ada could abide Mrs Sam, who followed them around the garden throughout their visit as though she feared they might take a blade of grass more than they were entitled to.

'I've got no time to be minding your plant-picking, with a family to be fed and a husband who makes more washing than any wife has a right to expect,' Mrs Sam grumbled at every visit.

'There's no need to stay by me. I can manage very well and let you know when I'm leaving,' Sarah suggested reasonably on her first visit.

'What, and have you traipsing over my grass and trampling my borders? I think not. I can't imagine where Sam's father got the idea that it makes any sort of sense to allow this arrangement. The sooner the growing season is over and I don't have to put up with this insult the better,' Mrs Sam said, hands on hips and her thin frame all but shaking at the indignity of it all.

Sarah had judged it best to bend to her work and pay no heed to these words, which were repeated on every visit as if learnt by heart. It didn't take long before she regretted ever having made the agreement with Farmer Platt, but until they no longer had need of these regular harvests she found herself unable to bring them to a premature end.

'Do you think you might dig up a little of the woundwort?' Ada asked her granddaughter prior to one visit. 'It's such a strong plant and I quite forgot to bring any of it with me. I'd be sad to lose it altogether.'

'You know how it is, Gran,' Sarah replied. 'Mrs Sam stands over me and watches me like a hawk. I'm sure she'll not let me take a plant from her garden, although come the autumn and the end of our arrangement I doubt that she'll keep a single thing growing there. She moans constantly about what a mess the beds are and wonders why anyone would want to grow such things. She'll have Sam dig everything out and plant cabbages and potatoes as soon as she can.'

Ada sighed but, as it turned out, she had no need to resign herself to the loss of her woundwort. On the next visit, Mrs Sam stood over Sarah as usual until the wails and cries from the infants within the cottage reached such a crescendo that she was forced to abandon her post, muttering a warning that she would be back directly. In her absence, Sarah managed to uproot a portion of the woundwort and hide it below the herbs in her basket, disguising the hole in the bed by overlaying it with lush foliage. She also took the chance to

236

have a word with the robin, who'd hopped down from the ivy hedge with the departure of Mrs Sam and was now perched close by, observing Sarah with his head crooked.

'I'm sorry,' Sarah said to the bird, 'I fear there'll be no more crumbs for you. Your new mistress is a harridan.'

'Who were you talking to?' Mrs Sam enquired, having arrived back in time to catch Sarah speaking but luckily without appearing to hear her words.

'Ah, just the robin. He's very friendly. I used to save a few crumbs for him every day.'

'Tssk! There'll be none of that now.' Mrs Sam's mouth was set in a thin line. 'Now, I'm going to have to ask you to leave. Charley has fallen and he has a swelling the size of an egg on his forehead. I need to be indoors with him.'

'I've quite finished anyway,' Sarah said, picking up her basket. 'And when I get home I will ask my grandmother for an ointment for Charley's bruises. I'll return with it at once.' She had waved away Mrs Sam's protestations that she had no need of it as she would be paying a visit to the apothecary. She hadn't seen Mrs Sam since she had left the medicines with her but clearly her mood hadn't mellowed, judging by Joe's mood after his encounter.

'The woman can't keep a civil tongue,' Joe said, with some heat. 'I was shocked to find you gone, and when I asked who the devil she was and what she had done with my wife and family she laughed in my face and said, "Some wife if she hasn't chosen to let you know she has moved away." And then she said that she neither knew nor cared where you might be living now but she hoped you might be done with her garden. It was only when she gave me to understand that 'twas her father-in-law, Farmer Platt, at farm on hill, that had put some arrangement with you in place that I saw where I might get a clue as to where you were. Farmer Platt put me right and so here I am.'

Joe looked around. 'You've fallen on your feet, I see.' He pressed on before Ada and Sarah had the chance to correct his mistaken impression that their home had been in this condition when they had taken it on. 'But tell me, do you not find it a little inconvenient to be so close to t'village after Hill Farm Cottage, which was nicely set away from prying eyes?'

'Inconvenient!' Sarah was startled. 'Why, we are much closer to the shops and Gran has found it beneficial for business to be so close to patients. And our neighbours have been invaluable; without Martha next door we could never have got this place set to rights.'

'Aye,' Joe was nodding in agreement but Sarah could see the lack of conviction in his eyes. Before she could question him further, though, Ada brought Alice in after her nap and Joe's full attention was turned on his daughter.

CHAPTER 37

Sarah looked back on the time spent with Joe that summer as one of the happiest times they had together. Perhaps it was the fact that there seemed to be more space to accommodate Joe; although Lane End Cottage was no larger than their previous home, the summer weather meant the garden was as good as another room in the house and most days found either Joe or Sarah outside with Alice. Despite being a narrow-boat dweller Joe proved able around the garden, happy to help Ada tend the plants, fix fencing or tie in exuberant summer growth as required.

Sarah was relieved to see that Joe's relationship had improved with Ada, who now seemed resigned to his presence. His devotion to Alice couldn't be faulted – he caught her up and took her into the garden at every opportunity and the pair of them were tanned golden-brown by the end of his stay, despite Sarah's repeated entreaties to keep their daughter out of the sun.

'Look at her: I'll wager she's nowt to do with me,' Joe teased, lifting a lock of Alice's hair. The sun had bleached her baby curls blonde.

'Don't be daft,' said Sarah. 'Her hair will be the colour of yours or mine when she's older. But keep her bonnet on her head, or she'll be getting a touch of the sun.'

Joe turned a bowl into a little pool for Alice, who shrieked with delight when he dangled her toes in it, or when he sat her in the water and surrounded her with sailing boats that he'd fashioned from leaves. At other times he caught her under her arms, making her squeal with glee, then, bent double, he supported her as she took fairy footsteps on tiptoe across the lawn, crowing with delight at her progress.

'You're making a rod for my back, Joseph Bancroft,' Sarah scolded as Alice, sitting on the grass and watching as her mother pegged out the washing, began to wail and hold out her arms beseechingly. 'She wants to be walked the whole time and she's barely six months old. My back will be broken before she can do it on her own.'

'Ah, she's a strong lass and she'll be up on her feet before you know it,' Joe said cheerfully, seizing his daughter and dancing with her around the lawn. Sarah shook her head but found it impossible to stay cross, especially as Joe caught her in to his side with his free arm and spun them all around until Sarah, quite dizzy and out of breath with laughing, had to beg for mercy. They collapsed in a heap on the grass and Sarah lay back and looked at the sky, complaining that her world was spinning.

'Look at t'bairn,' Joe said. Sarah propped herself on her elbow and saw that her daughter was resting against Joe's knee with a tremulous smile on her face, while her bottom lip quivered.

'Bless her, she's dizzy and doesn't know what to make of it,' Sarah exclaimed. She hugged her daughter to her and showered her with kisses. Joe repeated the action from the other side, managing to land a good many kisses on Sarah until she called a halt, declaring she couldn't breathe from all the laughing and the kissing.

Night after night, their happiness by day translated into passion. Joe's ardour was as strong as it had been when he'd courted her. Sarah clung to him and in a whisper, to avoid waking Alice, declared herself the happiest she had ever been. If she noticed a lack of response, she put it down to his aversion to talking about those 'soft things' as he liked to call any conversation about love. Sarah was convinced that she would be with child again before the summer was out, a thought that wasn't entirely welcome to her.

It wasn't until much later that she looked back and realised that Joe barely left the house during his stay, except in the evening. Shortly after his arrival at Lane End Cottage she had persuaded him to accompany her to Nortonstall, to Sutcliffe & Sons, to put his mark on the lease. Sarah had been dreading this, worried that Mr Sutcliffe Senior or Junior might see fit to quiz Joe about his suitability as a tenant. To her relief, both were in court on the day of her visit and the clerk who attended to them seemed in a hurry to get the job done so he could return to his work.

Joe was also impatient, wanting to get back to Lane End Cottage he said, so they had taken the path back to Northwaite through the wooded valley, without meeting a soul. Sarah had taken his arm, enjoying the rarity of having him all to herself, but if she suggested that they walk out as a family, he would always find some reason to excuse himself. Happy that he wasn't frequenting The Old Bell in the afternoons, she never thought to question his apparent transformation into a homebody and so three blissful weeks passed before Joe announced that he must go back to the canal.

'So soon?' Sarah fell silent.

'Tha' knows it must be,' Joe said, reasonably. 'Otherwise, how am I to support you and t'bairn?'

Sarah couldn't find fault with this. He'd handed over his wages when he had arrived and for the first time she had known what it was like to have money. Money that wasn't there to be frittered away, of course, but to budget with and to use to plan for the future. It had given Sarah a good feeling, and if the trade-off for this was that Joe could not be hers full-time, so be it.

'I'll be back afore tha' knows it,' Joe cajoled her. 'And I reckon young Alice'll be on her feet by then. Talking an' all, no doubt.'

'Don't leave it that long!' Sarah protested. It was

with a heavy heart that she waved him off on his last morning, she and Alice standing at the gate to watch him out of sight. He turned to blow them kisses every few yards until he reached the corner and was gone from view.

'I think a return to your studies would serve you well,' Ada said briskly after Sarah had moped for a day or two.

Sarah demurred. 'The wages Joe brings in will mean there's no need any more,' she said, the feel of what it was like to have money still fresh in her mind.

'That's as may be,' Ada replied, 'but times change and work dries up. You've an aptitude for this work and you should carry on learning while you have no need of it. It will always be there for you in the future, should things change.'

As the glorious early summer gave way to a wetter July and August, confining Sarah to the house with Alice, there seemed more point in getting to grips with learning once more. In addition, within a matter of weeks of Joe's departure the onset of nausea in the mornings confirmed what Sarah had suspected. Joe's visit had left her expecting, with a baby brother or sister for Alice due early in the coming year.

PART V

SEPTEMBER 1875 – OCTOBER 1877

CHAPTER 38

As the summer of 1875 became autumn, life in Lane End Cottage settled into a rhythm similar to that in Hill Farm Cottage the year previously, only Sarah had a lively would-be toddler to contend with as well as her studies and her pregnancy. Her sickness this time around was much worse and Sarah veered between thinking it must be because she was expecting a boy and fearing that she was over-tired and that this was the root cause.

'You're young and you're healthy,' Ada said firmly but with some sympathy. 'It will pass. My mother would have said that it was a sign that the baby is settling itself.'

Sarah fell to thinking about her own mother, lost to her, and whether she would have had any useful advice to offer her daughter. She feared not, for she had left the upbringing of her daughters very much to her own mother, Ada. She felt sure that her sisters, Jane and Ellen, would have longed to be involved, though. How they would have loved a niece to dote on!

'If the new baby is a girl, she shall be Jane,'

Sarah decided. 'Or perhaps Janet, or Janie.' It struck her all at once that using her sister's exact name felt somehow wrong. Surely, every time she used it, it would remind her of her loss until that sense became dulled as the new baby took over the name as her own. It was far better to have a name that served as a reminder, rather than as an echo, Sarah decided.

'Don't worry,' Ada said, misconstruing Sarah's silence to signify she was dwelling on her sickness. 'I'm reluctant to prescribe a draught for you until more time has passed and it is safe for the baby, but if the nausea becomes unbearable we will think of something.'

Sarah was about to reassure her grandmother that she hadn't been thinking of this at all when a sharp knock at the kitchen door startled them both. Patients would arrive on Ada's doorstep at all times of the day and sometimes even into the night, so they weren't unduly concerned – although this knock had a sense of urgency about it.

'I'll go,' Sarah said, rising from the table where they were labelling jars of leaves that they had dried from the last harvest from Mrs Sam's garden. She was puzzled when she opened the door. There was something familiar about the man on the doorstep but she couldn't place him at first. He was small, scrawny and unkempt, and there was an odour about him that suggested a lack of washing, no doubt because he had been sleeping rough if his appearance was any guide.

'Can I help you?' Sarah asked, holding the door ready to slam it shut if he should prove troublesome.

'You be Sarah.' It was a statement rather than a question, and when the man opened his mouth to speak Sarah knew at once who it was. The missing front teeth were the only clue she needed: it was Joe's best man, last seen over a year ago.

'Oh, it's . . .' Sarah couldn't bring his name to mind as her thoughts flew to Joe. Had something happened?

'Alf, missus,' he helpfully supplied.

'Alfred, of course. Do you want to come in? Do you have a message from Joe?'

Sarah overcame her reluctance and stood back, opening the door wider to make way for him, but he remained on the doorstep.

'I'll not stay, missus. I just came to tell thee . . .' The man hesitated, looking at his feet and all the while twisting his cap in his hands.

'Tell me what, Alfred?' Sarah asked, adding, 'Can I get you a glass of water?' for he seemed tongue-tied and at a loss all of a sudden. She felt a stab of anxiety and wished he would hurry up and speak. Had something happened to Joe?

'Joe's in prison, missus. He asked me to tell thee.'

'Prison!' Sarah's exclamation brought Ada to the door.

'For pity's sake, come inside, man. The doorstep is no place to be discussing such matters.' Ada's voice was harsh with shock.

'No, missus, I can't stay.' Alfred was already preparing to make his getaway down the path.

'Please, just a moment longer,' Sarah begged him. 'Why? Where? What . . . what did he do?'

'He were caught tekking cabbages from market garden at canal side. When they searched him he had taters, too, and in t'boat they found a pheasant all plucked and ready for pot.'

'But is that so bad?' Sarah asked, relieved that it was no worse and that no violence was involved. She thought guiltily of the poaching that Joe had done for them back in the spring.

'Aye, well, see, he'd bin caught afore.' Alfred was shifting from foot to foot, clearly worried by the tale he had to tell. 'So wi' his record he's gone and got six years.'

'Six!' Sarah could hardly believe her ears.

'Aye, missus.' Alfred remembered the rest of his message. 'He's in Leeds prison. But tha' won't be able to visit.' He was almost at the gate by now. 'Sorry, missus.' He doffed his cap and all but sprinted away from the gate.

Sarah felt her legs begin to give way beneath her and she would have fallen to the floor if Ada hadn't caught her round the waist and supported her to a chair.

'Six years . . .' Sarah repeated, in a kind of wonder. How could this be so? There were so many questions she wanted to ask, but no one to ask them of. Alfred, the only person with any answers, had left the scene.

Sarah became aware that Ada, who was looking more than a little shaken herself, was regarding her with concern.

'Do you think it's true?' Sarah asked, her mind fogged with the implications of it all.

Ada shook her head, as if to clear her thoughts. 'I think it must be. Why else would Alfred have chosen to pay us a visit?'

Both women subsided into silence then Sarah burst out, 'It seems like a harsh punishment, doesn't it? Six years for a few vegetables.'

'And a pheasant,' Ada answered mechanically.

Sarah started to pace the floor. 'I must visit him. Leeds, Alfred said.' She halted. 'Can I just turn up? How do I find out? Why did Alfred run off like that?'

Ada's thoughts were turning in a different direction. 'Six years, and not a penny earned in that time. And you with another baby on the way. 'Tis a mess, without a doubt.'

'I should start for Leeds at once,' Sarah said, as though she were about to leave the house as she was, without bonnet, shawl or money.

'No, no, we must discover more before you undertake such a journey. I will go and visit Mr Heaton, the magistrate, if he is at home. I hesitate to share our ill fortune with him but I can think of no other way. He will know about such things.'

Ada was tying on her bonnet as she spoke. 'Stay here and look after Alice. I won't be long.' Flinging a shawl around her shoulders she was on her way before Sarah could argue with her.

CHAPTER 39

Sarah tried hard to keep busy during her grandmother's absence, getting Alice up from her nap and tidying away the work that had been occupying her and Ada when Alfred came calling. Her thoughts, though, returned over and over again to Alfred's news. Try as she might, she couldn't imagine how things would be with Joe. Prison wasn't something she had had any reason to concern herself with during her life so far, and she realised that she had no knowledge of what his sentence might involve.

Ada returned to find Sarah very distracted and barely paying attention to Alice, who was grizzling to be put down and didn't want her mother pacing the floor with her and patting her back.

'Was he there?' Sarah demanded, as soon as Ada had stepped through the door.

'He was. And it's a sorry business indeed.' Ada was grim-faced. 'It turns out Mr Heaton was the presiding magistrate on Joe's case, so he was able to tell me a good deal. Alfred spoke the truth: Joe is in Leeds jail and the sentence is indeed six years. It is only a matter of the greatest good fortune that it isn't longer.'

Sarah, bewildered by this latest news, was rendered speechless.

'It seems Joe has previous convictions for petty thieving. He's served more than one six-month term already. If the items thieved were deemed to be worth over a shilling then the jail term handed out is longer. In addition, he has stolen from the same market gardener on more than one occasion, and this time the man was determined to exact a higher penalty.' Ada shook her head. 'It seems that Mr Heaton was only too well aware of Joe's link to this family and felt a duty to save him from an even harsher punishment for my sake as well as yours. Mrs Heaton has been a patient of mine for many years,' she added, almost as an afterthought.

'When can I visit him?' Sarah demanded.

Ada had turned away and was carefully folding and smoothing her shawl. Sarah had a feeling she was hiding her face from her.

'It's not likely that you will be able to,' Ada said. 'Mr Heaton told me that contact with home and family is seen as unhelpful in the eyes of the law. You have to apply for permission to visit and it *may* be granted once or even twice a year, but you can write four times a year.'

'Unhelpful . . .' Sarah echoed, trying to take in what she had heard. 'How can it be seen as unhelpful to have contact with your wife and family? And it's all very well to say that I may write – but Joe can neither read nor write so what use is that to us?'

Ada, who had endured a humiliating interview with Mr Heaton in which he had not seen fit to spare her his opinion of her granddaughter's feckless husband, was torn between anger at what Joe's actions had brought upon the family and a wish to ease the situation for Sarah.

When she turned around, Sarah could see how drained and tired she looked.

'I'm sure that there will be those in jail who will make it their business to read and write on behalf of those who can't. I suggest the best thing would be to make haste and write so that Joe knows you have received Alfred's message, and perhaps he can tell you more of his situation when he replies.'

Sarah put pen to paper that very evening, but it took more than one attempt to produce a letter that she was happy with. On reading back her first effort, she felt that there was too much anger set down there and not enough sympathy for Joe's predicament. Her second attempt petered out in tears, which stained the paper.

'Self-pity,' she said to herself, angrily. She didn't want Joe to fret about her being upset so she started again. She tried hard to deliver the news that they were to have another baby without imparting any of the anger she felt, not least at having to share such news in a letter to prison. She expressed a wish that his sentence would not be too hard and would pass before they both knew it. Even as she wrote, she felt this to be madness. If she looked back on her life six years previously, why, she could barely remember it. So much had happened since then. She had been but a child six years ago, living with her sisters and her mother in Hill Farm Cottage. Even two years previously seemed like a lifetime ago. She had met Joe, got married, lost her mother and sisters, had a baby, moved home. How might things change in the six years still to come?

She laid down her pen. Alice would grow up without knowing her father, and it would be even worse for the new baby. And Ada had been right. How would they manage for money?

With the letter sent on its way, Sarah had ample time to reflect. Her future suddenly looked very different. The home life that she had envisaged with a husband and family had already turned out to be but a dream, and she had had to adapt to Joe's lengthy absences. No sooner had their life fallen into some sort of manageable pattern, with Joe spending what time he could with them, then that had been ripped away from her too. If she thought about it too much it was almost unbearable. Six years without her husband was too long, and for such a petty crime. Sarah was torn between anger at Joe's folly and rage against what seemed like a sentence out of all proportion.

Ada was tight-lipped. After his last visit she had

started to thaw out a little towards Joe but now her opinion was reversed. She was still smarting from her interview with Mr Heaton and the revelation of Joe's current, and past, misdemeanours. Once again, he seemed like a foolish choice for her granddaughter to have made, and she could see only too clearly the path that lay ahead if they could not, in future, make ends meet.

Thankfully, Joe had already put his mark to the contract for Lane End Cottage and so there was no need for the solicitor to know anything of their changed circumstances. Unless, that is, gossip or news of the court case and sentence appearing in the local newspaper put paid to that. Ada tried to put that thought aside: further worry served no purpose at this point.

By unspoken consent the two women devoted their efforts to ensuring that Ada's herbalism could support them. Sarah tried to stop her mind straying to thoughts of Joe by focusing as much attention as possible on learning whatever she could from Ada, and so it came as something of a shock when, two weeks after she had sent her letter to Leeds jail, the reply came back. When Ada handed her the letter she took it wordlessly and put it in her pocket, then took her bonnet from the hook.

'Would you mind Alice for me?' she asked Ada, barely waiting for a reply before she slipped through the door and down the path. She had no destination in mind when she left the house, but her feet took her away from the village, following the road out of town. Walking rapidly, she ran her finger along the folded edges of the letter in her pocket. The thought of what lay within made her tremble and when she reached the five-barred gate where her labour with Alice had begun, she came to a halt, feeling nauseous and light-headed. Leaning on the gate for support she took the letter from her pocket and opened it with shaky fingers.

'My dearest Sarah,' it read. *'I would that I could turn back the clock and undo what has come to pass. You may be sure that I am paying the price for my folly. I wish I had known that another baby was on the way and all I can do is to beg you to look after yourself, and Alice too. I know you will have no knowledge of what it is like in here and so that you might think of me by day, and know what I am about, I thought I would describe prison life to you.*

'We rise at 6am and must take a turn around the yard before breakfast. Then after a bowl of gruel we must work for 4 hours (I have been given the task of helping clean the jail) until we have our midday meal. It is hard to believe that soup and bread or meat and potatoes can be such a high point of the day, especially when you see how little meat is served to us and how hard the bread is that accompanies it. The afternoon is for hard labour – I must walk a treadmill each day until I all but drop. Every

night we get a watery soup or more gruel then it is back to our cells to sleep, before we begin all over again.

'I miss the canal, the daylight, the freedom of being outside but most of all I miss you, Sarah.

Your loving husband, Joe.'

CHAPTER 40

At first reading, Sarah was delighted by Joe's letter and its apologetic tone and by his thoughtfulness in sharing the details of prison life with her, even though it sounded hard and difficult to endure. Then she fell to wondering how much of the letter was actually in Joe's words. It didn't sound like his voice at all and, on rereading it, she began to wonder whether in fact it was a standard letter that prison scribes copied out, adding a few personal details here and there to make it sound authentic. It was impossible to tell since none of it was in Joe's hand but the suspicion, once aroused, was impossible to eradicate.

Sarah's nervous excitement, then elation, dissipated and she was left feeling ruffled on her walk home, which she took at a slower pace than her journey out. Her headache and the nausea had returned with such force that she had to stop and rest before covering the last few yards.

Sarah was barely through the door before Ada burst out with a piece of her own news. 'Daniel is coming to visit next weekend.' She had also received a letter by the same post that brought Joe's, and had been waiting impatiently for Sarah's return. Then Ada noticed her granddaughter's pallor and, laying her hand on Sarah's forehead, she exclaimed over how clammy it was.

'Sit down,' she ordered, before fetching her a glass of water, which Sarah gulped gratefully, wondering whether this was all that was required to drive away the nausea. She drew Daniel's letter, which lay open on the table, towards her. It was brief and to the point:

> *'I have business in the area at the end of next week and so I will call by, if convenient, to see how you are settling in. It seems as though too many weeks have passed since I last saw you and I hope all is well at Lane End Cottage. I often imagine you there while I am at work in Manchester and look forward to seeing you all – I am sure I will find Alice grown already.*
> *Daniel.'*

Sarah was reminded painfully of the nature of Joe's letter – this one was undoubtedly all Daniel's own work.

'It's been weeks since we've seen him,' Ada remarked, as Sarah read the letter. The gladness in her voice at the thought of Daniel's visit was a reminder of the closeness that existed between Daniel and Ada, Sarah thought. She could not imagine her grandmother exhibiting such delight at the announcement of a forthcoming visit from Joe – impossible though that now was.

All at once overcome with weariness, Sarah was forced to ask her grandmother whether she would mind if she went to lie down for a little while. Ada, musing aloud about Daniel's visit and what she might cook for him, was pulled back to the present and regarded Sarah with concern once more. She helped her granddaughter up the stairs to bed, where Sarah fell instantly asleep, although it was a restless slumber, filled with dreams.

She awoke to find that dusk had fallen; she could hear the murmur of Ada and Alice's voices from below, and smells of cooking were wafting up the stairs. As Sarah sat on the edge of the bed, readying herself to go downstairs, another wave of nausea hit, this time accompanied by a terrible cramping pain. She bent double, whimpering. After a few minutes she straightened up slowly, praying that whatever it was had passed, and after five more minutes she cautiously attempted to rise. The time she was successful and she reached the top of the stairs before the cramps struck once more, making her sink to her knees.

'Gran,' she called, once the worst of the pain had passed, but she lacked strength and her voice barely rose above a whisper. She closed her eyes and gritted her teeth with the effort of trying again. 'Gran.' This time the call was loud enough to carry down the stairs and she heard her grandmother pause in her conversation with Alice.

'Sarah?' Her grandmother had appeared at the foot of the stairs, calling back in response whilst keeping half an eye on Alice in the kitchen. Ada turned to look upwards, as if to listen for a reply, and visibly started as, once her eyes had grown accustomed to the gloom, she made out Sarah's crumpled figure. 'Good heavens!' Ada began to mount the stairs. 'Whatever is wrong?'

It was late that night before Ada rose from beside Sarah's bed and told her that there was nothing more to be done.

'The baby is lost,' she said. 'Now you must concentrate on regaining your strength because you have a lively, healthy daughter to care for. There'll be time enough for another child when that husband of yours is out of prison. You may yet come to see this as a blessing – for now, try to sleep.'

Sarah heard her through a haze of pain and exhaustion, drifting into a deep sleep as Ada gathered bloodied cloths and towels together and left the room. She woke at dawn, hearing rain beating against the windowpane and, before the household awoke, she wept for the loss of her baby, of her hopes and for her marriage. On that September morning the world seemed to Sarah Bancroft like a very hard place indeed.

CHAPTER 41

Sarah's emotions veered between anger and sadness in the days to come. She was angry with Joe for having been foolish enough to get caught stealing, leaving her alone in this way to deal with the loss of their baby. Then, as she got on with day-to-day life with Alice, sadness would overwhelm her. There would be no brother or sister for Alice now, not for a very long time. This feeling then precipitated the onset of anger at Joe and his folly, and so it went on. She both dreaded and longed for the arrival of Daniel, fearful that she would be unable to disguise her unstable emotions but also longing for the distraction that he would provide.

Daniel arrived at midday on the Saturday, carrying a bag over his shoulder. He proceeded to unpack it, revealing all manner of goods from the shops in Manchester. It felt a bit like Christmas all over again, Sarah thought. She wondered briefly whether Ada had written to him, explaining what had befallen the family, and perhaps the gifts were a special effort to cheer her up. Daniel didn't seem unduly solicitous towards her, though: he was absorbed in showing Alice a wind-up toy he had brought for her. Sarah was just thinking how much she would like to take a closer look at it when Daniel looked up and said, 'My work will bring me to Northwaite more often in the future.'

Ada, who was setting plates out for dinner, paused and waited for him to continue.

'The owner of my mill in Manchester has joined forces with other mill-owners in the area to try out a new type of engine for power. Hobbs' Mill is one of the main partners in this, so I will be spending more time here in weeks to come.'

Ada positively beamed at the news and was quick to insist that Daniel must stay with them at Lane End Cottage whenever he was in Northwaite.

'I couldn't impose on your hospitality like that,' he protested. 'I will stay at the inn but will visit you every time I'm in Northwaite, of course.'

Sarah had said very little since Daniel's arrival but now she spoke up. 'You would be doing us a favour if we could provide you with board and lodging, rather than the inn. I don't know whether Ada has told you what has befallen me? With regard to Joe,' she added hastily, catching the sharp look her grandmother directed her way.

Daniel, who had been crouched on the floor with Alice, sat back on his heels. 'I hope he is not ill?' he asked, concerned.

'Would that were the case,' Ada muttered.

Sarah ignored her. 'No. I'm afraid to say . . .' She hesitated, feeling the shame in what she was about to reveal. 'I'm afraid to say that he has been imprisoned.'

Daniel rose to his feet, causing Alice to protest at the loss of her playmate. 'I am indeed very sorry to hear that,' he said gravely. 'I cannot believe he has done anything of consequence. I hope you may expect to be reunited very soon.'

'His offence is hardly great,' Sarah said with some bitterness, 'but the punishment is harsh.' She went on to outline what had happened, glad all at once to share the burden with someone else.

'I am very sorry,' Daniel repeated, when he had heard her out. 'Justice seems prepared to strike at the man of little means the hardest. Is there anything I can do?' He looked doubtfully at Sarah. 'I do not think that Leeds jail will be a suitable place for you to find yourself. Can I visit him on your behalf?'

'I'm resigned to hearing little from him, other than the four letters a year we are allowed to exchange,' Sarah said. 'I will apply to visit but have been told not to expect that the request will be automatically granted.'

No more was said on the subject as Ada declared dinner should be served. Sarah was happy to concentrate on getting food on the table and avoid any further discussion about what had happened to Joe. It felt like there were too many things that must be kept hidden from Daniel during his visit. Talk turned to how they were settling in, and after dinner Sarah washed up while Ada proudly showed

Daniel what they had achieved in the house and garden since his last visit.

Sunday proved to be a windy but strangely sunny day, still with a hint of warmth unusual for autumn. To Sarah and her grandmother's surprise, Daniel announced his intention of attending church that morning. He hadn't done so when he had stayed with them before and Sarah had made the assumption that he wasn't a churchgoer. He looked as though he felt his actions required an explanation.

'I took to going after Ellen died,' he explained. 'At first I was very irregular in my attendance, but gradually I found I took comfort from it and now I would miss it if I didn't go.'

Ada and Sarah saw him off and welcomed him back without comment but, while he was away, each was occupied with her own thoughts. Sarah wondered how different things might have been if her sister had lived. No doubt she and Daniel would be married by now; perhaps even with a family. Ellen might have been able to give up working at the mill as Daniel's prospects improved. Perhaps they might even have lived in Northwaite since Daniel's work increasingly brought him here. Her sister living in the same place as her again – how wonderful would that have been!

In her imagination Sarah once more saw the fields where they had played as children, filled with sunshine on a summer's day. This time, the children in the field belonged to her and Ellen, and she was leaning over the gate with her sister, watching them and laughing about the time they had tried to pick all the flowers in the field. Her daydream was so absorbing that it was an effort to pull herself back to the present and to the realisation that this could never be.

For her part, Ada felt chastened by Daniel's church attendance. She hadn't set foot in the Methodist chapel since the deaths of her daughter and granddaughters, and the minister's visit in March hadn't persuaded her otherwise. She fell to ruminating on the loss of her faith and, like Sarah, her thoughts turned to her lost family. She felt little hope that Mary's future would have been a bright one, but the loss of her granddaughters so young was a bitter blow.

If Ellen had lived, it was inconceivable that she and Daniel wouldn't have married. Daniel's place would have been cemented within the family. As it was, he was a welcome visitor and always seemed content to spend time with them, but that would no doubt change once he found a bride. Ada was struck by the thought that he might even meet someone suitable during his visit to the church – one of the village girls, someone who worked at the mill, perhaps. Ada tried to suppress a shudder. Daniel deserved happiness, but selfishly she would have liked to keep him as part of their family.

If Daniel sensed a sombre mood on his return to the house he made no comment, instead turning his attention to Alice who, no sooner had he stepped through the door, was laughing in delight and holding her arms out to him.

'Look, it's Uncle Daniel,' Sarah said, conscious that he was now the only man in Alice's life. She would need to reinforce this idea, otherwise Alice would perhaps start to think that Daniel was her father. The new title conferred upon him must have made the same idea occur to Daniel, for he flushed slightly but covered up his discomfort by entering into a noisy game of tickling with Alice.

After dinner, Daniel suggested that they might take a walk as the weather was still fine. By mutual agreement, they turned left out of the gate, heading out of the village before taking the steep path down into the valley. As they descended, the air grew cooler and Sarah was glad they had all wrapped up warmly, despite the sunshine. Alice was sitting on Daniel's shoulders and at first Sarah cried out a warning every time they approached a branch hanging low. Then, seeing what care he was taking of his precious burden, she let him alone.

Alice squealed in delight as they went along, unused to the view afforded by such an elevated seat and thrilled by the novelty of the expedition. Sarah lagged behind so that she could watch the progress of the little group. Daniel led the way, calling back a running commentary to Ada: 'Mind the branch,' 'Watch out for the brambles,' 'Loose stones here.' Ada looked happier than Sarah could ever remember seeing her.

Sarah felt a terrible pang. This should be Joe walking together with Alice yet, even as the thought struck, she knew Joe would never have suggested such a walk and, even if he had, Ada would never have joined them.

'Joe,' she whispered, as the group ahead of her descended further down the path and passed out of view. 'Joe, why have you left me alone?'

'Sarah!' The calls floated back along the path. 'Sarah. Where are you?'

'Coming,' she called, shaking off her melancholy and hurrying to catch up.

'I had a stone in my boot,' she offered by way of explanation when she joined them. They had reached the broad, dark pool at the bottom of the valley, the one where Sarah always believed that spirits must dwell. Although, now she thought about it, that was probably a story told to her and her sisters to stop them straying this far alone. No one would have wanted to be worrying about them falling into the water in such a remote spot.

Daniel, knowing none of this, was busy telling Alice that it was home to fairies. 'Look.' He pointed to where skeins of traveller's joy were festooned around low branches of the trees edging the pool. 'Fairy bowers. They sleep here by day and when dusk falls they come out to bathe and drink.'

Sarah wasn't sure how much Alice could understand of this but her daughter was wriggling so much in Daniel's arms that she was fearful she might fall in the water. Daniel had tight hold of her, though, and distracted her by pointing out what he called the fairy slide where the passage of feet had worn the path on the hillside into smooth grey undulations, which it took little to reimagine as a fairy playground.

Ada and Sarah settled themselves on a low rock and watched Daniel and Alice, now playing among the stones at the water's edge. Within a quarter of an hour, Sarah noticed that her grandmother had started to shiver, and so she summoned Daniel and Alice to return home. The steep climb back up the path in the fading light, and then on to Lane End Cottage, left them all breathless. The onset of dusk brought with it a sharp drop in temperature and they were glad of the warmth of the kitchen, although they were all rosy-cheeked after their exertions.

'Thank you for suggesting the walk, Daniel,' Sarah said, conscious that she rarely took walks that weren't for a set purpose. She went to the village to buy food, to Nortonstall to the market, to deliver herbs locally or collect herbs further afield. She never went out just for a walk, for recreation and exercise, and she felt all the better for it.

As did her grandmother, if one could judge by her relaxed and carefree appearance as she chatted with Daniel while the kettle boiled on the range. She looked ten years younger, Sarah thought, trying to shake off the feeling that her own marriage had brought them more problems than she could ever have anticipated, had she given it a moment's thought. Which, of course, she hadn't.

CHAPTER 42

Over the coming months, Daniel became established as part of the family, spending two weeks out of every four at Lane End Cottage. The arrangement suited them all. The extra income from his board and lodging went some way to alleviating the anxiety that Ada and Sarah felt over the loss of Joe's earnings. And there was no denying that, although Ada and Sarah were quite self-sufficient, they were glad to make use of Daniel to do some of the heavier work, such as chopping wood, and for fixing things about the place.

Soon it became habit to save such tasks for his visits. The most benefit, though, was undoubtedly gained from his company. He brought with him tales of the big city, which Ada and Sarah were always eager to hear, enjoying the glimpse of a world quite beyond anything that village life offered. He also brought levity and humour to lives that had become accustomed to difficulty as the state most likely to prevail.

Sarah was almost startled when spring came – it had felt throughout the winter months as though life was somehow filled with light, even when it was dark and cold outside. Alice, in particular, benefited from the extra attention that Daniel's visits brought. At one year old, she had become a confident walker and the proud possessor of a vocabulary of ten words.

When Sarah wrote to Joe, she told him of their good fortune in having Daniel as a regular boarder. She played down the ways in which the family profited from his presence, not wanting her husband's mind made uneasy over the part Daniel was starting to play in the family. For herself, it felt as though she had lost her sisters but gained a brother.

Through the summer Daniel's visits were frequent enough to guarantee the family a steady source of income, yet infrequent enough to be eagerly awaited. Each time he left, or rather failed to return from work after spending a few days with them, Alice would follow Sarah around asking for 'Uncle Da-da' and becoming disconsolate when she was told, 'No, he'll be back again in a few days' time.' Sarah had given up trying to discourage Alice's use of 'Da-da' for Daniel. After all, she reasoned, by the time Joe returned, Alice would have long given up on baby talk and she could tell that it pleased Daniel to be given this nickname.

Sarah's studies of herbalism continued at Ada's insistence. 'Although we have this extra income from Daniel, the time will come when I can no longer practise,' she said. 'And you will need to be ready for that day, to take over where I leave off.'

Sarah nodded her agreement, but for her the urgency had abated once more. She had Alice to take care of and although she helped her grandmother as before, she wasn't always as focused as she might be. Ada held her counsel, deciding that Sarah could absorb a great deal of what she needed to know by working alongside her, and so the summer progressed harmoniously enough. Sarah felt as though their lives were happy and settled for the first time in a long time and she allowed herself to relax and enjoy it.

She wrote dutiful letters to Joe but after her suggestions that she should visit were turned down on more than one occasion she decided it was for the best. Joe was where he was and there was no point in fretting about it. They would pick up again when he was released – in the meantime, her life must go on.

So Sarah was totally unprepared when, in the second spring since Joe's imprisonment, Daniel arrived to stay, seemingly ill at ease. He was his usual self with Alice, now two years old and already very good at managing to get her own way with him. He avoided Ada and Sarah's eyes, however, which immediately caused Ada concern. Sarah wondered whether they had upset him in some way but it wasn't until that evening, when Alice was asleep, that he felt able to reveal what lay behind his awkwardness.

'My work is done at Hobbs' Mill,' he said abruptly. 'I won't have need of staying with you in the future. Although I hope I may still visit,' he added hastily, seeing the shocked expressions on Ada and Sarah's faces. 'But I won't need regular board and lodging.' The last few words were uttered barely above a whisper and the misery on Daniel's face showed that he was only too well aware what this meant to them.

There was a silence, which lengthened as Ada and Sarah struggled for words. The loss of income was not uppermost in Sarah's mind; instead, her concern was for Alice, who was at her happiest when Daniel stayed with them. And she worried for Ada, too, for whom Daniel was the grandson she had never had.

Both women spoke at once: 'You mustn't . . .' 'Please don't . . .' Sarah paused and Ada gave a rather shaky laugh. 'You mustn't apologise,' she continued. 'We have all benefited from having you here with us and we're just so sorry that it must come to an end.'

'Please don't worry,' Sarah added. 'We always knew that this would happen, but as time passed we had forgotten that the arrangement wasn't a permanent one.'

'But the money . . .' Daniel's voice faltered. He knew how much they relied on the relatively small amount he paid them.

'You mustn't think about it.' Ada was firm. 'Far more important to us is the loss of your company.

I hope I can rely on you to honour your word and still find time to visit us whenever you can?'

'Indeed.' Sarah was as eager as Ada to gloss over the impact of the loss of money. 'Alice will be quite lost without her Uncle Dan-dan,' she said, Alice having decided to adopt a new name for Daniel, in keeping with her greater age. 'We can't expect to impose on your time,' she added hastily, 'but you must remember you will be welcome here whenever you would like to come.'

'I hope that will be often,' Daniel said. He looked a little forlorn. 'I've come to view this as more of a home than any other I've had.'

They all fell silent again until Daniel made an effort to divert their attention by relating an incident from the mill and the rest of the evening passed in general conversation. That night, however, Alice was the only one to rest easy. The others tossed and turned in their beds, struggling to comprehend what the new situation would mean to them. Ada's thoughts spun between the loss of money and of Daniel's company, Sarah's between what Alice's reaction would be and how she herself would miss Daniel, whilst the man in question was racked with guilt by the impact of his news. Ada, Alice and Sarah occupied his thoughts. The latter would have been startled to know that she occupied the greater part of them.

CHAPTER 43

Despite everyone's best efforts to make Daniel's final stay at Lane End Cottage as normal as possible, none of them could prevent moments of sadness descending, quickly smoothed over by hasty conversation. Sarah had decided that Alice shouldn't be told of the change that was about to befall them, hopeful that a young child's hazy sense of the passage of time would allow them to pretend that it wasn't long since Daniel's last visit and not yet time for the next. So Daniel made his departure very early one morning, before the rest of the household was up. Having told Ada and Sarah of his intention the night before, he left without any major farewells but with the promise of a social visit to be made very soon.

Yet as the weeks passed, although Daniel continued to write on a weekly basis, he failed to put in an appearance at Lane End Cottage. Alice had given up asking for Uncle Dan-dan but Sarah was sure that she hadn't stopped missing him. She went often to the gate as if looking for someone, and looked up hopefully whenever patients knocked at the door. It hurt Sarah to see her like this and she wondered what was keeping Daniel away.

What surprised her even more, though, was how much she herself missed Daniel. She found herself saving anecdotes to tell him, then remembering that it was pointless to do so, as she didn't know when she would next see him. She longed, too, for adult company other than that of her grandmother.

She had Martha next door, of course, and she was as steady and as reliable as ever. She had commented that Daniel hadn't been to visit in a while and when Sarah explained, out of earshot of Alice, why that was, Martha had looked at her with a good deal of sympathy.

'You must miss him very much.'

'Yes, we do. Not just because of the money, of course, but for his company. And he was so good with Alice.' Sarah watched as Alice trotted around Martha's garden in determined pursuit of a cat, who had chosen Martha to be his new owner after moving out of the farm up the road.

'And he was good for you, too.'

Sarah looked up. 'Yes, his company is much missed. And he was a great help about the place.'

'Sarah, he was more than that.' Martha slowly shook her head. 'Look at you, barely twenty years old and with that husband of yours no use to you at all, locked away in jail. Daniel clearly doted on you. I wouldn't be surprised if he took himself off on purpose.'

Shocked, Sarah bent to her task of shelling peas and hoped that her blush wasn't visible. She hadn't considered Daniel's absence in this light before and now that she had, the thought quickly took root in her mind. Could there be any truth in it? Surely not – after all, he'd explained how he was no longer needed at the mill, his project successfully completed.

'I'm sure you're mistaken,' she finally managed to say. 'Daniel is like a brother to me. And in any case, in his most recent letter he promises to visit as soon as his work in Manchester permits.'

Martha wasn't to be so easily put off. 'You'd have been a good match for each other if things had been different,' she said, taking the bowl of shelled peas from Sarah and returning with a jug of barley water and three glasses.

'If things had been different he'd have been married to my sister Ellen,' Sarah replied, with some spirit.

Martha let the comment lie. 'Have you heard from Joe of late?' she asked.

Sarah was glad to change the subject, but less glad of where the conversation now led. 'Yes, I had a letter just this week. I'd asked him again about a visit but he said his sister Kitty had been to see him quite unexpectedly and he didn't think another visit would be granted any time soon.'

Martha paused as she poured the barley water. 'His sister? Did you know anything about this?'

Sarah, who had been taken aback and upset by

the news, had to confess that she didn't. As soon as Kitty had been mentioned in the letter she realised that she and Joe had never discussed his family and she had no knowledge of the whereabouts of either parents or siblings. She intended to ask Joe for more information in her own reply.

'Could his sister be of any help to you, I wonder?' Martha asked, handing a glass of barley water to Alice, who had given up on her attempts to play with the cat and had flopped beside them in the shade.

'Help? In what way?' Sarah asked.

'Money, perhaps.' Martha had moved to tying back roses that had become unruly around the back door and had her face turned away from Sarah. 'I fear that if the three of you try to manage on what Ada alone can make from her herbalism it might be too much for her. On the other hand, it might be good for you to take some work out of the house.'

Sarah was surprised. She wondered whether her grandmother had said something to Martha. Could she have asked her to drop a hint in this way?

'I think we manage well enough. But did you have some work in mind?'

'I hear they're hiring at the mill,' Martha said. 'The success of whatever it was that Daniel was working on means they have taken on more orders, and more orders means more workers are needed.'

'I'm sure it isn't necessary but I will think about

it,' Sarah said, having no intention of doing any such thing. She changed the topic by asking Martha about her recipe for the barley water. Shortly after, she made her excuses and left with Alice, on the pretext of needing to help Ada. She found that what she really needed was a little time to think about what Martha had said. There was a lot to take in.

Had Daniel really stopped visiting because of the feelings he had for her, knowing her to be a married woman? Her astonishment at this notion was beginning to be overtaken by another feeling, one that she hadn't experienced in a while. To be admired by a man was both surprising and appealing, and even as she tried to push these feelings aside they were taking root and growing in intensity.

Yet, once her thoughts turned to Martha's second pronouncement, it was easy to deflate her unseemly excitement at the first. Martha's suggestion that she might work at the mill, to ease the burden of being a breadwinner that had fallen on Ada once more, was an unwelcome one. She had shrugged it off at the time but it, too, had taken root and started to grow.

CHAPTER 44

Sarah had reason to regret the feelings that her conversation with Martha had aroused. She wrote to Joe, asking him to share the details of his family with her and expressing her sadness that she hadn't had the chance to become acquainted with Kitty. But she paid far less heed to that letter, once posted, than she did to the correspondence between Ada and Daniel.

Daniel was still making vague promises to visit as soon as he could manage it, and with each postponement of his appearance it felt to Sarah that she missed him all the more. But as summer passed and autumn came upon them she found herself writing to him, although not in the way she had sometimes imagined in her daydreams. This letter was emotional, but carried no expression of Sarah's feelings, confused as they were. Instead, it was written on behalf of Ada, who had fallen ill at the start of autumn and was now confined to her bed, in great pain from a bout of rheumatism. Sarah had administered the remedies that her grandmother had instructed her to make but they had brought her little relief. Her letter to Daniel was brief, but heartfelt.

'Dear Daniel,
'I hope this letter finds you well. You must be a little surprised to receive a letter in a hand other than my grandmother's but I am sorry to have to report that she has taken to her bed this past week or so, having felt unwell since the beginning of September, and she now finds herself unable to hold a pen, such is the pain of her rheumatism.

'If you were able to find some time to visit her I know she would be very grateful. Alice and I would be glad of your company, too. If this proves impossible then please do still write – my grandmother will be as happy to hear from you as ever.
Yours,
Sarah Bancroft'

She had agonised over what to say at first but after a false start or two had let the words flow as they would. With the letter despatched she fell to wondering how long it would be before she could expect a reply, resolving neither to keep constant watch for the postman, nor to count the days. Daniel had, after all, made it very plain how busy he was and his failure to keep his word over his visits was surely testament to this.

So it came as something of a shock to find

Martha loitering by her gate one afternoon later that week as Sarah returned from delivering remedies around the neighbourhood. She had managed to maintain the practice as well as she could while Ada was ill, taking instruction on any remedies she wasn't yet experienced in making, but she had noticed that some patients, wary of change, had ceased to make their regular visits to Lane End Cottage.

Sarah spotted Martha as she walked up the road and wondered why she was out in the garden on such a dreary October afternoon. It was impossible to see whether she had Alice, whom she'd happily agreed to mind, outside with her but Sarah rather hoped not. She hadn't left any outdoor clothes for her daughter and there was a dampness in the air.

'There you are!' Martha exclaimed as Sarah drew closer. 'I wanted to catch you just in case you went home first before you came looking for Alice. I wanted to warn you.'

'Warn me?' Sarah's hand flew to her mouth in horror. Had something happened to her grandmother while she had been out? Or to Alice? For Alice was nowhere to be seen.

Martha saw Sarah's gaze sweep across the garden and guessed who she was looking for. 'Don't worry, Alice is perfectly safe. She's at home.'

'At home? Is Gran feeling better?' Sarah, struggling to make sense of the situation, already had her hand on the latch of the gate.

'Before you go in I should tell you something,'

Martha said. 'Alice is with Daniel. He's come to visit Ada. He knocked at your door and, getting no reply, he didn't like to walk in and risk frightening Ada so he came to see me to ask when you were expected home. Alice was so delighted to see him and so insistent on taking him to see her gran that I thought it would be all right to let them both go. I hope I didn't do wrong.' Martha, having recounted her news, looked anxious in case Sarah disapproved.

'Thank you, Martha. I'm sure Gran was delighted. You did right.' Sarah was already heading up the garden path and flung the words back over her shoulder as she went. In truth, she felt slightly piqued that she hadn't been at home to welcome Daniel. Why hadn't he written first? Her heart started to thump with the anticipation of seeing him and by the time she was through the door she felt a little shaky. She had longed to see Daniel for so long and now that he was here she felt embarrassed, as though her thoughts might be written plainly across her face.

'Hello,' she called up the stairs, finding the downstairs rooms quiet and peaceful.

'Hello,' Daniel called back. 'We're with Ada.'

As Sarah climbed the stairs Alice appeared on the landing. 'Dan-dan's here,' she exclaimed in great excitement. The sight of her daughter calmed Sarah. Her delight in Daniel's appearance put her own feelings into perspective and by the time she stood on the threshold of her grandmother's bedroom she felt sure that she was ready to greet Daniel as though she had last seen him just a week or two before.

The sight of him, though, as he turned towards her from his seat by the bed threatened to undo her resolve. He looked as he always had – his face frank and open and creased into a smile at the sight of her. His freckles stood out against his pale skin and his hair was perhaps a little longer than it ought to be, curling over his collar, but she experienced a great urge to rush over and fling her arms around him.

Instead, she contented herself by returning his smile and saying, 'I'm so pleased that you were able to come. Gran must be too. And it goes without saying that Alice is very happy, as you can see.' She bent down to pick up her daughter, who wriggled and protested, demanding to be put down so she could return to Daniel's side.

Daniel clearly thought a rebuke was implied in her words and he coloured up a little. 'I'm very sorry that it has been so long since I was able to visit you all.' He paused and Sarah flapped her hand at him to signify dissent.

'No, no, you mustn't apologise. You have work to do, and besides you are here now and you have clearly over-excited Gran and tired her out already.'

Sarah, determined to lighten the tone, indicated Ada, who had indeed fallen asleep, worn out by two hours of Alice's chatter.

Sarah lowered her voice. 'Let's leave her to rest

for a while. Come down to the kitchen and I'll get you something to eat after your journey. And I want to hear all about what you have been up to since we last saw you.'

CHAPTER 45

Daniel's presence that evening continued to cause Sarah to veer between delight and embarrassment. Her pleasure at seeing him again was tempered by the new realisation of how her feelings toward him had developed. She feared that this might be too clearly read in her face. She wondered now whether she had been blind in the past. She'd thought of Daniel as akin to a brother, being unable to conceive of an easy relationship with a man in any other way. But where did this new realisation leave Joe in her life? As the hours passed, though, she was able to push such unwelcome thoughts away and concentrate solely on the joy of having Daniel there.

Their conversation initially was disjointed. One or other of them would remember something they wanted to ask or tell the other and embark upon it, only to be interrupted by Alice, or the fact that food needed to be cooked and Ada tended to. In the end, Sarah was glad that Alice took Daniel away to insist he did some drawing with her, leaving Sarah to get food on the table and marshal her thoughts. She wasn't sure how long Daniel's visit would last but the prospect of having his company to herself that evening was both welcome and novel. She'd never experienced it before, her grandmother having always been present.

By unspoken consent they put aside any further attempts to catch up on news while Alice and Ada still had demands on them, concentrating their attention instead on grandmother and great-granddaughter until they could finally relax into each other's company as the house slipped into the quiet of evening.

'So, what has been happening? What has kept you away from us for so long?' Sarah asked, having determined in the hours running up to this moment that she would ask him outright.

'I have so little to report,' Daniel protested. 'My life consists in the main of going to work and coming home again, and repeating this day after day. It's far too dull. I want to hear about what's to be done to make your grandmother well again, how Alice does and all the gossip from the village. And about you, of course,' he added.

Sarah, now alert to every nuance of their conversation, wondered whether there was some evasiveness on his part – but a memory of something that Alice had done, and her wish to recount it, quite put the thought from her mind.

'And what of Ada's illness?' Daniel demanded, once the topic of Alice was exhausted. 'How long has she been like this?'

Sarah told him of the illness's progression and

290

Daniel frowned when she answered 'no' in answer to his question as to whether a doctor had been called.

Sarah shook her head. 'It's no good, Daniel. Gran won't hear of consulting a doctor. Imagine how it would look if any of her patients heard of such a thing. She's right, of course. There's little that she doesn't know about illnesses and their treatments. It would serve no purpose.'

Daniel looked unconvinced but turned to another issue that was on his mind. 'How are you managing for money?' he asked bluntly.

Sarah flushed. She'd hoped this topic wouldn't be raised. 'Well, Gran has been instructing me on how to make any of the remedies that I'm unfamiliar with. But she can hardly see patients in her bedroom and they are less inclined to accept what I have to say to them.'

Sarah stopped. The numbers of patients falling away had been of such concern to her earlier in the week that she had taken a step she had hoped she would never need to take. Mindful of Martha's words in the summer, she had approached Hobbs' Mill about taking work then, once her engagement there was confirmed, she had spoken to Martha about whether she would be prepared to take care of Alice during the long mill day. She cherished the hope that Ada might soon be well enough to share part of the responsibility. It was news that she feared Daniel would not like to hear.

'I have a plan,' she said finally. Daniel was looking at her expectantly and she looked away as she spoke again. 'On Monday I start work at Hobbs' Mill.'

'At the mill?' Daniel pushed his chair away from the table where they were still sitting, the remnants of their meal waiting to be cleared away. He got his feet, then sat down again. 'Have you no other option?' Then, as another thought struck him, 'Who will look after Alice?'

'Martha has kindly said she will look after Alice. I will pay her, of course,' Sarah added. 'Then, if . . . when Gran gets better she can help out part of the time.'

Daniel opened his mouth as if to speak but Sarah cut in quickly. 'Even if Gran gets better I doubt she will be as fit as before. She's getting on and the strain of providing for us all is too great. It makes sense for me to take on that role.'

Daniel looked concerned as he listened to her. 'Sarah, could you not take over your grandmother's work? She has been training you for some time now.'

Sarah shook her head. 'It seems as though it will be hard to get the patients to accept me instead of Gran. We would earn less than before, and I would still have to pay Martha to take care of Alice for some of the time. I've thought long and hard but I can't see another way to make this work, for the moment at least.'

'The mill work is hard, Sarah,' Daniel warned.

'You'll be on your feet all day. And the mill folk are . . .' He hesitated.

'I'm used to working hard – and besides, I have no option.' Sarah knew that she sounded defiant. 'And if you mean the mill folk are rough, well, yes, I suppose that's true of some of them. But many of them are from the village, from families I know through Gran's work.'

Daniel was up and pacing the floor, shaking his head. 'Sarah, you can read and write. You could do so much better. You've got a good head on your shoulders. In Manchester . . .' He stopped.

Sarah's expression was mulish. 'I don't live in Manchester. Nor do I intend to do so. Gran is here; Alice needs to be cared for. After the experience of my mother and sisters I don't see what Manchester has to recommend it.' Fired up, she was on her feet too, clearing the plates and piling them in the sink.

'But you loved to hear about city life,' Daniel protested.

'Hear about it, yes. Would I want to live there? No.' Sarah realised that her rising temper was making her clearing-up efforts noisy and she made an effort to be quieter for the sake of her grandmother and Alice, sleeping upstairs.

'You're wasted here,' Daniel declared fiercely. 'You'll not find mill work to your taste at all. It's dull and repetitive – take it from me. I've seen how it is. You have a brain and you should be using it.'

Sarah's passage between sink and table coincided with Daniel's pacing and for a moment or two they stood facing each other, both flushed and with expressions of grim determination on their faces. Daniel yielded first. His expression softened and he reached out his hand to fleetingly brush Sarah's arm. His fingertips lingered for a second or two and Sarah swallowed hard, feeling her anger, so swiftly kindled, in danger of turning just as quickly to tears.

'Don't let us quarrel,' Daniel said softly. He made no move to step from her path but held her gaze, while her heart thumped so loudly in her breast that she feared he must notice.

Neither of them spoke for what seemed like an age but must have been barely half a minute. Sarah felt she must break the spell, although every fibre of her being was yearning for Daniel to reach out and touch her again.

'Since your opinion of me is so high, what work do you suggest I should get?' she asked lightly, making to step round him to collect the last of the dishes from the table.

This time Daniel prevented her by taking her shoulders in a firm grip and holding her slightly away from him. 'You are right to point out the folly of my suggestions. I look to force my own ideas on you, without any clear idea of the sense of them, because I am filled with guilt. I can no longer stay with you but I can afford to help you by offering you a similar monthly sum. It would be a favour to me,' he added hastily, seeing Sarah's expression. 'You could view it as a loan.'

'Daniel, we couldn't be beholden to you in that way. We must make our own way in life, and you will need whatever money you have to secure your own future. You will marry before long and have your own family to support.'

Sarah's last words were provocative, issued in the hope of a denial. She hoped that her face didn't reveal how little appeal the picture she had just painted of Daniel's future held for her, but he hardly appeared to be listening to her.

His expression was filled with anguish when he spoke again. 'It is true that there is another reason why I have stayed away,' he said. 'I *have* met someone in Manchester, and I suppose in the fullness of time we might be wed.'

Sarah closed her eyes briefly, feeling for all the world as if he had struck her.

'I feared you would despise me for paying scant attention to Ellen's memory.' Daniel sighed, but didn't relinquish his grip on Sarah's shoulders. 'But even worse, Sarah, I have to confess that I have fallen in love with you.'

Sarah gasped and tried to move back but Daniel hadn't finished. 'With you, with Alice, with Ada and with the life you have here.'

Sarah's mind was reeling as she tried to make sense of Daniel's words and so she was hardly aware that he was drawing her in to his chest and holding her there. Then, almost before she realised what was happening he tilted her face up towards him and kissed her lips, softly at first then with a passion that made her stagger back when he finally released her.

They stood facing each other once more, speechless. Sarah knew that what had just taken place should never have happened. Yet she wanted to experience it again even though it was wrong. For a few euphoric moments she didn't even care that it was wrong. Then reality began to impose itself on her thoughts. Daniel had just confessed that he was all but engaged. And not only that, she herself was a married woman. Whatever would Joe think if he knew? The thought made her glance around nervously, as though someone might see and report back to him.

'I'm sorry, Sarah.' Daniel reached out and caught her hand but held it gently and didn't try to pull her to him again. He looked slightly stunned by his own actions. 'I shouldn't have done that but I'm not sorry that I did. Can we set it aside and carry on as before, do you think?'

Sarah considered. Could she carry on seeing Daniel and forget that this moment had ever happened? Could she welcome his wife-to-be into the house without remembering what had passed between herself and Daniel, wishing for it to happen again, yet knowing she had no right to do so? Her eyes filled with tears as she slowly shook her head. Daniel gently pressed her hand to his lips and let it fall.

'I knew I had no right to ask such a thing. I must do as I did before and leave you – otherwise both our lives will be a torment. My offer to help you with money until Joe returns will always stand.'

Sarah shook her head again. That could never be right, even less so after what had just passed between them. A great weariness overtook her.

'I must clear up so all is ready for the morning. I wish you a good night's rest.' She turned away from Daniel to busy herself at the sink.

'I will be gone in the morning, Sarah,' he said, hesitating before turning towards the stairs. 'I will say goodbye to Ada before I leave, but you and Alice must not disturb yourselves.'

Sarah bent over the sink as she listened to his tread on the stairs. How would she explain to her grandmother and to Alice that Daniel had gone once more, never to return? It would be a cruel blow, one that was hard to contemplate.

CHAPTER 46

'Is that you, Sarah?' Ada's voice was querulous as Sarah made her way upstairs a few minutes later. Sarah hesitated, scrubbed at her face in an effort to wipe away any traces of her tears, then stepped into her grandmother's bedroom.

'Are you all right, Gran? Can I get you something?'

'What have you been doing downstairs until this hour? Was that Daniel I heard just now going up the stairs?'

'It's not that late,' Sarah said. 'Daniel and I were just catching up on news – it's such a long time since we've seen him. Now, it's time for you to rest if you want to make sure that you get better all the sooner.'

She made a fuss of straightening Ada's covers and plumping her pillows to disguise the agitation that her grandmother's words had caused her. Imagining how she would have felt if Ada had been witness to what had passed between Daniel and herself in the kitchen, she felt a wave of embarrassment wash over her.

Yet that night, as she lay in her bed while Alice

298

slept peacefully in her own over by the window, that feeling receded. She was tortured instead by the thought of Daniel's proximity. He lay in the next room, with just a wall to separate them. It was as though she could sense him, wakeful, just a few feet away. Sarah sat up in bed, her face hot. She turned to look at the wall behind her bedhead, as if it might open and offer her passage to the room next door. Reaching out, she laid her palm flat against the wall and closed her eyes. She stayed there until the stiffness in her shoulder obliged her to move and so she lay down again in bed, curled up tightly and wishing fiercely for the oblivion of sleep.

When she awoke, cramped and stiff from the position she had held for a few hours, the room was perceptibly less dark. For a moment she couldn't think why she was sleeping so awkwardly until the memories flooded back from the evening before. She sat up quickly, listening. The house was still. Had Daniel left already? Or was he still asleep? Would she have a chance to speak to him before he went?

She got out of bed and tiptoed to the door, taking care to tread lightly. Pausing on the threshold she listened. Still no sound. She stepped onto the landing and saw immediately that Daniel's door, closed last night, was wide open.

'Daniel,' she whispered. But she knew at once he had gone. She crept along the landing and looked into his room where the bed, neatly made, looked as though it hadn't been slept in. Sarah went quietly across to her grandmother's room and peeped in. Ada was sleeping peacefully, the covers pulled up under her chin. A folded note lay on the table beside her bed. Sarah stared at it. Was this the farewell to Ada that Daniel had promised? She had to stop herself from going into the room and retrieving the note; her fingers itched to open it to see what it contained. She clenched her fingers and turned away. It was not her place to read it. She must swallow her bitter disappointment and resign herself to the fact that she had seen the last of Daniel and that it could only be for the best.

Sarah lay sleepless in bed for another hour, staring at the ceiling and trying to talk herself into believing that the phase of her life that was about to begin would be a good one. Then, when she judged it to be an acceptable time to rise, she went quietly downstairs and sat at the kitchen table, looking out as the light lifted and wishing that she could turn her thoughts to what Joe, rather than Daniel, might be doing now.

Finally she roused herself and set the kettle to boil, making up a breakfast tray to take to Ada. The thought of the letter lying there on the bedside table was filling her head by the time she mounted the stairs. Childish chatter alerted her to the fact that Alice was awake and had no doubt woken Ada, too. As she expected, when she entered Ada's room she found her grandmother half-propped on her pillows and Alice snuggled into the bed beside her.

'Good morning,' Sarah greeted them cheerfully, determined not to give any hint of the gloominess of her thoughts. Putting the tray down on the bedside table, she picked up the note. 'What's this?' she asked, showing it to Ada, before laying it on the bedcover. Then she moved over to the window to open the curtains, determined to hide her agitation.

When she turned around, Ada was holding up the note and regarding it suspiciously. 'I don't know,' she said. 'Where can it have come from? You'll have to read it to me.'

She held it out to Sarah, who delayed by settling Ada so that she could sit comfortably against the pillows and manage her breakfast tray. Then, with trembling fingers, she unfolded the piece of paper. It looked as though it had been torn from a notebook. Would Daniel, no doubt imagining that Ada would read this herself, reveal anything of what had happened to cause his sudden departure? Would she find herself reading out shaming words referring to herself?

Taking a deep breath, Sarah read,

'My dear Ada,
'I was so glad to have the chance to spend time with you yesterday even though I was, of course, very sorry to find you unwell and confined to bed. I hope that Sarah's very good care will

301

have you back on your feet again in no time at all.

'It was delightful to catch up on all the family news from Sarah and to hear about her future plans. I have some plans of my own that I couldn't bring myself to share with you yesterday and I hope you will forgive me. I am shortly to depart for America to study the ways in which they operate their mills there and I am none too certain when, or if, I will return. I wanted the time we spent together to be untainted by this. I am particularly sad that I do not know when I will next see Alice, who has grown greatly since my last visit.

'I must also ask forgiveness of you all for departing in what you may think a cowardly manner, although I hope you will come to see it as having the intention of sparing us all from sad and uncomfortable farewells.

'Your friendship over these last few years has been invaluable to me and it has brought me much joy. I will treasure those memories and hope that the future will bring great happiness to us all.

Your loving friend,
Daniel.'

Sarah didn't know how she had made it to the end of the letter without breaking down. She hoped that her pauses could be read as astonishment at the revelations contained within it. Indeed, she was at a loss as to what to make of it.

'Did Daniel tell you anything of this last night?' Ada asked. Her brows had knit together in a frown and she was plucking at the sheets.

'No, he did not,' Sarah said. 'I am as shocked as you are.'

'And what did he mean by referring to your future plans?' Sarah's grandmother had lost none of her sharpness despite the pain of her illness.

Sarah looked down at the note, silent while she tried to gather her thoughts. 'I'm taking work at the mill. From Monday. You're not to worry – Martha will look after Alice and come in to keep you company during the day, too.'

Ada opened her mouth to speak but no words came out. Alice, who had been looking from her mother to Ada throughout the reading of the letter and the subsequent conversation, had understood very little of what was going on but could sense that it was something that she might not like. The corners of her mouth turned down and she showed every sign of getting ready to wail until Sarah scooped her up, saying 'Time to get dressed.' She hurried her out of the room, leaving Ada to digest the startling news of the last half-hour.

PART VI

NOVEMBER 1877 – SEPTEMBER 1881

CHAPTER 47

Sarah would always look back at the time she spent at the mill as one of almost unremitting unhappiness. It didn't help that, starting work as she had in November, her walks to and from work were in the dark at each end of the day and always, or so it seemed to her, in wind, driving rain or snow. Despite getting up early to make sure that everything was ready for Martha, she invariably set off late. It had been agreed that it was better for Martha to come to Lane End Cottage to look after Alice and Ada there.

'It's no hardship,' Martha had protested in an attempt to stop Sarah fretting that it was an inconvenience. 'I just have to step next door. It's not as though I have to travel any distance, unlike you.'

Sarah had subsided, only too aware that rousing Alice before dawn to take her to Martha's would be problem enough, while leaving Ada alone and unattended at home for long periods was likewise inadvisable. So she persisted in making sure that meals were prepared in advance, even though Martha had declared herself more than happy to cook. Sarah knew it was guilt that made her do this – guilt at leaving two family members who were unable to fend for themselves for someone else to care for.

Each morning when she left the house she was already late, hurrying to catch up with the tail end of the mill-workers who were already well on the way along the road and out of the village. She would listen for the sound of their voices ahead of her, straining her ears to hear them over the noise of her clogs ringing on the road. She knew that if she caught up with them just before they turned down the path into the valley, she would make it to the mill just in time. If they were already on their way down, her success was less assured.

The path was steep and worn away in places by the passage of so many feet. Taken in company, the pace was a little slower and, with a number of lanterns to guide the way, a little safer. Taken at speed, with the fear of wages docked for lateness and the humiliation of a public scolding lying ahead, the path seemed more hazardous. Loose scree made it precarious in places, the wind invariably blew out the lantern even if Sarah had managed to light it before she left, and rain made the stones slippery lower down the path so that a hurried descent risked causing Sarah to skid or take a tumble. After the first week or so, some of the mill-hands had taken to keeping a watch for her arrival, sending up an ironic cheer as she made it to the mill yard, which only served to draw attention to her lateness.

Ramsay, the mill manager, who knew something of Sarah's situation, was inclined to leniency at first, whispering to her to 'Hurry along in and straighten your cap for goodness' sake. Be on time tomorrow and we'll let no more be said.' But with Sarah late five days out of six he had no option but to dock her pay. 'It grieves me, Sarah,' he said. 'Your grandmother was my mother's saviour with the remedies she prescribed for her, but I can't keep making allowances for you. You'll have to buck up your ideas if you want to keep your job.'

Lateness wasn't Sarah's only problem. She seemed to have no aptitude for the work, being intimidated by the machinery, the noise and the sheer size of the mill floor. On her first day she watched in awe as the spinners manoeuvred the carriages of their spinning-mules, deftly sending the frames back and forth, drawing out the thread while doing several things at once without ever breaking the rhythm. Sarah started as a bobbin-carrier, ferrying the reels from the carding room to the mill floor. Her first sight of the vast space captivated her and she was enchanted by the fine cotton fibres floating everywhere like fairy gossamer.

She was quick to realise that appearances were deceptive – the floating fibres caught in everyone's clothes and hair and, even worse, clogged their breathing. On top of that, the heat and humidity necessary to prevent the cotton thread from breaking as it was spun, and the noise of the great machines, stunned her. Children darted everywhere.

309

They picked up the drifts of fibre from under the machines to prevent them creating a fire hazard, used their small, nimble fingers to mend thread broken during spinning, or acted as runners between the different areas of the mill.

Daniel had spoken the truth. After being on her feet all day, hurrying from the carding room to the mill floor and back again, Sarah was exhausted and there was an uphill walk home still to be faced. She longed to spend time with Ada and Alice and hear news of their day, but she could barely manage to eat her food and utter a few monosyllabic answers to her grandmother's questions before sleep claimed her and the whole process had to be started all over again before dawn the next day.

After two weeks, Sarah had become more used to the routine and less exhausted by it but her skills as a mill-hand were still woefully inadequate. She looked in envy at the women around her who managed their machines with a supple grace, turning, bending and twisting as they moved along the great framework, all the time conducting a low conversation with their immediate neighbours. Her own attempts to stifle squeaks of fear when the great carriages of spindles rolled towards her as she made her way amongst them didn't pass unnoticed. She was consigned to the carding room where the bobbins were prepared, a lowly job in the great hierarchy of the mill.

The number of people that the mill employed

had taken her by surprise. Its population of workers was considerably larger than the village of Northwaite, sitting on the hillside up above it. It attracted workers not just from there, but also from Nortonstall and all the surrounding villages.

It soon dawned on Sarah that the relatively solitary life she had led up until now had made her ill-suited to the noise and bustle of the mill and the banter of the workers there. Once her mother and sisters had left to join her father in Manchester, she and Ada had been thrown very much on each other's company. Hill Farm Cottage had been a little remote and Sarah's trips to the village were for supplies or to deliver remedies, and not for social reasons.

At first she had found it hard to understand the closeness of the friendships among the women who had worked at the mill together for years. She observed them as they walked along in the morning, arms entwined, chatting as they went. Conversations were randomly set aside and picked up again throughout the day, as work allowed, while the journey home saw the same women walking together again, arm in arm, weary but still chatting. Sarah came to realise that they spent so much time together, they mostly knew one another better than they knew their own husbands and families.

Just a few of the women walked alone, keeping themselves to themselves, and Sarah saw how this sometimes happened when a spat between friends saw one of them cast out from the close-knit group. It rarely lasted longer than a day before everything would be back to normal. Sarah, though, was acutely aware that she walked alone each day more often than not.

CHAPTER 48

During Sarah's early days at the mill, she felt her isolation keenly. None of the women offered to welcome her into one of their tight-knit groups and at first she didn't have the confidence to introduce herself to them. After a few days, she thought she recognised some of the children she had once known in Northwaite, now grown up, amongst the women workers. She was getting up the courage to go over to them one day in her dinner break when, to her annoyance, a man settled himself on the hard wooden bench opposite her, obstructing her view.

'New here, are you?' he asked.

'Yes,' Sarah said. She didn't offer anything else, hoping to discourage further conversation.

'From hereabouts?' he asked, smiling and not in the least put off.

'Yes, from Northwaite.'

'I'm from there mesen and can't say as I recognise you,' he said, his brow creased into a frown. 'And I'm sure I would ha' noticed if I'd seen a pretty lass like you around.'

Sarah, aware that the women seated further along

313

the rows of bench seats had stopped their chatter to listen, became increasingly uncomfortable.

'Well, being a married woman perhaps I don't frequent the same places as you.' Her frosty response drew giggles from the listening women.

The man, far from being put in his place, seemed to be enjoying their exchange.

'Oh, aye. And who's t'lucky man then?'

'Joe Bancroft,' Sarah said.

The man frowned. 'Don't know anyone o' that name from Northwaite.'

'He's from Nortonstall,' Sarah said.

One of the women leant forward. 'Joe Bancroft, from Nortonstall?' she asked. 'And you're his . . . wife, you say?'

She paused deliberately and the other women nudged each other and giggled.

Sarah flushed. The dinner break usually seemed far too short but today she was relieved when the bell sounded to send them back to the mill floor.

'Yes, his wife,' she said. She felt instantly wary and she'd have asked the woman why she wanted to know, if the overlooker hadn't been shouting at them that it was time for them all to get back to their places. The opportunity lost, Sarah couldn't find a reason to reopen the conversation, but she became acutely conscious of nudges and giggles whenever she passed that little group at home time or clocking-on time, until before long something else engaged their attention and she was forgotten.

Sarah's spirited response to her dinner-time inquisition had an unexpected benefit, however. Other women – ones from Northwaite village – had been witness to it and that night, on the way home, one of them approached her.

'Well done for tekkin' no nonsense from t'likes of our Will.' The woman who spoke was so well muffled against the cold that Sarah couldn't recognise her but that overture was all that it took for the other women to register their acceptance, too. From then on, Sarah was offered friendly words of greeting when she joined the group on the walk to the mill in the morning and was invited to sit with them at dinner-time.

It turned out that Edie, who had spoken up first, was sister to Will, the forward chap who made it his business to try it on with every woman who worked at the mill, regardless of age or marital status. Edie had ceased to pay his actions any heed although one dinner-time she was heard to express the wish that there was surely one woman in the whole of the mill who'd be prepared to take him in hand and relieve her of the obligation.

'I had high hopes of you,' she confided in Sarah, 'until you opened your mouth and we could tell you had your nose up in t'air.'

Sarah protested, to much laughter, and Edie gave her a nudge. 'Aye, well, we know you now and you're one of us. Although 'tis a shame. You're a sight too dainty for this work – an' you can read an' write an' all.'

315

There was a murmur of agreement from the other women. Sarah shook her head to negate their comments but in her heart she felt it to be true. Gaining their acceptance had helped her to feel more settled at the mill but it still took every ounce of resolve to get her there each day.

At night she watched Alice sleeping peacefully – her arms flung free of the covers and cheeks flushed – and marvelled at her perfection. Alice was now nearly three years old and Sarah felt it deeply that she was missing so many stages in her daughter's growing up. Yet there was food on the table and money put by, so that whatever the future might bring she would hopefully be ready for it.

Although she continued to write dutifully to Joe every three months, she found it harder and harder to know what to say to him. He'd been gone for virtually the whole of Alice's life now and Sarah had given up asking him whether she could visit. In any case, a six-day working week left precious little time for prison-visiting, especially to see someone who felt like a stranger to her. Daniel, though, was another matter.

Despite all her resolutions to forget him, it was Daniel she thought about before she went to sleep at night; Daniel's face that came to her unbidden when work was unbearably dull. Daniel, alas, wasn't there to save her when her daydreaming caused her to neglect the thread as it spooled, leading to unevenly wound bobbins or, even worse, broken threads. Sarah veered between shame that she was unable to master what was apparently the most basic skill in the mill and a kind of triumph at her unsuitability for the work.

CHAPTER 49

December 1877 felt like an endurance trial to Sarah, as she walked to work through rain and snow, fog and frost, always wishing herself somewhere else. The days crept by but, as the month progressed, Sarah sensed a change in atmosphere at work. There was an air of excitement, even of friskiness, at the mill. They would have two days' holiday at the Christmas period, as Edie explained with delight, and there would just be three days at work after that before they got their Sunday off as usual.

'The master usually lets us leave early on Christmas Eve an' all,' Edie said. 'He has guests at his table in t'evening and he likes his workers to be well out of t'way so we don't spoil his party.' Edie snorted to express her contempt then added, 'I'm not complaining, mind. I've enough to do in my own home to get ready for Christmas. An' if it's been a good year we get something extra in our pay packets the Friday afore. I've got my hopes pinned on it – I've my eye on a new bonnet and I've asked Bessie in t'shop to put it by for me.'

Having Christmas in the offing gave the workers

something to talk about at dinner-times and the women were eager to share plans and recipes with each other. Sarah listened, smiled and nodded but didn't have much to add to the conversation. It would be a quiet Christmas with just the three of them at home this year, she reflected. No Daniel and no Joe – it would seem odd. She realised that she ought to come up with some ideas of her own, otherwise the day that would be special to her for being a mid-week holiday would simply seem boring to Ada and Alice.

The arrival of mistletoe in the mill the week before Christmas whipped up a frenzy of excitement. It was frowned upon by the management, but the men were wise to this and kept it well hidden, whipping out a sprig whenever the opportunity to demand a kiss from an often reluctant victim presented itself. The whole mill was astonished when the tables were turned on Edie's brother Will – one of the worst mistletoe offenders. Carrie Banks, a petite and pale wraith-like girl with a mass of dark hair, and possibly the quietest worker at the mill, presented herself to Will with a sprig of mistletoe all of her own and procured from who knows where. She stood on tiptoe, the sprig held aloft, puckered her lips and closed her eyes. Will, astonished by the turn of events, was seen to blush deeply, then bend down to kiss her on the lips, to a round of applause from all those nearby.

'Can you believe it?' Edie asked Sarah a day or

two later. 'That little minx Carrie has only gone and turned our Will into some sort of mooncalf. He's chased after every bit of skirt in t'mill, wi'out success. Then this little madam turns tables on him. I swear he's in love. Can't stop talking about her.'

Despite Edie's bluster she looked delighted and Sarah noticed Will walking home by Carrie's side that evening, his head bent down to listen to her and a slightly stunned expression on his face. Sarah chuckled at the sight and nudged Edie.

'See, I tell't you!' Edie exclaimed. 'It beggars belief. An' I never heard that Carrie utter a word afore, yet now our Will can't get a word in edge-wise, the daft fool.' It was said with great affection. Sarah felt sure that some Christmas magic had rubbed off on the pair and she already had high hopes for their future.

As Edie had predicted, the workers were let off early on Christmas Eve and, as everyone hurried to shut down their machines and tidy their work areas there was a hum of excited chatter. Sarah came down from the carding room and caught up with Edie in the yard.

'It's slinging it down,' Edie complained, as the driving rain looked set to dampen everyone's spirits for the homeward journey.

'Aye, it'll be snow afore long.' Will and Carrie had caught up with them. Sarah shivered. She wondered whether he was right. The air was much colder than it had been on the way to work that morning and the thought of the fireside at home was very appealing. The walk back to Northwaite was quieter than usual, everyone concentrating their energy on staying upright on a path made slippery by rain and mud. As Sarah reached Lane End Cottage, the first house on the route back into the village, she was startled to receive a chorus of Christmas wishes from her fellow workers.

Holding back sudden tears, Sarah stopped at the gate, holding her lantern high, and called, 'And a merry Christmas to you all,' to their retreating backs. Edie, Will and Carrie waved before hunching against the rain and hurrying on.

Sarah hastened up the path, unlatched the kitchen door and stepped into a kitchen full of delicious aromas of nutmeg, cinnamon and cloves.

'Now, you're not to lift a finger,' Ada said before Sarah could speak. 'Get those wet things off you and go and sit by the fire in the parlour. I've made you a hot drink to see off that cough of yours and we've all sorts of good things to eat.' Ada's health was much improved and she was determined to demonstrate this to Sarah by taking on the burden of all the Christmas preparations.

Sarah didn't argue but went upstairs and changed out of her work clothes into her second-best dress in honour of Christmas Eve, then she went down to the parlour to find Martha and Alice already settled there. Alice held out her arms to her mother and Sarah scooped her up and seated her on her lap. A paroxysm of coughing seized her as she did so and Martha frowned, then rose, went out to the kitchen and returned with a steaming glass of dark-coloured liquid. As Martha set it down beside her, Sarah caught a waft of the aroma she had noticed as she entered the kitchen.

'There, something special made by Ada for Christmas,' Martha said, before adding in a lower tone, 'with the addition of a nip of brandy from me. To help your cough.' She winked at Sarah who was prevented from replying by the entrance of Ada bearing a plate of mince pies.

'Mmm, these smell good.' Sarah took one for herself and one for Alice from the plate. 'Were they a gift from one of your patients?'

Ada shook her head. 'They were from Daniel.'

'From Daniel?' Sarah was startled. 'But he's in America, surely?'

'It seems not.' Ada took a note from the pocket of her apron. 'He writes to say his departure has been delayed as the mill in Manchester still requires his presence. So he has sent us a parcel of all sorts of good things and he says . . .' Here she paused to put on her spectacles to read his letter. 'He says that he now hopes to depart before the summer is out and in the meantime he sends Christmas wishes to one and all.'

Ada looked downcast for a moment. 'Why didn't he come to spend Christmas with us, as he has done for the last few years, I wonder?'

'No doubt he has good reason,' Martha said

briskly. 'Now, can I try one of those mince pies? And Sarah, drink up before it gets cold.'

Sarah took a deep draught of the drink and was grateful for its soothing effect and the warmth that spread through her as the alcohol took hold. She was shaken by the news of Daniel, having thought him long gone away. It unsettled her to know that he was still here, not too many miles distant in Manchester. Or was he perhaps spending Christmas elsewhere, with his fiancée's family? It was a most unwelcome thought.

CHAPTER 50

That night, perhaps prompted by the brandy – another measure of which Martha had succeeded in adding to a second glass of the spiced Christmas punch – Sarah dreamt that Joe and Daniel, combined into one man, had arrived on the doorstep on Christmas Day. She was perturbed by the merging of their facial characteristics, Daniel's pale skin combined with Joe's dark curls, while Joe's teasing charm sounded odd issuing from a mouth shaped like Daniel's. Her initial delight soon turned to uncertainty and then alarm, due to the unnerving behaviour of this person who appeared to be both friend and husband, yet was actually a stranger.

Sarah woke with a start, uncertain whether she had actually cried out or not, but Alice slept on undisturbed in her small bed by the window and there was no sound from Ada's room. It was still dark so Sarah attempted to compose herself to sleep, morning clearly being some way off, but a fear of tumbling back into the nightmare kept her awake for a while longer. When she came to again it was to find Alice snuggled into bed beside her, whispering loudly, 'Wake up!'

The day passed well enough, despite Sarah's worries that her grandmother and daughter would find it dull without Joe or Daniel present. Ada was determined to keep Sarah out of the kitchen as much as possible and the day started with a special breakfast of ham and eggs, eaten in a leisurely fashion and a far cry from the rushed bowl of porridge that Sarah had become accustomed to before heading to the mill each morning.

By the time they had finished, the bells were ringing to call the villagers to church and chapel but Ada had remained steadfast in spurning religion since her daughter and granddaughters had died. Sarah felt no inclination to take Alice along, but Martha called by on her way to church, with a promise to come and help with the dinner as soon as she returned.

Martha's husband had proved the village gossip correct by simply failing to return from Leeds the previous Christmas. He had eventually sent word to say that he wouldn't be coming back, and although it became apparent that he had moved in with a lady-friend, Martha didn't seem unduly put out. She professed herself better off without him, taking in laundry to supplement the little she earned from her part-time care of Alice.

'He was a lazy good-for-nothing when he was here,' she said. 'I do very nicely on my own, thank you.' Her children had long grown up and moved away, and would not be with her for Christmas, so she was joining Ada, Sarah and Alice, who were more than happy to have her company.

By the time Martha returned from the Christmas Day service, a light fall of snow sprinkled the ground. The joint of beef was cooking in the oven, the vegetables were all prepared and the plum pudding was steaming gently on the range. Alice and Sarah were kneeling in front of the parlour fire, a large box open before them while Ada, seated by the fire, looked on. Martha came to sit with them, a small glass of brandy in her hand. Her cheeks were flushed from the cold outside but also, as she confessed, because she had joined some of her fellow churchgoers for a glass of something festive at The Old Bell on the way home.

Sarah saw Ada give Martha a sharp look but her attention was distracted by Alice, now burrowing into the box to see what she could find. It contained the Christmas gifts from Daniel, all varieties of food so far, much to Alice's disappointment, but Ada assured her there was something in there that she would like. After pulling out a jar of marmalade, a box of dates and a tin of pilchards, she had been partly mollified by a wooden box containing jellied fruits, attracted by their bright colours and sugary coating. A packet of tea, despite its pretty packaging, was not considered worthy of notice, while a tin of toffees with a Lakeland scene painted on the lid was set aside to be opened after dinner.

Finally, just one package remained, taking up the whole of the bottom of the box. Sarah helped Alice to lift it out and was surprised by how light it was. Surely it must be empty? She hoped her daughter wasn't going to be sorely disappointed, although she could think of no good reason why Daniel might have enclosed an empty box in his Christmas parcel.

As Ada and Martha watched, Sarah helped Alice to lift the lid and they both exclaimed at the contents. Cylinders of crepe paper, in alternating bright red and green, lay within, each one with a brightly coloured paper wrapper around its middle, illustrated with a different scene. There was a perky robin, a church in a snowy landscape, children in bright coats throwing snowballs, a pile of wrapped gifts, a sprig of holly and a candle, burning strongly and dripping wax.

'What are they?' Martha asked, leaning over to look more closely as Sarah lifted one of the cylinders from the box. Each one was pinched in above and below the illustrated wrapper and when Alice lifted another one up and shook it, it rattled.

Sarah picked up the lid of the box. 'Christmas Crackers. A gift and a motto in every one. Make your Christmas go with a bang.' She looked doubtful. 'I'm not sure what that means.'

She looked again. 'Oh, there's a drawing. See, Alice. The crackers are piled in the middle of the dining table. Then it looks as though two people each take one end of a cracker and pull.'

Alice seized a red cracker and held it out to her mother, looking hopeful.

'I suppose we can try one. There are six crackers so there will still be enough for one each.' Sarah was herself keen to see how this was going to work so she grasped one end of the cracker firmly, telling Alice to hold her end with both hands.

'One, two, three, pull!' she instructed. There was a bang, Alice fell backwards, Ada screamed and Martha nearly dropped her drink.

'Goodness!' Ada said. 'Whatever was Daniel thinking of? Does he want to frighten us out of our wits? I'm sure I don't want one of those things, thank you.' She went quite pink in the face but looked less cross as Sarah quickly shook out the contents of the cracker in an attempt to mollify Alice, who looked as though she was going to burst into tears from the shock.

'What's this, I wonder?' Sarah unrolled a tube of gold paper that had fallen from the cracker. 'A crown. For princess Alice.' She smoothed out the folds and set it on Alice's head, where it promptly slid down over her face.

'Mummy wear it,' Alice said firmly. Sarah set the crown on her own head and retrieved a brightly coloured piece of metal that had fallen beneath Ada's chair. Further investigation proved it to be a tinplate frog, which leapt high in the air when pressed on its back. Sarah read the motto then slipped it into her pocket, unobserved, as Martha and Ada got up to cook the vegetables and make the gravy. The words – *The magic spell of love can never die, Its spirit floats o'er earth and sky* – seemed too personal to share, somehow, on a day when there would be absences from the dinner-table.

'Come on, Alice, let's put the rest of the crackers on the table,' Sarah said.

Alice, however, was content playing with the frog so Sarah left her to it and piled them in the middle of the table herself, noticing as she did so that Martha was pouring herself another drink from the brandy bottle that she had tucked into the lower shelf of the kitchen dresser.

The Christmas dinner felt very special after all the effort Ada had put into it and they all sat over it for a long time, apart from Alice. She was excused to play with her frog, as well as all the other little gifts that had come out of the crackers. Ada had eventually been persuaded to pull one, shutting her eyes as she did so and professing herself delighted with the miniature pack of playing cards, which she immediately donated to a hopeful Alice.

The crackers were a thoughtful gift on Daniel's part, Sarah reflected; an exciting novelty for the adults, they had produced six small gifts that had entertained Alice far more than a single larger present might have done. She also treasured all the wrapper illustrations, carefully peeling them away from the paper crackers and smoothing them flat. Sarah had promised to make a scrap-book for her and stick them in.

329

Ada refused Martha's offer of a drink but Sarah had a couple of small glasses, more out of a wish to please Martha and to save her from drinking the whole bottle to herself, than out of any desire for it. The plum pudding had to be saved until the evening, when it was served with dates and nuts – another gift from Daniel – as everyone was too full to consider eating it after such a splendid dinner.

Ada and Sarah declined all offers of help with the washing-up from Martha, and watched without comment as she made her unsteady way home at the end of the evening. Alice went to sleep with her treasures from the day lined up on the bedroom windowsill so that they would be the first things she saw on waking the next morning. Seeing how exhausted her grandmother looked, Sarah sent Ada to bed shortly after her daughter, then finished tidying up before sitting in front of the dying embers of the fire.

She had one more day before it was work as usual: something to savour. It was hard to contemplate the resumption of her routine after such a lovely Christmas Day, but there it was. At least the working week would be short and there was still the New Year to look forward to. She found it hard to imagine how Joe would have spent the day in prison, although his letters in previous years had spoken of a relaxing of the regime with no hard labour and meat served in recognisable portions at dinner-time. A carol service in the evening provided a welcome distraction and a chance to stay up later than usual.

Joe had served over two years of his sentence now, but there were still nearly four years left to go. So much had changed already in the time that he had been away – what might still be to come? Sarah sat on and stared into the dying fire, wondering just what the future might hold.

CHAPTER 51

Winter turned to spring and spring to summer, when there was at least some joy in being out and about so early, with warmth already in the air, the birds singing joyously and sunshine creating the illusion that better things were on the horizon. Ada, only too aware of Sarah's great unhappiness at the mill, despite her best efforts to disguise it, tried to persuade her to give it up.

'I'm fully recovered,' she said. 'I don't see the need for you to carry on. I'm looking after Alice most days now, without Martha's help. I can bring in enough of an income – and a little bit extra if you are there to help me, too.'

Sarah, though, despite her dislike of the work, had got the taste for setting money by and became stubborn when her grandmother pressed her case.

'I'll give it another month or two,' she conceded in the end. But the months passed and before Sarah knew it, another whole year had gone by. The year 1878 became 1879 and winter was on the horizon once more, yet Sarah still remained at the mill. Her cough had become persistent with the damp autumn weather, refusing to respond to the coltsfoot syrup that her grandmother had made up for her, which had proved efficacious in the past.

'It will pass,' she said. 'There's a lot of coughing to be heard all around the mill. It's just the change in the weather.'

Sarah and Ada both knew, though, that the cotton fibres that floated in the air at the mill had started to affect her lungs. At night, Sarah lay in bed attempting to stifle her coughing, to avoid waking Alice and hoping that her grandmother couldn't hear. It would only reopen the debate about her continuing to work, while it had also become apparent to Sarah that once again Ada wasn't as well as she could be. The colder, damper months had brought her rheumatism back and Sarah worried about leaving her in charge of Alice although Ada was adamant that she could manage. Sarah feared that Ada was hiding something worse from her, for she seemed to be growing frailer, but her own obstinate desire to prove her worth by bringing in an income from the mill caused her to put this down to the simple fact that her grandmother was getting older. Martha promised to keep an eye on things, which provided a little reassurance, although Sarah was unsure just how much her neighbour might be drinking during the day.

In the end, it was Edie who talked some sense into her.

'Some women are never rid once the cough takes hold,' she warned. 'And some of them find themselves staring into an early grave. You've got a bairn to take care of and you're the only one she's got, what with your husband put away and Ada getting on in years. You must consider whether you can make ends meet any other way.'

It was quite a speech for Edie and Sarah was suitably chastened. She promised her workmate that if the end of the month came and the cough was no better she would take her advice. Fate, however, intervened before the month was through.

Sarah made her way up to Northwaite from the valley as fast she could, the words of the overlooker ringing in her ears.

'There's been a message come to the office. You're to get yourself home as fast as you can.'

He shrugged when Sarah asked for more details. Had something befallen Alice? Or Ada?

'I can't rightly say. But you'd best be on your way.'

Sarah wasn't sure whether he simply didn't know what was wrong, or did know but wasn't prepared to tell her. One thing was for sure: his usual sharpness had been replaced by a gruffness that was the closest he came to showing he had a softer side. As she hurried to collect her shawl and her lamp, even though they wouldn't be needed for the journey home today given the early hour, he called after her, 'Don't be worrying 'bout getting in to work tomorrow, neither.'

The wind caught her full in the face as the path began to flatten out at the crest of the valley. The icy blast of it burnt her cheeks and froze what she realised were tears trickling down them. All the way along the path up the valley the over-looker's words had been worrying away at her. What could be wrong? It must be something serious. No one was ever sent home, let alone excused work for a second day, over some trivial issue. Ada? Alice? . . . The names ran on a loop in her brain and it was only when she stopped, gasping for breath with a stitch in her side, that she thought to add another name to the litany. Joe. Could something have happened to Joe? It had been several months since his last letter but there was nothing unusual in that. Or was it longer than that? She tried to think back: the repetitious daily toil at the mill seemed to have robbed her of all sense of the passage of time.

She'd reached the gate of Lane End Cottage now and she paused for a moment, casting her eyes around as if hoping for some clue. All looked as usual; there was nothing outwardly to show that there was anything wrong within. At that moment the kitchen door at the side of the house opened and Martha peered out.

'Is that you, Sarah? Thank heavens you're home. What a to-do we've had!'

She bustled Sarah into the kitchen and pulled out a chair at the kitchen table for her.

'Here, I made some tea and kept the pot warm

for you,' and she poured a cup from the big teapot warming on the hob.

Sarah looked around: all looked peaceful and as it should be, but where was Alice? And Ada?

'Is it . . .?' She paused, not sure who to enquire about first.

'Alice is with Hannah, next door to me,' Martha said. 'I thought it best to get her out of the way. She's well, you mustn't worry. You know how Hannah dotes on her.'

All at once, Sarah knew. Her grandmother hadn't been looking well for days; she'd grown paler and greyer as the weeks went on. Sarah had been worried about leaving Alice with her while she went to work but Ada had been emphatic.

'There's nothing wrong with me that one of my tonics won't cure. I'm just not as young as I was, that's all. It's just the weather. You'll see: once the first primroses are out next spring I'll be as right as rain.'

Sarah had taken from that what she wanted to hear, rather than trusting the evidence of her own eyes, because she didn't want to think about the potential problems if Ada wasn't well enough to mind Alice.

'It's Ada, isn't it?' she asked. 'What happened?'

Martha rubbed Sarah's shoulder, in a sign of brisk sympathy.

'Aye, I'm afraid it is. Mrs Sykes came to collect her remedy and found the door ajar. When there was no reply to her knocking and calling she went in.' Martha hesitated, as if weighing up how much information to give. 'She found Ada collapsed here in the kitchen, on the floor.' Martha indicated the spot and Sarah's hand flew to her mouth to stifle a cry.

'Mrs Sykes ran round to bang on my door and I came at once. Poor Ada, I could tell she'd breathed her last.'

'And Alice?' Sarah whispered.

Martha looked uncomfortable. 'We couldn't find her at first, until we looked upstairs. Then we found her huddled under the quilt on your bed.'

She patted Sarah on the back as she started to cry. 'Don't fret. Alice has had a shock but she's young. She'll forget about it very quickly.'

Sarah found little comfort in her words. She was consumed with guilt over what Alice had witnessed, and anguished over the loss of her grandmother. Martha let her sob for a bit then asked gently, 'Do you want to see her?'

Sarah, whose thoughts had been wide-ranging as she cried, looked at her in some bewilderment.

'Ada. Do you want to see Ada?' Martha repeated.

Sarah nodded slowly, then she got to her feet and followed Martha as she led her through to the parlour.

'I had to call out the doctor to make sure all was as I thought. He got me some help to carry her through here.' Martha paused before opening the parlour door.

Sarah stepped hesitantly over the threshold.

Somehow a coffin had already been acquired for Ada and she lay within, looking so tiny and shrunken that it seemed as though it had been made for a giant. Sarah approached with some trepidation. The figure in the coffin bore little more than a faint resemblance to her grandmother. The hair looked right, as did the clothes, but as all breath had left her body it had clearly taken with it whatever it was that made Ada who she was. The diminished, grey figure lying there looked much older than the woman Sarah had been used to seeing on a daily basis, and fresh tears flowed at the sight of her.

'She was all alone,' she whispered between sobs.

Martha tactfully refrained from referring to the fact that Alice had been there, but reassured Sarah that, according to the doctor, Ada wouldn't have known a thing.

'He said it would all have been over in seconds,' she reported.

The stark details brought on another fit of sobbing, as Sarah reached out to touch Ada's hand. It felt cold and waxy to the touch. She was too late. The Ada of that morning, of just a few hours previously, had gone. She could no longer say all those things she should have said before, nor thank her for all the love and care she had bestowed on Sarah over the years.

'I'll leave you. There'll be things you want to say. And don't think she can't hear you,' Martha said, preparing to make a tactful withdrawal.

'Her presence is still strong in this room. I can feel it.'

Sarah was torn: she wanted to see Alice, to make sure that she was all right, but she also wanted to say some last meaningful words to her grandmother. Except that now she couldn't think of a single sensible thing to say. She sat beside the coffin and tears flowed again. She felt very alone. With Ada gone, it seemed to Sarah as though she had lost the final family member who could offer her any support. Her father didn't count; he hadn't been a presence in her life for years. There was Joe, of course, but he was never there when she needed him. It was very clear that she was on her own now. She needed to be strong, for Alice and herself. There was no one left to rely on.

Sarah sat beside Ada for a few more minutes, her tears now dry. 'I wish I had listened to my own worries this morning and hadn't left you alone. I'm sorry,' she said. Her shoulders started to shake with fresh sobs but she fought them down. 'You taught me well,' she whispered. Then, as a thought struck with her with increasing clarity: 'I'll continue your work.'

She bent over the coffin to kiss Ada's forehead but in her heart she felt it was too late. There was nothing to be done now except to make sure that she put into practice everything that her grandmother had taught her. Sarah resolved in an instant that she wouldn't continue at the mill; in any case, who could be trusted to look after Alice with Ada dead and Martha now a sight too fond of the bottle? Instead, she vowed that she would become the best herbalist that she could possibly be, in honour of her grandmother.

CHAPTER 52

The days up to, and after, the funeral passed in a blur. Ada was welcomed back into the fold of the Methodist Church for her final resting place although this caused Sarah some heartache for she'd had no guidance from her grandmother as to her wishes. Sarah stuck by the resolution she had made by Ada's coffin and gave notice at the mill. She was too troubled by Martha's drinking to feel that she could leave her in sole charge of Alice all day, and so she felt that in a way the decision had already been made for her. She was encouraged in her tentative plans when, at Ada's funeral, which was well attended, several of the mourners approached her to say that they hoped she would continue in her grandmother's footsteps.

'Ada spoke very highly of you as a herbalist,' one of her grandmother's long-term patients confided. 'She felt sure that you would be a more than worthy successor to her once you applied your mind to it.'

Sarah felt both proud and ashamed. It was true that she had worked at the practice of herbalism in fits and starts, distracted by the birth of Alice, by Joe's imprisonment and by the necessity of earning a regular income through Ada's previous illnesses. Now, though, she told herself how very lucky she was to have this to fall back on: something that would allow her to look after Alice while she worked. She felt guilty at first, giving up her job at the mill, but Edie gazed at her in astonishment when she confessed these feelings.

'Do you not think I'd be away from here in a heartbeat if there were aught I could do instead?' she demanded. 'I know grief does strange things to a body but I fear it's addled your wits. You go and get on with what you're good at. I'll be sending Carrie along for something to help her in childbirth. She suffers something terrible, poor lass.'

Will and Carrie had been married within six months of the mistletoe incident and their first baby had been born in the October of that year. Their second child was now well on its way. Sarah privately thought that Carrie's petite frame was the likely cause of her difficulties, but making up some raspberry-leaf tea for her in the latter weeks of pregnancy could do no harm.

So it was that, with Ada barely in the ground, Sarah found herself trying to get to grips with taking over Ada's practice and patients. She devoted herself to a thorough study of the few books that Ada had possessed, then, resolving to bring something of herself to this venture, she made contact by letter with other herbalists spread throughout the country: in Scotland, Plymouth, Nottingham and London. At first she was hesitant, fearing that these established herbalists would view her as an upstart, but her correspondence allowed her to seek advice and support which, much to her surprise, was readily forthcoming. Before long she felt confident enough to adjust existing remedies to suit the changing needs of her patients.

In the weeks following Ada's death, Alice was subdued. Gran's 'falling down', which had resulted in such sadness and in her vanishing from her life, had made her anxious. She was very clingy at first, so much so that Sarah despaired of being able to get any work done at all during her daughter's waking hours. With time, though, Alice's anxiety lessened and she relaxed as she accepted that her mother was now at home taking care of her. She became better at amusing herself when Sarah was busy and the regular stream of visitors proved to be a welcome diversion in what was now such a small family.

That first Christmas without Ada, barely a month after her death, was one of such unremitting gloom both in the weather outside and in the mood within the house that Sarah preferred not to remember it. Ada's death had left her with no other adult to talk to on a daily basis, no one with whom to share chores and worries, nor triumphs, when they came.

At first, Sarah left her grandmother's bedroom untouched. Then one day, after six months had passed, Sarah decided that it was time to pack a few of her grandmother's things away. It wasn't that she had a use for the room: simply that it felt wrong to leave it just as it had been on the morning that Ada had died. Her brush and comb were set down just as she had left them, a few items of inexpensive jewellery lay in a box next to them on top of the chest of drawers, while her clothes were still neatly folded in the drawers below.

Having decided to make a start Sarah hesitated, suddenly unsure of what to do. Ada's clothes were well worn but still serviceable. She supposed they could be packed up for the workhouse. Then she remembered the patchwork quilt she had made with her grandmother just before their move to Lane End Cottage. Suddenly she felt happier: she would make a quilt using the fabrics, and that way she would retain memories of Ada. Sarah began to sort the clothes into piles of plain and patterned fabric, then she further grouped them into colours that worked together. As she burrowed down into the final drawer, the deepest one at the bottom, her fingers struck something hard.

She cleared the folded clothes away from around it and uncovered a tin box, which had once held biscuits. It rattled as she lifted it out; thinking that perhaps it held buttons or pieces of costume jewellery that had fallen from favour, Sarah casually prised off the lid. To her astonishment, the tin contained sovereigns – many sovereigns – as well as a folded sheet of paper.

Sarah sat down on Ada's bed with the box before her, then unfolded the paper.

'My dear Sarah,' the note read, 'if you are reading this then I am no longer with you. The money in this tin is all I can leave you by way of a legacy. It came to me from my mother, Catherine Abbot, who earned it from the sale of her paintings. I haven't spent any of it – in fact, I have been able to add a little to it over the years – and I know that you will use it wisely to safeguard your, and Alice's, future.'

The signature was in Ada's familiar, neat handwriting. Sarah tipped the sovereigns onto the blanket and counted the coins, trying to take in what she had read as she did so. There were fifty sovereigns, an enormous sum for Ada to have kept all this time. With tears in her eyes, she read the note again, moved by her grandmother's thoughtfulness and this final contact with her from beyond the grave.

Then it struck her that the wording of the note was significant. There was no mention of Joe. Sarah thought about what this might mean. Joe had played so little part in her life in these past years that it was hard to imagine how they might go on when he came out of prison. She felt a sudden stab of anxiety that she had never visited him – indeed, she hadn't really tried to after he had refused her initial attempts. She had been prompt and dutiful in her letters to him but had felt constrained; she knew that someone else was reading them to him and it was hard to include anything personal beyond details of how she, Ada and Alice fared.

She had written to let him know about Ada's death, and to his credit a letter sent by return had expressed concern over how she was coping and a wish that he could be with her to support her at such a time of sorrow. Now that she thought this over again she wondered, not for the first time, how much of that came from Joe, and how much was suggested to him by his scribe.

She immediately felt disloyal to have such thoughts. Yet, if she looked back over the years since her marriage, how much had she been able to rely on Joe? That she and Alice could call Lane End Cottage home and had survived thus far was entirely due to her own efforts.

Although Ada hadn't spelt it out in her note, the implication was there by omission. She didn't trust Joe to provide for the family and so she had taken it upon herself to ensure that they had something to fall back on. They couldn't live off such a sum but, if times were hard, it offered them some protection. She knew instinctively that Joe should never learn of it. Which left her with the problem of where to keep the tin box. Storing it amongst her own clothes would be risky, and now that she had cleared out Ada's chest of drawers it couldn't be hidden there.

Sarah took the box down to the parlour, lifted the hearthrug and located a floorboard that was a little looser than all the rest. She used a kitchen knife to prise up the board, placed the box in the cavity revealed below and nailed the board back in place. It felt firmer than it had previously, making it harder to judge which board it was, so she fetched a piece of chalk and rubbed it along the short edge of the board. She hoped it would neither be conspicuous nor wear off under the pressure of the rug.

In the end, the tin didn't remain in place as long as Sarah had planned. Around eighteen months later, an unexpected visitor caused her to change her plans.

CHAPTER 53

As the year turned, Sarah grew quietly more confident in her practice of the herbalist's art. She had been dispensing Ada's remedies to the long-standing patients without a problem and her initial worries over diagnosing new patients, or new complaints in existing patients, proved groundless. She discovered that she enjoyed the challenge and was delighted when a remedy that she had created proved successful. A lot of the skill lay in drawing out of the patient exactly what the problem was: sometimes a diagnosis that appeared immediately obvious proved to be false under further probing. More than once Sarah found that a patient presenting with a stomach complaint hadn't necessarily eaten something that had upset them but, as like as not, was suffering an anxiety related to another area of their life and it was this that was causing the problem.

Sarah had no small success in getting new patients from her time spent at the mill. Edie had been an early loyal supporter of her in her new role, while Carrie had been enthusiastic in her praises of her to friends and relatives. Sarah began to see more and more cases of the persistent cough caused by the fine cotton fibres that clogged up the atmosphere in the mill and she resolved to try and find a remedy that worked long-term, not least because she herself continued to suffer in the winter months.

As her knowledge grew, Sarah began to develop the herb garden further. In addition, she drew up lists of where in the surrounding countryside she might find reliable sources for herbs that required the sort of growing conditions she couldn't replicate in the garden. Going on collecting expeditions gave her an excuse to be outside with Alice when the weather was good and stopped her feeling too much confined to the house.

It was on one such trip, in the late summer almost two years after Ada's death, that Sarah and Alice were to be found sitting on the shady edge of Tinker's Wood, high up on the hill, enjoying a picnic. This time, the focus of their collecting had been blackberries, rather than herbs. Alice, now aged six, was gazing down into the valley as she licked her fingers to remove the sticky sweetness of the fruit she had consumed.

'Look,' she said, pointing. 'There's a hat moving along all by itself.'

Sarah followed her finger and spotted a straw hat bobbing jauntily along, level with the top of the hedge. She laughed. 'You're right. That's Tinker's Way. It must be set on someone's head but the hedges having grown so high, it makes it impossible to see. How odd it looks.'

She was quiet for a moment, reminded of that day over seven years ago when she had first seen Joe, down there on Tinker's Way, and how she had at first thought him very forward and then irresistible. So much had happened since then. And even though she was now married to Joe, how little she had seen of him during that time!

To shake off unwelcome thoughts, she began to gather their things together.

'Time to go home,' she said, stalling Alice's protests by promising that they could make a repeat visit before the week was out.

Alice set off at a great pace down the hill, ignoring her mother's warnings to be careful and not to catch her foot in a rabbit hole. Sarah watched her daughter's dark curly hair bouncing down her back as she leapt from tussock to tussock, screaming her enjoyment as she ran. When she caught up with Alice at the bottom of the hill, Sarah scolded her for her disobedience.

'But it was fun,' Alice protested. 'And see – I came to no harm. I'm sure you did it when you were young.'

Sarah was silenced. It hadn't been that long ago that she had roamed freely around these hills and fields, without a care in the world. Now here she was, just twenty-four years old and, she reflected, living a life filled with responsibility. Pushing the thought away, she took Alice's hand in hers and they set off along Tinker's Way, Alice chattering non-stop until they were in sight of Lane End Cottage, when she stopped abruptly.

'Who's that at our gate?' Alice asked.

Sarah, squinting against the low sun, saw that there was indeed a figure at the gate, deep in conversation with Martha. As they drew closer, she observed that it was a man, holding a pale-coloured straw hat in his hands.

'I don't know who it is,' Sarah replied, at the very same moment as she recognised the visitor for who it was – Daniel.

Surely, though, Daniel was in America now? Whatever was he doing here in Northwaite? With barely fifty yards separating them, and the memory of their last meeting suddenly uppermost in her mind, she was seized by the inclination to turn and flee even as her feet took her mechanically forwards.

'Sarah, here you are at last!' Martha called out as they approached. 'Look who's come to visit! I was trying to persuade him to step inside but he insisted on waiting for you.'

Fleetingly, Sarah saw Martha as if through Daniel's eyes. Even if the slurring of her words hadn't given her away, her florid complexion and stoutness, both relatively new acquisitions, bore witness to the fact that daytime drinking was now habitual for her.

Alice sidled behind her mother's skirts, overcome with shyness, as Sarah greeted Daniel.

'What a surprise! I thought you long gone to

America. What brings you to these parts?' Without waiting for an answer she opened the gate. 'Won't you come in? You must be hot from your walk – I do believe Alice and I saw you as you passed along Tinker's Way.'

She could sense that she was prattling, out of pure nervousness, but didn't seem able to stop herself.

'Alice, come out and show yourself. This is Daniel. You were very fond of him when you were small.' Sarah attempted to extricate Alice, who had now buried her head in the folds of her mother's skirt, necessitating an awkward crab-like shuffle to the kitchen door.

'Martha, thank you so much for looking after Daniel. I'll call round later to see how you do.' Sarah politely but firmly made it clear that her neighbour's company was not required. She knew only too well how Martha, made jolly by the drink, would dominate the conversation before either falling asleep or becoming aggressive. She took good care of her neighbour, though. She was in the habit of checking on her every evening, to make sure that she had eaten and that she hadn't fallen asleep leaving the house in danger of burning down from a neglected fire or lamp while she slept.

Martha, who had begun to follow them up the path, turned away muttering. Sarah ushered Daniel into the kitchen and closed the door firmly.

'Let's go and sit in the garden. It's so hot for September but there's some shade out there.'

Sarah busied herself with glasses and set these and a jug of elderflower cordial on a tray. Daniel, who had been trying to coax Alice into overcoming her shyness and making friends again, moved quickly to take the tray from Sarah. She followed him into the garden, despatching Alice to fetch a blanket that they could sit on. Sarah's heart was beating fast and she hoped that she was managing to disguise how unsettled Daniel's visit had made her. Casting covert glances at him while she prepared the tray, she had noticed that he appeared to have filled out a little and gained some frown lines on his forehead. Other than that, the passage of time had left him largely unchanged.

'So,' she said, when they were all settled with glasses of cordial, 'what brings you here?'

Daniel took a deep draught of his drink. 'Why, I've only just discovered that Ada has died. And that it happened nigh on two years ago. Why ever didn't you let me know, Sarah?'

Sarah was taken aback. Why hadn't she let Daniel know? She thought back. She supposed it was because she had no address for him in America and, perhaps, had been reluctant to try to find one.

'It was so sudden, Daniel. It happened without warning. She was buried within the week and my mind was in turmoil. It never occurred to me to try to track you down in America.'

Sarah and Daniel looked at each other. The mixture of emotions that she had felt on seeing him was replaced by a wariness of his mood, which bordered on irritable.

'So, how did you hear about Gran?' Sarah asked, trying to unravel what had brought him there.

'I was in communication with the mill at Northwaite. I asked the manager how you did and he wrote back that you had left some time before, after your grandmother died. I felt that there was no time to write and await a reply from you, when I was due to visit Manchester anyway, so here I am.' Daniel's expression and words implied that he was still put out by the manner in which he had discovered what had occurred.

'I'm so sorry, Daniel.' Sarah was contrite, then a thought struck her. 'Did you and Gran not correspond regularly? Did you not wonder why her letters ceased?'

Daniel looked a little uncomfortable. 'I was so busy on arrival in the United States, finding somewhere to live and getting my wife settled.' Sarah gave what she hoped was an imperceptible start. 'Some months passed before I wrote to Ada with my new address and, when I didn't hear anything in return, I assumed that my letter or her reply had gone astray. I resolved to write again but I confess a year or more must have passed. Then a trip back to the mill in Manchester became necessary so I thought it would be more easily done from here.' Daniel looked despondent. 'I had no idea that it was all too late.'

'I'm sorry,' Sarah said again. She described a

little of what had happened on that fateful day, taking care not to cause upset to Alice, who had wandered away but was now back, clutching her rag doll Tilly.

'Will you stay and eat with us and tell us about your adventures?' Sarah asked.

'My return passage is booked from Liverpool the day after tomorrow but I must say that I have little wish to make the return journey to Manchester this evening,' Daniel said. 'If I can impose on you to let me stay in my old room I will be up and on my way before daybreak tomorrow.'

Sarah was surprised to find that Daniel would be leaving England so soon. They hadn't seen each other in nearly four years and she thought that she had successfully shut him out of her mind in that time. Now that he was here, she was no longer sure. She turned away from him and fussed over Alice, tugging her rumpled pinafore into a semblance of neatness, to hide her own expression.

'That's settled, then,' Sarah said. 'You can sleep in your old room.'

She was relieved that Alice had, as yet, refused to move into the room that Daniel had once used. If she had, Daniel would have had to sleep in the room that still remained her grandmother's, in Sarah's mind, despite the passage of so much time.

Daniel unbent a little now that it was apparent he hadn't purposely been denied knowledge of Ada's passing. The rest of the afternoon passed swiftly, with Alice deciding that Daniel could be her friend after all. She conducted him around the garden, Tilly in tow, to show him all her favourite hiding places while Sarah watched briefly, a smile on her lips, before quickly moving on to prepare some food for them all.

CHAPTER 54

With dinner eaten and Alice tucked into bed, despite her sleepy protests, Sarah lit the fire in the parlour in honour of Daniel's visit and to drive away the evening chill that had set in under clear September skies.

'I must say I expected to find Joe back here with you now,' Daniel said once they were settled by the fire.

'Not yet,' Sarah said. She was reluctant to be drawn into discussing Joe with Daniel, feeling a sudden shame at the thought of her husband. How different he was from Daniel! She had managed to successfully shut Joe out of her thoughts on the whole. Since Ada's death it had become obvious to her that she must be entirely self-sufficient and, right at this moment, the thought of Joe's return was an unwelcome one.

'How are you managing, Sarah?' Daniel asked suddenly. 'How are you earning a living now that you've left the mill?'

Sarah explained how she had taken over from Ada and built the practice so that she was now the best-known herbalist for miles around. She felt a sense of pride as she described her achievements to Daniel. 'Also,' she added as an afterthought, 'Ada did leave me a small legacy to help provide for the future.'

'A legacy?' Daniel's expression was hard to read.

'Yes, she'd inherited a little from her own grandmother who was an artist and had kept it untouched, even adding a little to it over the years.'

'Do you mind me asking where it is now?' Daniel asked.

Sarah hesitated, colouring up. 'It's in a safe place,' she said.

'In the house?' Daniel pressed.

Sarah was puzzled. Did he mean to ask to borrow money? His manner of dress suggested prosperity so it seemed unlikely but even so . . .

Daniel spoke again, breaking into her thoughts. 'You must excuse my blunt questions. They were only intended to help you protect your money. I wonder, had you considered putting them into a savings account, at the Post Office for instance?'

'A savings account?' Sarah was doubtful. 'Surely the money is safer kept where I can see it?'

'Well, that's the popular opinion,' Daniel conceded. 'But what if the house should catch fire or someone should discover your hiding place and take your money?' He didn't specify who that 'someone' might be but they both knew that he meant Joe.

'I'll think about it,' Sarah said, having no intention of doing so. Daniel persisted, explaining how she could earn money on her legacy by, in effect, lending it to the Post Office who would pay her interest in return. Intrigued by such a novel idea, but still wary, she promised again to look into it, although this time she actually meant it.

The rest of the evening passed in more wide-ranging discussion, Daniel describing his journey by steamer to New York from Liverpool, how the city he found on arrival was bigger than Manchester, set on a great waterfront along the East River and with every square inch of space seemingly crammed with buildings as far as the eye could see. He spoke of a great bridge that was being built across the water, with towers of brick set in the river and huge loops of steel holding up what would be carriageways for pedestrians, horse-drawn carriages and steam trains running in both directions, side by side. Sarah shook her head in wonder, trying hard to imagine the marvels his words evoked.

Daniel was frustrated with himself. 'I'm not doing it justice. I should have thought to bring a newspaper with me from New York – there are always photographs of the city, and of the bridge as it grows. And I hear there are plans afoot to build some of the tallest buildings in the world there, even though it already has some that are higher than I ever saw in Manchester.'

Such modern developments were clearly very much to Daniel's taste, Sarah thought.

'And where do you live?' she asked tentatively. She wasn't sure that she wanted to know too much about where Daniel lived with his wife but felt it would be polite to enquire.

'Not in New York as you might expect. The mills are in New England so we had to travel further north, to Rhode Island.'

As Daniel described the wildness of the ocean bordering the land and the great cities growing there, then went on to describe the technical advances being made in the American mills, Sarah sat back. She found herself nodding, understanding less than half of what he said but captivated by watching and listening to him. She had a feeling that Daniel had moved a long way from her in life, not just in geographical miles, and he would move yet farther still. Nevertheless, she was enjoying the evening, and Daniel's company, so much that she kept finding new questions to ask him to delay his departure for bed, only too conscious that in the morning he would be gone.

'Do you have children?' Sarah asked finally. It was the closest she could get to the topic she had been skirting around all evening, that of his wife.

A shadow crossed Daniel's face. 'No, we don't.' He hesitated, then said in a rush, 'And I fear we will not. My wife came back with me to England but she will not be returning to America. She has chosen to stay here, instead. With her parents.'

There was a long silence as he gazed into the fire. Sarah didn't know how to respond and the silence deepened. Daniel looked thoroughly miserable and she longed to reach out to him, but held herself back.

At last, he spoke again. 'It hasn't been a happy marriage, Sarah.' He turned to look at her, and his expression was sombre. 'My thoughts were too caught up in you and I hoped that by leaving the country and marrying I could suppress them. It was a mistake.'

Sarah was unable to withhold a gasp at his words. Agitated, she rose from the fireside, and Daniel did the same, both of them aware that words had been spoken that now could not be unsaid.

Daniel hugged Sarah to him suddenly, making her gasp once again. He held her so close that she could barely breathe and then he kissed her on the cheek. He didn't let go and she half-feared, half-hoped that he might turn her face towards him and kiss her on the mouth. She knew she would be lost if he did and so she broke free, heart hammering, and stammered that she needed to check on Martha before turning in.

As she stumbled down the garden path in the dark, quite sure that Martha would be either abed or fast asleep in a chair at the kitchen table, she felt her cheek burning as though branded by Daniel's lips. She let herself into Martha's house, trying all the while to make sense of Daniel's words. Listening to his description of life in America she had felt no envy – it was so far beyond her understanding that she couldn't find it in her. But she had felt a terrible pang when she thought of herself and her own future. Was her destiny always to be hard at work and caring for others? Was she to be forever denied the happiness that she once thought would be hers when she married Joe?

Now, with Daniel's revelation about the unhappiness of his marriage, she was forced to re-evaluate. Suddenly she felt on a more equal footing with him – both of them trapped in marriages that were a mistake, both of them doing their utmost to make the best of things. Reaching a decision all at once she felt strong in a way that she hadn't since her single-minded pursuit of Joe, so many years before.

She checked that Martha was safely in bed, with no candles left burning and the fire already low in the grate, before quietly moving the empty bottles to the kitchen sink. Perhaps they would serve as a reminder to Martha of how much she had drunk when she awoke, although, if they did, Sarah doubted she'd heed the warning beyond mid-morning, when she'd already be feeling the need of her first drink of the day.

Sarah returned home and quietly tidied up before preparing to mount the stairs to bed. She hesitated on the landing, all previous certainty draining away. Daniel had already told Sarah that he would be gone before she and Alice awoke in the morning, needing to return to Manchester first before journeying on to Liverpool. If she crept silently past his room, without stopping to check whether she could hear his sleeping breath, then all would go on as before.

But, as she tiptoed past his door, it opened silently and Daniel stood there, a dark outline in the doorway. It was impossible to make out his features but Sarah stared for a moment before tentatively stretching out a hand towards him. She laid her palm flat against his chest, feeling the warmth of his skin beneath his shirt and his heartbeat, fast and strong, echoing her own.

This time, when he drew her towards him, she was sure. He stepped backwards into the room, quietly closing the door with one hand as he kissed her mouth. She lifted both hands to her head and pulled the pins from her hair, feeling a sense of release as it tumbled free.

Sarah was glad of the darkness. It allowed her to feel that she was someone else, somewhere other than in her own home, her daughter asleep in the next room. It allowed her to immerse herself in the sensations of Daniel's hands in her hair and on her body and to give back to him the pleasure that he was giving her. She wished that every minute of their night could be a day, while at the same time not allowing herself to think at all.

When she finally fell into a light sleep, Sarah dreamt of Daniel. She saw the pair of them as though observing a painting, his freckled face flushed lightly with heat, his hair darkened and damp with sweat. She saw his arms wrapped around her; arms that were far paler than Joe's because of the hours he spent indoors but nonetheless muscled because of the work he did with heavy machinery. She awoke with a start to find Daniel standing at the bedside, already dressed, the thin light of dawn breaking into the room.

'Come back to bed,' she whispered, before she could stop herself.

Daniel shook his head slowly, biting his lip. Then he bent forward and kissed her forehead, her shoulders and the dip of her collarbone before he raised her hand to his cheek. He held it there for a moment, his eyes closed, before gently resting it down on the sheet. Then he stepped swiftly to the door and was gone, without looking back.

Sarah lay awhile, watching him in her mind's eye as he walked down the path then headed into the village before taking the road down to Nortonstall and the station, to await the first train of the day. She could hardly bear to leave the warmth of the bed, and the memories of what had passed there during the dark hours of the night, but she must make her way to her own bed before Alice awoke. She closed her eyes briefly, hugging the memory of Daniel to herself, catching the faintest scent of him still there on her skin. Then she arose, gathered her clothes up from the floor where they had been scattered, and crept cautiously to her own room, taking care to avoid waking Alice.

Sarah slid between the sheets and shivered in the chill that she found there. She knew sleep would not come now and so she concentrated on remembering every moment of the night just gone, to store and treasure into the future. She blushed as she remembered her own behaviour, then she allowed herself a small smile. What she and Daniel had done was wrong, without a doubt, but she wouldn't take back a moment of it. She hoped Daniel felt the same.

PART VII

SEPTEMBER 1881 – AUGUST 1882

CHAPTER 55

Sarah nursed her secret, fobbing off Martha's questions. It hurt her to do so but she wanted no word of Daniel's overnight stay being spread around The Old Bell by her old friend. Instead, she explained to Martha that his return journey to the States was imminent, without explicitly stating when he had left, and distracted her by repeating Daniel's tales of the wonders of New York.

'It's a shame you didn't marry him rather than your Joe,' Martha exclaimed. 'Why, just imagine, it could be you living the high life out there with him.'

Sarah smiled but made no response. Despite Daniel's best efforts to describe it to her, such a life as he was living was beyond her ken. She would keep him safe here in Yorkshire instead, in her heart.

It was just a few days later, as she rolled out the pastry for a rabbit pie, that she heard someone coming up the path, whistling. The footsteps paused briefly at the kitchen door, there was a knock, then, before she had time to answer, the door swung open and a figure stepped inside.

For a moment, Sarah had the absurd belief that it was Daniel, unable to bring himself to depart from Liverpool, returning to her. A split second later she recognised the visitor as her husband, paler, gaunt and with a bushier beard than when she had last seen him. Lines were etched deeply in his face and he looked weary.

'Joe!' She let the rolling pin fall from her hands, clattering to the table from where it bounced to the floor. The noise brought Alice down from the bedroom, where she had been putting Tilly, who had apparently been very naughty, to bed without any supper.

'Well now, who's this then?' Joe said, stopped in his tracks at the sight of his daughter. 'You'll not be telling me 'tis Alice, a bairn barely bigger than a hand's breadth when I last clapped eyes on her?'

Sarah, rendered speechless by Joe's unexpected appearance, could only nod. Joe's face broke into a grin and Sarah noticed the gaps in his smile, where teeth had been lost.

'Come say hello, then.' Joe held out his arms as Alice shrank back.

Fearing that Alice's shyness might upset or anger Joe, Sarah quietly pulled out a chair for her husband.

'Sit down and I'll make us some tea. Why didn't you tell me that you'd be back? We'd have been ready to give you a proper welcome.'

'Aye, she don't remember me.' Joe, made despondent by Alice's reaction, sank into the chair.

'Not that I can blame her, with me gone so long.' He looked around the room, taking it in as though he'd never set eyes on it before, as Sarah busied herself making tea.

'Did you not get my letter, then? I tell't you of my return in it.'

Sarah shook her head. 'No letter. If only I'd known . . .' She looked at the mess of flour and half-rolled pastry on the table. 'This can hardly be the welcome you were expecting.'

'I'll be bound that thieving rascal in prison took my post money and kept it, knowing he wouldn't see me again. No wonder you had no letter.' Joe's flash of anger subsided as suddenly as it had appeared. He took Sarah's hand. 'Anyways, it makes no odds. If you knew how much I'd longed for my freedom . . .' He couldn't go on, his eyes filling with tears, and Sarah found herself wiping her own eyes with the corner of her floury apron.

'Here,' she beckoned to Alice. 'Come and get to know your father again.'

Alice hung back at first, her eyes like saucers, but when Sarah suggested that Tilly could be reprieved from her punishment and brought to meet Joe, she was quick to hurry upstairs to fetch her doll.

Sarah cleared the flour and pastry aside and sat down at the table with Joe. She had often wondered how she would feel on seeing her husband after so long apart. Now that he was here unexpectedly, with no chance for her to prepare herself, it felt mainly as though he had been away on one of his long trips. He was changed, though. He looked a good deal older, and she noticed a tremor in his hand as he raised his cup to his lips. She was at a loss as to what to say to him. Reminding him of his spell in prison by asking him about it didn't feel like the right thing to do.

She wanted to avert questions about her own life, though – the remembrance of Daniel's recent visit bringing a blush to her cheeks as she thought of it. Alice was the obvious diversion: she busied herself describing their daughter's last six years to the father who had missed all but the tiniest fraction of it.

Alice herself listened in, fascinated and full of questions, and by the time Sarah had finished she was standing close to the seated Joe, clearly taken with his luxurious beard. At the end of Sarah's history of Alice, Joe sat a while and then yawned, stretched and declared himself in need of a rest after his journey home.

As he climbed the stairs, Sarah reflected uneasily on the changes she would need to make. It would be best to move Alice out of the bedroom, for a start. It made no sense for the three of them to be sharing one room with two others available. As she finished making the rabbit pie, thankful at least that there would be some good food to offer Joe that evening, her thoughts turned to Daniel. He would no doubt be halfway across the seas, heading back to his home. She pushed the thought aside. Joe was home now and he must be her priority. She must direct her energies to making sure that they could be happy as a family, although she was fearful it wouldn't be easy.

Despite having no forewarning of his homecoming, Sarah made a big effort to make Joe's first evening back with them as welcoming as it could be. She lit the fire in the parlour and resolved not to be resentful if he disappeared off to The Old Bell before the pie was cooked. But when Joe came downstairs again after his nap he seemed subdued and showed no signs of wanting to do anything other than stay home.

'Where are your belongings?' Sarah asked, wondering whether he had left them outside –for there was no sign of any bag in the house.

'I have none,' Joe said.

'Nothing at all?' Sarah was astonished.

'We wore a uniform inside and anything else that I had was but rags after six years inside. I threw it away. I have what I stand up in.'

Sarah was diverted from further questioning by the urgent memory of something she needed to say.

'Joe, I'm sorry that I didn't come to visit you. You refused to let me come at first but I should have persisted.' She felt guilty as she spoke, remembering how easily she had given up on the idea.

Joe looked uncomfortable. 'Aye, well, I didn't want you to have to trek all that way to find yoursen in such a place. 'Tain't for the likes of you.'

'Even so, I'm your wife. I should have been there for you.' Sarah felt the truth of this keenly as she spoke.

'Nay.' Joe was emphatic. ''Tis me that's at fault. I shouldn't have got meself into such a mess, what wi' you and the lass to provide for.' He was silent for a moment. 'I can't blame you if you're mad at me. I left you to tek care of everything.'

Sarah considered. She wasn't angry and she wasn't sure why. She supposed that she had been, when times had been particularly hard and she had felt so alone – when she had been forced to take work at the mill, or when Ada died. Now, though, she had learnt the hard way not to expect too much from Joe.

He was fast asleep when she finally slipped into bed that night, after she had cleared up the kitchen, tidied the parlour and been next door to check on Martha for the night. Sarah lay awake a while, listening to his breathing, before turning on her side and falling into a fitful sleep. She was awoken again by the sensation of Joe's arms around her. She thought to deter him by pretending to sleep on, then thought better of it and turned towards him.

'How often I thought of thee,' Joe murmured in her ear, moving to kiss her cheek and then her lips.

Sarah fought hard to erase the memory of Daniel and tried instead to conjure the excitement of her early, secret meetings with Joe. 'He's my husband,' she told herself. 'God knows what he has had to endure these past few years.'

She put her arms around his neck and kissed him back and, cloaked by the darkness, they were once again the lovers who sought out the hidden reaches of the deer pool, all traces of the tribulations of the last few years briefly erased.

CHAPTER 56

When Sarah awoke later that morning, she could hear voices from downstairs. Neither Joe nor Alice was in the bedroom so she lay for a while, dozing in the warmth of the bed. It wouldn't hurt them to get to know each other a little better, she decided. Just as Sarah was thinking that she really should get up, Alice ran up the stairs and into the room.

'Come and see. We have a surprise for you!' Sarah, realising that Alice was about to blurt out what it was, clapped her hands over her ears and shook her head at her daughter.

'I'm coming now,' she said as Alice rushed down the stairs ahead of her.

Father and daughter had been busy. The table was laid for breakfast, the tea was already in the pot and Joe was cooking eggs on the range. A new loaf of bread had been cut, albeit into rather thick slabs, and Alice proudly pointed out the arrangement of leaves, autumn flowers and berries that she had created in a jug on the table. Chattering away all the while, she used all her strength to drag out one of the heavy wooden chairs so that

Sarah could sit down. As Joe turned from the range with the eggs, Sarah met his eyes and smiled. If this was a glimpse of the future, it would suit her very well.

It was soon apparent, though, that Joe's return to his family wasn't going to be as straightforward as it first appeared. He managed to be sociable and happy for two or three hours at a time, then he would withdraw, taking himself off into the garden to chop wood, or to go for a walk. Sarah watched him go, observing that he didn't turn towards The Old Bell but instead took the road that headed either out into the country or down into the valley.

She thought about it and decided not to question him. He probably needed time to adjust to life outside prison, she reasoned, where he had been constantly surrounded by other prisoners and had to abide by the daily routine. She told herself that he just needed to get used to his old life once more.

At the end of the first week, Joe announced that he would be gone for a night or two. He was going in search of his old master, to try for work.

'But I can support us well enough for now,' Sarah protested. 'Having one extra mouth to feed makes no difference.'

'That's as may be but I can't just be sitting all day watching you. A man needs to work.' Joe was quite firm.

Although Sarah understood his feelings, she

didn't want him to return to the canal. She didn't want him to be away for lengthy periods, as before, and – if truth be told – she feared that he might fall into the same trap of stealing once he was back in his old routine.

When she put this to him, they came close to having their first quarrel since his return.

'Don't you think I've learnt my lesson? I'll not be caught a second time.'

It struck Sarah that he didn't say he wouldn't thieve again – just that he wouldn't be caught – but, before she could take him up on this, Joe was talking again, banging the table to emphasise his points.

'And what would you have me do, if not work the canals? I'm not fit for owt else.'

'You could work on the land. Or get a job at the mill,' Sarah suggested.

'Aye, earn a pittance on t'farm and be out of work half the year. What use is that? As for mill, nay, that's not for me. Trapped indoors all day – 'twill be too much like prison.'

Joe refused to discuss it any further and, sick at heart, Sarah watched him go off.

'Where's Daddy going?' Alice, having so recently found a new playmate, looked disconsolate.

'He's looking for work. He'll be back in a day or two,' Sarah promised.

Joe was as good as his word, reappearing a couple of days later and seemingly in much better humour. He hugged his wife and daughter, before sharing the news that he would be away again within the week.

'So you've found work on the canals?' Sarah tried hard to keep the disapproval out of her voice.

'Aye, it's what I know best. It's the right work for a man like me. The boss is right happy to have me back.' Joe caught Sarah round the waist and waltzed her around the kitchen while Alice squealed in delight at the sight.

'Can you ask him to let you do shorter runs?' Sarah asked when she had got her breath back. With Joe so recently home, she was determined to try to maintain some semblance of a family life.

'Aye, I can ask but I'm not in best position to bargain.' Joe chuckled.

Sarah sighed, her dreams of a family life with Joe, the sort of life she had so rarely experienced, vanishing into dust once more. They would go back to the way they had been before, only this time at least she knew what to expect. And this time she knew that she could provide for her daughter.

A day later Joe came to her, somewhat shamefaced.

'Canst thou loan me some money?' he asked. 'I've a need to buy some clothes to tek with me on canal.'

Sarah felt a mixture of emotions. Guilt, at not having thought that he might be in need of money after leaving prison, tinged with anger that they were falling into old habits so soon.

'I'll pay it back,' Joe added.

Sarah went to her cashbox, where she kept the

payments made by her patients. As she unlocked it, a sudden memory came to her of the discussion she had had with Daniel about her legacy. She extracted a handful of coins from the box, resolving to visit the Post Office in Nortonstall the following week, once Joe had departed on his trip.

'Will this be enough?' she asked, handing over the coins. Joe barely glanced at them before pocketing them and kissing her on the lips, causing her to protest and him to laugh.

His good humour extended over the following days and showed itself as ardour at night. It was as if he needed to reacquaint himself with every inch of her body and to store the memory of it for when he was away. Sarah was thankful that she had moved Alice into Daniel's old room, for she was finding the transition from live-alone mother to wife and lover a hard one to make.

In the end, she was relieved to wave Joe off to start work, his bag of newly acquired clothes slung across his back. He had been an intense companion over the last few days, full of wild humour and outlandish schemes to amuse her and Alice. She was glad of the chance to return to the more settled routine they had had before. Until, that is, she opened her cashbox to take payment for a remedy and discovered it to be all but empty.

Trying to disguise her shock in front of her patient, Mrs Burton, she wondered how such a thing could have happened. There was only one explanation: Joe must have taken the key from her chest of drawers one night while she slept, replacing it before she awoke. Her thought flew to Ada's legacy, tucked away beneath the floorboards. She could hardly bear to wait for Mrs Burton to leave before rushing into the parlour and raising the rug. A fine film of chalk dust at the end of one of the floorboards suggested that her inheritance remained untouched but she didn't feel secure until she had levered up the board, removed the box and checked inside it.

That night, she slept with the box in Joe's place beside her in bed and the next morning found her in Nortonstall, following Daniel's advice and relinquishing her sovereigns to the care of the Post Office.

CHAPTER 57

Sarah's anger simmered for days. How could Joe have just taken the money? What did he expect his family to live on? She wondered briefly whether someone else might be responsible. Could they have got into the house and stolen it? She even considered Martha and then felt ashamed. It didn't take her long to realise that if someone else had been responsible they would either have taken the whole cashbox or just smashed it open. Only Joe knew where she kept the key.

It was lucky that several patients paid in instalments and so, gradually, she was able to amass the money again, but not before an anxious couple of weeks had passed in which Sarah and Alice had dined mainly on the vegetables that were growing in the garden, along with whatever was in the larder. Alice didn't seem to be bothered but at night, when Sarah lay in bed, stomach growling for lack of proper sustenance, she raged against Joe and rehearsed what she would say to him when next he showed his face in the house.

Her vengeful plans were disrupted when, less

than six weeks after Joe's departure, she realised that she was with child again. By this time, the household was back on an even keel. The dark days and nights of winter were upon them but Sarah was working hard and there was food on the table. As the reality of her position dawned on her, though, she felt fearful. How would she manage with a new baby to care for, this time without her grandmother to help her? Martha, who had been so reliable last time, looked likely to be worse than useless. Sarah's night-time ruminations, previously all channelled into her anger at Joe's actions, found a new focus.

Yet, as the weeks progressed Sarah gradually became accustomed to the idea and began to put practical plans in place. Alice would be seven years old when the baby was born. She was a calm and sensible child and Sarah felt sure that she would be a help to her. After five months, when it was no longer possible to disguise her shape under the bulky layers of winter clothes, she told her daughter that she would have a baby brother or sister before too long. Alice was delighted and immediately set to planning where the baby might sleep and whether or not she might share Tilly with him or her.

Against all the odds, the prospect of a new baby seemed to give Martha something to engage with and Sarah observed that her drinking had slowed and her neighbour showed every sign of making an effort to sort herself out before the baby was due.

In a practical move, Sarah had started to put a weekly amount from the cashbox into a new account at the Post Office, one that she could access whenever she needed to with her passbook. She knew that Joe would be back before too long and it seemed safer to put temptation out of his way. There was a conversation to be had when he did show his face but, until then, she could only prepare as best she could.

When Joe next appeared at Lane End Cottage in late March he was unexpected, as ever. He arrived whilst Sarah was sitting at the kitchen table on a sunny Saturday afternoon, talking to a patient about her new remedy. Sarah was flustered by his appearance and the presence of Mrs Sykes meant that she was, of course, unable to say any of the things that were on her mind.

Alice, though, was delighted to see her father and, after he had made a cursory greeting, as though he had just returned from stepping out for the afternoon rather than an absence of five months, they both made a hasty exit, Alice intent on showing Joe some chickens that Martha had acquired. By the time they returned half an hour later, Mrs Sykes had left and Alice had spilled the beans to Joe about the new baby.

'So, I hear I'm to be a father again,' Joe said, almost the minute he had set foot through the door. 'How long must I wait to see the new arrival?' He laid his hands on Sarah's belly as he spoke and she stiffened, causing him to draw back a little in surprise.

There was no chance for Sarah to tell Joe what she thought about the theft of her money until Alice had gone to bed. She had to content herself with monosyllabic answers to his questions, directing glares his way to register her displeasure with him. Joe looked puzzled but wasn't able to ask her outright what was wrong until Alice was safely tucked up in bed.

'Sit thee down,' Joe said, pulling out a chair as Sarah came back into the kitchen. 'Now, tell me what 'tis that ails you. 'Tis a fine welcome for a husband working away nigh on six months, to come home to a sour face and short answers.'

Sarah was made so cross by his injured tone that she could barely speak. She opened and closed her mouth more than once, without being able to utter a sound, before she finally managed to say, 'Did you truly think that taking money from my cashbox, leaving your wife and daughter with barely a shilling to provide for themselves, could pass unnoticed?'

'Ah.' Joe looked down at the table and Sarah saw that at least he had the grace to colour up.

'Well?' she demanded, when he didn't say anything further. 'What do you have to say for yourself?'

''Twas for my sister, Kitty,' Joe said. The words tumbled out in a rush. 'She came to see me in prison and tell't me how desperate she was, with the bairns to feed and her husband dead. I couldn't bear to think on it an' I promised that as soon as I was out I'd find some way to put bread on her table.' He paused for breath and raised beseeching eyes to Sarah.

'Your *sister*?' Sarah said. She was reminded that he had mentioned her in one of his letters and she wanted to ask him how it was that his sister had been able to visit him in prison, when his own wife hadn't, but Joe was speaking again.

'Aye, well, I hadn't seen her in a while. She got back in touch when I were in prison and she were in need.' Joe's eyes were back on the table again, then he looked up at Sarah as he appealed to her.

'What could I do? I had no money when I got out. I had to ask you for some to buy me some work clothes, as you well know. When I saw all money in that box it were too much temptation. It were a way to make things right for her.'

'And what about us?' Sarah demanded. 'Did you not think how we would go on, with nigh on all the money gone?'

Joe was silent for a while. 'Aye, well, there we are. That's my trouble. I don't think, do I? Can you forgive me?' He looked hopefully at his wife. 'A wife's money is her husband's, after all.' Seeing he had overstepped the mark with his final words he added hastily, 'But I'll pay it back. Only I don't rightly know how much it was. I've got money though, see. The boss paid me.' He fished in his pockets and brought out a handful of coins, with the promise of more to come from his bag.

Sarah wasn't really mollified. She still felt that he had done wrong but his reminder that her money was also his made her glad that she had taken precautions to safeguard not only her legacy but the small savings she had been able to make from her regular income. Mindful that Joe was likely to be gone again before she knew it, she scooped up the coins and said she would take these as a contribution to the repayment for now. He could pay her the housekeeping money once he had unpacked.

The rest of the evening passed with Sarah in a calmer frame of mind but, as she fell asleep that night, she vowed to ask Joe more about his sister and her children before he left again. If they lived nearby and they were in need then, of course, it was only right that Joe and Sarah should try to help.

CHAPTER 58

Sarah was thwarted in her intentions regarding Joe's sister because the very next morning, as they settled down to breakfast, there was a knock at the door. Joe answered it and Sarah caught a glimpse of Alfred, his best man, outside. There was a muttered conversation, an exclamation from Joe and then he shut the door and turned back into the room looking grim.

'I've been summoned back to canal. The boss has a delivery he needs run through to Manchester urgent-like. Seems I'm t'only one not already out with a boat so it has to be me.'

'But you only got back yesterday!' Sarah was at a loss. 'Surely you can have more than one night's break?'

'Aye, well, 'twould appear not.' Joe was already halfway up the stairs. 'Alf's waiting at end of road. I said I'd be there in ten minutes.'

Sarah still hadn't formulated an argument to prevent him going by the time he reappeared at the foot of the stairs, pack in hand.

'I'll try to swing it so I'm back in time for t'new one,' Joe said, patting Sarah's bump and kissing her full on the lips. He planted a kiss on Alice's head. 'You look after your mam, mind.' Then the door opened and shut and he was gone, leaving Sarah feeling as though he hadn't been there at all. It was only later, as she looked in the cashbox, that she remembered Joe hadn't given her the promised housekeeping money after all.

As Sarah's confinement date approached, Martha began to cluck around her like a mother hen. Sarah felt very well, although her tiredness increased as her belly grew and the weather turned warmer. Most nights she went to sleep at the same time as Alice so she felt well able to shrug off Martha's advice to get more rest.

One morning she awoke extra early, ready to blame the twitter of birds for dragging her from her sleep. After she had been awake for a couple of minutes she realised – with the advent of a second one – that it was a strong contraction that had woken her.

She struggled to sit up in bed and tried to decide what to do for the best. She should go downstairs to boil water in preparation, and to make herself some tea although she felt a little nauseous. She simply couldn't summon the energy, though, to get out of bed. Next, she contemplated going to Alice's room to wake her so that she could go and fetch Martha. This thought was overtaken by another strong contraction. Fearing the baby's arrival was imminent, she called for Alice as loudly as she could, praying that her daughter wasn't in a deep sleep. Just when she was ready to resign herself to managing things alone – a by no means welcome thought – Alice appeared in the doorway, sleepily rubbing her eyes.

'Did you call, Ma?'

'Can you go next door and knock for Martha? If she doesn't come to the door, you can go inside and shout for her. I doubt the door is locked. Tell her I'd like her to come over.' Sarah tried to keep the urgency out of her voice.

Alice hesitated, looking doubtfully down at her nightgown.

'There's no need to get dressed. Just wrap my shawl around you. Off you go.' Sarah did her best to disguise a gasp and a groan as another contraction took hold, but a glimpse of Alice's white face as she ran from the room told her she had failed. Sarah tried to remember to breathe as Martha had taught her all those years before during Alice's birth, screwing up her face in concentration, and so it was that her neighbour found her five minutes later.

Martha had been roused from a deep sleep but she assessed the situation at a glance and took charge at once. She put water to boil on the kitchen range, asking Alice to watch over the pots and to call her when the bubbles rose from the bottom, but on no account to touch anything. Then she set about making Sarah comfortable, preparing the room and the bed as best she could.

'The midwife?' Sarah asked weakly after a particularly strong contraction.

'I don't think there's time,' Martha replied briskly. 'I think you'll be welcoming a new arrival into the world before I've managed to tell Alice how to go about finding her.'

Within the half-hour, Martha was proved right. The latest addition to the Bancroft family arrived an hour before Sarah would normally have been awake. Mother and daughter were soon washed and tucked up in bed, with Alice settled in beside them, quite fascinated by her sister's tiny fingers and snub nose.

'So, another daughter,' Martha said, hands on her hips as she eased the strain from her back. 'Have you and Joe a name in mind?'

'*I* have,' Sarah said. 'She's to be Ella, after my sister Ellen.'

She gazed down at the wisp of reddish-blonde hair peeping out from Ella's swaddling blanket, feeling quite overcome, before she succumbed to the exhaustion of an early awakening and a rapid birth and fell into a deep sleep.

Over the next few days, as she became accustomed to having a new baby to care for once more, her thoughts turned to Joe and his reaction. When would he return? Would having two children make him more inclined to seek work that didn't take him away for such long periods? As the days turned into weeks, she discovered that her fears as to how she would manage on her own were unfounded. Alice was like a second mother to Ella and didn't want to be parted from her. Martha was insistent that Sarah took a daytime nap so that she could spend some time with the new baby, and many of the patients, particularly those with children or grandchildren of their own, were only too eager to hold her when they visited.

At eight weeks old, Ella was proving to be an easy-going and good-natured baby. The family had already settled into a new routine and so when Joe put in an appearance at last, Sarah was a little disconcerted. He arrived without warning one evening when both children were asleep. Sarah herself was about to head upstairs to bed but she knew she must make an effort to show willing and to offer to make Joe some supper.

'Aye, bread and cheese and a glass of ale will do me,' Joe said, sinking into a chair at the kitchen table and stretching out his legs. Sarah had to step over them as she busied herself fetching the loaf, a knife, butter, cheese and pickles.

'We have no ale,' she said, setting the food down in front of him. 'If I'd known you were coming . . .' She trailed off, hoping it didn't sound too much like an accusation. Joe didn't seem to want a quarrel and accepted tea without demur.

'So, don't keep me guessing,' he said, once he'd wolfed down several slices of bread and cheese. 'Have I a son or a daughter?'

'Another daughter,' Sarah said.

'Let's be seeing her, then,' Joe said. He looked up at her expectantly.

'She's asleep,' Sarah protested. 'I don't want to fetch her down. Can it not wait until the morning?'

Joe frowned. 'I've been away working to put food on the table for this family and now you say I can't see my new bairn of how many weeks?'

'Eight weeks.' Sarah was tight-lipped.

'Aye, eight weeks. Come on now, a peep at the little lass can't hurt.'

Sarah could see Joe was not to be deterred so, rather than bringing Ella downstairs and risk disturbing her, she persuaded Joe to go up and see their new daughter in their bedroom, where she slept under the window in the crib that had once belonged to Alice.

Sarah held her breath as Joe gazed down at Ella, who moved restlessly in her sleep as if she sensed a presence but couldn't quite bring herself to wake up and acknowledge it.

'Does she look as Alice did? I can't rightly tell in t'dark.' Even Joe's whisper had a rumble to it that Sarah feared might wake Ella so she put her finger to her lips and shooed him back down the stairs.

'She looks a lot like Alice did, but with lighter hair,' Sarah said. 'You'll see her properly in the morning.'

Sarah told him a little more about the day of Ella's birth and remembered to share their new daughter's name with him, but before long Joe was yawning and declared his intention of going to sleep. Sarah was thankful that he hadn't wanted to look in on Alice, who would surely have woken, but in any case they had been abed but five minutes before Ella was awake and demanding a feed.

It seemed that no sooner was she settled – Joe, of course, fast asleep and snoring throughout – and Sarah back to sleep than Alice bounced into the room. Her delighted cries on discovering her father was home woke Ella earlier than normal, and so their first day as a family of four was a little ragged around the edges. Ella grizzled, which was most unlike her, and regarded Joe with deep mistrust, wailing whenever he took her from her mother.

'I thought thou tell't me she was an easy child,' Joe chuckled, holding the irate bundle at arm's length. 'Ten to one the fairies swapped her in t'night.'

Thankfully, the next day was easier, and the next. Sarah was settling into the enjoyment of having Joe around when, all too soon, he announced that he must go back to his boat. This time, he handed over some money without being asked and Sarah, who had intended bringing pressure to bear on him to find local work, found she could do no more than make a tentative suggestion.

'Alice would love it if you were here more frequently. Ella, too, when she's old enough,' Sarah said on his last evening. 'Will you at least think about what else you might do to earn money?'

'Aye I'll think on it but I'm not sure 'twill make any odds.' Joe was quite cheerful. 'Working on boats is t'only life I know. I ain't fit to do owt else.'

PART VIII

AUGUST 1882 – MAY 1890

CHAPTER 59

And so life in the Bancroft household carried on over the years with a routine of sorts whereby Joe continued to appear at irregular intervals. He was glorious company when he was there, making a fuss of the girls and occasionally producing surprise gifts for them or for Sarah, some of them more successful than others. Sarah was less than impressed by the frog that he brought for Alice on one occasion, captured in his handkerchief along the road. He proudly presented it to her, only for it to escape and leap around the kitchen – to Sarah's consternation and Joe's delight. The Zoetrope was more successful – a revolving metal wheel with regularly spaced slits in the side, it was designed to view strips of paper placed within, printed with various images that appeared to move continuously when the wheel was spun. The dancing man and galloping horse kept Alice amused for days, although Sarah was uneasy as to where Joe might have come by such a thing. His claim to have bought it in Manchester might have been true, but for the lack of the accompanying box.

Generally, Sarah felt, Joe was like a boisterous uncle who swept into their lives, amused them all, then left again, leaving them to settle back into the familiarity of their everyday routine. She always had mixed feelings about his visits, which initially involved anger that he could drift in and out of their lives as he pleased, followed by resignation and then relaxation into enjoying his company, not least for the sake of the girls.

As a rule, she was glad to see him go again after the upheaval of his visit; she was out of the habit of having male company about the place. When she confided this to Martha, fearful of what she would think of her, she was relieved by her reaction.

'Lord bless you! It's no wonder you feel as you do. The man's gone for weeks at a time then there he is, under your feet all day. In the normal way of things, he'd be away at work during the day, good for nothing but his supper and bed after a hard day and with plans of his own on a Sunday. Don't go fretting yourself. 'Twould be enough to drive most women to distraction.'

Martha's speech left her quite pink in the cheeks with indignation, but it made Sarah feel better. There was little love lost between Joe and Martha, who seemed to have inherited Ada's antipathy towards Sarah's husband. Sarah had asked her once why she felt as she did, but Martha's emphatic shake of the head had put her off pressing her for an answer, fearful all at once of what might be revealed.

A lasting consequence of Joe's irregular visits over the years, though, was the addition of two more children to the family. Thomas was born barely two years after Ella and much doted on by his two big sisters. When his birth was followed two years later by that of Annie, Sarah declared to Joe that their family was quite big enough now. Managing four children with their father away much of the time, and with a herbal practice to run, was more than enough for her. She could have added that this absent father also frequently neglected to pay his share of the expenses for a growing household.

Sarah was just about managing to keep their heads above water on the money she earned but she was only too well aware that, should there be any alteration in their circumstances, the balance could be tipped irredeemably. The thought of her nest-egg tucked away in the Post Office made her hold back from further scolding: she knew it didn't work on Joe who would simply take himself off. Instead, on his first visit after Annie's birth, Sarah refused to share the marital bed and simply removed herself to sleep in the younger children's room at night, citing the need to nurse Annie and to get a good night's rest.

There was another reason for her choosing to absent herself from Joe, too. Once Sarah was seeing patients again after Annie's birth, she received one of her regular visits from Ramsay, the manager at Hobbs' Mill. She had long been supplying him with a remedy for his mother that she swore was the only thing keeping her alive after all these years. It was a mild nerve tonic, faithfully replicating Ada's original recipe, and had successfully kept her tendency towards dark thoughts and anxiety at bay. Now he was keen to consult Sarah about his daughter, Molly, whose cough was proving troublesome.

Ramsay always shared whatever news and gossip he had from the mill although Sarah, having left there over six years ago, sometimes struggled to remember most of the people that he referred to. This time, though, was different.

'I had some sad news this week,' he said, as Sarah stoppered the bottle of tonic for his mother.

'Oh?' she said, looking up, her attention caught.

'You'll remember the lad that lodged with you and your grandmother for a while when he was working at t'mill here? He were based in Manchester – Daniel Whittaker, his name was. Went off to work in mills in America.'

Sarah tried to make her response casual, although her heart was beating wildly. 'Has something happened to him? You mentioned sad news . . .' Her voice trailed off.

'Aye, he were caught up in an accident at sea. The ship he were on got hit by another in the fog and down it went. He were three days out of New York, on way to Liverpool. It were in t' paper,' Ramsay added, in case Sarah needed reassurance that he was telling the truth.

'There were no survivors?' Sarah struggled to raise her voice above a whisper.

'Oh, aye. One boat of about twenty souls. But all the rest lost. A terrible tragedy.'

Ramsay went on to tell Sarah more about the report in the paper and how Daniel's name was on the list of those drowned, news that had come to him from the manager of the Manchester mill where he had once worked.

'Daniel had arranged to visit them while he were back. They were right shocked an' upset,' Ramsay proclaimed, solemnly.

Sarah could barely remember anything about Ramsay's subsequent departure, other than his apologies for not delivering such distressing news 'with a sight more tact', and a promise to get his wife Ivy to bring their sick daughter to see him at the first opportunity. She had shut the door on him then rested her head against it.

She had heard from Daniel only once after he had left her, that September morning nearly five years before. A letter had come with an American stamp and she had been terrified, sure that the village would find her out in her guilt. She had to remind herself that Daniel had been a friend to the family before he had become anything else, and there was no reason why she shouldn't receive a letter from him.

'My dearest Sarah,' it read. *'I have thought long and hard about writing to you, and have*

tried so very hard not to do so. If only you knew how many letters I have begun and discarded, fearful of causing you problems or pain. But perhaps I am being thoughtless in attributing my own feelings to you, too. Yet, when we parted, I felt sure that our feelings were entwined. Sarah, you are married, with a beautiful daughter. I know that I can never be part of your life but I wanted you to know that you will always be part – a major part – of mine. I love you, Sarah, even though you can never be mine.

  Daniel.'

The letter had arrived a month after Daniel had left. Sarah had read it every night, alone in her bed, and kept it under her pillow. After another month it was beginning to tear along the creases and a month after that, fearful that she would be unable to find a safe hiding place for it before Joe next returned, she threw it on the fire. By then, every word of it was committed to her memory and treasured in her heart. The letter had upset her equilibrium and added fuel to the anger she had felt when she discovered that Joe had stolen from her cashbox, shortly after his return from prison.

Yet when Ella was born, Sarah had once again resigned herself to the way things were. Daniel was, without doubt, a better man than Joe, but Daniel lived in the United States and she wasn't married to him. She was married to Joe and must make the best of how things were, for the sake of her family. She could at least carry the memory of Daniel's words with her and know that, wherever he was, she was never far from his thoughts.

Sarah took that comfort from Ramsay's revelation. The routine of her days and the demands on her time by the patients, her family and Joe meant that she could push the worst of her thoughts away until it was time to go to bed. Then, with Annie tucked up beside her and Thomas sleeping peacefully on the other side of the room, she could silently indulge her grief and sense of loss. Her dreams were filled with the crash of waves against the side of a great ship as it foundered, cries of panic muffled in the fog. She was there in the cold greyness, desperately searching for Daniel's familiar features among the faces of those thronged on deck. She tried to push her way through them, calling out his name, but they didn't move, turning their backs on her and shutting her out until they faded away into the fog and she was alone.

Time and again, she awoke weeping, fearing that she had called Daniel's name aloud. But the children slept on, undisturbed, and Joe's regular snores sounded along the landing.

CHAPTER 60

If Joe was aware that anything other than the birth of their fourth child was keeping his wife from his bed, he didn't show it. He tried his best to win Sarah round and, although his visits were no more frequent, he was at his most charming when he was there. He didn't push or wheedle or make demands and the passage of time allowed Sarah to mourn in secret. She was grateful to him for that, although she took care not to make it apparent what was going on in her head.

After a year had passed she could no longer use the excuse of needing to nurse Annie as a reason to stay away from his bed. Yet she did not want to risk having another baby. Although they were managing well enough as a family of four children, due to Alice being so much older and able to help care for the younger ones, Sarah found that her own health was increasingly bad in the winter. The cough that had afflicted her at the mill returned as the weather worsened and on some winter mornings she could barely drag herself out of bed to prepare breakfast. The remedies that she created for herself had only partial success yet, as the weather improved in the spring, so did her health.

So Sarah had returned to the marital bed but had become quite adept at managing Joe's advances, generally making sure that she didn't go up to bed until she knew that he was asleep. The household settled into a new pattern and, although Joe's homecomings remained un-announced, Sarah found herself starting to look forward to having him around again. The children were all getting older and life was becoming a little easier to manage; at times Sarah wondered whether Daniel's death had contributed to this. There was no longer any prospect of escape, no matter how improbable; no reason to believe that things could ever be other than they were.

A hot summer's evening when Annie was three years old was to change all of that once more. It was the last day of Joe's leave before he had to return to his boat, and the sunny weather, after a disappointing summer, proved irresistible to the family. A picnic lunch in the garden, with a joint of cold ham, pickles, cheese and bread, turned into an indolent afternoon. Alice and Ella sprawled in the shade on a blanket while Thomas poked things in their ears and Annie pulled their hair to get their attention.

After a while, Alice was persuaded to take Thomas off to the field to watch for rabbits. Annie curled up between Ella and her mother and fell asleep, while Sarah herself dozed. She awoke to the sensation of someone stroking her arm and the curve of her collarbone and she lay for a moment without opening her eyes, enjoying the sensation. She thought that it was one of the children and a small smile played on her lips but, when she opened her eyes, it was to find Joe's face very close to her own.

Startled, her instinct was to pull away but Joe put his fingers to his lips and shook his head, indicating the sleeping family at her side. Unable to move, she closed her eyes again and let herself relax. It was a long time since any hands other than small ones had stroked her face. She was almost sorry when she heard Thomas's chatter as he and Alice climbed over the fence and came back up the garden. Joe squeezed her hand and smiled ruefully as she struggled to rouse herself fully and sit up.

That evening as the family sat over a late supper, Sarah watched Joe as he teased Thomas, who was sleepy again and inclined to crankiness. Joe's face was more lined now with age and his hair was increasingly grey, but the memory came back to her of how she had felt about him when they first met. That was more than fifteen years ago now. Could it really be so long?

She shook her head as she thought of her innocence back then. She had been drawn to his smile and his confident pursuit of her and she had responded, without a thought of what lay ahead. She had been young and foolish, with a notion in her head about what marriage meant that bore no relation to the reality. It had been a hard life with Joe but they had got this far and she knew she must look to the future and hope that what lay in store was a promise of many happy and fulfilling years.

That night, Sarah didn't wait for Joe to fall asleep before she went up to bed. He seemed surprised by her presence when she slipped between the sheets beside him and she took his hand and pressed it to her cheek. He turned to her, wordlessly, and she felt as though her love for her husband had returned and with it an ardour that she had never experienced before. When he woke at dawn to set off for the canal she clung to him and he was reluctant to part from her.

'I'll be back afore long,' he promised. 'Mebbe you're right. 'Tis time to find work that doesn't keep me apart from you and the bairns for such a length o' time.'

He sighed and Sarah found herself moved by the despondent expression on his face. She went down to the kitchen and packed up some of the leftover ham and cheese so that he would have some supplies to send him on his way, then she stood on the doorstep and waved him off as the sun rose, casting shafts of misty light through the trees. It promised to be another fine day. Sarah, too wide awake to return to bed, took herself out into the garden and tended the herb beds, snipping off dead leaves and flowers and enjoying the aroma of the crushed vegetation before returning to the house to greet the family as they awoke.

Six weeks later, as strengthening winds blew the few remaining leaves from the trees, Sarah had to accept that what she feared would happen had come to pass. She was with child again. Her face was grim as she thought of the discussion she must have with Joe when he was next home. She must persuade him to look for work locally with some urgency and they must agree that there would be no more children.

Her small frame showed this, her fifth pregnancy, at a very early stage. She thought Alice had noticed it, for she seemed to have increased her efforts to be a helpful daughter. She was not only consistently patient with the little ones but had started to help her mother by logging all the dispensing of remedies, and the payments, in the ledger, which was a vital part of Sarah's work.

Christmas came and went with no sign of Joe's return. The weather was harsh and Sarah put his absence down to the fact that once again his boat must be stuck in the ice, waiting for better weather to release it. She resolved to go down to the canal in the New Year and ask whether anyone there knew of his whereabouts, although part of her felt that he would be sure to arrive before she would need to do so.

By the time that the snow and frost had eased

it was March and Sarah was too big with child to undertake the journey. She considered sending Alice, but balked at the thought of sending her alone on such a mission, and so she persuaded herself that Joe would be back at any moment. Several times a day she was convinced that she heard him whistling as he came along the road. Surely that was the sound of the latch on the gate as it opened? Weren't those his footsteps coming up the path?

She caught Alice watching her closely on more than one occasion, so she tried to stop herself showing any signs of the growing unease that she was feeling at the length of Joe's absence. When Beatrice, or Beattie as she very quickly became known, arrived in a bit of a rush two weeks early, Joe had still not shown his face at Lane End Cottage. Sarah's emotions veered between anger and fear. Martha, who had been on hand for the birth as she had for all of Sarah's babies, pursed her lips and shook her head as she swaddled the latest arrival.

'You need to track down that husband of yours and have words with him. He can't be going gallivanting off like this with nary a word and you having five mouths to feed now. Your grandmother will be turning in her grave. I don't know how you get by . . .'

The truth was Sarah had ceased to rely on Joe's money, which was always erratic in appearance, a long time before. She knew, though, that she needed to be well enough to be up and out of bed and able to see her patients within a week or two. She couldn't afford for any of them to start looking elsewhere – to the new doctor in the village, for example. She thought it unlikely, as they all swore by her remedies and had stayed loyal to her, but she mustn't give them the opportunity.

It was hard to conjure up the warm feelings that she'd had towards Joe when she'd last seen him. Martha was right: she needed to make him see that things must change, once and for all.

'I'll get back to work first,' Sarah told herself, 'and then I'll make that trip to the canal to see what they know down there about the whereabouts of Joseph Bancroft.'

CHAPTER 61

'I wonder, could you tell me where I might find Joe Bancroft?'

Sarah hoped her request sounded polite but firm. The man had stepped out from his hut on the towpath by the locks, seemingly intent on barring her passage. Sarah didn't know whether the towpath was a public right of way, but she wanted to impress on him that she had genuine business there. She was nervous he would deny her, though; his dog, which had been curled up inside the tiny hut, came to the door and growled at her.

The man regarded Sarah with some suspicion. 'Tha'll not find him here,' he said. He paused, observing her, and Sarah, suddenly aware that she had been twisting her wedding ring on her finger in a state of anxiety, stopped and clasped her hands in front of her. During the walk down to the canal she had become increasingly nervous. She'd left Alice in charge of the children and for the first time, alone and away from the house, she had allowed herself to speculate at length on what might have kept Joe away from them for so long.

Such reflection had just caused her agitation to increase.

The man considered, then decided to take pity on her. 'Ask down there.' He jerked his head towards the row of narrow-boats moored along the bank.

'Kitty,' he bellowed suddenly, startling Sarah, then he tipped his cap to her and retreated back inside his hut, shushing the dog.

Sarah set off uncertainly along the towpath, not sure where she was meant to go until she spotted the figure of a woman who was watching Sarah approach from the cabin of a boat moored a little way along.

When they were first married Sarah had been curious about Joe's lifestyle on the boats, and his work there. He'd answered her questions but hadn't encouraged her when she'd suggested that she might accompany him there one day and she had long ago stopped asking to visit the canal. Bringing up Alice – and then Ella, Thomas and Annie – very much on her own had taken up all her time. She had ceased to think of the canal dwellers as a community of which Joe was a part and, instead, had come to regard it as a place of work, which she resented for taking him away from home so often. Now, she was struck by what she observed as she made her way along the towpath.

The boats were closely moored, nose to tail or in some cases side by side. It looked as though the only living space available on each boat was a tiny cabin at one end – the rest of the space was given over to a hold to store cargo. Clearly the community was making the most of being moored up for a while: washing was strung along the towpath hedgerows to dry in the spring sunshine and children of all ages were running up and down, playing tag, while dogs, excited by the activity, barked from the decks where they were chained.

The woman, who Sarah presumed must be Kitty, was now standing on the towpath with her hands on her hips and regarding Sarah with apparent hostility as she approached.

'I was looking for Joseph Bancroft,' Sarah said, dispensing with any niceties of greeting for the woman really did look quite formidable.

'And what might you be wanting with him?' Kitty demanded.

Sarah was taken aback. 'He's my husband. I believe he works on one of the boats here.'

Kitty's expression changed. She no longer looked so menacing. In fact, Sarah thought, she looked shocked. Surely Kitty was the name of Joe's sister, the one who had visited him in prison when she was in desperate straits? Could this be her? Although Sarah had managed in the end to suggest meeting her and seeing what help they could offer to her and her children, Joe had brushed the suggestion aside. He had never mentioned that she had become a canal dweller, too.

'You'd best come in,' Kitty said at last, stepping back onto the boat and pulling aside the curtain that separated the cabin from the tiller. 'I was afeared you were an inspector, coming to check on the children. Although those inspectors are usually men, 'tis true.' She seemed to be talking to herself as she stood to one side, jerking her head at Sarah to indicate she should get on board.

Three or four of the children, wearing clothes noticeably more ragged than the others, although clean, had gathered by the boat, their curiosity piqued by the visitor. Kitty shooed them away with some vehemence.

'Clear off. Come back at suppertime. And mind that you bring something that we can eat back with you.'

As she clambered clumsily aboard, Sarah was reminded of what Joe had said about the theft of eggs, or even chickens, as well as fruit and vegetables from the gardens of those nearest the canal when the boat people were moored up. His own thieving, learnt along here as a child, was what had landed him in prison. Then she registered the interior of the cabin where she was standing and it drove all other thoughts from her mind. It was tiny, with seemingly just enough room for the two of them standing side by side. Even though Sarah was petite, she suddenly felt like a giant, filling up all the space. However did they manage when the all the children were on board? she wondered.

Kitty pointed to a bench seat. 'Sit you down,' she said. She made no motion to offer Sarah refreshment; she was probably unused to entertaining anyone other than family, Sarah thought. Yet when she took a closer look at her surroundings, she was struck by how neat and clean it was. Crocheted strips edged every cupboard and shelf, plates that were clearly just for show decorated the walls and there were few signs that the space was anyone's living quarters, let alone the sleeping quarters, too, for what appeared to be a large family. On closer inspection, though, there was a stove in the corner, with a narrow chimney stretching up and out of the cabin. And some of the panelled wood interior clearly hid the necessities for everyday living; as Sarah's eyes got used to the gloom of the interior after the brightness outside she could make out cupboard doors that hadn't completely shut against the fullness of their contents.

'So it be Joe that you're after,' Kitty said. Sarah noted uneasily that the menace seemed to have returned to her tones. She nodded, mute, wondering whether to ask the woman whether she was indeed his sister although now she came to look at her more closely she could see little family resemblance. She looked careworn and considerably older than Sarah herself. Kitty's hair, all but grey, was loosely bundled back under a faded blue scarf and her sack-like clothes disguised the sort of bosomy figure that Ada would have described as 'mature'.

'Joe's dead,' Kitty said.

Sarah, her thoughts otherwise engaged, at first didn't register what she had said.

'Dead, do you not hear me? Gone these six months

past, leaving me with this boat to manage and all the bairns too.' Kitty looked defeated suddenly.

Sarah, still unable to fully comprehend what she had been told, could only focus on the latter part of Kitty's speech. Had she shared the boat with her brother? Why had Joe never mentioned this?

Kitty shook her head impatiently. 'Do you not understand? This Joseph, this man you say was your husband, well, he was *my* husband Joe. I long thought he had a fancy woman in town but I didn't know he'd been and married her.' Kitty's eyes were fixed on the wedding ring that Sarah was once again twisting in some agitation.

'How many children do you have?' Sarah's head was filled with so many questions she hardly knew where to begin but she blurted out the first one that came to mind, the memory of the ragged children on the path returning to her quite forcefully.

'There be four living with me here on the boat and two lent out to t'other boats, to bring in a mite of earnings,' Kitty said. She looked at Sarah's face and an expression of horror crossed her own. 'Don't be telling me you're with child?' she said, her eyes flitting over Sarah's figure.

'No,' Sarah declared. 'But I have five already, the youngest not yet a month old and never seen her father.'

Both women sat in a kind of stunned silence while they contemplated the enormity of what they'd discovered.

CHAPTER 62

Neither Sarah nor Kitty had stirred from their silent contemplation for some time. Sarah's thoughts ranged here and there and although she had an over-riding urge to get up and leave the boat she wasn't sure whether she might regret not seeking answers to some of the questions that plagued her.

'So what happened?' she asked at last. 'To Joe,' she added, as it was clear from Kitty's puzzled expression that she, too, had been wrapped up in her own thoughts.

'He were crushed,' Kitty said. Sarah couldn't suppress a gasp of horror but Kitty's tone was matter-of-fact. Of course, Sarah realised, she had probably known of Joe's death for a while and had had time to come to terms with it.

'How? When?' she asked.

'Unloading in Manchester. The chain snapped as it were lifting the cotton bales and Joe were caught underneath. There were nowt they could do for 'im.' Kitty's mouth was set in a straight line. 'Course it were no one's fault. So we haven't seen a penny or owt. We're just meant to get on wi'out 'im.'

'And when did it happen?' Sarah all but whispered.

'Like I said, it were six months ago now.'

Another silence fell. Joe had been killed even before she first expected him home, Sarah thought. Why hadn't she been able to sense the loss of him? How come nothing had told her he was gone?

The two women sat on, bound by an awkward alliance. They shared a common grief and an awkward secret – the same husband. As they contemplated what the news meant to them, each in turn sighed at intervals. Sarah could have sat on like this, in difficult kinship, until darkness fell, but the fact that she had left Alice to look after the family, and Beattie still so young, suddenly struck her.

'I must go,' she said, but made no move. She wondered whether she should offer to meet Kitty again, then thought better of it. It was best for both of them that their relationship to the same man remained unknown. Kitty seemed less surprised by it, Sarah reflected. She said she had suspected something. It made her wonder whether Joe had given her cause for suspicion before.

Finally, she stood up. She hardly knew what to say. 'It was nice meeting you' was barely appropriate. How did you say goodbye to a woman whose situation you understood only too well, yet despised because it was that very situation that had kept your husband apart from you? Sarah wanted to hate Kitty but she couldn't. Kitty had surely been as much wronged by Joe as she had.

Yet she had no wish to know her better, either. It would have been better for both of them if the other had never existed, she thought bitterly as she made her way back along the towpath.

'Goodbye. And good luck' had seemed the only appropriate thing to say to Kitty in the end.

'Found what you were looking for?' The man had come out of his hut as she approached. This time the dog was quiet but watchful.

'You might say that,' Sarah said. Her tone sounded grim, even to her own ears, and she moved swiftly on before he could ask further questions.

She had solved the puzzle of the whereabouts of Joe Bancroft. She knew now why he had never returned to his family from his last trip. As she walked back towards Northwaite, willing her feet to carry her faster than they seemed inclined, she realised she hadn't thought to ask where he was buried. She wasn't sure whether or not it mattered. Like so many things in Joe's life it would remain a mystery. Perhaps that was for the best. She had a feeling that Kitty believed that she had prior ownership of Joe and maybe it was better to let her have that small victory, at least. She, like Sarah, had precious little to remember him by other than the children.

Sarah was heartsick for some time after the discovery of Joe's duplicity. She had no one with whom she could share her burden. She would have turned to Martha, but her neighbour had announced that she'd found love again late in life and planned to go off to set up home in Leeds with a butcher. Martha had been so clearly delighted by her good fortune that Sarah couldn't let her see that her own instant reaction was a selfish worry as to how on earth she would manage without her. Sarah also came to see that it was better that no one knew the shame of her situation – married to a man whom another woman described as her own husband.

Sarah couldn't show her distress in front of the children, either. Although the three little ones were too young to understand, she didn't want any of them to carry bad memories of their father through their lives, despite everything. They were, of course, used to Joe's long absences: the most recent one had stretched to nearly a year. She resolved not to say a word until they asked and, if and when they did, she would imply that he had left them. It seemed safer to reveal as little as possible, certainly not the shameful truth.

During long, sleepless nights, Sarah had ample time to look back over her life with Joe. Were there clues as to what had been going on that she should have spotted? She had racked her brains but come up with very little. There was his puzzling anger in the early days of their marriage when she had darned his socks and sewn on some buttons – was that because he was going back to Kitty, rather than to the solitary life she had imagined for him on a boat? He must have been worried that Kitty would notice. The occasions that he had been late in arriving, or absent, for Christmas – was this another sign of him sharing out his time between two families?

Who had he gone to see first when he came out of prison? She was convinced that he must have come straight to see her and Alice, until she remembered his lack of belongings and her heart sank. Had his tale of leaving prison with no possessions been a lie? Then she remembered how he had left them after a short time, returning a couple of days later in a happier mood. Had he been to see Kitty then, rather than immediately after prison?

The money he had taken from her locked cashbox – he had told her he had given it to Kitty and her children, but Kitty wasn't his sister, as he had maintained. And the children weren't his nieces and nephews, but his own. No wonder he had discouraged Sarah's suggestion that they should offer further help. He couldn't risk his secret life being uncovered. Sarah felt a blinding rage at the thought. The money that he had taken was her money, money that she had earned to support herself and Alice. He had no right. She had to turn her face into her pillow to stop herself from crying out into the night.

When the thought finally occurred to her that Joe most probably hadn't spent as much time away on his trips as she had believed, she was quite beside herself. Of course, it made sense that he had spent equal amounts of time with Kitty. With a great uneasiness, she tried to remember the ages of the children she had seen on the towpath. Were any of them the same age as her children, she wondered? Horrible though the idea was, it seemed likely. She was filled with a terrible despair. She hadn't known this man at all.

It came to her that when she first met Joe, he must already have been with Kitty. His easy manner, his wooing of her – he couldn't have intended anything other than taking advantage of her naivety and moving on. 'Did he take me for a fool?' she thought. Unbidden, his face appeared before her, his skin tanned and crinkled into laughter lines around his eyes, the blue of corn-flowers and always merry. Joe had never taken life too seriously and only now could Sarah fully appreciate the consequences of that.

Would she have felt the same about him if they had met on a cold winter's day, not on a bright spring one when her heart was full of the promise of the summer to come? Looking back on those heady few weeks, she saw everything in vivid colour. The grass was surely a brighter green than ever before or since, the sun shone out of a cloud-less sky more times than one dare hope for in a Yorkshire spring, while the birds puffed out their breasts and poured out their song as though their hearts might burst with joy.

Yet he had returned time and again and he had married her. Would he have done so if Ada had given him no other choice? Sarah wondered. These were questions to which she would never have answers now. Ada had been right about Joe, but she would never have the satisfaction of knowing it, nor would she have welcomed such a discovery. For the first time, Sarah had reason to be thankful that her grandmother was no longer with them.

In the rare better moments, when something gave rise to a fleeting fond memory of her husband, she tried to reason with herself. Joe had been horribly misguided. Perhaps there had been times when he had resolved to leave one or other of his families, then couldn't go through with it. But he had, at least, tried to do right by both of them.

Still, it was to take many months before Sarah could think of Joe with anything other than anger. Caring for her family filled up so much of her time that there was none left over to spend worrying about the past. Beattie, the new baby, had proved to be a tranquil child, no doubt as a result of having three sisters and a brother to vie for her attention and carry her around. Sarah had been able to attend to her patients and her herb garden within a week of Beattie's birth and for this she was thankful. It meant they would not need to fall back on her legacy, safely tucked away. And, after she had learnt of Joe's treachery, her work gave her a focus – something to take her mind away from the treadmill to which it was bound.

Sarah had been absorbed in her thoughts while she stood at the sink, working her way through a pile of laundry. She looked up from rinsing out the final bits of washing, through the window to where Alice and Ella had spread a blanket on the grass and laid Beattie on it, with Thomas and Annie seated on either side of her. It looked as though Alice was telling them a story. Ella had been despatched to fetch something but she had been waylaid – by birdsong, a sunbeam or a dragonfly dancing through the air, perhaps – and had stopped stock still, gazing upwards, rapt.

Sarah looked at Ella, then looked at her other children. Ella's reddish-blonde curls were the only thing that set her apart from the other dark-haired Bancroft children. Facially, they all resembled each other but Sarah knew, had known from the moment of her birth. If ever her belief began to waver, a gesture of Ella's such as a shake of the head or a pensive look reconfirmed it.

Other than her own memories, Ella was all she had to remember of the man who might have been her one true love. If Daniel's ship hadn't foundered, would he have made the journey from Manchester to visit them? Would he have taken one look at Ella and would he have known, as she had? And if he had, would it have made a difference? Then she put the thought firmly away, for it was of no use to her now, and she went outside to the only people who mattered in her life.

'Room for another one?' she asked, settling on the blanket with Beattie on her lap and Thomas and Annie cuddling into either side of her. 'Now, what shall we play?'